OUTLIER

OUTLIER

The Second Derivative

Penny Lane

This is a work of fiction.

Any similarity to real people, living or dead, and any resemblance to actual events is purely coincidental.

The mention of names, places, institutions, or organizations is for fictional purposes only, and their inclusion does not imply any relationship to the events recounted in this book.

Published by Tryqit LLC in the United States

ISBN 978-0-578-39755-9 eBook

ISBN 978-0-578-39571-5 Paperback

CONTENTS

But Mousie, thou art no thy-lane,
In proving foresight may be vain:
The best laid schemes o'Mice and Men
Gang oft agley,
An' lea'e us nought but grief an' pain,
For promised joy.

Still thou art blest, compar'd wi' me!
The present only toucheth thee:
But Och! I backward cast my e'e,
On prospects drear!
An' forward, tho' I canna see,
I guess an' fear!

Robert Burns (1759-1796)

PART 1

THE ENCOUNTER

CHAPTER 1

Bad things happen at night. At least that is the fear planted in the root directory of our consciousness. The night brings the possibility of things unseen and unknown. We retreat to the safety of our house and bed, thinking we will deal with the monsters tomorrow in the daylight. But the future encompasses both day and night. The future is the unknown, the foundation of all fear.

The thing about the future is that it doesn't exist yet. How can you know anything about something that doesn't exist? How many people woke up today with a plan, and have no idea they won't live to see the sunset? Death has a nasty way of surprising us. How many people go to bed at night and expect tomorrow to be another day in their routine life? Some may not make it to daylight. Others will be surprised when their life spins out of control and suddenly travels down an unforeseen path. Such was the case for Sam Barron.

Sam was startled awake from a deep sleep. His eyes opened to a view of the digital clock on the bedside table. The bright red numbers glowing in the darkness told him it was ten minutes after two o'clock in the morning. His heart was pounding in his chest. Instinctively, he rolled over and searched through the pitch black in the direction of the opposite wall of the master bedroom. There, by the door, the little red LED light meant the house alarm was set. Nobody could be in the house, so what had awakened him? He lay still, stiff and alert, listening intently. Not a sound. His heart continued to race.

Had he been dreaming? Was it a dream that woke him? He couldn't remember dreaming. He reached for his cell phone on the bedside table and checked for any texts or messages that might have triggered a sound alert. Wait. There! Noise coming from downstairs. Instantly, he threw back the covers and swung his feet to the hardwood floor. He silently glided to the bedroom door and tiptoed into the hall. He could clearly hear noise now, rising up the stairwell from below. It sounded like someone was opening and closing drawers in the dining room sideboard. How could that be? How did someone penetrate the perimeter alarm? The interior motion detectors were turned off when he was home at night, but a door or window alarm should have been activated. Soundlessly, he moved across the hall and inside the doorway of the guest bedroom located at the top of the stairs. Sam wanted to yell down the stairs, "Get the fuck out of my house!", but he resisted the impulse. His one advantage was his knowledge of the house, combined with the element of surprise. He didn't want to give up the opportunity to startle and shock the intruder.

Sam thought about going back to the master bedroom closet to get the knife he kept there, but he didn't want to get into a fight. The intruder might have a gun. If anyone came upstairs, they would most likely head straight toward the master bedroom. His best hope was to let the intruder pass by the guest room, then run downstairs when the intruder was in the master. He could hit the alarm panel by the back door as he ran outside and into the clear. Why hadn't the alarm gone off? How did anyone get in?

The noise in the dining room stopped. After a moment of silence, steps crossed to the foot of the stairs. He slid back into the darkness behind the doorway, but he could still see the landing halfway up the stairwell. A window above the stairs cast a dim light into the stairwell. A shadowy figure approached the landing from below. Sam froze in place. As the intruder walked across the landing, his silhouette revealed a slender profile of average height, maybe five-eight. Something about his lithe movement made Sam think teenager. Change of plan! Sam quickly pulled back further into the darkness of the bedroom and turned on the home app on his phone. He could have spoken a command, but that would have given away his position. He was careful to shield the light from his phone against his chest while he positioned his finger over the icon for downstairs lights. As the intruder reached the top of the stairs, Sam tapped his phone. The lights went on, and the stairwell lit up from below. The guy spun around to look down the stairs. Sam leaped from the darkness onto the back of the burglar.

They would have tumbled down the stairs together, but the intruder pushed back hard off the handrail. Sam had his left arm fully around the guy's neck and was getting ready to use his right arm to complete an unbreakable headlock, but he was surprised at how slender and light the man was. Sam was having no trouble holding on with just his left arm. Instead of focusing on a debilitating choke, he took advantage of the shift in weight from falling down the stairs to leaning back. Sam took several more steps backward and pulled his opponent off his feet. As the intruder fell backward, Sam went with him and sat down, pulling the guy on top of him. Instantly, Sam wrapped his legs around the body above him and squeezed it in a scissors lock. The fellow was wriggling and thrashing about, waving his arms wildly. Sam wrapped his right arm over the intruder's arm and chest to try to quiet him down. As he reached across the body on top of him, Sam's right hand grabbed onto a breast. Sam froze. The intruder froze.

"You're not a man, you're a woman!" Sam exclaimed. "What the fuck are you doing in my house?"

There was no response.

CHAPTER 2

Earlier that same Friday evening, Sam Barron sat at his kitchen table and considered how disenchanted he was with his life. Through the doorway, he could see his travel bag sitting in the hall. He had recently flown back into town, only to be greeted by his desolate existence. Probably like most people, Sam had great expectations when he was young. He wasn't sure what he would grow up to be, but he assumed he would be important and have a successful life, perhaps a famous life. Now, at forty-four years old, he wondered, "Is this as good as it gets?" Sam had a nice life. He had every reason to be satisfied. On paper, he had what looked like a very successful life. But nevertheless, he felt he had fallen short of his potential.

He had performed everything expected in life. He married, raised a family, and earned a good living. He owned a lovely house in Seahaven, Massachusetts, an upscale seaside resort town that he was proud to call home. But now he was coasting, and it felt hollow. Worse, he now viewed his prior accomplishment of building a family as a failure. His marriage had fallen apart and his family disintegrated. His responsibility as a provider and protector was gone. Little more was expected of him by anyone except himself. Other than the occasional special project with personal risk involved, no great life challenge lay ahead for him to rise up and meet. Compared to others around him who struggled to stay on life's treadmill, Sam was so accomplished that his daily existence had become way too easy — and that translated into boring.

He married right out of college, and his daughter was born within a year. Although a financial strain for him and his wife at their young age, she was an absolute delight. A son was born a year and a half later, and that completed his preconceived notion of fulfillment. Sam spent two decades being totally absorbed with his family and building his investment adviser business. Then it all fell apart. Two years ago, his daughter became a casualty of a contentious world. As an intelligence officer in the navy, she had been killed overseas under circumstances never fully revealed to him and his wife. Her death was surreal, and the lack of explanation left him with no closure, suspended in a sad, painful emotional limbo.

His son married a lovely English woman while he was in college. Immediately upon graduation, they decided to live outside of London. Sam was lucky if he saw them once a year. Sam's family life had dissolved, and much of his happiness along with it. He held his personal hurt inside, like a burning ember under a pile of dead ashes. Sam was never taught to share his pain. He couldn't understand why anybody would want to share their pain.

While struggling with his own grief, Sam didn't know how to comfort his wife. It was frustratingly clear to Sam his wife had changed from the lively, loving, intelligent woman she had been when they were younger. She had become introverted, depressed, and not just uninterested in life, but downright bitter. She had a generally sour demeanor. They had grown apart and shared less and less. Their love diminished to the point where they were little more than roommates. It was a gradual process over a period of months. Sam always assumed that they would eventually get back on track, but he didn't understand what his benign neglect was costing him. He couldn't manage to give her the comfort she needed, so it was inevitable that she would find it elsewhere.

The final nail in the coffin of their sex life was when Sam found out he had prostate cancer. In his mind, sexual performance was part of the definition of his masculinity. He was dismayed that, at his relatively young age, his manhood was threatened, and worse, even his life was threatened. Surgery was prescribed immediately. Sam and his wife had not had sex for a long time, but in the days prior to his surgery, he had asked her directly, "Would you like to have sex with me?"

Without even looking at him, she replied, "No."

"This might be your last chance ever."

"It's not going to happen."

To Sam, it felt like a complete repudiation of their love. Rejection translated to an acceptance of loneliness, and he stopped trying to rescue the relationship. It was no surprise to him when she had an affair with a wealthy entrepreneur who also happened to be a trust fund baby. When she asked for a divorce, Sam didn't contest it, as long as he could keep the house. Maybe the guy could give her more emotional support than he could, but Sam suspected the man's money had a lot to do with it. Now, as he sat alone in an empty house and looked back over his life, it felt pathetic. Brooding over his situation, he blamed himself for his downward spiral, but he couldn't come to grips with why it needed to happen.

It took Sam a long time to fully recover from his surgery. He had experienced minor surgery before, and he was usually up and around immediately. This time, although released from the hospital within twenty-four hours, it was weeks before the shock to his body subsided, and even longer before he felt normal in any sense of the word. He was terrified they wouldn't be able to get all the cancer. His worry was eased by postoperative reports and further tests, but the question of quality of life came into play. What kind of a life was he going to have if he couldn't control his bladder and had to wear diapers forever? It was distracting to have a constant obsession with urination. He watched what he drank, stayed close to bathrooms, carried extra pads in his briefcase, and worked on the pelvic exercises the doctors gave him. It was two months before he could dare to believe he might be able to control his bodily functions in the way that he had always taken for granted.

Eventually, his sexual desire returned, but for the first time in his life, he experienced the erectile dysfunction he had always scoffed at when he saw ads for cures on TV. Regardless of the desire he felt, he couldn't believe his penis refused to stand up and get hard. Even with the Sildenafil prescribed as a normal part of his recovery, he wondered if he would ever be able to perform with a woman. Very slowly, the trauma to his nerves subsided and more function returned. It was well over a year before he felt confident that he could sufficiently hold an erection without taking any pills. But now he felt the loneliness and frustration of not having a partner. His divorce was officially concluded more than a year ago. In all those months, he still hadn't been out on an actual date with a woman. An after work drink with associates didn't count. It was Friday night. He should be out having a good time.

Sam was shaken out of his reverie by the doorbell. He walked to the front door and peered through the sidelight. He saw the grey hair and worn face of John Cooperman. Although the years had not treated him well, his visage retained an aura of kindness with a hint of jovial mirth. Sam opened the door with a smile on his face, and swung it wide.

"Coop! It isn't Halloween. Why do I have a spook on my front doorstep?" Sam loved teasing Coop at every opportunity. "Is that the best you can do for a costume? That doesn't look like Agency attire, and it doesn't work for Halloween."

Coop glanced down at his chinos and cashmere sweater,

then shrugged. "The privilege of being semi-retired."

"You never believed in a dress code anyway. Who let you out of your cage?"

Coop chuckled. "I was driving by and saw your car in the driveway. I called you last Sunday to see if you wanted to go sailing. Turns out you missed a nice day, considering how wet it has been so far for the month of May. You must have been away."

"Driveway, day, May, away, you're rhyming your sentences, Coop. Are you turning into a rap artist? I was away. I just flew back last night. I was on a project for the Bureau in DC."

Coop held out his hand, palm up, and gestured toward the hallway behind Sam. "So, are you going to invite me in? Where I come from, it's customary to offer a beer to a guest."

"Jesus Coop, you cut right to the chase, don't you?"

Coop was a friend and a mentor. He was twenty years senior, and had worked in one capacity or another for almost every major intelligence agency in DC. He gave a playful nudge to Sam as he moved past. "So, the FBI still has its talons in you after all these years. I can remember when they talked to you at a college job fair. Boy those were the days! I can't picture any of the agencies setting up a table and recruiting under a banner on any college campus now. We aren't PC anymore. I'm surprised anyone ever thought we were."

Sam followed Coop back to the kitchen and pulled two beers from the fridge. He pointed toward the table, indicating a chair. "Yeah, well, as you know, I turned them down even then. The FBI has always been too bureaucratic and too structured for my taste. It's probably a good thing, because that's why they hire me now. They need someone who can think outside the narrow borders of their world."

Coop had a nostalgic smile on his face. "When I saw your resume and interview notes, I told them to keep track of you. I knew someday you'd turn out to be useful." He raised his beer toward Sam. "Cheers!"

Sam reciprocated. "Cheers!" He took a gulp and sat down across from Coop. "Yeah, I guess I can thank you for all the shit I've gone through over the past twenty years. It's been interesting though. Homeland Security, FBI, CIA, NSA, the alphabet soup of agencies... It's an incestuous swamp, but I don't have to tell you that."

Coop leaned forward with interest in his eyes. "What did the Bureau have you working on this time? I assume it's not a state secret."

"No secret, but an interesting case. I helped get a really nasty guy off the street. We called him Teflon Jack. This guy had been up on three priors and the charges just slid off him, like a greased egg off a Teflon pan. He's a consummate liar. Teflon Jack was brought up on robbery, assault, interstate trafficking, fraud, and everything else they could throw at him. Law enforcement tends to get motivated when innocent people are maimed during a crime. A bank job was involved, so the FBI set up a joint task force with the local police to nail this guy. I actually worked under the assistant U.S. attorney. For the fourth time around, the AG was not going to allow this guy to walk again, but they didn't have the resources to sort out a coherent prosecution."

Coop shook his head. "I don't see the difficulty. If it's just about a lie, all you have to do is find a conflict in the testimony or find evidence that can disprove his statement."

"Yeah, no. The problem was, they couldn't find anything to refute his lie. They had no surveillance video, no witnesses, he left his phone in his office so they couldn't track his location. They had his fingerprints on a gate post at the scene of the crime, but he claimed he was there at a different time for a perfectly innocent reason.

"A trial takes place in a reconstructed world. The jury only gets to see what's shown to them by the lawyers. When Teflon Jack said he was having a private meeting with someone in the middle of the day, and he happened to lean against a gate post, there was nothing in the picture to make the jury think it wasn't plausible. The prosecutor was stuck because he wanted irrefutable evidence, and there was none. My job was to collect new information and deliver a different picture to the jury, a more complete picture, to convince them they were being fed a lie."

"And the prosecutor couldn't do this himself?"

"The prosecutor was distracted by all the other evidence and details of the trial. He wanted to place the perp at the gate at two in the morning when the crime was committed. There was no evidence to do that. Furthermore, he had no hard evidence to disprove the perp's claim he was there during the day. How do you prove that Teflon Jack didn't leave his fingerprints in the middle of the day when he had a meeting with someone who was conveniently unavailable to confirm the meeting?

"Evidence would have been nice, but disassembling the lie was all it took. I sidestepped the issue of evidence and had the prosecuting attorney walk the jury through a logical analysis of choices. I collected the weather for that date, and found out it was ninety-eight degrees with eighty-six percent humidity. It was a bright, sunny day. The location was a side alley directly across from a glass-walled office building. The sun at noon would have reflected off the glass back onto the gate. Why would anyone hold a private meeting outside when it was extremely hot and miserable? The meeting would have been in full view of people in the office building, so it certainly wasn't private, and it wasn't soundproof. Thus, I gave the jury good reason to question the plausibility of his story. Next, we provided the jury with a selection of much better alternatives. The meeting could have been held in the conference room, in the lounge, in the restaurant, or in his airconditioned car with privacy glass for windows. Once the jury was given enough information to see the full picture, I hoped it was obvious that Teflon Jack was lying. There was no meeting."

"So how did the trial come out? Did the jury see through the lie?"

"They found him guilty, and the judge gave him twenty-six years. Furthermore, he's going back to trial on a technicality for one of his former crimes. I feel good about it."

"Well, chalk one up for the good guys!" Coop drained his beer, walked over and tossed the bottle in the trash. "I better be getting home to the wife. She's going to start wondering what happened to me. If the weather is decent, maybe we can go for a sail on Sunday? I'll give you a call."

"Sounds good. Thanks for stopping by." Sam walked Coop back to the front door.

Because it was Friday night, Sam might have gone out in a fruitless search for female company among the local bars, but he didn't feel like it. He had work to catch up on, and traveling had sucked the energy out of him. He ate a TV dinner, shuffled some paperwork, checked his emails, watched the news on TV, and went up to bed. On his way upstairs, he picked up his luggage which he hadn't unpacked since yesterday. He also remembered he forgot to stop at the post office and pick up the mail he had asked to be held. Oh well, he could unpack tomorrow and stop at the post office on Monday. He was tired and only wanted to go to bed. He had no reason to think this night would put into motion events that would change his life and threaten the security of his country.

CHAPTER 3

If Nancy Forrester had known how devastating her weekend was going to be, she would have stayed home. Things started to go downhill on Thursday. With a cup of coffee in hand, Nancy walked out into the fresh morning air and got into her car. She inserted the key and turned it. Nothing happened. She turned the key back and forth several times, and still nothing.

"No, no, no! Shit!" She slammed her palm on the steering wheel. She bought her little blue BMW about three years ago. Even though she bought it used, it had been an extravagance for her. Now, it was simply an old car draining her financially. She tapped the horn. It still worked. She turned her headlights on and walked around to the front of the car. They worked, but they were dim. She was sure the problem was the battery. She popped the hood to look at the battery cables. The connections were dirty, but tight. She took a photo of the battery label with her phone so she would know what to buy.

Nancy was twenty-eight and successful by most measures, but her life was a mess. Each morning she tried to start out with a fresh attitude and see her way clear to a better future. It was a pull yourself up by the bootstraps kind of existence. She had recently moved to the coastal town of Sea Haven and rented the little two-bedroom house she was parked next to. She hadn't had an opportunity yet to get to know any of her neighbors. There was nobody she felt comfortable asking for a jump start. She closed the hood and returned to the house. Now she was going to be late for work.

As soon as she was inside, she opened the Uber app on her phone to order a ride to work. A driver was ten minutes away. She checked Google Maps for an auto parts store close to the post office where she worked. She could walk there after work, purchase a new battery, and take Uber back home. Replacing the battery herself was a hell of a lot cheaper than getting a tow and having the dealership do it. In spite of his neglect, her father had managed to teach her a few useful skills.

Nancy worked at the post office, but she didn't work for the post office. She was a government contractor on assignment. As a software engineer, she was tasked with moving from one post office sorting center to the next around New England for the purpose of installing updates to the program used for the processing of mail. It was menial work compared to the last contract she had with the government, but she needed the work. Furthermore, Sea Haven, Massachusetts was a lot nicer than Washington DC in the summertime.

The company Nancy worked for was based in DC, and she considered northern Virginia to be her home. Her work had its ups and downs. Her prior contract was with DARPA (Defense Advanced Research Projects Agency). DARPA is one of the government's idea factories, and a cool employer for contract work. One of the DARPA programs invented a chemical that naturally wrapped around water molecules. When the tainted water was sprayed on the ground, certain light frequencies reflected differently off this chemical compared to unpainted terrain. The idea was to seed clouds and make rain with this chemical, or to fly over existing rain storms and introduce the chemical into the rain. When the fallen rain dried, everything would be coated with this invisible chemical. If something moved after the adulterated rain had fallen, cameras in space saw a dark spot in the place where that thing had previously sat. Comparing satellite photo sequences after a rainstorm allowed an artificial intelligence algorithm to identify and map movement on the ground for up to a week after the rain had dropped on a site of interest. Nancy had worked on the software, and it was a dream job. But all contracts must come to an end, and she now worked for the post office.

Once she finally arrived at work, Nancy settled into her routine. The post office had cleared a workspace for her where she could set up her laptop and have a surface to set her coffee down. That was about all she needed, along with a good internet connection. She had free run of the post office facility, which was a natural part of the job. She wasn't the kind of person who liked to sit still for long periods, so she found excuses to get up and walk around.

Since it was Thursday, she needed to make plans for the weekend. Weekends were when she pursued her "hobby". The postal delivery people spent the early morning sorting mail for their routes and loading their trucks. By ten o'clock, they were all out on foot or in their trucks. Nancy strolled by the work area filled with little cubbies where the delivery people sorted their routes. Whenever someone requested a temporary halt to their mail delivery, a big yellow postcard was taped above the appropriate pigeonhole. When nobody nearby was paying attention, Nancy snapped photos of four of these cards with her phone. She sauntered back to her desk and looked up the addresses on her laptop. She could guess the economic strata of each location from the section of town. If she wasn't sure of the quality of the neighborhood, she could go to satellite view and zoom in to get an idea of the size of the houses. Street view showed how well the properties were maintained.

The house at 1637 Ridgeview looked the most promising. Most of the houses in the neighborhood were on half-acre or full-acre lots. That meant she was less apt to be noticed by a nosy neighbor. Larger houses usually meant more potential entrances, which meant a greater probability of finding a weak spot. And of course, the bigger the house, the more likely she was to find valuables inside.

When she was still in grade school, Nancy learned to shoplift from the other kids she ran with. Without a mother, she was brought up on military bases by her father, who was away most of the time. He had a network of base families that he would park her with, but there was a general lack of adult supervision. She learned the meaning of the word fungible at a young age when her friend Keri was caught stealing. Keri had pocketed a silver dolphin necklace. Being one of a kind, it was easy to prove she had stolen it when she was caught. From that event, Nancy might have learned that stealing was wrong, and a bad idea. Instead, she learned the number one rule was to never get caught. The second rule was to only take things that are fungible. If you are caught, and you only have cash, or something so generic it could have come from anywhere, it's harder to prove you stole it.

Nancy didn't realize it at the time, but her introduction to shoplifting tapped into an impulse control disorder. She became excited and aroused leading up to a theft. Stealing provided gratification, followed by remorse and fear of arrest. The cycle started over again and repeated with the classic symptoms of kleptomania. Eventually, she came to realize that she had a compulsion problem and tried to work on self-discipline.

As she matured, Nancy grew out of her kleptomania phase and never planned to return to stealing. She told herself that her weekend "hobby" had developed out of necessity. She had spent two years living with a guy named Steve who effectively ruined her life. The first six months was a tumultuous period of romance when they moved in together in Washington DC. Decent apartments in DC were expensive. Even though they had two incomes, paying rent was a drain on their desired lifestyle. Ownership would give them a tax deduction and a chance to build up equity. Steve came up with the plan to purchase a fourplex in northern Virginia. They could live together in one unit and rent out the other three. When tax deductions were factored in, they could live almost for free.

The building they settled on was relatively cheap because it needed work. "No problem," said Steve. He could supervise subcontractors and do much of the work himself. This was going to be their ticket to a better life. Instead, it was a ticket to hell.

Steve needed Nancy's income to qualify for a mortgage and a construction loan. They formed a partnership and each signed on the dotted line. Construction was delayed and had major cost overruns. Without an occupancy certificate, they couldn't rent the units and get any income. The debt was killing them. When Steve should have been working on the building, he was at a bar drinking. His mood soured and their relationship deteriorated. Nancy feared his violent temper. When their savings dried up and their apartment lease expired, Nancy called it quits. She didn't want to be with him anymore.

Without obtaining the proper legal help, Steve arranged for a short sale of the fourplex. As a signatory to the loan, Nancy did not understand the full collateral damage that comes with a short sale. The money from the sale went to pay off the mortgage, but they came up short by over a hundred thousand dollars. Since the property was secured by a deed of trust, and since the lender agreed not to foreclose under the mortgage laws, there was no deficiency judgment. Being excused from their debt seemed like a win, but Nancy now had a black mark on her credit record. Worse, because it was an income property, the sale didn't qualify under the Mortgage Forgiveness Debt Relief Act, so the IRS came after her for almost twenty thousand dollars of tax. Nancy didn't realize being excused from a debt is treated the same by the IRS as if she had earned income. An income tax was owed on this imputed phantom income. Nancy's savings were depleted, so she couldn't pay the tax. When the IRS threatened to garnish her wages, her employer got involved. Nancy held a high-level security clearance. Financial troubles negatively affect government security clearances. Nancy stood to lose her clearance and her job. Her employer arranged for legal help from their in-house counsel, and monthly payments were structured to satisfy the IRS. This all seemed fine on paper, but Nancy couldn't make ends meet and needed to supplement her income. She thought about various side hustles. Mining cryptocurrency was a promising idea, but it took a lot of capital that she didn't have to buy the computer equipment. Besides, it was boring. Manual labor wasn't her thing, and a job like waitressing was far less attractive than reverting to her old habit. There was a thrill attached to being a cat burglar. It energized her in a way nothing else did, and it held the potential of easy money. Thus, her weekend hobby was born.

All through elementary school and junior high school, Nancy had been a gymnast, until she grew too tall in the middle of high school. She had the right kind of build, lean and powerful, but her increasing height disqualified her from ever being on the national team. The loss of a potential payoff undermined her motivation. The dedication required by the sport simply wasn't worth it. By the second year of high school, Nancy moved on to boys and more rigorous academics. Her athletic career had always served her well. As a gymnast, she gained confidence and learned discipline. It was easy for her to believe she could be a successful cat burglar.

She preferred going out on Friday or Saturday night so she could use the remainder of the weekend to catch up on her sleep and laundry. She remembered her childhood lesson, and disciplined herself to take only cash and small generic items she could easily sell online. The idea of fencing more expensive, one-of-a-kind items involved additional risk she didn't want to assume. If she only averaged two hundred dollars per robbery, it would take her one hundred robberies to pay her debt to the IRS. That was not a viable business plan, but until she had a better idea, she had to depend on luck. If she was lucky enough to score a thousand or two thousand dollars from a job, her progress would be much faster. She was climbing a mountain of sand, with little hope of reaching the top.

She did think about the ethics of what she was doing. She knew it wasn't right. She hoped it was temporary. She told herself her victims were insured, so the damage to them would be minimal. This was morally corrupt thinking, but she could blame it on her childhood or lack thereof. Maybe her target this weekend would be her lucky break.

CHAPTER 4

The plan was coming together. After she had replaced her car battery on Thursday evening, Nancy drove to Sam Barron's house on Ridgeview to check it out. Her target property was ideal, located on a slight curve in the road with empty land across the street. Only one neighbor could possibly see his driveway, and they were pretty far away with trees blocking their view. Street lights were spaced far apart, so she was sure she could find shadows in which to park her car.

On Friday night, Nancy went to bed early. At one in the morning on Saturday, she anticipated her alarm and turned it off before it could ring. Nancy flipped the covers back and stretched. She needed to wake up and get focused. She had developed a stock uniform she wore for her nighttime activities. She put on black socks and black yoga pants. She preferred not to wear a bra. Her breasts weren't large. She found boys' black sleeveless compression t-shirts on the internet that were comfortable and kept her breasts from bouncing. She pulled on another loose-fitting black t-shirt, and topped this with her black hoodie. She had also bought black Vans perf leather slip-on shoes on the internet. She painted the white-trimmed soles with a black magic marker. These were light, quiet, and had a good grip. She twisted her shoulder-length black hair up into a quasi-bun and stretched a black wool beanie cap over it. Her outfit was completed with a small fanny pack that held a flashlight, Leatherman multi-tool, black nitrile gloves, and a folded nylon bag she could use to carry found items.

It was a cool spring night in New England, with a minimal moon. Street numbers were difficult to read, so Nancy used her GPS to get her to the right section of Ridgeview. As she had planned, she was able to find a good spot to pull off the road in the shadows. She had previously taped shut the spring switch on her car door so the interior lights would not go on when she opened the door. Silently, she jogged across the street and down the driveway. She headed immediately for the shadow under the eve by the front corner of the house. The front door was the least likely entry point. She worked her way along the side of the house, inspecting windows as she went, and turned the corner at the back. There, next to the kitchen door, built into the side of the house, a doggie door! Perfect. A dog should not be home if the owners were away. She approached it cautiously.

The doggie door was the more expensive type with two flaps, one on the outside and one on the inside. When she lifted the outside flap, she found the middle space stuffed with insulation. Even better. Now she was confident there was no dog. She pulled the insulation out and pushed against the inner flap. It was solid. She took out her flashlight to inspect the situation. A plexiglass sheet had been locked over the inside flap. From the outside, she couldn't find any screws, slots, catches, or anything she could work with to remove the plexiglass. She turned around and stuck her foot in the hole and pressed. The plexiglass was solid and didn't want to give. She stomped once, hard. The plexiglass cracked down the middle and popped from its frame. It made more noise than she expected. Nancy froze and waited. No movement came from inside. No lights went on. She took a deep breath and let it out slowly. Nobody was supposed to be home.

It was easy for her to crawl through the doggie door and into the kitchen. She liked what she saw in the beam of her flashlight. The owners must have money. The kitchen was updated with slate floors and nicely veined top-quality granite countertops. The cabinets were a high-end cherry wood.

She headed for the dining room filled with replica late eighteenth-century furniture. She learned to appreciate antique furniture styles from all the moving she did as a child. She found a china cabinet and what appeared to be an original Hepplewhite sideboard. She opened the drawers in the sideboard and, using her flashlight, found silver napkin holders. They would be perfect to take, but they were monogrammed. That disqualified them. Nothing else looked promising. Nine times out of ten, the best score was in the master bedroom.

The main staircase was in the front hall. Six steps up alongside the wall, a landing at a right angle with a window behind it, and six more steps up alongside the opposite wall. Enough faint light came through the window to see her way up without the flashlight. Just as she reached the top of the stairs, lights went on behind her. Startled, Nancy spun back toward the light.

Bam! Something slammed into her from behind. An arm went around her neck, choking her. The force of the hit knocked her forward, off-balance. She grabbed the railing and pushed back hard to avoid falling down the stairs. She expected resistance, but found herself being pulled backward. She couldn't help falling on her back with a body beneath her. Instantly, legs wrapped around her thighs and squeezed with a vice-like lock. She flailed her arms, trying to hit the face of whoever was behind her. Before she could get a piece of him, an arm came across her chest, locking her right arm by her side and grabbing her left breast. She stopped moving.

This was the worst possible situation. The number one rule was to never, ever let anyone get close. As long as she had distance between herself and an attacker, she had options. This guy was clearly much stronger than her, bigger than her, and by being directly behind, he offered no target for her to attack. There was nothing she could do. No doubt, surprised by the female anatomy he found in his hand, he stiffened and lay still. He practically shouted in her ear, "You're not a man, you're a woman! What the fuck are you doing in my house?"

She didn't know what to say.

CHAPTER 5

Sam's heart was racing. He was still trying to figure out the situation. Their heads were side by side and his mouth was right next to her ear. With a determined and threatening voice, he whispered, "Who's with you?"

No answer.

He choked her with his left arm, gave a quick squeeze with his legs, and asked again, "Who else is here?"

"No one," she croaked. "I'm here by myself."

Sam waited and listened. "Is there anyone waiting for you outside?"

"No. I told you I'm by myself." She struggled to speak over the arm choking her.

Sam relaxed his grip slightly and waited. He was listening for any hint of movement downstairs. Finally, he said, "This is what's going to happen. You're going to reach out and pick up my phone which is in the doorway next to you. Then, we're going to get up slowly, together, and take a short walk. I don't want to hurt you, but if you fight me or do anything unexpected, I'm going to choke the daylight out of you. Do you understand?"

"Yes," said the girl. Sam watched in the dim light as she reached over, barely able to touch the phone, and pulled it toward her with her fingertips.

"Okay, here we go." Sam released his legs, sat up and ooched back enough so the girl was sitting on the floor and not on him. Together, they got their legs under them and managed to stand up while Sam kept his left arm firmly around her neck. He guided her through the master bedroom and into the master bathroom.

"There's a light switch to the right of the door. Turn it on."

She flipped the switch and suddenly they could see. Sam guided her to a second door that led into a water closet where the toilet was located. It was a tiny space designed for one person. He needed a small space to safely contain her while he sorted things out. The door opened inward, so Sam had to push her against the wall in the corner to get the door closed behind them. Once the door was closed, he turned on the light, then released his grip on her. He took a step back so his back was against the door. The room was too small for her to wind up for a punch or a kick. No way would she get out without a wrestling match, which she would lose.

Slowly, the young woman turned around. They saw each other face to face for the first time. Sam held his breath; he couldn't believe how attractive she was. He reached above her, and she ducked until she realized what he was doing. He pinched the top of her cap and pulled it straight up. Glossy black hair tumbled down over her shoulders.

Sam's heart was still thumping, and he was in emotional turmoil. He was angry someone would break into his house, but seeing this beautiful young lady, he was restrained from causing any harm to her. If she had been a man, he might be tempted to beat the crap out of him, but he couldn't do that to a woman. It would be like severely disciplining a puppy when your natural instinct was to pick it up and cuddle it.

Sam didn't have a conscious plan. Everything had happened so fast he was working from instinct. Now, a critical decision point had arrived. He didn't feel good about calling the police, but what else could he do?

Sam reached out and took his phone from her. "Here's the deal. You've violated my personal space. You've intruded on the sanctity of my house and invaded my privacy. I'm very upset. Now I have to call the police and turn you over to them. I don't want any more trouble from you."

He saw a look of shock and trepidation came over her face. Her eyes glanced around, like a trapped animal looking for a means of escape, but there was none.

Nancy was trapped. There was a long silence as they lay on the floor together with his head next to hers. He spoke directly into her ear in a low menacing voice.

"Who else is with you?"

She was tempted to say she had an accomplice downstairs, but where would that get her? She would continue to be a hostage until the ruse was discovered. Deceit would not endear her to her captor.

She desperately tried to think of any possible means of escape. This disaster was not going to have a good end unless she could break away and get out of the house. No way could she fight this guy while he had her pinned. She might as well cooperate and look for an opportunity as things developed.

Following his instructions to pick up his phone, she got to her feet with him. She assumed he would probably tie her up and call the police. She needed to escape before that happened. If she couldn't escape, she needed to figure out how to talk her way out of being arrested.

She was surprised when he took her into the bathroom water closet and closed the door. The space was so small it provided little opportunity to do anything. If he released the chokehold, she could turn and scratch his face and knee him in the balls, but he was blocking the door that needed to be opened inward. She had no escape. All she was likely to do was piss him off.

When he finally let her go and she was able to turn around, she suffered an unexpected shock. How dare he be so handsome? He was perhaps a dozen years older than her, mid-forties. He was four or five inches taller, and lean, as best she could tell under his baggy t-shirt and pajama bottoms. He had a classic all-American beach boy face, blonde hair, a strong jawline, piercing blue eyes, and a feeling of youthfulness about him, in spite of his apparent age. Her girlfriends in Virginia would label him a sex magnet.

She ducked as the man reached above her, until she realized he was just removing her cap. For a brief moment, a look of surprise registered on his face.

Then the inevitable happened. He reached out and took his phone from her. "Here's the deal," he said. "You've violated my personal space. You've intruded on the sanctity of my house and invaded my privacy. I'm very upset. Now I have to call the police and turn you over to them."

Holy shit! If he calls the police, she loses her security clearance, loses her job, and probably goes to jail. That is not an option. Nancy reached out and gently pushed the arm holding his phone to the side. "Wait! Can we take a minute to talk about this?"

"What's there to talk about? You made a bad choice breaking into my house, and now you have to pay the price."

Nancy put on her best coquettish smile. "I didn't take anything. I haven't done any harm. You could simply let me go."

She saw the hesitation in his eyes, but his voice was firm. "That isn't the way things work in my world. You're responsible for your actions and their consequences. You have intruded on me in a very personal way. I refuse to be your victim. I think the law should take care of this."

Nancy was crushed. She had to turn him away from this course of action. "Isn't there something I can do to make things okay? You'll ruin my life if you call the police. I'll do anything to make this right with you."

As she was saying she would do anything, she suddenly realized what that classic line meant. He was going to think she was offering him sex. Did she mean that? It wouldn't be too difficult. She'd probably had drunken one-night stands with guys who weren't half this good-looking. She was outraged to be caught in this situation, but she was more terrified of being arrested. Sex might be her only ticket out of this mess.

Nancy could see some confusion and uncertainty grip her antagonist, like he was performing some kind of mental calculation.

He looked intently at her with a troubled face. "I'm not sure what you have to offer me. Are you suggesting trading sex for your freedom?"

"If that's what it takes, I would consider that a fair trade."

He looked flabbergasted. "I'm not too keen on calling the police. That causes a lot of trouble for everyone. But I can't simply let you walk away scot-free. You owe a penalty, but I'm not sure I want to have sex with you. Let me rephrase that." He smiled with a feral, sexy expression. "You're attractive, and of course I would love to have sex with you, but are you sure that's a choice you want to make?"

"Getting arrested is the choice I don't want to make. I'm not saying I'm going to enjoy the alternative, but if that satisfies your sense of justice, I can live with it."

"Okay."

"Okay what? You're going to let me leave after you have your way with me?"

He looked sheepishly embarrassed. "Yes." After an awkward pause, she realized he had more to add. "At least you won't get pregnant or catch a disease from me. I've been celibate as a monk."

Here was proof once again, a sexual urge motivated all men. Nancy was devastated by the absence of better options, but was this really so bad? Since time immemorial, women have given their bodies to men in exchange for protection, food, and shelter. She was simply using the currency she had available.

Sam was in emotional turmoil. He felt vulnerable and violated due to a stranger breaking into his house. But he couldn't believe how beautiful she was. And now she was offering to have sex with him? Alarm bells were going off in his head. This was wrong in so many ways. His instincts told him he should call the police and be done with her, but the temptation was too great. She was offering him what he most wanted. He couldn't walk away from that.

Sam had trouble reading the expression on her face when he said yes to her offer. He thought he saw resignation and acceptance morph into seductive acquiescence. Desire had crept into his decision process and clouded any remaining judgement.

Heart pounding, he played it cool. "It begins by getting naked. I expect you to honor the bargain, but my theory is you aren't likely to try to run out of the house if you're stark naked." He let that sink in for a moment while he waited for her to react. "Do you want me to undress you?"

He reached toward her, but she shrugged him away.

"I'll do it myself."

She unzipped her hoodie sweatshirt and let it fall on the floor, followed by stripping off her outer t-shirt. She stepped out of her shoes, unclipped her fanny pack, and pulled off her yoga pants and socks. Then she paused and stared at him with her soft grey-blue eyes. Her pretty face and big eyes made Sam want to melt, but he held his ground and stared back. Reluctantly, she pulled the compression t-shirt over her head and then stood with her arms by her side.

Sam was dumbstruck at how incredible she was. She had the kind of stunning beauty that compelled a man to stare. Her expressive face had the angles and the developed features of a mature adult, but her skin was smooth and pure like that of a child. She had emotional eyes, a delicate nose, expressive lips, and a narrow jaw. Altogether, her features combined to give her a look of innocence. Her alert focused attention and calculated movement gave Sam an impression of intelligence and mature reserve hidden behind the facade of youth. Toned and shapely arms joined shoulders slightly wider than her narrow, gently curving hips. Her cute, petite breasts were perfectly symmetrical and looked like they had been molded from two champagne coupe glasses. They were firm and small enough to project straight out without any sag. Their proportion was ideal for her trim body. Clearly an athlete, her flat stomach and tight thighs all added together to give her a lithesome and alluringly nubile appearance. She was left with only a pair of silky white bikini panties and black nitrile gloves on her hands. It was an absurd clothing combination.

Sam slid his two index fingers inside the waistband of her panties. "Naked means no clothes."

She flinched as he slid each finger along the waistband to the outer edge of her hips, and then slowly pulled her panties down as he crouched down himself. He was kneeling when her panties reached the floor. His face was even with, and only six inches away from, her crotch. The tang of her scent filled his nose with a primal perfume to match their wildly inappropriate bargain. Much to his surprise, he didn't see a single pubic hair. He had never known a woman who shaved completely. The whole effect simply added to his confusion from the emotional turmoil churning within him.

Sam stood up and admired her while she peeled off the black nitrile gloves. As if to make a concession to her nakedness, he stripped off his t-shirt. He realized that he knew nothing about this woman, but he didn't care. It was lust at first sight, and he didn't want anything to get in the way of his good luck. In times past, he would have been embarrassed by an erection so powerful, his pajama bottoms would stick out. Now, he was worried the warm sensation of swelling between his legs might not result in him rising sufficiently to the occasion.

Sam turned and opened the door. He had to push back

against the young woman to give room for the door to swing past them. Her breasts pressed into his back, her belly and thighs touching him lower down. A shiver crossed his skin, and his penis pulsed momentarily. He wasn't sure what to expect from her, but she seemed docile. He turned and took her by the wrist with one hand to lead her through the bathroom and into the master bedroom. The bathroom light coming through the doorway cast a beam across the bedroom. He pointed to the king-size bed and gently led her toward it. As she got in and slid across, he set his phone on the bedside table, stepped out of his pajama bottoms, and followed her.

Nancy was worried about the prospect of going to bed with a strange man. But if she had to do it with anyone, this hunk would be her first choice. She was startled to find herself turned on by the thought. She hoped he would say yes to her proposition, yet she was surprised when he accepted. She knew it meant a shift in the balance of power. If he was thinking with his dick, then she could lead him around like a bull with a nose ring. She only had to survive this ordeal to gain her freedom.

She thought she could see desire in those beautiful blue eyes of his. "It begins by getting naked. I expect you to honor the bargain, but my theory is you aren't likely to try to run out of the house stark naked." A long pause stretched between his words. "Do you want me to undress you?"

She certainly wasn't going to give him any more control

than she had to. She bumped his hand away. "I'll do it myself."

She slowly unzipped her sweatshirt. She pulled off her t-shirt, stepped out of her shoes, unbuckled her fanny pack, and peeled off her yoga pants and socks. That was where she intended to stop. She assumed they would move to another room, but when she looked at him, he stared back with a look that said he was enjoying this and it wasn't going to stop here. She resented giving him any feeling of conquest, but reluctantly, she pulled the compression t-shirt over her head.

Her breasts were on full display and he wasn't shy about staring at her. It had suited her fine to not have breasts to contend with during her gymnastic career. Probably because of her intense workouts, puberty came late for her, and her chest remained flat. When her breasts did finally fill out in high school, they never grew to the size of many of the girls around her. She wouldn't have cared, except size seemed to be a measure of worth, particularly in the eyes of the boys. For her whole adult life, standing naked in front of a man had always made her feel lacking. She knew that many women would kill to have her slim body, but confidence for a woman seemed to come with big breasts.

The man reached out with his two index fingers toward her stomach.

"What is he doing now?"

She flinched and caught her breath as he slid his fingers inside the front waistband of her panties. "Naked means no clothes." He slid each finger along the waistband to the outer edge of her hips, then slowly pulled her panties down as he knelt. Nancy shivered, nipples tightening. She had lost control over her destiny. She could knee him in the face and try to kick him while he was down, but that would be futile. She still couldn't get through the door with him blocking it. Resigned to her fate, she grabbed her shoulders by crossing her arms over her chest to hide her nipples while he exposed the rest of her body. There was nothing for him to see that she was ashamed of, but she didn't like being held hostage to a bargain that required giving up control. At least he was being gentle and mastered his emotions so far. She hoped he was not going to become brutish and bestial. She didn't want to do anything to aggravate him.

When he stood up again and stared at her, she self-consciously removed the gloves she no longer needed. She was surprised when he spontaneously stripped off his t-shirt. What little body hair he had was transparent, like filaments of glass. It contributed to his youthful appearance. He had well-developed shoulders and arms with muscles that rippled beneath his skin. His stomach was flat with a washboard effect, but not like the extreme pictures of abs in the muscle magazines. He had a solid core, probably from years of athletic pursuits.

When he reached for the door handle and pulled the door inward, he had to press back against her. His buttocks pressed into her groin, and his back brushed against her breasts. His touch felt warm and solid. He took her by the wrist and led her into the bedroom. He pulled her forward, indicating she should get into the bed first. She slid across the large bed and immediately pulled the covers over her naked body. She turned her head on the pillow to watch him.

The man stood by the bed in a shaft of light cast from the door of the bathroom. As he released the drawstring and stepped out of his pajama bottoms, ripples of light and shadow played across his sculptured body. His figure reminded Nancy of a Greek statue. He looked like the work of a great artist, a hero carved in marble, except he had a partial erection.

As he turned toward the bed, she realized there was no getting out of this now, but she was determined to maintain control.

CHAPTER 6

Was he sure about this? Sam didn't expect her to suggest sex. Now he was nervous. He got into bed and lifted the covers over himself as he slid next to her. She was lying on her back with her legs together and arms by her side. He tentatively reached out a hand and rested it on her stomach. His body tingled with excitement at the touch of her smooth skin. Slowly, he moved his hand up to her breast. He cupped the firm mound and massaged it gently. She lay stiff and unmoving, staring at the dark ceiling. This was incredibly awkward.

He tried to convey a polite, soothing tone to his voice. "What's your name?"

There was a long pause before she acknowledged him. "Nancy".

"What's your last name, Nancy?"

This time there was an even longer pause. He had her body, but Nancy did not want to give him control of anything more.

"That's not part of the bargain, is it?"

Resistance to all intimacy troubled Sam. "I guess not," he mumbled.

What was he thinking? This wasn't a date! Her response made him even more embarrassed. He wanted her participation.

"My name is Sam."

"I know." She hesitated and let that sink in. "Sam Barron."

"I see you've done your homework."

"Not well enough. You weren't supposed to be here. I thought you were away."

"I was away. I just returned. Bad timing on your part."

None of this conversation was having the desired effect of putting her at ease and making this less awkward. Sam moved his hand to her other breast in a futile effort to do something different to get a response from her.

"You said you wouldn't get me pregnant. I don't see any condoms. How does this work?"

"Don't have any. I didn't know you were coming tonight. But you don't need to worry."

Sam pulled the covers down to his hips and pointed at a spot about an inch below his belly button. "I don't know if there's enough light for you to see this scar. I was abducted by aliens and they put a probe in me here. They removed things from my insides. Now, when I have an orgasm, nothing comes out. I'm upset they tampered with my sex organs, but on the plus side, I can have sex with no muss and no fuss."

Wondering if he was a nut case, she snorted, "Sure! I'm

supposed to believe that?"

Sam pulled the covers back over them. "You can trust me or not. Your choice. This whole thing was your choice. It's not too late for you to change your mind."

Nancy got caught up in the dilemma of him asking her to trust him. Was trust relevant if she didn't have another viable alternative? Even if she didn't trust him, she still had to go forward with her first decision to agree to get in bed with him, which also wasn't a choice. Trust or no trust, none of this was free will. Thank God for the morning-after pill.

Sam rolled over and reached for his phone on the bedside table. He sat up and pressed the microphone icon. It was now recording. He spoke into the phone. "I'm with Nancy, and she has agreed to have consensual sex with me. Actually, I guess that's redundant. If she has agreed, then, by definition, it is consensual. Anyway, it was your idea to have sex. Is it true you have agreed to have sex with me?" He held the phone out to Nancy.

She stared at it.

"You're supposed to say, 'Yes, I agree,' unless you don't."

"Yes, I agree."

"And I have given you several opportunities to say no. Is that true?" He held the phone out to her again.

"Yes, that's true."

"Good," said Sam as he turned off the phone and placed it back on the table. He then snuggled back under the covers.

"Was that really necessary?"

"Under the circumstances, yes. There can be no question

that you agreed to this."

"Under duress," grumbled Nancy.

"The situation is of your own making. They say the choices we make determine who we are."

"Yeah, well that assumes we truly have choices. Sometimes we are simply the victim of other people's choices."

Sam squinted with a frown. "Well, I'm the victim of your bad decision to break into my house."

Nancy saw no point in continuing the conversation. The guy clearly did not understand what it meant to be a woman.

Sam's hand found its former place on her breast. As he gently massaged it, she lay stoically stiff and tried to ignore him. It actually felt quite pleasant. Every time he brushed the nipple, a tingle passed through her from her clit to her finger-tips, but she was not going to allow him any satisfaction. She wasn't sure if she was mad more at him or herself for getting into this situation, but she was determined not to reward his indulgence. If he was going to get his jollies at her expense, she wasn't going to contribute.

Maybe she could refuse to participate, but Sam was now driven by a primal desire. He pulled the covers down to expose her closest breast and bent his head down. At first, he mouthed the tip with his lips. Then he gently sucked. He tickled her nipple with his tongue and tried every trick to get her engaged.

Her body was reacting to the sweet sensations, but mentally, she was undaunted in her resistance. She had every intention of lying still and playing the frigid bitch. Who was he to think he could seduce her after agreeing to her desperate bargain? Her mind flashed back to the statuesque body that had stood in the shaft of light beside the bed. *Stop it,* she told herself, as another thrill rippled through her body.

Sam believed he was fighting a hopeless battle. She didn't offer him the slightest response. He might as well get on with things. He moved his hand across her stomach and down between her legs. Her legs were still rigidly straight and locked together, but her thin thighs left plenty of room for his fingers to work their way below her mound and caress the folds of skin that covered the warm sweet spot he craved. He was surprised at how soft and smooth her skin was. He expected to feel razor stubble where all her hair had been removed. Women had secrets he had never bothered to explore. How all that hair was removed from such a delicate area was a mystery to him.

Slowly, he stroked and caressed the folds of skin while his fingers gently probed in between. Eventually, her body produced the slippery lubricant needed. He probed deeper while his strokes became longer. He found the knob of her clitoris. He lightly stroked it and circled it until she quivered. He wanted to kiss her, but her tightly clamped lips indicated he would be rejected. She lay straight and stared blankly at the ceiling. Her will seemed indomitable, but the hitch in her breath at his touch said otherwise.

Finally, he pushed himself up and placed one hand behind each of her knees. He lifted and separated her legs, and moved in between them. She braced herself for the first thrust which she expected to be uncomfortable, even painful, but it never came. He held his penis with one hand and stroked it up and down her slit. It glided easily in the warm slippery wetness. He applied pressure, as if he was going to penetrate, but then he would slide forward across her clit. He jiggled, tapped, and probed in a delightful, teasing way. His other hand massaged one nipple, fingertips squeezing in time with the pressure from below. It was hard for her not to squirm in reaction. Desire was overtaking her resistance.

His penis swelled bone hard. When he did slide into her, it was so easy and gentle, her body welcomed him. Her insides engorged to encompass him in a firm but slippery grip. She folded around him as he pressed deep inside her. Nancy's body was betraying her. The feeling was exquisite, and her lust was in full acceptance, but a corner of her mind still was not. She hated this false closeness. She had the will to resist, but not the ability. Her self-esteem depended on her inner strength. She stared into his eyes with defiance, refusing to wilt under his dominance.

Slowly, Sam moved his hips to draw his penis in and out in long strokes. Her determination faded as she held Sam's gaze. Her feigned indifference gave way to awe as she absorbed the amazing sensations that coursed through her body. Her eyes glassed over. Against her intention, her knees pulled up toward her chest and her hips thrust up toward him. She wanted him to fill her completely with as much contact as possible. Her vagina throbbed in pulsating waves.

Sam was finally getting the response from her he craved. The striated muscles in her vagina grabbed hold and encased him. Regular contractions gave way to spasms of chaotic trembling and quivering. The sensation drove him over the edge. He strained into her, his pubic bone pushing against hers. She grabbed his back in a reflexive move, then turned her head sideways and moaned. Sam couldn't contain himself any longer. His balls contracted as the head of his penis expanded to its limit. Starting with a tingly surge deep inside of him, a spasm beginning near his tail bone swept through him and along the full length of his penis. He thrust uncontrollably while she had him clenched tightly with her hips locked to his. She gasped and bit her lower lip in a grimace as her body shuddered with paroxysms of pleasure. Her head swam with the surge of blood from her pounding heart. The room spun as lights and shadows swirled in her eyes. Like sweet salt air, she breathed in the scent of his perspiration.

"Hallelujah!" thought Sam, as joy swept over him. The doubts he had about his sexuality had been put to rest. In spite of how awkward the situation was, he really cared about this woman. As much as he wanted to dominate her because of her misdeeds, he also wanted to please her. It actually mattered to him that she would think well of him.

Sam supported his weight on his elbows as he lay on top of her, catching his breath. Her face was flushed, and she was panting. She still had her arms clasped around him, but her legs had relaxed, with her knees fallen out to either side. Sam was still inside her, and he wanted to stay there. He wanted this moment to last forever as waves of relief and satisfaction consumed him. She lay so comfortable and natural in his arms, soft and fitted to his body. But his erection was fading, and her muscles were naturally contracting and pushing him out. She let her arms fall to her side, and he finally rolled off of her. He kept one arm resting on her stomach.

Nancy was ashamed at her loss of control, and mad at herself. She had found herself in an untenable position. He clearly wanted to engage her in his lust, and she had not wanted to participate, but her body had been disloyal to her will. To his credit, he did not give up, and was skilled enough to elicit her participation. And the way he looked into her eyes… No man had ever done that before, like he was probing into her soul. At least he didn't treat her as an object. He wasn't simply masturbating into a woman. He acted as if he cared for her. But the whole thing was wrong. Just plain wrong.

She rolled away from him and sat up. "Are we done?"

The cold tone of her voice cut into him, bringing him back to reality. "I guess so…" Suddenly he was filled with regret and guilt, combined with tender feelings for her. "I wish we had met under different circumstances. I would have liked to have had the opportunity to get to know you."

She said nothing as she got up and walked to the bathroom. She closed the door. Sam walked to the closet and pulled on jeans and a sweatshirt. The toilet flushed and the door opened. She was fully dressed, inaccessible to him as a stranger.

"I'll walk you out," he said.

She said nothing.

When they walked through the kitchen, shattered plexiglass glittered on the floor by the doggie door. "So that's how you got in without tripping the alarm. If I hadn't been here, you would have set off the interior motion detectors. What would you have done then?"

Nancy shrugged. "Then it becomes a smash, grab, and run operation. I'd be long gone before anyone arrived."

"Seems like a precarious way to make a living."

They walked out to the street together. Sam followed her to her car. His conscience was talking to him, and he wasn't liking what it was saying.

"I hope you can live with your decision," Sam said. "I'm not so sure I can."

She took a breath, like she was going to make a retort, but she didn't. When they got to her car, Sam chewed on his lower lip, the tension between them terribly awkward. "Well, I guess this is goodbye. I don't expect I'll see you again."

"Not likely." Darkness hid the expression on her face as she got into her car.

Sam was going to snap a photo of her license plate, but didn't want to be too obvious. Instead, he memorized the number, then copied it into his phone after she drove away. At least he could find her if he needed to, but he couldn't imagine she would ever want to see him.

Sam returned to his empty house. He felt more alone than

before, and he carried a sense of disappointment and loss. This whole encounter was messed up.

PART 2

THE CHASE

CHAPTER 7

For the next few nights following his encounter with Nancy, Sam had vivid dreams involving this mysterious woman. The dreams were filled with tension and confusion, ultimately resolved sexually. Sam would wake up in the morning with an erection, confronted with disappointment it was only a dream. His constant loneliness was painful. Whenever the memory of her surfaced, it came with a combination of desire and guilt. He worked hard to push her far back into the dark recesses of his mind, and occupied himself with his daily routine.

He replaced the broken plexiglass and added a metal sheet to the outside of the doggie door. He continued on with his dull life as if nothing extraordinary had ever happened. He enjoyed his work, and he enjoyed his acquaintances, but with an element of disappointment in the background that he no longer had anything exciting or meaningful in his life. He had no close friend or lover to take comfort in. Nobody to laugh with, nobody to share with, nobody to care for or feel attached to. He missed his son in London. He maintained a social facade, but he was a desperately lonely person in an anonymous world.

About one month later, when summer was coming into full bloom, Sam received a call at his office. "Hello," said the female voice. "This is Nancy."

Sam was expecting a business call and he had to think for a moment. He didn't know anyone named Nancy. Then it hit him, and he stammered, "Oh, yes, hello." His gut was suddenly gripped with anxiety.

"I would like to meet with you."

Sam paused to digest what she said. "I don't know… I didn't expect to hear from you… I have a feeling you are trouble with a capital T —"

"Please!" she interrupted. "I'm not trouble, but I'm in trouble. I need your help!"

Sam would have said yes if he had been allowed to complete his sentence. Now it made him appear more gracious to say yes.

"Okay… I'll give you the benefit of the doubt. When are you thinking?"

"I can meet you right now."

Sam looked at his watch. Just after ten. "How about we meet at noon at the coffee shop on Elm Street? Do you know the one I mean?"

"Yes. I'll meet you there at noon." She hung up.

Sam held onto his phone wondering what this was all about. His insides were churning with a combination of worry and excitement. He thought focusing on work for the next hour would be difficult, but some more phone calls filled the time.

Sam left his office sooner than necessary and had to deliberately drive slowly so he wouldn't arrive too early. When he got to the coffee shop, he went straight to the counter and ordered a medium coffee. He selected a table in the front corner and sat with his back to the wall. No one was nearby. A young couple was giggling at a table across the room on the other side of the front door. Two tables away from them was a group of four older men who were clearly retired, and probably hung out here on a regular basis.

Nancy came through the door at exactly noon. When she looked around, Sam raised his cup of coffee with one hand and pointed toward the counter with the other. She got the hint and walked over to the counter to place her order. When she arrived at his table, Sam stood up awkwardly out of ingrained deference. He didn't know what to say, but she saved him the worry.

With a short burst of intensity, she said, "Thank you so much for seeing me!"

Sam sat back down. "This seems weird. I didn't expect to ever hear from you."

"I know. Maybe it is weird, but you're the only person I can turn to. You're the only one who knows what I do and – I hope – won't make things worse for me."

She was even more gorgeous than Sam remembered, if that

was possible. His body was telling him he would do anything for her, but his mind was more circumspect. "I'm worried you are going to involve me in something I can't afford to be involved with, but I'm listening."

"I think some men are trying to kill me, and I really, really need some help!"

This was not what Sam was expecting to hear. "What? What men, and why?"

"It's kind of a long story," she replied. "I don't know who they are, but I might know what they're after. My house was broken into, and then later, some men with guns came back to look for me. I can't go to the police, and I can't go home. I don't have any good options. That's why I hope you can help me."

"What do you want from me?"

She leaned forward, sliding her hand out to rest on his forearm. "First off, I need a safe place to stay. I need a place to hide out while I make sense of this. I called you because I have no connection to you that anybody will be able to figure out. If you can keep me hidden, I'll be so, so grateful."

Sam was skeptical. "So, I assume you did something illegal? Will I be aiding and abetting a fugitive?"

"No, no. The police aren't after me. I simply took something I shouldn't have, and now the Russians are looking for me. I don't think I can just give it back. I think they want me dead. I really need to hide!"

"Russians? What exactly did you take?" Sam sat back with his arms crossed.

Nancy reached into her purse and pulled out a USB flash drive and a small notebook. "I took these because they were carefully hidden, so I assumed they have value. I'm still not sure what they are. I looked at the files on the flash drive and mostly found algorithms and a lot of computer coding. There's one brief explanation, which I printed. The notebook is full of URLs and passwords for computer farms all over the world. It appears to give access to tremendous computing power through the likes of Amazon, Alphabet, Oracle, IBM, and Microsoft.

"I spent most of the night trying to figure this out. There's a lot I don't understand yet, but I think that the simple explanation is that someone has discovered a kind of time machine —"

"Come on," Sam scoffed.

"Actually, better than a time machine. Let me explain it this way. One use for a time machine is the ability to jump forward and see the future. If you don't like the future you see, you can come back to the present and make changes. The nice thing about a time machine is you don't have to waste time waiting and wondering about how changes you make now will affect the future. You can experiment with choices now, jump forward to the future and see what your changes do to the world, and keep going back and forth over and over until you get the results you want. Make sense?"

He set his coffee down and leaned back. "You are suggesting you could build your idea of the perfect future?"

"Right, but going back and forth through time would be a lot of work. Furthermore, I'm not sure it's truly possible."

Sam's eyes grew big as his eyebrows stretched upward. "What the... Are you nuts? You're talking about controlling the future? How are you going to change a future that hasn't happened yet? Anything can happen in the future."

Nancy waived the USB flash drive in front of his face. "That's exactly my point. How can you change the future if you don't know for sure what the future will be? I think this computer program might be better than time travel. This program purports to give you a virtual view of the future based on current data. Mathematically, it can jump forward without the constraint of time. Through prediction, you can get a view of the future before everyone else, without having to actually travel into the future."

Sam shook his head. Was this the same Nancy who had broken into his house and had hot sex with him? He tried to catch up to the idea she wasn't deranged, and her education and intellect were far greater than he had assumed. He admired the intensity in her eyes as she continued to explain.

"I'm jumping to conclusions here based on the **README** file I discovered on the flash drive." She pulled a page out of her pocket. "This is what I printed." She handed the single piece of paper to Sam.

D2

The name of this project is D2, which is shorthand for the second derivative*. The symbols of mathematics allow a virtual world to be constructed that has the same properties as the physical world, but without the constraint of inertia. Inertia prevents infinite speed. Inertia is that property of mass in the real world that effectively creates time. Time is simply a metronome that provides a benchmark for sequential change. Change of any type must occur in sequence to be meaningful. If change could happen instantaneously, time would not exist and the world would just be a meaningless blur. Inertia is the governing constraint that creates time.

In the world of mathematics, a computer program can process symbolic information at immense speed without the limitations imposed on matter. Thus, it is possible to get to the future faster in a virtual world than in the physical world, which is constrained by inertia. Depending on the mass of the system being analyzed, the future can be seen sometimes minutes or hours in advance. For high inertial systems, the future can be seen sometimes, days, weeks, or even years in advance. Generally, the quality of the view of the future is determined by the quality of the data input and by how far into the future one tries to look. The big difference with D2 is vastly better accuracy.

Most people view the world as a linear "cause and effect" series. The classic model is the billiard ball rolling across a table, causing one ball to bump into another, and then the next to bump into another, and so on. In fact, our world is far more complex. Almost nothing travels at a constant speed and in a constant direction. Almost everything is accelerating and decelerating, and there is a lot of simultaneity. The second derivative is a calculation of how the rate of change is itself changing. This calculation is essential to accurately model a progressive sequence into the future.

D2 is an artificial intelligence program that can "see" into the future of complex systems. The knowledge gained can be used to position oneself in advance to benefit from the future, or, alternatively, to change system inputs to create a different future.

Robert Drury, PhD

* In the Leibniz notation, the second derivative is denoted $\frac{d^2 y}{dx^2}$

The intensity in Nancy's voice increased. "I've worked for DARPA in the past and seen all sorts of futuristic projects. I think I understand some of the implications here. Do you realize how incredibly valuable this is if it really works? The person who can control the future holds the power to control the world. This is the kind of thing that can build and destroy nations."

Sam sat in silence, staring at the document, pondering what it meant. Finally, he looked Nancy in the eyes. "This all seems unbelievable. Truly unbelievable. Who is Robert Drury?"

"I checked him out on Google. He's a professor of astrophysics at Oxford University in England. News articles say he was recently murdered."

"Murdered!" Sam gripped the table. "And people are chasing you?"

"Yes." Nancy's large gray eyes were pleading.

"Okay. You owe me much more of an explanation, but for now, I do have a place where you can stay. I'm having some minor renovation done on my house, which makes it difficult to have you stay there, unseen. If you are being followed, I don't want to be exposed to that problem either. I own a forty-two-foot sailboat that I keep in a slip at Bartlett's Landing. She's hooked up to shore power and has all the comforts of home. You can stay there for a few days until we can figure this out and come up with a plan."

"Oh, thank you! Thank you!" Nancy gushed.

Sam stared off in the distance and lightly tapped the table. "If it's really possible to accurately predict the future —"

Nancy jumped in. "If it is, you could become fabulously wealthy. You could design battle plans that are guaranteed to work. You could influence elections. You could manipulate and control everybody and everything."

"No wonder people are after you." Sam ran a hand through his hair while he thought. "We have two problems. First, we have to know if this program works. Second, we have to figure out what to do with it. It can't fall into just anybody's hands."

Nancy looked at him with puppy dog eyes. "Right now, I'm just trying to stay alive. I appreciate anything you can do."

"Give me your phone." Sam held out his hand.

"What? Why?"

Sam pulled his phone out of his pocket and removed it from the wire-cloth pouch where he kept it. He handed the pouch to Nancy. "This is a Faraday cage. Put your phone in it. If people really are chasing you, they can track you through your phone. Just turning it off isn't good enough. This material will kill any signal. Don't ever take your phone out of this sleeve unless you're in a public place where you won't stay for more than a minute or two. In general, plan on not using your phone. If you need to get online, use a laptop — preferably not yours. If you need to make a call, borrow someone else's phone or use a public phone. And while we're on the subject, stop using your credit cards."

She sank into her seat. "Wow. I guess I hadn't thought through what this really means. How do you know about this stuff?"

"We'll get into that another time." Sam looked at the clock on his phone. "I have things I need to wrap up at the office. It'll take me about an hour. That'll give you time to gather up anything you might need. If you're in as much danger as you say, I wouldn't recommend going back home. Buy what you need, but only use cash. If you don't have enough cash, make a list and I'll go shopping for you later."

He looked through the window of the shop, then lowered his voice. "Listen carefully. If these people have any brains, they'll know what you're driving. There's a Walmart about five-hundred yards from Bartlett's Landing. Are you familiar with the marina?"

"Yes."

"I want you to make sure you aren't followed, then park in the Walmart parking lot. Walk from there to the landing and wait for me on the bench by the entry gate to the docks. I'll see you there at 1:30. Got it?"

Nancy nodded. "You don't know how scared I am. I can't thank you enough for helping me!"

"See you soon." Sam got up and left.

CHAPTER 8

Trouble for Nancy started shortly after she broke into Sam's house and got caught. She tried working for the next few weeks, but she couldn't focus. Her productivity ground to a halt. She was so distraught, and in such turmoil after that surreal experience, she told her employer she needed some time off. She had weeks of accumulated vacation time, so she returned to her home base outside Washington, DC, and tried to make sense of her life.

For several days she found it hard to get out of bed. Her mood swung from rage, to guilt that she had brought this on herself, to a "who gives a damn because my life is fucked anyway" attitude. She was barely clothing and feeding herself. Then she bumped into her friend Shelley at the grocery store.

"Whassup Nancy?" Shelley grinned. She wore a perpetual smile and was always enthusiastic about whatever she was doing. Today, that grated on Nancy's nerves.

"Just chilling." Nancy forced a smile. "I've taken some time off from work. What are you up to?"

Shelley's face brightened, if that was possible. "I've got this big embassy party tonight. I'm here picking up a few things for it now. Business has been crazy!"

Shelley ran a catering business and finally hit the big league after years of struggling. "Hey! If you aren't doing much, want to come help me set up? In fact, you can also help me work the party tonight if you want to. There'll be all kinds of good-looking foreign guys there. These things are usually blowouts. It'll be a lot of fun!"

"I don't know…"

"Sure you do!" Shelley bumped a fist against Nancy's arm. "It's going to be a blast! Come over this afternoon and help me set up. It's an amazing building. You'll love it. You can make up your mind later if you want to come to the party."

Nancy shrugged. It wasn't as if she had anything else planned. "Okay. I'll help you set up."

"Great!" Shelley wrote 3100 Mass Ave on the back of her business card and handed it to Nancy. "Take an Uber because you aren't going to be able to park. It's the British embassy. You'll love it. Meet me there at two this afternoon, and wear a simple dress. Wait at the main gate, and you'll see my truck pull up. Bring your license and passport. This is exciting, girl! See you soon!"

Nancy couldn't believe she had gotten herself sucked into this, but it might turn out to be interesting. At least it would take her mind off other things, and perhaps Shelley's perpetual sunshine would rub off on her.

Nancy used Lyft instead of Uber and arranged to be dropped at the Winston Churchill Memorial at 1:45. She spent ten minutes wandering around the statue of WC, then slowly sauntered toward the main gate of the British ambassador's residence. At two o'clock sharp, Shelley pulled up in her catering van. Her window was down and she called out, "Get in," pointing to the passenger seat.

"Good timing." Nancy hopped into the passenger seat, tucking under the skirt on her black sheath dress. "If I hung around much longer, I was afraid the guards would think I was casing the place."

Shelley pulled forward to the guard station and handed her credentials out the window. She stretched a hand toward Nancy. "Give me your passport." She handed Nancy's passport to the guard and told him, "She should be on your list."

The guard looked at their IDs and compared them against a list he had on a clipboard, then handed them back. "Pull through the gate and park to the right. Your truck needs to be inspected before you can pull up to the kitchen entrance." Uniformed men with rifles were strategically positioned on the driveway inside the gate.

Shelley did as she was told, then she and Nancy unloaded supplies into the kitchen. Their immediate objective was to set up the dining room with a buffet of hors d'oeuvres. As long as the weather held, this was going to be a garden party on the terrace overlooking the beautiful gardens. Guests would be served drinks and hors d'oeuvres by waiters on the terrace, but the main bar and food station were set up inside, in the dining room of the residence.

Nancy worked as a gofer, doing whatever she was told. The building was a wonderful example of elegant aristocratic life, and she could get used to that. Unfortunately, that dream would probably never come true.

During the whole setup process, a chief housekeeper, named Bidwell, oversaw everything and watched everybody with an eagle eye. If it weren't such an elegant setting, Nancy would have felt like she was in prison being watched by guards. But it was an embassy, and thus normal to have security stationed around.

She thought they made a mistake when they sent her for more linens. Bistro tables were being set up on the terrace, and they didn't have the right tablecloths for them. Bidwell directed her to the "servants' stairway" and told her she would find a linen closet on the third floor where appropriate-sized tablecloths could be obtained. She couldn't believe she was being sent upstairs unescorted.

When Nancy got to the second floor, she realized why she didn't have an escort. The door in the stairwell was painted with a notice that said, "Do Not Enter – Alarm". She shrugged, bummed she wasn't going to get to see the second floor. The stairs ended at the third floor where she was presented with a long hallway. The first room on her right was a laundry room.

After that was a series of cabinet doors, clearly "the linen clos-et". She worried it would take her all day to find what she was looking for, but fortunately, the shelves were all labeled.

Across from the laundry was a small sitting room. A series of doorways continued down the hall which Nancy suspected were bedrooms. The first door beyond the linen cabinets was slightly ajar. Nancy couldn't resist taking a peek.

It was indeed a bedroom. It didn't have the same elegance as the lower-level furnishings, but was above the standard she would expect for servant's quarters. The decorating was 19th century English, and the quality of the carpet and draperies were better than typically found in most upscale houses. The room was definitely occupied. Her old habit of hunting for treasure kicked in. Suits and shirts hung in the closet. A suitcase on a stand was locked. Nothing personal had been left on the bureau top or the bedside table. The bureau had a wavefront to it with a burl veneer on the drawers that displayed the gorgeous grain in the wood.

Nancy pulled open the top drawer, revealing men's socks and underwear. The burgundy color and goldcrest of a dip-lomatic passport caught her eye. She opened it to a picture of a rugged, handsome face – perhaps early thirties. The name said, Joseph Campbell. She quickly put it back and closed the drawer. She thought about opening the other drawers, but then her gaze went to the bottom of the bureau. Beneath the bottom drawer was a four-inch bar of wood that looked like part of the frame. Nancy had grown up with old furniture, so she knew better. Although there were no knobs to pull, sometimes that bottom piece hid another "secret" drawer. She reached down and pulled from underneath. Sure enough, a thin drawer slid out. An envelope was inside, containing a small notebook and a USB flash drive. She would never know what possessed her to take it. It must have some value if it was hidden, but it was against all her rules about only taking cash or unidentifiable generic items that could easily be turned into cash. She was driven more by curiosity than profit. If she couldn't make sense of its value, she had no problem simply getting rid of it.

Nancy was only wearing a sheath dress. She hadn't put on an apron, like Shelley. She had no pockets and no purse with her. Hands trembling, she hid the envelope between the tablecloths, and returned down the stairs. At the bottom of the stairs, along the hall leading back to the public rooms, there was a niche in the wall with a decorative urn in it. Nancy slipped the envelope out from between the linens and dropped it in the urn. She thought she would be able to return to retrieve it, but Bidwell's eagle eye prevented that. When Shelley asked her if she wanted to work the party that evening, Nancy was quick to reply yes.

The party that night was lively, elegant, and everything she expected of an embassy party. Washington, DC was better than Hollywood. Everyone was an actor. Everyone was hiding behind a façade, except perhaps the ambassador himself. Who knew how many secrets he was privy to?

Nancy was kept continuously busy. With all the serving she did, she saw virtually every face there. With her good looks, she received a dozen solicitations of various kinds which she was adept at brushing off. If she had been in a different frame of mind, she would have had fun pursuing some of the offers. She even saw Joe Campbell, and felt strange stealing from him. She didn't know for sure the envelope belonged to him, but it seemed probable.

Later in the evening, when the commotion died down and most of the guests were out on the terrace, Nancy was able to slip away and go back down the hall to the stairway. This time she was prepared. Shelley had provided her with a uniform and apron. When she was sure she was alone, she took the envelope out of the urn and slipped it into the pocket of the apron. By now, the excitement of the adventure had worn off; she wondered why she was doing this. She had no idea how much trouble this was going to cause her.

Being a government contractor with a high-level security clearance, Nancy should have realized that cameras are everywhere. Her head just wasn't in the game. She had no idea how easily she was going to be identified. She left the embassy party thinking she had gotten away clean. After two more days in Washington, she headed back to New England. It didn't occur to her that she was being chased.

CHAPTER 9

Nikolai Andronovich did not intend to kill his taxi driver. It simply became necessary. When Nikolai arrived at the airport in New York City from the United Kingdom, he and his two accomplices took a classic Yellow Cab. Using Uber would have necessitated registering on an app that could possibly be traced to a phone, and then back to him.

When the taxi driver opened the trunk for their bags and realized there were three of them, he said, "No. I can only take two in the back."

Nikolai reached into his pocket and pulled out two twenties. He held them out and said, "I'll give you an extra forty dollars if you let me ride in the front."

The cabbie looked at the bills and shrugged. "Okay. Let me unlock the door for you."

When Nikolai was getting into the passenger seat of the cab, and the driver was holding the door for him, his small satchel dropped onto the sidewalk and fell open. Among other things, his Russian passport fell out along with a fake UK driver's license. The taxi driver, trying to be helpful, picked up the driver's license, looked at it, then handed it to Nikolai. Although it was a small risk, Nikolai couldn't afford to have his whereabouts known and his identity compromised. Instead of going to their hotel, he gave instructions for the driver to take them to the Cathedral of St. John the Divine. As they got close, Nikolai told the cabbie to drive around behind the cathedral and let them off on Morningside Drive. The taxi pulled over into an empty parking space on the side of the road. As soon as the driver put the cab in park and looked to his left to get out of the car, Nikolai slipped a wire garrote over his head and pulled until it cut into his windpipe. The driver slumped across the front seat as the three Russians got out of the cab and casually walked away.

Nikolai had followed Joe Campbell to the United States, but he was more than six hours behind. It had taken that long for his handler to coordinate with their American contact and determine where Mr. Campbell was going. Eyes on the ground were supposed to track Joe when he landed in New York, but Nikolai didn't know who was running that operation or how they would communicate with him. After the fiasco in England, this whole thing was turning into a shit show.

Shortly after Nikolai arrived at his hotel, his cell phone pinged with a text message. All it said was, "Subject on the move. Flight booked to DC. Presumably British Embassy."

"Crap!" Nikolai thought to himself. "We aren't going to get any sleep tonight." He immediately booked a flight to Washington.

Nikolai was among the guests at the embassy party, mixing inconspicuously with the other attendees. His contact had arranged an invitation for him to accompany the Russian ambassador, so he could confirm that Joe Campbell was there. He couldn't touch Joe while he was in the embassy, but he managed to tag his coat with an RFID at the party. Now it would be easier to track him when he left the embassy.

CHAPTER 10

Joe Campbell slept late the day after the party. He spent the afternoon developing his strategy. He was struggling with how to proceed. Joe worked for MI6, but it had become clear to him MI6 had been penetrated and likely compromised by a double agent. Someone was after him and the information he had. He would have preferred to get the information back into secure hands in the UK, but he had no idea who he could trust. After all, that was why he was in the United States. Sharing this information with the CIA did not sit well with him, but he didn't see any alternative. How was he going to reach out to the right person at the CIA? He couldn't go through normal channels if his organization was compromised. This wasn't the kind of information that could safely pass through numerous lower-level hands. Somehow, he had to reach the right person. Who said it should be the CIA? Between the Department of Defense, Homeland Security, DARPA, Department of Energy, National Security Agency, FBI, DNI, and numerous other agencies, the United States has so many confusing overlaps in intelligence, it's hard to know who is really in charge of the overall security of the country. Joe knew he had to act, but he needed to make the right choice.

A day later, Joe discovered the envelope was missing. He went apoplectic. Assuming it was someone who worked at the embassy, he contacted the chief security officer immediately. He requested a complete review of all the sign-in sheets and duty rosters, and a complete review of all security videos for the last four days. By the following day, the most probable suspect to be identified was Nancy, a temporary employee of the catering company. From her passport, and with further research that revealed her as a federal contractor, and thus automatically in the database as a person of interest, it was easy to obtain Nancy's residence and work information. They didn't need to bother questioning Shelley.

Joe went straight to Nancy's apartment in Arlington, VA. Nikolai had his people posted outside the embassy, and they spotted Joe immediately when the RFID triggered an alert. It was easy to follow him. Nancy's place was off Virginia Square. After her split with Steve, she found an airline flight attendant to share an apartment. The arrangement worked out well because neither of them was there much. Kim came and went more often than Nancy did; but generally, they each had their privacy. Joe planned to break into the apartment and search it, but as a matter of standard operating procedure, he rang the bell first. Surprisingly, Kim was home and opened the door with a sleepy-eyed expression. When Joe said he was a friend looking for Nancy, Kim explained she had left for Massachusetts. Joe was sure Nancy took his envelope with her, so there was no need to search the apartment.

While Joe was talking to Kim, the Russians stuck a magnetic GPS beacon on Joe's car. They didn't know where he might go next. The effort would have been wasted if Joe decided to fly to Massachusetts, but it was too much of a hassle for him to turn in his rental car, purchase a last-minute plane ticket, and then have to rent another car. It was easier to simply drive.

Joe drove north with the Russians right behind him. He arrived at Nancy's rental house in mid-afternoon. There was no sign she was there, and the neighborhood was quiet. After failing to find an unlocked opening, Joe easily picked the lock on the kitchen door in the back. He was in no mood to be subtle. He tossed the house, looking in every conceivable place she could have hidden his envelope. He spent more than an hour and a half pulling out drawers, pulling books out of shelves, tossing sofa cushions, tipping over furniture to check for things taped underneath, pulling up carpets, and pulling out vents. Nothing! The place wasn't big and had only a limited number of places to hide things. He was going to have to confront her. He installed a camera in a corner of the living room where it wasn't likely to be seen immediately. He then went to find a motel to check-in for the night.

The Russians sat in a car parked discreetly down the street

from Nancy's house. They had been researching the addresses Joe led them to. It wasn't hard to come up with Nancy's name, but it wasn't clear what her relationship was to Joe. Why was he chasing after this girl? When Joe finally came out of the house, Nikolai said, "Let's follow him. We can always come back to this house."

Not long after Joe checked into the Twin Birch Motel, he had a knock on his door. He assumed it was a motel employee. Nobody knew his whereabouts. He looked through the peephole and saw three rough-looking characters. "Oh shit!" he thought to himself. The trouble with motel rooms was they didn't have back doors. It hadn't occurred to Joe he was being followed. Before he had a plan, the big Russian kicked in the door and three men were all over him.

Joe was tied to the desk chair and one man held Joe's belt around his neck. "Where is the information we want?" asked the big Russian in a thick accent.

"What information?" Joe gasped and choked. "I don't know what you're talking about."

The Russian walked over to the desk and picked up three magazines. He rolled them up into a tight cylinder and walloped Joe on each side of his head.

"I have your attention now?" The Russian slammed the roll of magazines across Joe's face. Blood gushed from his nose and ran down onto his shirt.

"We know about you and that Susan Drury woman. We know about the professor. We have been following you for a long time, so don't give me the shit that you don't know what I want." The Russian stared at him menacingly, then punched him in the gut for good measure.

"Okay, okay," Joe sputtered. "I know what you want, but I don't have it. It was stolen from me."

The Russian didn't look surprised. "Does the girl have it?"

"I don't know, maybe."

Nikolai pulled his phone out of his pocket and dialed a number. Joe recognized the 571 area code as northern Virginia, because he had recently used it himself. "We have the guy and he say he not have it. He think girl have it."

A voice at the other end of the call gave a clipped order Joe couldn't discern.

"You sure?" asked Nikolai. "Okay."

Nikolai put his phone back in his pocket and looked at Joe. "You no use to me." He pulled out his gun and shot Joe once in the head and once in the chest.

Nikolai turned to his companions. "Let's go back to that house."

CHAPTER 11

When Nancy returned to New England, she thought the best thing to do was to keep busy, so she went right back to work. Everything was normal, and she had no idea anyone was looking for her. When she came home from work, she found the inside of her house in shambles. Somebody had actually broken into her house. Ironically, she experienced the violation felt by her victims. Some of her favorite things were broken or strewn around on the floor. Someone had not just robbed her, they had vandalized her. She tried to figure out what was missing, but everything was out of place. She didn't own much of real value, so it was difficult to know what they might have been after. Her TV was still there and unbroken. Her jewelry appeared to be intact, but it was mostly all costume jewelry anyway.

"Oh shit!" She looked in her purse at the envelope she had brought from DC. She had forgotten she was carrying it around with her.

"Is this what they're after?" She surveyed the destruction around her. "Somebody wants this really badly. How did they find me this far from Washington?" A whirlwind of thoughts raced through her mind. All of them were bad. Whoever did this, knew who she was. The good news was they didn't find what they wanted here, so they probably wouldn't come back – unless they came back for her. She now had every reason in the world to be very afraid. She grabbed a bag and started throwing clothes in it. She needed to get out of here now! She tossed her bag and laptop in her car, then ran back inside for her purse, and a bottle of water.

She heard a car pull up out front. She ran to the front window and peeked out along the edge of the curtain. Three men got out of the car. One of them had a gun in his hand. Nancy grabbed her purse and bolted for the back door. She ran out into the backyard to a small shed by the back fence. As a former gymnast, she was tempted to vault the fence, but it was overgrown with vines and fronted by thorny shrubs. There was no guarantee that she could get over quickly. She opted for the shed. Amid rakes and a lawnmower, she tucked herself into the darkness and closed the door to a crack so she could see the house.

The guests at the Twin Birch Motel heard a ruckus followed by gunshots. They called the front desk, and the front desk called the police. It was a slow day in a small town, so the police were there in a matter of minutes. They weren't expecting what they found.

"Jesus!" said Sergeant Maddox. "What a fuck'n mess! Billy, call the coroner; also, we're going to need a forensics team. Ask the Captain if he wants help from the state."

Maddox pulled on a pair of vinyl gloves. He searched through the suitcase on the bed. Nothing interesting except a UK diplomatic passport. This vaulted the situation into a whole new category with international ramifications. On the other side of the bed, he found a laptop computer on the floor. It was open, turned on, and had a video running on the screen. It showed a room that had been tossed, and three men with guns poking through the rubble.

"Oh shit!" Maddox squatted to look closer. "Billy! Come here and look at this."

Officer Bill Beck came around the bed and looked at the video. "This is real-time." Maddox pointed to the time signature in the corner. "Can you tell where it is?"

Billy squinted at the screen. "Can you make it any bigger?"

Maddox moved the cursor down to an icon with a plus sign to zoom in. He clicked on the speaker icon to unmute. In thick Russian accents, the men on the screen said, "It has to be here. That asshole just didn't know where to look. Keep searching. Use your training. Anton, keep watch at the window. If the girl shows up, we need to grab her."

Suddenly Billy said, "Look on the counter. Do you see that

bag? Only postal employees have bags like that."

"Okay," said Maddox. "So we know the resident is female and probably a postal employee. Is that enough? I don't think so."

"Look on the fridge," said Billy. "That's a frigg'n big birthday card! Lucky for us because I can read Happy Birthday Nancy!"

"Got it!" Maddox grabbed his phone and called the local post office. He got the evening supervisor. He quickly explained he had an emergency situation and needed the home address for an employee named Nancy. The supervisor was skeptical. "We can't give out personal information."

"Look, either you give me what I need now or I'll have squad cars down there in five minutes to arrest you for obstruction. Believe me, you don't want to be having this conversation with me at the police station!"

"Alright, alright. We don't have an employee named Nancy, but we have a contract worker by that name. She lives at 1735 Aspen Street."

"Thank you!" Maddox hung up. "Let's go, Billy!" They ran for the cruiser.

Nancy was terrified. She was trapped with no way out. Sooner or later, those men were going to come and look in the shed. She had no good options. From raised voices and crashing around, she guessed they were getting increasingly frustrated. By the time they found her, they would be in a really bad mood. She debated making a break for it, but it was unlikely she could get down the driveway past the house without being seen. She could make it to her car, but guns could shoot through car windows. She didn't like her odds. As she was working through her choices, the back door opened and one of the men stepped halfway out. He turned and said something in Russian to the others still inside. At least Nancy guessed it was Russian. It could have been Albanian, or Croatian, or anything else. Nancy did not have a good ear for languages. If he was telling them about the shed, then she was totally screwed.

Then a miracle happened. She heard police sirens. Not just one siren, but several. The man returned back through the kitchen door. Nancy burst out of the shed and ran to her car. The men in her house scrambled out front to their car ahead of her. She backed out of the driveway. She was barely a hundred feet down the street when police lights appeared in her rearview mirror. As she watched the police come to a stop in front of her house, her hands were trembling on the steering wheel. She drove to the next town over and pulled into a restaurant. She needed a place to compose herself and think.

Nancy sat in a booth at the back of the restaurant. She couldn't stop shaking. She hoped it wasn't too obvious to the waitress. Because of a stupid lark, she had managed to totally trash her life. She didn't know what to do. She couldn't go back to her house. She didn't dare go to work. Night was coming on and she had no place to stay. She knew she was hungry, so the first order of business was to eat. While she was waiting for her food, she pulled out her phone and searched on the internet for a motel. Since she didn't know who all was after her, including perhaps the police, she found a cheap place twenty miles away, where she would probably be safe for at least one night.

Once she was at the motel, she breathed easier. Fortunately, she had her laptop. She spent hours at the motel with the USB flash drive plugged into her computer, trying to understand what was on it. Mathematical formulas and functions were written into computer code with comments referencing Greek letters and strange symbols unfamiliar to her. She thought to herself, "I'm a smart girl with education and training, but this is way beyond anything I understand."

She walked down to the motel office and paid the clerk a dollar to borrow his printer. She printed out one page from a README file. That one page was enough to make her realize she probably had something worth killing for. She had seen too many crime movies to believe she was going to be safe staying at a motel if they had already tracked her to the rental house. She needed a better place to stay, and she needed help figuring this all out. Her resources were limited, and she was painted into a corner.

Nancy had trouble sleeping. Every time she woke up, her mind worked on the problem of where to go and what to do. Finally, she had a desperate answer. At six in the morning, she was up and out of the motel, driving toward Ridgeview Road. She parked in front of a neighbor's house, hopefully far enough down the road from Sam Barron's that he wouldn't notice her. When Sam finally pulled out of his driveway, she followed him at a safe distance into town. He pulled into a parking space in front of a relatively nondescript office in a strip mall. Big letters over the front door said CIA, and below them the words Coastal Investment Advisors. "Are you kidding? CIA? Really?" It was absurd, but she figured it was at least memorable from a marketing standpoint.

Nancy drove to Sadie's Diner, on the outskirts of Sea Haven, where she got some breakfast. It was easy enough to look up Coastal Investment Advisors on the internet and get a phone number for Sam. This was a long shot, but he was a complete non sequitur in her life. If he could help her, it was unlikely anyone could trace her to him.

The idea of finding herself associated with Sam again was a most peculiar situation for Nancy. It was incredibly awkward to be asking him for assistance after their unusual bargain. Yet it also seemed like the most natural thing in the world, when confronted with the limited choices available to her. She needed a safe place to hide where there was no chance of being traced.

CHAPTER 12

W hen Sam pulled into the parking lot at Bartlett's Landing, he saw Nancy sitting on the bench right where he told her to be. As he walked up to her, he forced himself to set aside her beauty and focus on the danger surrounding her. "You're sure you weren't followed?"

"I'm sure."

"Then come with me." He kept glancing around as he punched the entry code into the lock on the gate to the docks. Bartlett's was a full-service marina with several dozen boat slips.

They walked along the pier, down the gangplank, and turned left onto one of the finger docks. Tucked in between two large powerboats, was a Hylas 42 sailboat with a dark blue hull. Sam unclipped the lifeline and welcomed Nancy into the aft cockpit. She waited anxiously while he unlocked the hatch cover to the companionway. When they went below, she saw a navigation table to the right and salon seating straight ahead.

The galley was on the left side. Behind it, toward the stern, was a stateroom with a queen-size bed.

Sam showed her how to use the toilet in the head, how to turn lights on and off, how to use the gas stove, and how to turn the stereo on. Since the boat was hooked up to shore power, she could use any amount of electricity without worrying about running the batteries down; and she could plug in standard 110 volt appliances. There was even a microwave.

"Give me a list of any food you would like," said Sam, "and I'll pick it up for you. There are already canned goods in the cabinet over the stove, along with basic staples. I can also buy any other personal items you need. I have clean sheets and towels for you, so you should be in pretty good shape."

Nancy clenched her jaw, fighting a threat from tears of relief. She took a breath and smiled at him. "Thank you so much. This is way better than I might have expected. I really have no place to go where I couldn't be found."

"So, let's talk about that. I need to know how I can help and what you expect from me." He moved forward and sat down on the cushioned bench seat in the salon. "Come sit down."

Nancy slid behind the dining table so she was facing Sam with the table in between. "I spent all night thinking about this. First, I need to figure out what exactly is on this USB flash drive. Once I know that, I can determine its value. I need to know who it is valuable to, and why. Then I can maybe figure out who is chasing me. Once I know all that, I can figure out how best to get rid of it and get my life back."

"Where did the flash drive come from?"

"It came from the British embassy. I would send it back, but people know who I am, and I'm pretty sure they want me dead. Probably, they think I know too much."

"Frankly, I am starting from zero here. I don't know anything about you except that you broke into my house. I don't know who you are, what you do, besides rob houses, where you are from, or how all this got started."

"Fair enough." Nancy nodded in agreement. "Those are all good questions and you deserve answers if you're going to help me. Let me start with my no-good ex-boyfriend."

Nancy recounted how her life went downhill after she met Steve. She explained why she had turned to a life of crime due to the problems Steve had left her with.

Sam held up a hand and interrupted for a moment. "You couldn't find something legitimate to earn more income?"

She thrust her jaw forward, defiantly, and tossed her hair. "Okay, so I could have made better choices. I did what seemed easy."

"What about your family? Can't they help you out with your debt? "

Nancy looked off to the side and took a deep breath. "My mother died an alcoholic when I was five, while my dad was off saving the world. He traveled all the time in the military. He recently passed away and left me with nothing but memories of good intentions.

"So, after my… visit to your house, I took time off and went back to Washington." She told Sam about her adventures in DC, about Joe Campbell, about how she had forgotten all about the USB drive in her purse until her house was broken into and foreign men with guns were after her. She explained how she had spent the previous night trying to understand what was on the USB flash drive, but the mathematics were unfamiliar to her. There was also a .exec file that was clearly a program, but she didn't dare try to run it. She didn't know what it was going to do. She looked at some of the coding, but there were thousands of pages of it and she couldn't begin to follow the logic. What she needed was a high-level mathematician and/or a computer scientist who could interpret the strange functions in the coding.

"So now you know a little bit about me," she said. "What about you? I don't know much about you." She looked at him with raised eyebrows.

"My daytime job is in the financial industry. I own a small investment company which gives me the flexibility to take random time off to come and go and operate without accountability to anyone."

"Yeah, your coming and going tripped me up."

Sam brushed off the comment. "I'm only accountable to myself to try to live the best life I can. Sometimes, like recently, I hit a rough patch, but I'm working through it. I tend to be pragmatic. In essence, life is simple: You get out of it what you put into it. If you don't plant, you can't harvest. The corollary is that you will most likely harvest what you do plant. If you give a smile, you're likely to get a smile. If you plant sarcasm, bitterness, and complaint, you will most probably reap the same in return. If you make no effort at all, you can count on being greeted with indifference.

"No day carries with it the guarantee of being a great day. But every day dawns with possibility. If you don't put forth the effort to participate, then you won't harvest the reward, be it great or small; and you'll miss something that you can never retrieve.

"You can live life to the fullest, or you can let it pass you by and blame bad luck for your paltry harvest. Regardless of the hand you're dealt, it makes sense to make the best of it. I try to keep my life interesting. I do participate in extracurricular activities to keep some spice in my life."

"Jesus! You sound like a motivational speaker. I could have used that a few years ago. Not sure it's what I need right now." There was an awkward pause as his expression said he was serious about his philosophy of life and did not appreciate her flip response. She frowned for a moment, then tried to lighten the mood. "By extracurricular activities, do you mean seducing young women? Or do you mean you're a thief like me? Or do you work for the actual CIA?"

Sam gave her a charming, boyish, embarrassed smile. Then his face got serious as he sat in silence for a minute. He wasn't sure how much he wanted to reveal about the next thing he was going to tell her. "In addition to my day job, I'm an Outlier for the US government. I do special projects from time to time."

A quizzical look came over Nancy's face. "An Outlier? What's an Outlier?"

Sam gave her another uneasy smile. "Mathematically speaking, if you can connect a group of dots on a chart to make a line, but one dot is separate and doesn't line up, that's an outlier. In my case, an Outlier is someone out of bounds, someone you aren't supposed to know about. I'm someone who is out of sequence, outside the system, and out of view. I operate for the government, but outside the government." He shrugged like he had broken his mother's china, but couldn't explain how it happened. "I've worked for an FBI joint task force as a logic analyst, giving them a fresh point of view from outside the bureau. I've worked for Homeland Security as an investigator of suspected money laundering. And I've worked for the CIA as a cutout. Information has been passed through me. I don't know who the messenger is. I don't know what the message is. I don't know who I'm passing the information on to. Since I'm an Outlier, I'm outside the system and constitute a complete break in the chain. Due to my unique position, I'm also used as a 'fixer' to take care of problems the government doesn't want its fingerprints on. It should be extremely hard for someone to find me if I have no connection to the larger government program. If I'm found, I have nothing useful to provide.

"I'm doing much the same thing for you. Since I'm an outlier to your sphere of life, you should be safe hiding with me. There's no way anyone looking for you can connect you to me. That's my function for the government."

"So, you have connections with the government. You know who to call?" she asked eagerly.

"Well, yes and no." Sam rocked his head from side to side as he paused. "The whole point of my position is I have no direct connection to the government."

After a long silence, Sam said, "Well, I did do a favor for Rick when he was Secretary of the Department of Energy. I could give him a call and ask for an introduction to the right people at Lawrence Livermore Lab. That's the home of some of the best and brightest. They've scaled up a super computer that can perform a billion, billion calculations per second. If we're talking about manipulating big data, that's where we'll find the experts."

Relief crossed Nancy's face. "Will you do that? We're really going to need help figuring out what this is, but they need to be able to keep a secret too."

"I'll see what I can do." Sam reached into a drawer and pulled out a pen and small notebook. "Now write down a shopping list for me and I'll get what you need. It's probably best you stay hidden for a while. Try to relax, and I'll be back before dinner."

True to all men of integrity, Sam's weakness was a beautiful young woman in desperate need of his help. That he already knew every curve of her body and the sounds she made in the throes of passion didn't help his judgement. A small voice was shouting a warning in the back corner of his mind, but he was deliberately ignoring it. He didn't care what continued entanglement with her was going to cost him. This was something he needed to do.

PART 3

THE DISCOVERY

CHAPTER 13

Two Months Earlier In Britain . . .

It all started with Susan Drury, a graduate student in advanced mathematics at Oxford University. As the daughter of Dr. Robert Drury, the head of the Astrophysics Department at Oxford, she was not an ordinary student, although she tried to be. Most of the time, she was preoccupied with her own studies and hanging out with her friends, but her father never hesitated to share his latest theories with her and occasionally asked her to check his calculations.

Joe Campbell first saw Susan at the Fox & Hound Pub. Perhaps in her mid-twenties, she stood out because of her red hair and friendly face that seemed to radiate joy. But before Joe had a chance to pick her out of the crowd, her infectious laugh and the lilt to her voice caught his attention over the din of the pub. He thought to himself she must have the nicest voice in the world. He could listen to her all day long. She was partying with friends, and Joe was content to sip his pint and watch her.

One of Susan's girlfriends leaned over and whispered in her ear. "You're being checked out by a gorgeous stud over your left shoulder."

"Oh, yeah? Tell me about him."

"Male model kind of rugged face, dark, sexy. I like his eyes. I see kindness there, but an aura of Celtic mystery. Something about him makes me think he's the real deal."

Susan scoffed. "You're making this up! I'm not going to turn around and look."

"I'm not kidding. He's the best-looking guy in here. Maybe five years older than you. I'd take him, but he definitely has a thing for you."

Susan shook her head. "Dream on! Been there and done that. They never turn out to be what you think."

Eventually, her friends left and she moved to a booth at the back of the pub and pulled out a book. Joe ordered a shepherd's pie, watched the crowd, and kept his thoughts to himself. He had come off an intense assignment, and all he wanted was downtime. But she was too exceptional, and he wasn't going to let her get away. Finally, he got up and approached her.

"Pardon me," he said. "I'm alone this evening and I'd love to have someone to talk to, if I may interrupt your reading."

She looked up with a puzzled frown. "I don't usually talk to strangers." Her English was highlighted with strong Irish overtones.

"That's probably a good policy, but I won't be a stranger for long if you let me tell you a story."

She looked hesitant.

"Trust me. I can be a lot more interesting than multivariable calculus matrices."

She smiled and closed her textbook. "You noticed." As the smile danced on her lips and her eyes twinkled, she continued with that captivating lilt to her voice. "I don't know… n-dimensional matrices can be pretty interesting."

"Is that so? Maybe you're the one who should be telling me the story. What do you find so interesting about calculus? By the way, I'm Joe." He held out his hand.

"Susan," she said as she took his hand.

"May I buy you a drink?"

"No thanks. I've had enough to drink for tonight."

It was clear she wasn't pushing him away, just declining the drink. Since she hadn't offered for him to sit down, he tried another approach. "How about we walk down the street to the bakery for pastry with coffee or tea?"

"I could go for that!" She smiled and gathered up her things.

That was how the relationship started. Little did Joe realize that Susan would literally be the death of him.

One thing led to another. Over the next six weeks, Joe and Susan became absorbed with each other. Susan would explain mathematics to Joe until his eyes glazed over. But he loved learning about her childhood and the rest of her life. When she asked the mysterious Joe Campbell what he did, he was evasive. Initially, she didn't get anything more than "I work for queen and country." Eventually, he was more forthcoming and allowed as to how he was a government employee, but he wasn't specific.

Joe Campbell had been recruited into MI6 when he was still in school. His father was a lifer in the military, and Joe had moved around the world with him. Joe's worldly experience made him perfect material to be molded into a spy. Joe didn't believe he was interested in a long-term relationship, and that was a good thing. The job did not allow for sharing. Joe would have to disappear for days, sometimes weeks on end without explanation. If one could not tell one's partner what one was doing, there was no basis for trust. Worse, anyone he was connected to became a liability. If a foreign agent wanted to get leverage, all they had to do was threaten a loved one. It was no secret that MI6 had one of the highest divorce rates of all the government jobs.

As he came to trust Susan, Joe finally promoted the lie that he worked in the Foreign Office. He said he had a security clearance and therefore couldn't talk about most of his work. The part he could talk about was dull paperwork, like the processing of documents such as passports and visas. It was enough to throw Susan off the scent so they could focus on other things — mostly sex.

They quickly became conjoined in a torrid affair. Neither could say it was true love, but the sex was spectacular. Joe was the epitome of masculinity Susan longed for. Most of her life, she had been surrounded by unappealing bookish academics. Joe was kind and gentle, but he was also strong, and physically dominant in a satisfying way. He triggered all the base animal instincts in her no one else had. She hungered for his body.

Joe relished Susan's soft and sensuous curves. She was pliable, like a ragdoll he could cuddle, bend, twist, and wrap. She was delightful in every way. Her nervous system was like a finely tuned instrument that would sing a different note to every different touch. Her wild Irish nature would come out during sex. She slipped into a relaxed, happy freedom he had never seen in another woman. She orgasmed with such intensity, her body would surge like a runaway train, and he could watch her stomach muscles ripple with spasms and her shoulders quiver as tremors swept repeatedly across her body. It gave him immense pleasure to know he could do that to her, and that she could do the same for him.

Susan was close to her father. The task of raising her fell to the professor when her mother died of cancer before Susan reached college. But growing up on a university campus was akin to having a large extended family. Susan knew most of the faculty and staff, and moved easily through the buildings as if she owned them.

Susan frequently dropped in on her father at his office after classes were over. She would fit a visit in before going out for the evening with Joe. Professor Drury always had a project going. He would use Susan as a sounding board to try out his hypotheses. Lately, he had been asking her to apply her mathematical skills to fluid dynamics problems.

At her most recent visit, Susan asked, "Why do you care about this stuff? I don't see the relationship to astrophysics."

"I grant you it isn't obvious. An important part of astrophysics is prediction. In some respects, because I'm dealing with large bodies moving over great distances during long periods of time, the physics is pretty straightforward. But at the same time, it's immensely important to be extremely accurate. Because of the long distances, an error of a tiny fraction of a degree can mean a miss of thousands or even millions of miles. And of course, gravitational acceleration is at the heart of this.

"So, you ask why the fluid dynamics? Think about traffic going down a crowded freeway. I'm sure you have experienced times when traffic has almost come to a standstill and you assume there must be an accident ahead. But when you reach the place where you expect to see the problem, there's nothing there. Sometimes traffic gets tied up in knots for no obvious reason. The same thing happens with fluids traveling down a pipe. Random internal turmoil will develop in the pipe for no obvious reason. It's a natural consequence of friction. Now, instead of fluid in a pipe, imagine a virtual 'pipeline' of information. What dictates how smoothly the information flows? How can we calculate when and in what order the information will arrive?"

"Wow, you don't pick anything easy to work on do you?"

Susan laughed. "I'll look at your calculations and get back to you. I have homework of my own to do, plus I'm going out to dinner tonight."

"Thanks. Have fun," Dr. Drury, already distracted by other thoughts, turned his attention to shuffling through papers on his desk.

Joe had a lot of free time on his hands. He was doing menial paperwork at the office while waiting for another assignment. He wasn't looking forward to having to travel again and be away from Susan. He wanted to spend all his extra time with her, but she was pushing back. She reminded him she had academic obligations. She worked as a teaching assistant and had her own research to do. She explained she also helped her father.

"Remind me what exactly your father does and why he needs your help?"

Susan tossed her hands, exasperated. "You know he's chairman of the department, but that's just a title. You have to understand who the man is. His mind never stops. He asks himself questions he can't answer. Then he fidgets and fusses until he can find an answer. And when he gets buried in abstract mathematics, he asks me to sort things out for him. Sometimes I can, but more often than not, just by formulating the question clearly to me, he figures out how to solve the problem himself. You really have to meet him to understand."

"Well then, why not?"

"Why not what? — Meet him?" Susan's eyebrows climbed into her hair.

"Sure, why not meet him? I'm not afraid." Joe smiled.

"Okay. The rest of this week is a disaster for me." Susan consulted the calendar on her phone. "How about next Tuesday after classes?"

"Tuesday it is. I look forward to meeting the source of all your beauty and wisdom." He grinned like a boy playing a prank, but he was earnest in his desire to meet her father.

On Tuesday, Joe left the office early and met Susan on campus. She walked him over to the Clarendon Laboratory, the temporary home of the astrophysics department offices. The Denys Wilkinson building, the true home of the department, was being renovated. Susan preferred the old-world feel of the Clarendon Building. Once inside the classic stone and red brick building, they climbed up three stories of stone steps with a wood-capped railing that was worn smooth and shiny from a century and a half of hands sliding along it. She took him down the hall to a heavy oak door with a glass window in it. Gold lettering on the glass simply said "Office of the Chairman". Dr. Robert Drury had never bothered to have his name put on the door. He simply didn't care about those kinds of details.

Susan pushed the door open. "Hi Dad!" she sang out. There was a special lilt to her voice that Joe hadn't heard before.

An older grey-haired man with spectacles looked up from

his desk. "Hi darling," he replied with a smile.

She placed her hand on Joe's arm. "Dad, this is Joe Campbell."

Dr. Drury came out from behind his desk and held out a hand. "Pleased to meet you!"

"I'm very pleased to meet you as well, sir. I've heard a lot about you."

"Have a seat." The professor pointed to a couple of leather armchairs opposite his desk. "Susan gives me the impression she's seeing quite a lot of you." He took a step back and leaned against the edge of his desk.

Joe smiled as he sat. "I enjoy her company very much."

Moving the conversation away from their relationship, Susan cut in. "Joe has been asking me about what you do. Rather than try to explain it, I thought I would let him meet you so you can tell him yourself."

"Oh, well," stammered the professor, looking uncertain. "Susan, you did mention you wanted me to talk about my project." He looked toward Joe. "Are you sure you want to know how an old man like me spends his time?"

Joe nodded and put on his best diplomatic poker face. He wasn't sure what he was getting into, but it was all part of caring about Susan. "I'm sure you're involved in very interesting things."

Professor Drury steepled his hands over his chest, the fingertips touching, and bent his head for a moment, as if in prayer. He seemed to be gathering his thoughts. He gave Susan a brief smile, and turned again to Joe.

"What do I do, you ask. Let me answer in a simple and general way you can easily understand. I feel my job, aside from teaching, is to learn how the universe works, in as much detail as I can. If I truly understand how the universe works, I should know how to meaningfully influence the future. It's like looking at a thousand pieces of a jigsaw puzzle scattered on a tabletop and being able to visualize the picture they'll make when assembled correctly. Imagine what you could do if you could accurately visualize tomorrow, as if you had a newspaper reporting on tomorrow. The future hasn't happened yet, but if you could know what the future will look like, you would know what to push and pull to influence the future. Sounds exotic, doesn't it?" Professor Drury smiled as if he was about to summon a genie from a bottle for the pleasure of everyone.

"I think this can be easily understood if we go back to basic concepts. The first thing to understand is that time depends on change. If absolutely nothing in the universe ever changed, time would not exist. In a place of absolutely no motion and no change of any type, you could not tell the difference between today and tomorrow and next year. Time would be meaningless.

"We have time because we have change. Change is always an orderly event, although it can happen rapidly in many places in many ways, and can occur simultaneously in different places. We recognize change as something that occurs sequentially through space and time.

"Just as important as the need for change, there must exist a maximum rate beyond which change cannot occur faster. Our current theories tell us that the maximum velocity is the speed of light, but this is a minor technicality. For our purposes, it doesn't matter what the maximum speed is, just that there has to be a maximum. If an object is moving sequentially from point A to point B to point C, it cannot instantly appear at point C from point A. If things could move instantly, an object could be at point C or B or even back at point A all in the same instant. In fact, any object could be anywhere in the world all in the same instant. Instantaneous change destroys the concept of sequence, which is essential to the definition of time. Space and time become meaningless if instantaneous change exists. So, we have two important conditions for time: change has to exist, and there must be a maximum rate of change."

"I have a question," interrupted Joe. "I understand it's common sense that there must be a maximum speed, but what determines how fast that speed is? What if the maximum rate of change were slower? Would that mean that time would go slower?"

Professor Drury grinned. "I see you're paying attention. Good! I don't know why the maximum speed is what it is, but I'm not sure it matters. Our perception of time has less to do with speed and more to do with density of change. Density has to do with how much of something you pack into a limited, or finite, container. In physics, if you place more mass into the same unit of volume, you have increased density. If you think of an interval of time as equivalent to a container of volume, and you think of the number of events as equivalent to mass, then the occurrence of more events in the same unit of time is an increase in the density of change. Imagine you're sitting on the porch having a drink with one friend. Compare that to standing in a room full of two hundred people at a cocktail party. So much more is happening at the cocktail party, I would say that is an environment of higher density of change. I suggest your sense of time would be different at a crowded cocktail party. Most of what we do is so far below the maximum rate of change, if the maximum rate were slower, we probably wouldn't notice. We might just increase the change in density to compensate. That seems to be the natural direction we're heading anyway. Technology is increasing the rate at which we do things, so our density of change is much greater now than it was a few hundred years ago. However, remember time is dependent on sequence. If the maximum rate were slower, an outcome dependent on a prior event moving at maximum speed would have to wait for that prior event. In that respect, perhaps we could say that time would move slower. Perhaps you can appreciate that I'm steering you toward the concept of relativity.

"Now we get to the interesting question. What governs the rate of change? Inertia is the answer I come up with. Inertia is that property of matter which resists change. In physics, inertia is a function of mass. If you want to change the motion of an object, its speed or direction, you must apply a force to accelerate its mass, which means energy is required. Specifically: force equals mass times acceleration. The faster you want an object to move, the more energy you have to apply. As you approach the speed of light, Einstein's relativity comes into play. Mass increases in accord with the Lorentz transformation and requires increasing amounts of energy. To reach the speed of light requires more energy than is available, and so, theory says no object can exceed the maximum allowable speed.

"Now that we understand the constraints that define time, it should be clear that time cannot move forward faster than the maximum rate of change. If you have any thoughts of time travel, you would have to move faster than time itself to jump ahead in time, and that is simply impossible. Another way to state it is, if you want to move faster than time, you would have to experience more change at a faster rate than time itself allows. Inertia constrains time, and inertia prevents you from moving faster than time. You cannot jump forward to see the future." A twinkle in the professor's eye belied this denial. "But you can do the next best thing!

"Mathematics is a universal symbolic language used to model our reality. If a person truly understands how a system works, then they should be able to model it by expressing it mathematically. A correct mathematical model leads to accurate prediction. And what is prediction? Prediction is a form of time travel without having to actually jump ahead in time. What I'm trying to explain to you is that, given enough accurate data, and given a clear understanding of how to arrange that data to symbolically model a particular system — think weather system, economic system, biological system, social system — it's possible to know exactly what's going to happen, just as if you could jump forward in time.

"One of the capabilities that we think separates humans from animals is autonoetic awareness. Our awareness of the past helps define who we are. This awareness makes it possible for humans to create a mental picture of the future and place themselves in it. You can travel to the future in your mind. I'm doing the same thing digitally. I'm assembling all of the pieces that will create tomorrow and, faster than time itself, creating a picture of the future so we can see it before we get there."

"Wow!" exclaimed Joe. "Are you telling me you can truly predict the future?"

"I am," said professor Drury with a smile. "I'm only constrained by the amount of data I have access to and the computing power I have access to.

"I'll admit that I'm still polishing up the program. There are a few equations I'm not happy with and some minor things to adjust, but I'm almost there. It's quite exciting!"

"And what are you planning to do with this?"

"Aah, that remains undecided." Dr. Drury pursed his lips. "There are obvious ethical questions, so I'm not publicizing this, and I trust you'll keep this information to yourself.

"I still have a bit more work to do on my model, so I'll cross the next bridge when I get to it. For me, it's not about what I can do with the model. The success of the model is simply a measure of my understanding of the universe. I take great satisfaction in knowing I've figured out certain things."

"Well, I'm very impressed." Joe winked at Susan. "Now I know where your daughter gets her brains from."

"I don't know about that." Dr. Drury chuckled. "I depend on her for some of the mathematics. She has something extra that didn't come from me."

Joe leaned forward. "So, does it really work? Have you tried it out?"

A grin slid onto the professor's face. "Of course it works." He continued to smile with quiet confidence. "I knew you were coming here today, so I prepared this." He reached for a sealed envelope sitting on his desk and handed it to Joe. "Open it up."

Joe slid a finger under the flap and tore it open. A timestamp at the top said 10:17 a.m. He read:

I know Joe won't arrive by car to meet Susan. I'm not sure how he will get here, but I believe it involves walking. He'll stop and buy a drink on the way – probably a coffee.
He won't be wearing his normal blue jeans. He'll be wearing proper trousers and an outer jacket – probably his black leather jacket. When he sits down, I expect him to sit to the right of Susan. Tonight, Joe is planning to go to a concert by the Jive Guys.

"Oh my gosh!" exclaimed Joe.

"Let me see it!" Susan grabbed the paper out of his hands. She scanned it quickly and then exclaimed, "A concert! I thought you were taking me to dinner."

Joe stammered, "I am taking you to dinner. Then I was

going to surprise you with the concert tickets."

Professor Drury waved his hand like a conductor bringing order to an orchestra. "So, I take it I got it right."

"You're dead on," sputtered Joe. "I don't know how you could've done this."

"It's pretty straightforward. I just entered your name and scraped the internet for every piece of information about you that's out there. This process is very data-intensive. By the way, I have questions about exactly what you do for a living, and who you work for, but we can talk about that another time. Anyway, my program reaches out to servers all over the world to aggregate the computing power necessary to analyze and assemble all the data needed to compute predictions. Obviously, I've never met you before and know little about you, so this is what the program came up with."

"That's incredible," Joe mumbled. "Just incredible"

"I must confess, there's no magic in the bit about the concert tickets. The program found the charge on your credit card. So that was an easy guess."

"Even so." Joe shrugged; he gathered similar personal information in his work for MI6. "I can't believe it. How did you know I would sit to the right of Susan?"

The professor threw up his hands. "I can't explain that. The whole point of artificial intelligence is the computer can manipulate massive amounts of data in a structural way our brains cannot follow. The computer can learn things and extrapolate behavior into predictions I can't backward engineer."

Susan grinned at Joe. "Pretty cool isn't it? I've been watching this develop for a while, but I still can't believe some of the results he gets."

"I must confess I'm dumbfounded," said Joe. "I understand the concept, but even so, I'm truly amazed to see it work. How hard is it to run?"

The professor began pacing. "I told you I'm still polishing it up, but the program isn't hard to run. The hard part is identifying the scope of the data that should be entered. Obviously, the more data the program has to work with, the better the prediction; but there are constraints. It takes massive computing power to run simple predictions. This is a perfect application for a quantum computer. If more data is collected, it takes more time to find it and organize it, and it takes more computing power. If it takes too much time to make a prediction, you might not have enough time to analyze it and act on it. I'm still learning the right balance between the quantity of data and the period of time and complexity of the prediction."

"Well, you've certainly given me a lot to think about," Joe said.

Susan stood. "Thanks for seeing us Dad, but we need to go."

The spark of intensity left the professor's face. "Porquoi fait tu partir si tôt?"

"We're going to be late for dinner and Joe's surprise concert if we don't get a move on."

"Aah yes." Her father nodded. He walked over and gave her a kiss on the cheek. He held his hand out to Joe. "Very nice meeting you, young man. I expect I'll see more of you."

"I hope so," said Joe with a smile as he guided Susan toward the door.

As Joe and Susan walked across campus to her place, Susan was eager to learn Joe's opinion. "So, what do you think? He's not really a people person, is he? He's so absorbed in his work."

Joe perked up. "Actually, I enjoyed meeting your father. He's an interesting guy. I wish I'd had him as a teacher. I could understand him." Then he paused in contemplation. "If your father's program really works, it seems like we need to believe in such a thing as fate. It means all of our futures are already determined and your father has simply figured out a way to look forward and see what fate has in store for us. What happened to choice and free will?"

"I've had this discussion several times with him. You're partly right. There is such a thing as fate. But you're also partly wrong. The future is not totally predetermined. It can be changed.

"At the turn of the nineteenth century, a French astronomer and mathematician named Marquis Pierre Simon de Laplace proposed that the universe was completely deterministic. If all events arise from a prior cause, then 'there should be an intelligence for which nothing would be uncertain and the future, as the past, would be present to its eyes.' Translation: if every event is caused by some prior event, then the future is predetermined by everything that has gone before. If you could understand all initial conditions and follow their path forward, you could know your future.

"If there's a predetermined fate, does free will exist? Is belief in free will a case of involuntary fiction? For example, we all experience situations where what we rationally know to be true is counter to our internalized belief. You may find it difficult to eat a piece of fudge that is shaped like a dog turd, even when you know there's absolutely nothing wrong with the fudge. Likewise, a fictional story or movie may deeply affect you and create internalized emotions that seem real to you, even though you know it's just a story. These types of autonomic beliefs are named aliefs by the philosopher Tamar Szabo Gendler. These aliefs create cognitive dissonance with our logical, rational knowledge. Aliefs can create internalized emotional reactions of joy, or sorrow, or fear just as if from a real event, even when we know there's no real cause for these emotions

"If you recognize and accept the mechanism of cause and effect, but believe in free will, then you're a victim of self-deception. You illogically accept that you have free will even though you don't believe that the process of cause and effect allows for free will. Free will is defined as a condition in which multiple options are truly available to you. But if you believe in cause and effect, there is no place in the causal chain of events for the will to act in an uncaused way."

Joe shook his head, confused.

Susan raised a hand, as if to interrupt herself. "Maybe actions are both free and predetermined. What you think of as choice may in fact be subject to your prior experiences and predisposition. Your action may be free, at least in your mind, even if you really could not have acted otherwise. For example, Benford's Law, or the law of anomalous numbers, says that numbers you think should be random, actually have a statistical pattern. If you try to cheat on your taxes and fill in the form with made-up numbers, the tax authority will be able to tell you're cheating. You may think you have free will to enter random numbers, but you will do it wrong. Your error is predictable and identifiable.

"William James famously remarked that his first act of free will would be to believe in free will."

Joe placed a hand on her arm. "It sounds like you are telling me free will is a fiction of our own making."

"If you were to ask my father, he would say the linearity of time allows present events to influence future events. However, the degree of influence, if any, becomes less certain the farther out into the future one looks.

"Furthermore, not all outcomes are input determined. There are several reasons why this should not be a surprise. In some cases, the influence of an input as it moves through a system or network of events is itself influenced in unpredictable ways. This is the covariance problem. In other cases, there are more initial conditions, including hidden or unexpected inputs, beyond those that are or can be identified. In yet other situations, internal random dynamics in the system can produce different results, even when the same inputs are applied.

"The variance of perception from reality is one of the major stumbling blocks encountered when trying to predict outcomes. Although it is frequently believed one can predict or control an outcome through the control of all of the inputs that can determine the outcome, a flaw centers around the perception of control. Rarely does one actually control all of the determinants of an outcome. It's wrong to confuse the appearance of control with actual total control. It's normal to think that if one controls the majority of the input, one should be able to control the outcome. Yet, majority control is different from absolute control. Sometimes the smallest, seemingly most insignificant factor can cause a major change in outcomes. In chaos theory, sensitive dependence on initial conditions is called the butterfly effect. Minute differences in input can cause overwhelming differences in output. The world is not as simple as we wish. Systems that never repeat themselves, aperiodic systems, nonlinear systems, are prone to constant, unpredictable change, regardless of the initial conditions.

"In the rare case when it appears there is absolute control over all the input, the Theory of Volatility introduces that niggling little problem of random motion which can put events into play beyond anyone's control. In other words, the lack of linearity in a complex system means, by definition, that the predictability of the outcome is not entirely input-dependent. This is why we get mutations, black swans, and other unexpected outcomes.

"So, to answer your question, yes, there is a predetermined fate, but it's not absolute and thus, isn't definitively predictable."

Joe looked exasperated. "That's hardly an answer. It sounds like professorial equivocation."

Susan smiled with chagrin. "That's what you get when you ask an unanswerable question. You might note that the Western legal system is one of the consequences of a rational belief in a world driven by cause and effect. Since the actions of an individual can influence future events, the legal system holds the individual accountable for his actions.

"Existentialism emphasizes the free will to make choices and the consequent responsibility of the individual. Jean-Paul Sartre was the most notable existentialist of the twentieth century. Sartre coined the word existentialism to define his view of the nature of man as a self-defining projection in a universe devoid of purpose.

"Although existentialism recognizes the injection of free will into the event sequence of time, how can the individual accept responsibility for his actions without also believing his actions will be the cause for future events? It seems existentialists must accept the premise of cause and effect. This points out that free will competes with fate to determine the future.

"It makes me wonder. If we think we have the free will to change the future, are we really changing the future, or simply helping it along its predetermined path?"

"Wow!" said Joe. "You have clearly spent too much time at a university!"

Susan chuckled. "Yeah, I tend to get carried away. Sorry."

Joe put his arm around her shoulders and gave her a quick

squeeze. "Let's focus on dinner. I have a fun evening planned!"

The next morning, Joe Campbell didn't waste any time getting to work.

Fortunately, his group leader wasn't at his desk, because Joe had no intention of talking to him anyway. Joe headed for his uber-boss and was confronted with a closed door.

"Is he in, Sally?" he asked of the attractive blonde stationed in a recess to the right of the office door.

Sally looked up from her computer and smiled at Joe. "He has meetings back-to-back this morning."

"I really need to see him." Joe tapped his fingers anxiously on his pant leg.

"You can't go in, love. He told me no interruptions. I can call you when he has a break."

"Do that. Please. It's important." Joe looked longingly at the closed office door, then turned and left.

It was irritating not to be able to move forward. Joe returned to his desk and dealt with the most basic tasks waiting for him. It was too hard to focus on anything that took real brainpower. His mind was totally distracted by the conversation he'd had with Susan and Dr. Drury the previous afternoon.

Joe was on his second cup of coffee at 11 a.m. when Sally called him. "Sir Reginald can see you now, but you best be quick. He doesn't have much time. I told him you said it was important."

Joe was effusive in his thank you. "I'll be there in less than a minute" He grabbed his jacket and headed down the hall.

Sir Reginald Huntsman was the public face of MI6. Higher-ups and numerous teams interfaced on a need-to-know basis, but Sir Reginald acted as the hub. He was the primary funnel for information, both coming and going.

His office was something out of the Victorian era. It had dark paneling with an aged patina, heavy red curtains with fringe, large pieces of leather furniture, oriental carpets, floor-to-ceiling glassed bookcases, and a large, intricately-carved partners desk behind which he sat. He didn't get up when Joe came in. He waved him to a seat in lieu of saying, "Sit down and get on with it."

"Thank you for seeing me, sir. Something has come up which I think merits your urgent attention."

"Well, you picked a bad day for it," scoffed Sir Reginald, "so let's get right to the point."

Joe quickly explained about his meeting with Dr. Drury and the project he was working on. He explained the doctor was at an advanced stage with the project and, amazingly, it appeared to work. The most troubling aspect was that it was an "off the books" personal project, apparently without any supervision or controls. If it truly worked as well as purported, it could be of immense importance to the intelligence community as well as its use in numerous other applications.

"In short, I don't think Dr. Drury has begun to consider

all the ramifications of what he has developed. Furthermore, I don't think he has considered what could happen if it falls into the wrong hands. I truly think this is an issue of immediate national interest."

Sir Reginald pursed his lips. "What do you propose?"

"The first thing we should do is secure the project and make sure it's protected. Once we've done that, we can run tests and learn how effective it is and how it might best be used. Right now, I'm not sure this knowledge is something we want released into the public domain. We need to make sure the wrong people don't find out about it. I'm not even sure who the 'right' people are. If the public learns of this, it could change the world in ways that are hard to imagine."

"Okay, okay. I'm going to toss this back into your lap because I can't deal with it today. I know Oxford University does research work for the government. I want you to investigate how we can catch this Dr. Drury in the net of qualifying as a 'government contractor' because of his employment with Oxford. Under the Official Secrets Act of 1989, as revised, any person who is not a Crown servant but who provides, or is employed in the provision of goods and services to the government can fall under the Act as a 'government contractor'. We can use that to shut his mouth and constrain what he does. We don't want to be seen as stealing his work, but I want you to explore ways we can properly supervise and control what he does so this doesn't get away from us before we know what we're dealing with. You understand what I'm saying?"

"I do."

"Well then, get on it and report back to me as soon as you have an actionable plan. I want to button this up and learn more. Please shut the door on your way out." Sir Reginald reached for the phone as Joe left

Joe spent the rest of the day researching the history of forced taking by the government. Ever since the Magna Carta, it had been illegal for the government to confiscate property without paying for what was taken. But that hadn't stopped the Crown from skirting the regulations in the past. Since the 1960s, there had been a clear path laid out for confiscation of real property. A Compulsory Purchase Order must be issued, followed by a well-defined process for substantiating the public need and paying compensation. The taking of personal property was a different matter. Unless the item was illegal, it was difficult to find a legal premise for confiscation. In this case, national security was the motivating cause. This would imply an order could be sought from National Security and Intelligence, or from the Cabinet Office. But this line of pursuit was all wrong. The whole point was to keep Dr. Drury's project secret. Jumping through all the legal hoops to obtain an order against him would defeat the effort to hide what he was doing. Susan was an additional complication. If Joe was behind a government attempt to strong-arm her father, it certainly was not going to help his relationship with her.

By the end of the day, Joe came to the conclusion the Official

Secrets Act could indeed be used to enforce the silence of Dr. Drury, but obtaining his cooperation to share his project with Intelligence would be more fruitful than trying to confiscate or take control of the project. Joe was going to need to use Susan to sell the importance of putting a security bubble around this project. Joe felt awkward about his position, but there was no doubt in his mind that national security came first.

By Thursday morning, Joe had a plan. He would spend the rest of the day getting all his ducks in a row and outline a detailed project management plan. He would take Susan out to dinner on Friday night and sell her on the plan. They would then have the weekend to meet with her father and solicit his cooperation. It was going to be tricky to explain to Susan his involvement with national security without revealing his true position in the government. He needed to vaguely refer to colleagues in the intelligence community. Perhaps he could suggest that her father was already under surveillance and he had been approached as an intermediary because they had observed his relationship with her and her father.

CHAPTER 14

Thursday evening, three men in trench coats walked into the office of Professor Robert Drury with guns drawn. As he raised his gaze from a manuscript and saw the guns, confusion and worry washed over him.

With a thick Russian accent, one of them said, "Stand up and give your program."

Dr. Drury placed both hands on his desk and lifted himself out of his chair. "You must be mistaken. I don't know what you're talking about."

A second man stepped forward and pulled the professor from behind his desk. "We don't have time to play games! You have a program we want. Where is it?"

Dr. Drury was still confused. "Do you mean a computer program? You're in the astrophysics department. We have lots of programs. Why do you want — "

The Russian grabbed him by the lapels of this jacket and

shook him violently. "Enough!" he shouted. "You have a program that makes predictions. We want it now!"

Dr. Drury tried to hide his surprise as he realized what they were after. "What makes you think I have anything like that? Who told you — "

The Russian smacked him with a fierce backhand across the face. Dr. Drury stumbled backward and tripped over a pile of books on the floor. He waved his arms wildly as he fell straight back. The corner of his desk was in the perfect position to clip his head as he crashed down to the floor. A dark pool of blood oozed onto the oak planks of the floor.

"Shit!" Nikolai stepped back from the blood. To Dimitri, he said, "What the fuck, you moron! See if he's alive."

The second Russian squatted down and pushed on the lifeless body. He removed his black glove and pressed two fingers to the man's neck. Then he shook his head and stood up.

"What the fuck we gonna do now?" Nikolai asked.

The third man had been pushing papers around on the professor's desk. On a small table next to the desk, he found a laptop computer. "This is probably it," he said as he held it up.

"Okay, check the file cabinets and other tables in case there's anything else," Nikolai instructed.

Within three minutes, the office was empty, leaving a dead body on the floor and papers scattered everywhere.

At ten p.m., Susan got the call. A watchman locking up the

building had found professor Drury and called the police. Susan called Joe in tears and asked him to meet her at her father's office. Joe was in such a panic, he actually arrived before Susan did.

When Joe was greeted by the police in the hallway outside the office door, he showed them his government credentials. "This is just between us. Nobody is to know who I am or why I'm here." The officer nodded and let him in.

The body was draped with a black plastic sheet. Books and papers were scattered all over the floor. Nobody else was in the office except for the officer at the door. He was waiting for a forensics team. Before Joe could make sense of anything, Susan burst through the door.

"Oh no! Oh no!" she cried. "Joe, what happened? How can this be?" Tears were streaming down her face and she held her hands out in a helpless gesture.

Joe took her by the arms, brushed papers off a chair, and pushed her to sit down.

The police officer approached them. "Ye canna' stay. Tis a crime scene. But we'd like tae have ye verify the identity of the deceased."

Joe nodded and walked over to the body. He bent down and lifted a corner of the plastic tarp. His heart sank in empathy with Susan's loss. Joe looked at the policeman. "This is Dr. Drury."

From the position of her chair, Susan could see her father's face when Joe lifted the tarp. She let out a wail and bolted toward the two men. Joe stood and grabbed Susan in a giant bear hug. "There's nothing we can do now." He struggled to contain her as he led her toward the door. She was sobbing uncontrollably.

When they got to the hall, Joe loosened his grip on her. He led her down the hall, away from the police. Then he held her face in his hands and looked directly into her eyes. "Susan, I'm so, so sorry, but I need to ask you something. I think this has to do with your father's prediction project. Do you know where he keeps the materials? Is the program in a computer somewhere?"

A look of horror spread across Susan's face. "Oh no! Do you really think that is it? Why would somebody… ?"

Joe continued to hold her gaze. "I think the program is far more valuable than your father realized. I'm worried it has fallen into the wrong hands. Did he use the university computers, or does he have a laptop he kept the program on?"

Susan tried to shake her head against Joe's palms. "No, no. My father has done government work in the past, and he felt strongly about not using university property for his personal research, because the lines get blurred between what's his and what belongs to the university. His laptop was given to him by the university, so he always kept his personal research on separate external drives."

Joe dropped his hands from her face to her shoulders. He still held her directly in front of him and looked deep into her eyes. "Do you know where the drives are?"

"He keeps a lot of miscellaneous backup drives at home, but his prediction model is on a flash drive in the Trojan horse."

"Trojan horse? What's that?"

"It's on the shelf in his office. Come. I'll show you."

As they approached the office door, the same policeman stepped in front of them. "Ye canna' go in there. I told ye, tis a crime scene, an' we need for it t' be processed."

Joe leaned toward him and half-whispered in his ear. "This is a matter of national security. I'll take responsibility. You can call the bureau if you need more reassurance. We won't touch your crime scene."

Without waiting for a response, Joe pushed past the policeman and pulled Susan with him. He half-closed the door behind them so the policeman would not follow.

Susan pointed to a decorative carved wooden horse sitting above head level on the shelves across the room. Joe walked her around the far side of the desk, positioning himself between her and the draped body to shield her view.

Joe reached up for the horse and gave it to her. She slid up a small panel on its chest a fraction of an inch. That was enough to allow her to then slide a panel on its stomach forward until a flash drive fell out into her hand.

"It's still here." She closed the panels on the horse and handed it back to Joe. He placed it back on the shelf.

"There's one more thing we need." Susan turned toward her father's desk and opened the top left drawer. She took out a small five-inch notebook and closed the drawer.

The noise of the desk drawer closing caused the policeman to push the office door open. Susan slid the drive and notebook into her coat pocket as he entered.

Joe looked at the policeman. "We're just leaving. You can

have your superiors get in touch with my office if there are questions. We'll leave you to figure out who did this." He and Susan skirted past the policeman to get out the door.

The policeman said to Susan, "Ma'am, I'm sure they'll be wantin' ta question ye. I wouldna' be goin' far."

The full reality of what had happened hit Susan again, and she started crying as Joe hustled her down the stairs and out of the building.

CHAPTER 15

By the time Joe got Susan back to her apartment, she was incoherent. Her grief was so great, she couldn't form a complete thought. Joe pushed a glass of wine into her while he tried to calm her down. There was no consoling her. Ultimately, she lay down on the bed and he held her until she sobbed herself to sleep.

Once Susan was asleep, Joe retreated to the armchair in the front room. With only a night light on in the kitchen, Joe sat in the dark gloom of night, pondering the disturbing events of the day. For Dr. Drury to be killed right after Joe had revealed the existence of the doctor's project to Sir Reginald was too much of a coincidence. Was it possible MI6 decided to go around him to secure the program? Did Sir Reginald pass the information to Government Communications Headquarters? Or was there a mole in MI6 who passed the information to someone else? All these possibilities were troubling. For something this important, if he couldn't trust MI6, who could he trust?

Joe thought about what it meant to be able to predict the future. It could mean unlimited wealth. It supplied the knowledge to intervene and control any future event. It provided the ability to manipulate the outcome of trade negotiations, battles, competition for essential resources or technologies. The power that would accrue to a person or nation was frightening. Who could possibly be trusted with that much power?

Joe realized he could end his quandary by simply destroying the flash drive and notebook, but he couldn't bring himself to do that. It would be like destroying one of the great treasures of the world. He reasoned that, like any tool, what might be used to do harm, could also be used to do good. He needed to find safe hands, a safe place for this treasure to reside. He knew one thing. He was pretty sure he couldn't trust his own nation of birth. The UK was a fabulous country, but, in spite of Brexit, was caught up in entangling alliances with the European Union, and was still fighting to get out from under the Victorian-era stigma of colonization. The UK spent too many years living off the fat of the former territories, now known as the Commonwealth, instead of preserving and cultivating the unique attributes and talent of the people who made Britain such a powerhouse in the first place.

In the morning, Susan woke fully dressed on her bed with a blanket pulled over her. She sat up with a nagging headache and clogged sinuses. When she remembered the night before, a pall of sadness fell over her.

She got out of bed and wondered where Joe was. She found him asleep on the couch in the living room. When she filled the kettle and put it on the stove, the noise roused Joe. He joined her in the kitchen and put his arms around her.

"I'm so terribly sorry about your father."

She sank against the warmth of his body and said nothing. This was a turning point. Nothing was ever going to be the same. She wanted to be held, as if his strength could suspend her in time and preserve all the wonderful things in life that had belonged to her in the past. She was afraid it was all going to wash away. She was staring into an empty black future she couldn't comprehend.

"I wish I didn't have to go." Joe kissed the top of her head. "But there is something extremely important at work I need to tend to. I shouldn't be too long."

"That's okay." She reached for the kettle. "I don't feel like doing anything right now. I'm fine just staying here."

Joe looked at the flash drive and notebook sitting on the breakfast bar. "Let's put these somewhere safe until I get back."

Susan reached for a white china canister sitting next to others labeled "flour" and "sugar". She took the top off, exposing a wad of Euro bills hidden within. Adding the items from off the breakfast bar, she put the top on and placed it back on the shelf. "They'll be fine there."

Joe grabbed his jacket. "I won't be long." He gave her a

quick kiss and headed for the door. "I'm sorry, but I need to do this."

+≒═·═≓+

Joe couldn't come up with any sensible explanation for Dr. Drury's death. The thought that MI6 was behind it was tearing him up.

He went straight to Sir Reginald's office. He didn't even acknowledge Sally as he walked past her and barged through the office door. Sir Reginald raised his head from his paperwork with a startled look on his face. "Joe?"

Joe was trying hard to restrain his emotions. "You heard what happened?"

"I received a police report this morning," Sir Reginald folded his hands together. "Was that your professor?"

"It was." Joe hardened his expression and crossed his arms. "I find it beyond coincidence this happened after I spoke with you. Can you tell me who else knew about our meeting?"

Sir Reginald looked perplexed. "I haven't spoken with anyone."

Joe fought exasperation. "Do you tape your meetings? Do you keep notes? Who else has access to your affairs?"

A wave of concern swept over Sir Reginald's face. "What are you implying? Standard procedure is always followed. Yes, I take notes. At the end of the day, Sally reviews my schedule with me and I give her my notes. I also dictate my thoughts and provide additional color to my notes. Sally types everything up and then it's archived by our records section. Everybody along the way has been vetted, and of course, everything is held as top secret. I don't know how you can think any information escaped from this office."

"I don't know what to say, but I can't come to grips with the chain of events that led to this man's death."

"Was anything taken? Do you have the professor's program?"

Joe had previously made up his mind he was going to lie. "No. I don't have the program. I don't know where it is. The professor's laptop is missing. I'm worried that whoever has the laptop might have the program."

"This's not good." Sir Reginald didn't seem as upset as Joe thought he should have been. "You need to see if you can find that laptop."

"I don't even know where to start. I suppose I'll just have to follow along with the police investigation." Joe shrugged, turned, and walked out of the office.

Joe's desire to know who was behind Dr. Drury's death was thwarted by the mysterious veil of secrecy that hung over all houses of espionage. He had no way of confirming a mole in MI6, but he had accomplished his primary objective. He had stated clearly that he did not have the professor's program. Whoever had access to the information from his first meeting, would have access to what he said in this meeting. His denial should have deflected any further pursuit of him or Susan, at least for a while. When whoever took the laptop realizes they don't have the program, they would explore other possibilities. Eventually, they would circle back to him. But by then, he hoped he would be well on his way to disposing of the program and removing himself from any further involvement.

When Joe returned to Susan, he found her in a daze. She appeared to be picking things up and straightening the room, but she wasn't accomplishing anything. Joe took her by both hands and sat her down.

"Whoever took your father's laptop will soon realize they don't have his project. We're both in serious jeopardy as long as we hold on to the program. We need to leave town immediately."

Susan bit her lower lip. "I have an aunt in New York City."

"Perfect." He kissed her. "I'll fly to New York with you and get you settled with your aunt. Then I'll fly down to Washington, DC and explore finding the 'right' people to become custodians of your father's work."

Within days, Joe found himself at the British embassy in DC, and Nancy found the flash drive and notebook in the hidden drawer of the dresser in the bedroom where Joe was staying. No good deed goes unpunished. Joe's involvement with Susan and his attempt to secure her father's program did indeed become the death of him.

PART 4

CAT AND MOUSE

CHAPTER 16

S am spent a tormented night at his house. He was having a hard time dealing with Nancy coming back into his life. He was immensely attracted to her, but he was also guilt-ridden over his previous encounter with her. What had possessed him to agree to a bargain that extorted her? He was so desperate for female companionship that he had taken advantage of the situation, and now it had come back to haunt him. All of that was bad enough, but now she was dependent on him. Once again, he was in the position of having leverage, and he wasn't sure he trusted himself not to misuse his advantage. And all this business about Russians chasing her? What was he to make of that?

Sam got out of bed early and was at the grocery store when it opened at seven. He made short work of buying supplies and was at his boat before eight. The companionway was locked from the inside, so he tapped on the plexiglass hatch cover. In a few moments, Nancy opened up for him.

"Good morning! I brought you breakfast," Sam said with a smile. He couldn't help being distracted by the sight of her. Beautiful bare legs disappeared at the lower edge of a large sweatshirt of his. He imagined nothing else underneath, sending a zing to his groin. Her hair was astray. He had obviously woken her up. She had an endearing disorganized look, like a puppy confused by its surroundings. He handed her one of the grocery bags, then carried the other bag down the companionway.

"I think I got everything on your list, plus a few extras." Sam grabbed a skillet from the drawer below the oven. "Are eggs and bacon okay?"

Nancy smiled. "Sure. I could do with coffee too."

Sam nodded. "Coming right up!"

"Give me a moment to get dressed. I hope you don't mind I borrowed your sweatshirt."

Sam couldn't hold back a grin. "Looks good on you."

Nancy walked into the stateroom and closed the door.

When she came back out, Sam was setting food on the table in the salon.

"I hope you slept well."

"Yes. I needed a good night's sleep." Nancy sat opposite Sam and reached for the coffee cup he had filled. "This is a nice boat."

"Thank you. It's my one real extravagance. My ex-wife never cared about sailing. She barely tolerated the boat."

Nancy looked up from her food. "You were married?"

"Didn't work out." Sam shrugged. "Our daughter died, and things fell apart."

Nancy grimaced at having wandered into territory where she didn't want to be. "I'm sorry." She pushed a strand of hair out of her eyes. "So, what's the plan for the day?"

Sam took a breath and brightened up. "The fellow I want to phone is a couple of time zones west of us. My plan is to go into the office and work until late morning. Then I'll see who I can find to help us figure out your puzzle. You're welcome to stay here and relax. The TV functions, and there's a small collection of books on the shelf in the forward cabin. I'd try to stay out of sight. Your presence will raise questions among other people at the marina who know this is my boat. And we certainly don't want the people who are looking for you to get wind of your location."

Nancy placed her hand on top of his and looked deep into his eyes. "Thanks, by the way. I really appreciate having a safe place to stay."

The physical contact was not something he expected. Sam's heart fluttered, but he resisted the warm feeling growing inside of him. He shrugged and looked past her. "It's no problem. I hope we can get to the bottom of what's going on." He glanced at the ship's clock, pulled his hand away, and rose. "I better get going. Time is moving on."

Nancy nodded. "Don't worry about the dishes. I'll clean up. Thanks for breakfast!"

Sam took a last glance at her and hoped his expression

wasn't giving away his burgeoning feelings. "Be careful. See you soon."

After he departed, Nancy cleaned up the remains from breakfast. She stuck her head up and out the companionway to enjoy the sunshine, but heeded his warning about being seen and retreated below. She wandered forward to look at the collection of books Sam said were there. Her gaze was diverted by a wood plaque mounted on the bulkhead with the words "Altissima Quaeque Flumina Minimo Sono Labi" carved into it. Nancy knew it was Latin, but the introductory class she had taken in high school was no use. She thought of asking for a translation on her phone, but remembered Sam's warning. She didn't think there would be anything wrong with using her laptop if she went through a virtual private network connection. So, she set her computer on the nav station and performed a quick search. The direct translation was, "The deepest rivers flow with the least sound." The common interpretation was, "Still waters run deep and much is not seen." That seemed a bit mysterious and possibly threatening. An optimistic interpretation was, "A quiet personality hides deep thought and passion." A darker interpretation was, "A quiet man is a dangerous man, compared to a shallow, noisy enemy." Who was Sam Barron? This was an intriguing quote to have mounted in his boat.

Bored and lonely, she drifted to the stern, flopped down on the bed, and thought about the peculiar situation she had found herself in. Here she was on a beautiful boat, owned by a handsome man who she thought she would never see again. She replayed the events of that night in her mind. How could she have been so careless? It wasn't in her game plan to ever get caught. And then they ended up in bed. How weird was that? She remembered his naked body and how gentle and persistent he was.

It had been a long time since she broke up with Steve, and she hadn't been to bed with a man between then and when she met Sam. She brushed a hand over her nipples, suddenly horny. She slipped a hand down to circle her clit, recalling the feeling of Sam's penis rubbing the same area. She crossed her legs and rolled over onto her stomach. She clutched the pillow, scrunching it beneath her chest. Oh my lord, she could use a good fuck right now! It didn't matter what her mind thought about it. Her body wanted Sam.

If only life were so simple. She had people trying to kill her, and she was thinking about sex? But maybe life was simple. What did a rabbit do? Eat, fuck, and try to stay alive — not get killed by predators. Maybe that summed up her life too.

It had been days since Nancy had been able to relax. As she lay there, the gentle motion of the boat worked its magic, and she fell into a deep sleep.

When Sam returned to his boat in the early afternoon, the companionway hatch was open and he found Nancy with a spray can of Pledge polishing the woodwork down below. "You don't have to do that!"

"I know, but it looks so nice, and I want to make myself useful."

"I have good news." Sam beamed like a little boy pleased with himself. "I talked to my friend from the Department of Energy, and he hooked us up with an expert. You absolutely won't believe his name!"

Sam paused and was greeted with silence.

Finally, Nancy spoke. "Is that a statement or a rhetorical question?"

Sam frowned, confused. "I guess maybe, either. Anyway, his name is Doctor Thermopylae Higgins! Can you believe it? Who names their child Thermopylae? — Never mind, that is rhetorical.

"So it seems Dr. Higgins is an expert on large data sets at Livermore Labs, but he's currently a guest research advisor this summer at Georgetown University. I didn't realize Georgetown was a private research university. It wouldn't have occurred to me someone like Dr. Higgins would be found there.

"Anyway, we have an appointment to meet with him in three days."

"Wow. That's good news," said Nancy. "Do you really think he can help us?"

"There's no way to know for sure, but Rick says he's one of the top guys at Lawrence Livermore National Laboratories. The fact that he's on the east coast makes it easy for us. This is not something I want to do over the phone. So, I'll get us tickets and we can fly down to DC the day after tomorrow."

Nancy looked vexed. "You know I can't pay for a plane ticket right now. I don't have the cash, and you said not to use my credit cards."

Sam shook his head. "Don't worry about it. I got this covered. I'm happy to do it, and we want to keep you under wraps. I'm nervous that we'll need to use your real name due to TSA security checks at the airport. You're sure you aren't wanted by the police?"

"No." Nancy paused for a few seconds. "I mean yes, I'm pretty sure the police aren't searching airports for me. Of course, they know my house was broken into, but I can't imagine they know much more than that."

"Good. Then we're all set." Sam smiled at her. "The day after tomorrow will be our travel day, so we have an extra day to kill. What do you say we take tomorrow off? Do you like to sail? We can go for a sail and give you a chance to get fresh air and sunshine. I expect you're going stir crazy from staying below deck all day today."

Nancy broke into a big smile. "I don't know how to sail, but if you're willing to deal with a novice, I'd love to give it a try."

"Excellent!" Sam grinned. "We have a date. I'm going back to my office to get things in order since I'll be away for several days. I'll plan to be here at eight tomorrow morning. We can have breakfast together again, then get going. Does that sound like a plan?"

"Sounds great!" An awkward moment passed when Nancy

almost hugged him. "I'm looking forward to it. Thank you."

+>==—==+

When Joe Campbell's body was found by Sergeant Maddox, along with a diplomatic passport, the FBI was contacted. Although the murder involved a foreign citizen, it was a domestic crime, the jurisdiction of the FBI. The FBI, which agreed to a joint task force with the Sea Haven police department, was the agency that contacted the British Embassy. From the British Embassy, word found its way back to Sir Reginald at MI6. Sir Reginald immediately connected the murder of Dr. Drury with the murder of Joe Campbell and became quite distressed. He called his counterpart at the CIA. Sir Reginald had lied to Joe when Joe asked him if anyone else knew about their conversation. Sir Reginald had called Director Angela Firestone at the CIA because he knew the US government had various projects underway using artificial intelligence to make predictions. He wanted to get a sense of whether Dr. Drury's project was likely to have any real value. Now, the director at the CIA was telling Sir Reginald she hadn't heard anything about the death of Joe Campbell. Of course, he hadn't told her Joe's name during their first conversation, and she had no reason to be advised of a random foreign national's death. But Sir Reginald was thinking too many coincidences were starting to seem not like coincidences.

CHAPTER 17

The Russians were tenacious. After they were scared away from Nancy's house by the police, they lost track of her. They spent the next few days using a vast array of resources. Of course they monitored airports, train stations, and bus stations. They hacked into the EZ Pass toll system to check for her license plate. They also hacked into street cameras and police license plate readers. They monitored her credit cards and her phone. They watched the post office where she worked, and searched in vain for friends and relatives. They had no success finding a clue. Finally, they put in a request for a satellite survey of a 500-square-mile area around Sea Haven. From directly overhead, they were not going to have a good angle to be able to see a license plate, so they simply looked for light blue cars. They could have used a drone, but that was going to take longer to arrange, and it was likely to draw unwanted attention.

There were lots of light blue cars, so they used an artificial intelligence program to scan the images, looking for a match to a BMW body style. The satellite could only make one pass per day. On the first pass, they came up with forty-seven color matches, but only twenty-three were confirmed shape matches. The others were only possibilities. They started driving from one car to the next checking the license plates. Often, by the time they got to the location, the car had moved. It was frustrating work, but it had to be done.

Sixty-two hours into the operation, they found Nancy's car parked at the Walmart lot. Now, all they could do was stake it out and wait, like a spider waiting for its prey. While at least one pair of eyes was on the car at all times, others were roaming nearby neighborhoods looking for Nancy or any logical place she might hide. There was a reason why people called Nikolai a pit bull. Once he got a bite of something, he wouldn't let go.

CHAPTER 18

When Sam showed up at his boat with breakfast, he found the companionway hatch cover open. He called down for Nancy, but received no answer. As he came down the stairs, he called out again. An aura of emptiness hung below deck, the silence indicating nobody was there. He set the grocery bags in the galley and walked forward and aft, searching. He knocked on the door to the head and pushed the door open. She was gone. There was no sign of a struggle, but that didn't mean much. Panic overtook him as he went back up on deck. He wasn't sure where to look. Would she have gone back to her car? He walked back up the dock toward the marina. At last he spotted her, carrying a ditty bag, and wearing a towel wrapped around her wet hair. She had gone up to the locker room to take a shower.

Sam ran up to her. "I was worried when I didn't find you on the boat."

"I'm sorry. I wanted to get cleaned up. It's easier onshore where I have more space and more water pressure." She hit him with a disarming grin.

"I understand. I was just worried. I thought something might have happened."

He walked her back to the boat and started laying out breakfast while she combed out her hair. He called out to her in a sing-song voice. "It's another beautiful day in paradise! Are you ready to do some sailing?"

"Absolutely!" She leaned around the doorframe and smiled. "But you're going to have to show me how!"

As she walked back into the salon, Sam's eyes swept over her from head to toe. Her white sleeveless blouse had the top three buttons undone. Her navy-blue shorts exposed the full length of her leg, and fit so snug, the curve of her hip was on display. The sight made his heart sing. "No worries. You're going to do fine."

After breakfast, Sam let Nancy clean up below while he unhooked the shore power, took off the sail cover, removed the instrument covers, brought the winch handles up on deck, hung the life ring on the taffrail, and put out the American flag. Soon, they were shipshape and ready to cast off. Sam backed the sloop out of its slip and turned into the channel to head out through the mooring field in the harbor.

Sea Haven was settled in the 1600s as a fishing village. It took over one hundred years to become incorporated as a town. Like many New England towns, fishing slowly gave way to cottage-style industry. There was a mix of leather tanning, metalworking, carpentry, and small shipbuilding, along with agriculture. It didn't have the right ingredients to become a real factory town. By the early 1900s, Sea Haven was discovered by the upper class and became a summer escape from the heat in the city. In the 1960s to '70s, the summer cottages were expanded into year-round suburban residences. As they motored out of the harbor, the McMansionized waterfront residences stood out along the rocky shoreline. Sea Haven had become a full-out resort town for the wealthy.

As they passed the red channel buoy that marked the harbor entrance, Sam turned into the wind and told Nancy to take the wheel. "It's just like driving a car, except you have rear-end steering."

Sam walked forward to the mast and raised the mainsail. There was a perfect ten to twelve mph wind. Sam told Nancy to bear off to port. When he saw the confusion on her face, he said, "Turn left, off the wind." He came back to the cockpit and sheeted the mainsail in tight. Then he turned off the engine. "We're sailing!" He reached over and grabbed the port jib sheet with his left hand while he popped the spinlock off with his right hand to release the roller furling. As he pulled on the jib sheet, the wind caught the clew of the sail, and the jib unwound rapidly. As it snapped full in the wind, Sam took three wraps around the winch and cranked it in to a close-hauled position. "Easy as that!" He smiled at Nancy.

He saw an expression of mild panic as she gripped the

wheel. "You're doing fine." He grinned. "Everything's good."

As they headed out to sea on starboard tack, he showed Nancy how to head up toward the wind until the sails started to luff, then turn slightly off the wind until the sails filled and the telltales flew out straight. She was a quick learner and adapted naturally.

When a puff hit them and the boat heeled over, Nancy grabbed on like she was preparing for a rollercoaster ride. Sam explained they had a heavy keel under the boat that would keep them from tipping over. "Pretty soon you'll get used to the motion of the boat, and even in a lumpy sea, it'll be second nature for you to walk around and compensate for the roll. But always hold on to something, just in case. I don't want to lose you overboard."

Nancy grinned. "I knew my gymnastics training would be useful."

The boat settled into a groove, and with the wind in her hair, and a smile on her face, Sam could tell Nancy was enjoying herself.

God, she looked beautiful. Standing at the helm with the sun beaming down on her wind-swept hair, she looked like a model at a photoshoot.

"I'm going below. Can I bring you up something to drink?"

"Water would be fine."

Sam reappeared with bottled water in one hand and a coke in the other.

"You're doing great. Just watch out for the lobster pot buoys.

We don't want to snag one of those. Are you sure you've never sailed before?"

"This is my first time. I was born in the Midwest, nowhere close to water. I told you before, my mother died when I was young. My father was in the military, so he dragged me around the country with him. We moved to Arizona, then California, and then finally ended up in Virginia when I was in high school. My father was away a lot, so I often stayed with my aunt Peggy in Virginia. I was pretty much on my own. My father gave Aunt Peggy money for me, but I think she spent more of it on herself than she did on me. I was mostly like a tenant in her house rather than family. Fortunately, I had gymnastics to keep me busy, at least until I grew too tall in high school."

"So, what do you do, besides breaking into people's houses?"

Nancy grimaced at the mention of her illicit hobby. "I think I mentioned I'm a government contractor. I specialize in computer science, specifically large system software. I like the elegance of math, and machines that can follow instructions without ever making a mistake."

Sam was surprised. "How did you get into that?"

"Well, I had no idea what I wanted to do when I entered college. I always assumed I would get a gymnastics scholarship for college, but I grew too tall by my second year in high school and ultimately left the sport. I went to a community college in Virginia and started out thinking I wanted to study economics. I took a computer coding course to fill out my requirements, and I really liked it. My sophomore year I packed my schedule with computer science courses. I applied to MIT and Harvard for my junior year. It's almost impossible to get into those schools as a freshman, but not many people think to apply as a junior. Natural attrition causes spaces to become available, so by junior year, it's sometimes possible to find an opening. MIT didn't take me, but Harvard said yes, and said they would help with my tuition. I had gender and geography going for me.

"When I graduated, I was advised to go where the money is, and it was easy to see the government has the money. That means they can do interesting projects, and they can pay well. They don't pay low-level government employees well, but there's a lot of opportunity to make good money if you're an outside contractor."

Sam said, "We have something in com — "

A big puff of wind knocked the boat down, interrupting. The bow naturally headed up into the wind, and Nancy wrestled with the helm, not quite sure what to do. There was a loud bang and the mast shuddered. Vibrations traveled down the shrouds and stays into the body of the boat. Sam looked around to see what was happening, and noticed the mainsail slumping down the mast.

He jumped across the cockpit and grabbed the helm from Nancy. He turned the boat directly into the wind and told Nancy to hold the wheel steady. Sam released the jib sheet and pulled on the jib furling line as quickly as he could. As soon as the jib was secure, he focused on corralling the mainsail. He pulled it the rest of the way down the mast and rapidly threw sail ties over it to keep it from flapping and blowing all over the place.

Nancy had no idea what had happened, but she did as she was told and held the wheel steady.

Relax," said Sam. "Everything's okay, but I'm afraid that's the end of our sail." He looked up the mast. "Unless…"

He walked toward the helm. "I'll take the wheel if you'll run below and grab the binoculars. They're in the starboard cabinet in the forward corner of the salon."

Nancy looked quizzically at him. "Starboard is where?"

Sam smiled. "On the right. The forward cabinet on the right."

While she was getting the binoculars, Sam started the engine and pushed the throttle to slow ahead. The boat had blown off the wind and was rocking from side to side in the waves. He turned back into the wind so she would head straight into the waves with very little pitch or roll.

When Nancy returned from below, he took the binoculars from her and looked at the top of the mast. "We're in luck. How would you like to climb the mast?"

Nancy looked up and sputtered, "How do you think I'm going to climb the mast?"

Sam grinned at her. "I'm just kidding. You don't have to. I can have it fixed at the marina. I didn't really mean climb anyway. I would winch you up in a bosun's chair. The good news is the shackle on the halyard broke. The remains of the shackle are keeping the halyard from falling back down inside the mast. We just need to grab the halyard at the top of the mast and pull it down."

"What's a bosun's chair?"

"It's not really a chair. It's more like a sling, part of a harness I can attach to the spinnaker halyard to winch someone up to the top of the mast."

"Oh." Nancy twisted her lips to the side with a cute, meet-the-challenge look. "I could probably do that."

"Really?" Sam was truly surprised. "I don't expect you to. The mast is more than fifty feet high. If you're at all afraid of heights, you won't like it."

"Heights don't bother me. If I don't actually have to climb, and if I'm safely in a harness, I don't see a problem."

"Wow." Sam rubbed his brow. "If you're willing to try it, it isn't complicated. All you have to do is grab the end of the halyard at the top of the mast and pull it back down with you."

"I'm game."

Sam put the boat on autopilot, slow ahead into the wind. He went below, retrieved the bosun's chair, and held it as he showed Nancy how to step into it. Her touch was warm, and stirred his insides. He worked hard to stay focused as he put his arms around her to strap her in. He attached both the port and starboard spinnaker halyards to the harness. He explained he would use the port halyard to winch her up, and the star-board halyard would be a safety line. "You need to hold onto the mast or a shroud at all times. If the boat rocks, you could go flying out ten feet away from the mast. It isn't the swinging out that's the problem. It's when you swing back in and slam into the mast that you're going to get hurt. So hold on tight. If at any time you're uncomfortable, let me know, and I'll lower you back down."

Nancy looked up to the top of the mast with a glint of determination. "Okay."

Sam took three wraps around the winch with the halyard and started grinding slowly. Once the harness snugged up tight on her, Nancy settled back into the sling. With a hand on each side of the mast, and her bare feet also holding onto each side of the mast, she worked her way up into the air. Where the lower shrouds came into the mast, she let go of the mast and grabbed onto the shrouds. Sam slowed down his grinding when she approached the radar dome because she had to work her way out and around the dome on the front of the mast. She was like a spider monkey the way she moved from mast to shroud and back to the mast, over the spreaders and up.

"You doing okay?" Sam shouted.

"Just fine!"

Finally, when she got within two feet of the top, she reached up and grabbed the broken shackle on the main halyard. Sam made sure the halyard wasn't cleated and was free to run. "If you can tie it to your harness, your hands will be free to hold on."

"No problem," she shouted back.

"Alright, I'm bringing you down."

When her feet touched back down on the deck, Sam left his position at the winch and ran up to her by the mast. He gave her a huge hug. "Well done! That was terrific!"

The feeling of her in his arms made his heart race. He was reluctant to let her go. He took her head in both hands and kissed her on the forehead. He wanted so much more, but he worried about taking liberties.

Nancy was embarrassed at the enthusiasm. With a demure smile, she said, "I'm glad I could help."

He took the halyard from her and assisted her out of the harness. "I didn't expect you to do that. I'm very impressed!"

The boat rocked on a wave and she put a hand on his chest as if to steady herself, but it wasn't clear she needed to. She looked into his eyes. "Any time you need me."

"You've saved the day. Now we can keep sailing!"

Sam pulled out his knife and cut the remnants of the shackle off the main halyard. He tied a bowline in the halyard through the head of the sail, and raised the mainsail. He turned off the engine, unfurled the jib, and they were back sailing again.

"It is too nice a day not to keep sailing, if that's alright with you."

Nancy flashed him a smile. "I'm having a great time!"

"Good! Let's think about snacks, or maybe lunch."

They continued to sail for the balance of the afternoon. Sam was entranced. Nancy was not only beautiful and sexy, she had a lot more to offer. The more she talked, the more he appreciated that beneath her reserve, she was intelligent, funny, practical, complex, well-read, but at times naive in terms of real-world experience. She was also troubled by her place in life at the moment. He wanted so much to help her, but he was having difficulty defining their relationship.

When they returned to the marina and got the boat ship-shape, Sam unfolded the mahogany dining table in the cockpit. It was a warm, balmy evening, perfect for drinks and dinner outside. For hors d'oeuvres, he only had crackers and cheese to offer, along with a bottle of wine, but that was more than enough to accompany their conversation.

After a moment of silence, Nancy brought the conversation back to something Sam said earlier. "You were saying we had something in common before the mainsail came down."

"Oh, yes. I was going to tell you I spent time at Harvard also. After the successful completion of one of my assignments, the agency I was working for offered to pay for my attendance at a management program at the Harvard Business School. It isn't quite the same as being an undergrad, but I became reacquainted with Harvard Square."

"Really? I don't suppose we were there at the same time."

"No. I was probably at least a half dozen years ahead of you." Sam cringed at the reference to their age gap. "I was just back in Cambridge a few weeks ago. I can't believe how much Harvard Square has changed since I was at school there. In fact, the changes started before I got there. When I started school, I was looking forward to getting a roast beef sandwich at Elsie's and a beer at the Wurst House, but they were gone. It probably means nothing to you, but those were landmarks for decades. My father used to take me to Elsie's and to the Pewter Pot muffin house when I was a kid. And I remember Tommy's Lunch too.

All of that was gone when I took classes there. Even now, a lot of the shops have turned over again since I was there."

"There's a store called Tommy's Value on Mt. Auburn."

"Yeah, I think that's in the same place as Tommy's Lunch used to be, but it isn't the same. Anyway, this talk is making me feel old. How about we change the subject and move on to dinner? The sunset is going to leave us in the dark pretty soon. I'm going to get some candles."

"That sounds good. What can I do to help?"

Sam was thrilled to have someone to share his boat with. This was how he had always imagined it should be, but his ex-wife had no interest in him or the boat. "If you're able to put together a salad, I'll throw steaks on the grill. Let me show you where everything is."

Sam went below to get matches, and to lay out for Nancy the lettuce, tomatoes, cucumber, cheese, avocado, and anything else she might want. He carried a couple of steaks up to the taffrail grill. As he cooked the steaks, he felt like a kid on his first date. On one hand, he was totally relaxed and having a wonderful time. But on the other hand, he had to remind himself that she was here out of necessity, not necessarily by choice. He wanted to make a good impression on Nancy, and was desperate to please her. He had been lonely for such a long time, he was wallowing in the joy of being with someone who truly appealed to him.

Nancy came into the cockpit with a bowl of salad and table settings. "That smells really good. I didn't realize how hungry I am."

"The steaks are just about done. Pour yourself more wine and we'll be all set."

"More wine sounds good. I guess I don't have to drive to get home." She smiled obliquely. "You don't have to drive either."

Sam understood the invitation, but he still wasn't comfortable it was an even playing field and a balanced relationship. "We'll see," was all he could muster.

The wind had died and the water was glassy, reflecting the lights that had come on around the harbor. It was remarkably quiet. The only sound was water lapping against the boats and docks. Occasionally, a launch engine could be heard across the water as someone was being delivered or picked up from a boat on a mooring. Their conversation dropped down to a murmur, with bouts of silence as they concentrated on eating. Both ignoring the elephant parked between them, they revisited the events of the day, and Sam provided a more detailed explanation of how a sailboat works.

"Thank you for taking me sailing today. I really enjoyed it."

"You're welcome." Sam smiled. "I had a good time too. You were amazing going up the mast. I'm very impressed you did that."

Nancy blushed and shrugged. "It wasn't as scary as some of the stuff I had to do for gymnastics." She described doing blind backflips on the balance beam, and performing vaults with a combination of flips and twists that meant she would lose sight of her landing spot.

When she was done eating, Nancy shivered. "I think all the blood is rushing to my stomach. And it's getting cooler now that the sun is down."

Sam got up and walked around the table. "Here. Put on my windbreaker. It has a fleece lining." He slid in next to her and held the jacket behind her so she could stick her arms in the sleeves.

"Do you mind if I sit here?" Sam perched stiffly, uncertain. "You have a much better view of the harbor. I'm tired of having the marina spotlights in my eyes."

"Sure, it's fine. I'm going to steal some of your body heat." She snuggled up next to him, and he put his arm around her shoulders as he relaxed against the seatback.

"I feel strange being here with you, considering the events surrounding our first meeting."

Nancy nodded her head against his chest. "We didn't have the most conventional start."

The light floral fragrance of shampoo in her hair stirred memories of teenage love and heartbreak.

Sam cleared his throat. "I'm glad I was able to meet you, but the circumstances produced an awkward agreement between us. I would call it suboptimal. No matter how much I try to rationalize what happened in my mind, I can't make the bargain feel right."

Nancy looked up at him. "I remember you saying we're all the result of the choices we make. That sounded harsh at the time, but you're right. I'm sorry I chose to rob people. That was a bad choice, but it didn't seem like I had a choice. I was boxed into a corner because of a prior bad choice I had made. I trusted a man who I thought I loved, but he wasn't trustworthy. I should have found a better solution to my problem. I brought a lot of this onto myself."

"I shouldn't have accepted your offer. You caught me in a moment of weakness, and I rationalized my acceptance by telling myself that you were making the choice. But it wasn't a fair choice for you to have to make. You deserved better."

They sat in silence brooding on what they had just shared.

Nancy turned to him. "What was that business about aliens?"

"Oh, yeah." Chagrinned, he chuckled in embarrassment. "That's a bit of self-deception. I had a prostatectomy a few years ago.

"A what?"

He sighed. "I had prostate cancer, so they removed my prostate."

Nancy touched his arm and looked up with a furrowed brow. "Are you alright?"

"My self-esteem was shredded, but the cancer is gone."

"You're a cancer survivor. That's awesome."

"It hasn't been five years, so nobody is saying 'cancer free'. Once you have had it, a cloud always hangs over you. The experience was a real takedown for me. I grew up being naturally good at everything. I always felt that if there was anything I wanted to do, nothing could stop me. That attitude has helped me enjoy success in my business, and it is why I am known as a 'fixer' for the government. I can usually get things done that other people don't have the drive or skill set to accomplish.

"I felt betrayed by my body when I was told I had cancer. Sex was so easy and natural, I never thought about the role it played in my life, but having my manhood threatened was debilitating. It was easier to say to myself it was something aliens did to me, because I couldn't understand why it happened. If I lost control of this, then what else? I want to be captain of my ship and master of my fate. I really needed to know I could still have sex with a woman. You were the victim of my loneliness, my fear, and my frustration. It didn't help that you're so friggin' gorgeous."

Nancy smiled. "You really think so?"

"Come on. You know you are!" Sam gave her a squeeze around the shoulders.

"Well, I'm glad you're helping me now. I don't know what I would have done if you hadn't taken me in."

Sam sensed her sincerity. She wasn't searching for flattery. He let a comfortable silence settle over them for a moment.

"You know," he said, "my experience with you has caused me to do a lot of thinking about right and wrong. I tend to think of all social interactions as transactional. Everybody is trading something for something else. Theft is simply a transaction with negative compensation for one party. It seems to me, almost all crime involves theft of one sort or another. Theft is the unpermitted taking of something. Even murder is the theft of a life. Using that premise, punishment is an attempt to exact compensation from the criminal, the thief, to balance out the transaction. Compensation under the law may involve a payment directly to the victim and/or payment to society. The objective is to teach the criminal a lesson by balancing the transaction."

"I can agree with that, but what's your point?"

"I didn't want to call the police on you. By accepting your offer to have sex, I deceived myself into believing I was balancing the transaction. I was claiming compensation and a penalty from you.

"Imagine someone robs a bank. That is blatant theft. Now, suppose you know who robbed the bank. You promise not to turn them in if they give you ten thousand dollars. Is this balancing the transaction? The law isn't assessing a penalty for the original crime. An illegal transaction, known as blackmail, has been introduced in addition to the theft. It might seem fair to some people for the bank robber to have to buy his way out of a problem he created, but it doesn't address the original crime of bank robbery, and doesn't compensate the original victim. The robber is himself being extorted, and thus becomes a victim. This is not in the best interest of a civil society. Two wrongs do not make a right."

Nancy reached up and gently placed a finger on his lips. "In our case, you were the victim and I owed you compensation. Getting hauled off by the police was not an option for me, so I offered you something in exchange."

Sam sighed and squirmed slightly. "You just stated the

problem. Losing your freedom was not an option, so you didn't have a true choice. It was not a fair way to value your dignity, and your self-respect, and all that you gave up to get into bed with me."

Nancy pushed away and looked him in the eyes. "Is any transaction ever perfectly balanced and totally fair? If I'm unbelievably thirsty and you charge me ten dollars for a small bottle of water in an airport waiting area, that might be viewed as extortion if I can't get water anywhere else. But if I agree to pay the ten dollars, then there's nothing wrong with the transaction. It's legal, and it happens every day."

Sam removed his arm from around her and shook his head. "No. I have trouble with that logic. You're saying, since you and I agreed to have sex, I didn't do anything wrong. But deep down, I know it wasn't right. I had leverage on you. I feel really bad about it, and I can't rationalize it away. I am truly sorry."

Nancy snuggled back in closer to him. "Apology accepted. I'm not sure you had much more choice than me, but it's in the past. I have put it behind me."

A silence ensued while Sam sought to change the subject. "Let's clear the table. We'll get you down below where it's warmer."

Nancy climbed down the companionway, and Sam handed things down to her. Then he folded up the table and joined her in the galley. Nancy washed the dishes, and Sam dried them. At one point, Nancy turned around to see what was left on the counter, and Sam reached across behind her to set a dry glass down on the other side of the sink. When she turned back, their faces were inches apart. One breath passed between them, then Nancy lifted her face up and kissed him. She slid her arms around him and gripped his shoulder muscles. She stood on tiptoes and pressed her body against his. Sam relished the sensation of her lips under his, her breasts pressing against his chest. He eagerly kissed her back. His hands reached around the curve of her hips and pulled her in. The bed teased him, visible through the cabin door behind her, and desire flooded through him. It would be so easy to take her to bed and relieve the tension that had been dogging him since the first time, but no — he couldn't do it.

Gently Sam pushed her back and cradled her face in his hands. "This isn't right. As much as I want it to be, this isn't right. Not now. You're dependent on me to help you, and I don't want to betray your trust and take advantage of the situation."

Nancy pouted. "I'm a big girl."

"I know, but we have a couple of important days ahead of us, and we should focus on that. I should get going and let you get organized. I'll come back in the morning and we'll fly south to see what we can learn from Dr. Higgins."

Sam gave her a quick hug, like a consolation prize, to express don't be mad at me, I still care. He turned and climbed up the companionway.

Nancy clenched her fists, bewildered and frustrated. She knew what she wanted, but she was still trying to figure him out.

CHAPTER 19

As if repeating a choreographed performance, Sam showed up with breakfast at eight in the morning. He loved catching Nancy with that rumpled, fresh out of bed look that made him desire to take her right back to bed. But today they had an agenda, so they couldn't linger over breakfast. He explained their travel plans, and then told her she should pack while he moves her car. "We can't leave it at Walmart indefinitely. Someone will notice. I have a large shed where I store my boat over the winter. I can put it there where it'll be safe and out of sight until we return."

"I don't have much to pack." Nancy handed him her car keys. "I'll be ready when you get back."

Sam started up the companionway steps, then stopped and returned. He handed his phone to Nancy and reached in his wallet for a credit card. "While I'm gone, would you mind reserving rooms for us at the Washington Plaza Hotel? Don't use your name. You can make up a name, or say you're Mrs. Barron. We don't want anyone tracking you."

"Sure, I can do that. See you soon."

Nancy finished straightening up and then searched the internet for the number of the Washington Plaza Hotel.

Sam walked to the Walmart store and found the parking lot two-thirds full. It took him a while to find Nancy's car. He looked around, saw nothing out of the ordinary, got in the car, and drove off. He needed to head back through the center of Sea Haven to get to his shed, on the other side of town. Typical of most old New England towns, Sea Haven had narrow winding streets. This made it easy for Sam to spot a black Audi following him. He made a few sudden turns onto side streets, both right and left. The Audi stayed with him until they realized he had spotted them. At a straight section of the road, they sped up and pulled up beside him in the oncoming traffic lane. One of the men waved a gun at him and pointed for him to pull over. A car in the oncoming lane made the Audi slam on its brakes and pull back in behind Sam. Sam sped up and headed for the narrowest streets he could find ahead of him. He wanted to keep them contained and off-balance, and he didn't want them pulling up beside him or passing him. He waited until the last possible moment before turning at intersections, hoping they couldn't make the turn and follow him. He wasn't having any luck shaking them. He checked the rearview mirror again, perspiring. "Where are the police when you want them?"

His wish brought to mind a solution. He cranked a hard right turn onto Maple Street, banged a left onto Winger Street, and a right onto Ocean Avenue. The Sea Haven police station was located about a half-mile ahead on the corner of Ocean Avenue and School Street. Sam pulled into the parking lot in front of the police station. The Audi pulled over to the side of the road facing south on Ocean Avenue.

Sam got out of Nancy's BMW and walked briskly through the glass front door into the police station. He found himself in a surprisingly small lobby with a glass wall on one side. Behind the glass partition sat the duty officer. Sam spoke through the small opening in the glass. "I hope you can help me. Some men are chasing me in their car. I don't know what their problem is. I think it's some kind of road rage. They're stopped out on the street. Can you talk to them?"

The duty officer pressed a button and leaned toward a microphone. "Mike, can you come up here? Need help in the lobby." After a thirty-second pause, a side door in the lobby wall opened.

The uniformed officer who came through the door looked at Sam. "What's going on?"

Sam pointed through the glass front door to the Audi still sitting on Ocean Avenue. "Those guys in the Audi have been harassing me. One of them pointed a gun at me. Can you talk to them?"

Mike called over to the duty officer. "Get backup. I'm going outside."

Sam followed Officer Mike out the front door. As Mike walked toward the Audi, Sam got in Nancy's car. When the officer had walked another 20 feet, the Audi peeled away from the curb, going south on Ocean Avenue. The officer stepped out into the street and tried to get the license plate. Meanwhile, Sam drove out of the parking lot in the other direction, west on School Street. Sam suspected there might be a tracking device on Nancy's car, so he changed his plan about taking it to his shed. He continued through town to the Mobil gas station with a convenience store attached to it.

Sam walked into the store and asked the clerk if they sold gas cans. The cashier pointed toward the back corner. "We have two-gallon and five-gallon plastic jerry cans."

Sam pulled forty dollars out of his pocket and handed it to the cashier. "I'll take a five-gallon can and apply the rest to gas. I'm on pump three."

Sam filled up the gas can and put the small amount of remaining gas he paid for in the car. Then he drove to the Sea Haven dump. The dump had been closed for the past two years. The location was used as a transfer station. Behind the bins for the transfer station, several acres of remediated land was getting overgrown with weeds and shrubs. Sam followed the dirt road into the old dump until it became impassable. He opened the glove compartment and found Nancy's registration and insurance card, which he stuffed in his pocket. He was glad to see her name, Nancy Forrester, confirmed by the paperwork. A corner of his mind doubted she'd given him her real name.

He took the gas can and splashed gas liberally over the front and back seats. He left the plastic jug more than half full on the back seat. Fortunately, the car was old enough to have an old-fashioned cigarette lighter. He pushed the lighter in until it was red hot. He stepped away from the car and tossed the lighter through the open window onto the soaked front seat. Flames immediately erupted in the front of the car.

The dump was located next to a forty-acre wooded conservation area, Deadman's Swamp. Sam trotted toward the trees. He reached the tree line when the black Audi appeared in the distance. It was heading straight for Nancy's car which was now billowing black smoke. The appearance of the Audi confirmed his suspicion. As the Audi approached the BMW, the gas tank in the back seat exploded, which ignited the car's gas tank. The double explosion sent glass, shrapnel, and flames shooting in all directions.

Sam disappeared into the trees and jogged through the forest. This was home territory for him. He ran for exercise on the trails through Deadman's Swamp. From the other side of the forest, it was only another two miles to his house on Ridgeview.

By the time he got home, Sam was soaked through with sweat. He headed straight for the shower. Then he packed a bag for the trip to DC and called an Uber to take him back to Bartlett's Landing.

When Sam arrived at his boat, he found Nancy lounging in the salon idly flipping pages of a magazine. Her expression was of a child forced to play inside on a rainy day. As soon as she saw him, she stood and gave him an unexpected hug.

"I guess you're right about the Russians." Sam untangled her arms from around him. "Actually, I don't know for sure if they were Russian, but men were definitely chasing me. Apparently, they staked out your car."

Nancy's brow wrinkled in concern. "Are you alright?"

"I'm fine, but your car isn't." Sam reached into his pocket and took out her registration and insurance card. "I want you to call the police and report your car as stolen. When they call you back and tell you they found it destroyed, you can call your insurance company."

"Seriously?" Nancy stared at the documents.

Sam shrugged. "We need to leave for the airport in twenty minutes." Then he told her the whole story of his morning's adventure.

Before Nancy gave Sam's phone back to him, she made a quick call to the police and reported her car stolen, as if it had happened the night before. The officer who took down the information didn't connect the dots to her as a person of interest.

CHAPTER 20

Nancy had no idea of the full extent of law enforcement activity surrounding her. She was correct when she told Sam the police had no reason to be after her, except for curiosity over why her house had been trashed. But the FBI and British intelligence were beginning to connect the dots. Other people were also looking for her. As soon as TSA entered a record of her ID at the airport, it was flagged by an agency that had full access to the system. It took three hours to be handed off and processed through channels, but the details of her airline ticket were eventually texted to Nikolai Andronovich.

"Crap!" he said to himself. "First, we have to drive all the way up here from DC, and now we have to go back. They couldn't send us plane tickets. No! We have to fucking drive back!" This operation had gone sideways from the start, and Nikolai was pissed.

There would be operatives on the ground at DCA when

she landed to track Nancy to her apartment or hotel. Details would be sent to Nikolai when they were known.

While they were waiting for their plane at the airport, Sam pulled out his laptop and asked Nancy for the flash drive. "I'm going to copy it over a VPN into an encrypted vault in the cloud so I can send a means of access to Dr. Higgins. That way, he'll have a chance to look at it before we meet tomorrow."

Sam also used his phone to take some photos of the pages in the notebook and place them in the same encrypted file. He sent an email to Dr. Higgins confirming their appointment, and giving him the password to the vault: "The nickname of our mutual friend, followed by the hour of our meeting." If anyone intercepted the email, hopefully, they would be stymied by a lack of information to figure out the password.

While Sam was on his computer, Nancy took the opportunity to visit the restroom. While she was sitting in a stall, digging around in her purse, she bumped against her mobile phone in the protective bag Sam had given her. It had been more than three days since she had checked her email. They were due to board the plane in ten minutes. What could be the harm in taking a quick look? When she turned on her phone, notifications of missed calls flashed at her. There were several from the same number, which she didn't recognize. There was also a voicemail. She played the voicemail.

"Miss Forrester, this is Sergeant Maddox with the Sea

Haven police department. We would like to determine your whereabouts and verify that you're safe. We found the body of a British citizen named Joseph Campbell in a room at the Twin Birch Motel, and he had a video feed to a camera installed in your house on Aspen Street. We found your house to be ransacked, and no sign of you. I also see you reported your car as being stolen. That phone call was logged in after we visited your house, so presumably you're still okay, but then we found your car totally destroyed by fire. We're very concerned about your welfare. Please call the Sea Haven police as soon as you receive this message, and ask for Sergeant Maddox. If we cannot clarify your situation, you will rapidly become a person of interest to the FBI, who is investigating the death of the foreign national."

"Oh shit!" Nancy whispered. If she hadn't already been sitting on the toilet, she would have peed her pants. Her hands shook so badly, she had trouble pushing the icons on her phone to close it down. She wondered if she had been the cause of Joe's death. Who killed him? Was it the same group that was after her? Terror wracked her body. Cold sweat broke out on her forehead and trickled down her back. She had to pull herself together. If she told Sam, he would be displeased she had turned on her phone. What would he think about the death of Joseph Campbell? Would he still continue to help her?

Nancy splashed cold water on her face. She freshened up her makeup and returned to the waiting area. As she was walking back, the loudspeaker announced the boarding of their flight. She put on her best smile for Sam. "I guess that's us. Time to go."

Their flight was uneventful, but it was always interesting to fly down the river for the landing approach to Reagan National Airport. On a clear day, there was a great view of the city. It was fun to pick out various government buildings and national monuments. Getting away from the problems in New England, and returning to familiar territory put both of them more at ease. They had no reason to suspect they might be followed.

Although Nancy was familiar with Washington, she had never been to the Washington Plaza Hotel. As they pulled up to the front entrance, it looked like any other glass-faced high-rise surrounded by a scattering of stone churches and old architecture from former grand residences.

When they were walking from the taxi to the front door, Sam leaned over and quietly said, "I hope this is alright. It's not a splashy hotel, but we don't want splashy right now. Inconspicuous is best."

As they approached the front desk, Nancy moved behind Sam. She knew what was coming.

Sam addressed the man behind the counter. "You have reservations for Sam Barron."

"Welcome to the Washington Plaza!" the clerk said. "Just a moment." He looked at his computer screen. "Yes, here you are. I see you have stayed with us before, Mr. Barron. I'm giving you a complimentary upgrade to one of our superior rooms. I hope you enjoy it. May I run your Visa card?"

Sam reached in his wallet and handed the clerk his credit card. Then he turned around to Nancy and silently mouthed the words, "One room?" His eyebrows went up with the question.

Nancy grinned. "Mr. and Mrs. – Right?"

Sam shrugged and turned back to the counter. The clerk handed his card back, asked him to sign an acknowledgment, and gave him two plastic magnetic room keys.

"Let me get you a bellman."

"That's okay. Our bags are on wheels. Thank you, but we can find our way."

Sam and Nancy headed for the elevators.

When they got to the room, Sam unlocked the door and pushed his suitcase inside in front of him. Nancy came up behind him and put her left hand on his neck. She swung around in front of him so they were face to face. With a sparkle in her eyes, she said, "I hope you don't mind, Mr. Barron. I thought it would be strange to have two rooms if we're married."

Sam smiled at the impish face she was making. "You could have been my assistant, or a colleague, but I'm fine with this arrangement. There are two queen beds."

Nancy raised an eyebrow at him, turned, entered the room, and flopped spread-eagle on the first bed.

Sam was uncertain what to do next. She was such a temptation. He looked at his phone. "It's only 4:30. Would you like to go for a walk before dinner?'

A shadow of disappointment passed across her face. "Sure. It would be nice to stretch our legs after that plane ride."

He helped her stand again and they left the hotel.

From Thomas Circle, Sam and Nancy strolled down Massachusetts Ave NW, otherwise known as Embassy Row. It was fun to look at the architecture and try to guess which embassy they were looking at, before reading the sign at the gate. When they passed Dupont Circle, Sam pointed to a large mansion. "Do you know what that is?"

Nancy shrugged. "No. I'm from here, and I should know more than you do, but I guess you spend more time here than you let on."

Sam winced. He didn't mean to put her down or be overbearing. He softened his tone. "In every city, there's at least one building that draws me like a magnet. In Boston, it's the Isabella Stewart Gardner Museum. In New York, it's the Frick. I just feel totally at home there. In London, it's the Victoria and Albert. You get the idea. So, this is the Anderson House.

"I don't know how much time you've spent in the Boston area, but you might be familiar with the name Larz Anderson. He and his wife lived there and had a prominent estate. He was an American diplomat, so he felt he also needed a large house in Washington to entertain. When he died, he gave the house to the Society of the Cincinnati. That is the nation's oldest and first hereditary patriotic organization, founded after the American Revolution in 1783.

"Technically, I qualify to be a member because I'm a direct male descendant of commissioned officers in the Continental army. I never felt it made sense for me to join, but I love visiting the place. It's an interesting museum about the American Revolution."

Nancy slipped her hand into his. "You keep surprising me. You know a lot. And there's much about you that I don't know."

Sam looked into her eyes. "My personal motto is, 'Tell everybody something, but don't tell anybody everything.'" He smiled at her. "For you, I might make an exception."

Nancy smiled back and squeezed his hand. They walked that way, hand in hand, until they got to the river.

Nancy pointed across the river along the extension of Massachusetts Avenue. "You know what that is down there?"

"No. What?"

"That's the British Embassy. That's where all my troubles started. Well, not all of them, but at least this most recent problem."

Sam studied the view for a moment, as if it could tell him something. "I don't think we need to go any further. We've walked pretty far already. I think it's time to head back."

When they got back to the hotel, Nancy said, "I feel kind of grubby. Do you mind if I take a shower?'

"Not at all. Let me ask you about dinner first. Do you want to go out, or do you want to stay in and eat at the hotel?"

"Well, if you're thinking of anything fancy, I don't have the clothes. If you remember, I left my house in kind of a hurry."

Sam sat down on his bed. "I'm happy with normal American comfort food. The hotel restaurant isn't too bad if you're okay with making a minimal effort."

"That sounds good to me. I'm hungry, but feel lazy too. I'm down for a relaxing evening staying in."

While Nancy was in the shower, Sam turned on the TV and watched Bloomberg market news. He had people at the office who could oversee things for him, but he didn't want to be blindsided by some major breaking news story that would shake the stock or bond markets.

He enjoyed having Nancy around. He was glad she had arranged the room situation the way she did. He felt young and enthusiastic about life again. He still couldn't get past the awkwardness of their relationship, but he wanted to be able to share his feelings with her. He couldn't deny the excitement of being in a hotel room with such a cute, beautiful, sensuous woman. She was everything he could dream of.

Nancy came out of the bathroom with a towel wrapped around her hair, and a larger towel wrapped around her body. Sam couldn't resist visualizing all that lay beneath the towel.

"I guess it's my turn in the shower." He scooted into the bathroom and closed the door, giving her the privacy to dress without him staring. The bathroom was steamy and smelled of women's perfumed soaps, shampoo, and cosmetics. The smell of feminine mystery. He breathed it in with joy and unquenched thirst.

When Sam was drying himself off after a quick shower, he realized he had been in such a hurry, he hadn't brought any fresh clothes in with him. He wrapped his towel around his waist and crept to his suitcase. Nancy, now dressed in jeans and a polo shirt, was sitting in front of a vanity mirror on the desk, blow-drying her hair. Sam thought maybe she would move back to the bathroom for the larger mirror, but she didn't. He grabbed a fresh pair of underwear and stepped into it with the towel still around his waist. As he pulled his underwear up, the towel fell away. Sam grabbed his trousers and hopped into them. He looked over at Nancy and saw her watching him through the mirror.

"Like the view?" He cringed at the defensive tone that came out.

She turned and laughed at him. "You have a nice ass."

"Glad to know I'm not totally over the hill." He reached for a fresh shirt.

When he was done dressing, they headed downstairs for dinner.

The service was slow, but that was fine with them. They didn't notice. They spent dinner talking, staring into each other's eyes, laughing, drinking, and leisurely sharing desert. The time slid past, until it was getting late when they strolled back to their room.

"Well, tomorrow is going to be an important day." Sam set the keycard on the bureau, took off his watch, and emptied his pockets. "I hope we have the right man to lead us through this puzzle."

Nancy shrugged. "I'm depending on you."

Sam's brow drew together in furrows. "First we have to

figure out the full potential of this program. I hope Dr. Higgins can do that for us. But the bigger question is what are we going to do with the program? That decision probably falls entirely on us."

Nancy set down her purse on a chair and sat on one of the two beds, smoothing the coverlet. "One thing is for sure. Until we can figure out what to do with this, we're in danger. At least I'm in danger. I'm not sure if anybody knows about you yet."

Sam felt slightly hurt she was still separating her position from his. "We're in this together. I'll be with you every step of the way."

Nancy looked up at him and smiled. "I'm glad I picked your house to break into."

Sam grinned and reached out. She stood, and he gave her a quick hug. When she tilted up for a kiss, he stepped away. "It's time for bed. Do you want the bathroom first?"

She pressed her lips together with a slight frown. "I'll be quick," She grabbed a few things and went into the bathroom.

Sam took advantage of her absence to get out of his clothes and into PJ bottoms and a t-shirt. Nancy came out of the bathroom in a jersey-style short nightgown with hearts on it. She reminded Sam of a co-ed in a dorm, except the cutest co-ed he had ever seen. He went into the bathroom, splashed cold water on his face, and brushed his teeth. When he came out, Nancy was in her bed, lying on her side, propped up on one elbow. Sam walked over and gave her a quick kiss on the cheek. "Good night." He climbed into the other bed and turned out the lights.

Nancy sighed. "Good night. Thank you for all you're doing for me."

"No problem." He turned on his side with his back toward her.

Nancy had thought she was tired, but her mind kept working, and she was restless. She worried over what was on the flash drive and who those men were who tore her house apart. The more she tried to concentrate on her problems, the more her mind kept wandering back to Sam. She thought she had figured him out, yet there were all kinds of things she didn't understand. He said she was hot, made her feel desirable, then tucked her in like a toddler and slept in a separate bed. What was that all about? She knew he was no monk, not after the sex they'd had. But since that time, nothing. She'd tried to be seductive, flirted incessantly. Nothing.

Anger and disappointment brewed. Self-doubt crept in. Why would he leave her aroused, but unfulfilled, pretending he didn't know every curve of her figure and want it still? She counted as many of his faults as she could to distance herself from her desire. He was older than her, but he was in great shape – better shape than many of the men her age. As far as she could tell, he wasn't attached to another woman. He was divorced, so she wasn't breaking anything that wasn't already broken. He had money, he had that beautiful boat, had his own company. He was fun and interesting. She pictured his body, piece by piece, and was having a hard time coming up with anything she didn't like. The more she thought about him, the more impatient she grew with his rejection. She listened to his regular breathing. It sounded like he was asleep. She slid from her bed, peeled off her nightshirt, and crept over to his bed. She lifted the covers and slid in next to him. He stirred and rolled over onto his back. She snuggled up next to him. He lifted his arm and put it under her head.

"I was lonely and couldn't sleep." She rested her hand on his chest, feeling his heartbeat.

Sam brought his free hand to her shoulder and brushed it down her torso, expecting her nightgown. He paused, then clutched her tighter. "That's okay, but be careful, because I'm horny."

Nancy put her hand flat on his stomach and slid it down between his legs under his PJs. She wrapped her hand around his throbbing member. "You're horny indeed, aren't you?" She slowly slid her hand up and down his penis. The skin moved with her hand, the smooth contours of his shaft gliding beneath the skin. She squeezed the ridgeline of its head and pulled his skin all the way up and over the tip, then back down again.

"That's alright, considering…"

"Considering what?" asked Sam.

"Considering I've been horny since that night."

Sam rolled toward her and kissed her.

She captured his lips and opened to welcome his tongue, pressing herself against him. "You're wearing too many clothes, mister."

"I think this is a problem I can fix," he said with a chuckle.

"I think you can, and that would make me happy."

Sam chucked his t-shirt and bottoms, coming back against her bare and hot to the touch. With his free hand, he cupped her breast gently like he was revisiting a treasured old friend. The electricity of his touch tingled along her body from toes to scalp. Impatient, she steered his hand down between her legs. She was moist and throbbing with desire. She shuddered as his probing fingers found sensitive spots. She wanted him. She needed him. She rolled on top of him and, with her hands on his chest, she settled down on his swollen cock. As it slid deep into her, she gasped with pleasure. The muscles inside of her spontaneously squeezed, and her whole body shuddered with pleasure. A giant smile spread across her face as she bent down and kissed Sam. Tenderness exuded from him, and he behaved as if his only mission was to give her pleasure. Both his hands were on her breasts now, and his hips were complementing her slow, rhythmic motion as she rocked forward and back. The pleasure was exquisite, and she quivered periodically with spasms, a string of mini orgasms.

Just when she thought it couldn't get any better, Sam sat up. With his arms around her back, and still within her, he swung his legs over the side of the bed and stood. He was a lot stronger than his slender frame revealed. He turned and gently lowered her head and shoulders back onto the bed. Blood rushed to her head, and her vision blurred as she was swimming in new sensations. Sam slid back onto the bed with her, and placed a pillow under her hips. He lowered her down onto the pillow and sank deep into her, his full length filling her entirely. As her insides stretched, the sliding contact increased, and the sensation took her to new heights. Her stomach muscles clenched, hard as a washboard. Waves of contractions swept through her as Sam slowly slid in and out, building up an unbelievable tension, her nerves ready to explode.

She cried out as waves of relief swept across her. Her whole body shook violently. Sam let out a gasp, and pushed one last time with a trembling spasm that swept from his hips to his shoulders. He collapsed on her, but spared her the full weight of his body. Nancy lay there dazed as he panted close to her ear. She ran her fingers through the hair on the back of his head.

"That was unbelievable!" murmured Sam. "I can't begin to tell you how meaningful this is to me. You have given me the greatest gift you possibly could."

"You're not so bad yourself." Nancy laughed. "I feel like you were made for me. You certainly rang my bell!"

"This feels so good. I wish I could stay in you forever – or at least for the rest of the night."

"I know. But if it were possible, I guarantee you we wouldn't get any sleep."

Sam gave her a tender kiss, and held her tight. He wanted to imprint forever in his memory the feeling of her smooth skin and taut body pressed next to him. He was overcome with the joy of having her for a lover.

Reluctantly, he moved over beside her and they spooned

together. As Sam was starting to fall asleep, Nancy quietly asked him, "What do I not know about you? Tell me something about yourself that most people don't know."

Sam thought for a minute. "I can ride a unicycle."

"Seriously? How did you learn to do that?"

"Well, I was kind of bored one summer when I was a teenager, so I decided I needed a challenge. I taught myself how to ride."

"Can you still do it?"

"Like riding a bicycle. Once you learn how, you don't forget. Your turn. Tell me something I don't know about you."

"I'm really flexible. I can put my ankles behind my head."

"Wow. It might have been useful to know that twenty minutes ago."

Nancy laughed. "Yeah. I guess we missed a potential opportunity."

"Next time," Sam murmured, kissing the back of her neck.

"Surprise me with one more thing." Nancy snuggled tighter against him. "What other secrets do you have?"

"You'll laugh. I play the bagpipes. Many people find it loud and obnoxious, so I usually play on the boat when I'm a bit offshore."

"I think that's cool!" Nancy hugged his arms around her. "You're an interesting person, Sam Barron."

"I'm also a tired person. Good night." He snuggled close and drifted off to sleep.

CHAPTER 21

Fortunately, Sam set an alarm, or they might have slept together well into the morning. Nancy was the first out of bed and into the bathroom. When Sam heard the shower running, he stuck his head in the bathroom and asked, "May I scrub your back?"

"Sure."

Sam stepped into the shower behind her and wrapped his arms around her shoulders, fondling her breasts.

Nancy leaned back into him. "Mmm." She reached behind and grasped his erection. "Someone wants to go another round."

"It'll need to be a quickie. We have places to go. But you've got me hooked."

Nancy bent slightly at the waist and guided him in from behind. He grasped her hips and pulled her tight. With her hands against the shower wall and the water spraying on her back, Sam pumped into her. The slap of wet skin echoed off the tile walls. Sam had an urge he needed to quell and he wasn't being delicate.

Amid the noise of the shower, he heard her gasp, "Yes, yes." This drove him on as he held his breath and strained into her. He groaned with a gasp and felt his legs go weak.

Nancy turned around and flung herself into his arms. She kissed him with a ferocious intensity. "God, you're unbelievable. That was great. Just what I wanted."

Sam rubbed his hands gently up and down her body, feeling all the curves, her smooth wet skin, and the texture of her muscles beneath. "I guess I failed the back scrub, but this was far better."

"Indeed, it was." She kissed him again.

After they were cleaned up and dressed, they headed downstairs for a quick breakfast. As they walked from the elevator to the lobby, two men sitting on opposite sides of the lobby in similar suits, each reading a newspaper, caught Sam's attention. The scene just seemed odd. Who reads newspapers these days? The men were large and bulky. They looked like construction workers, stuffed into Sunday suits.

Sam whispered in Nancy's ear. "Do you have the flash drive and notebook in your purse?"

"Yes." Her grip tightened involuntarily on her purse.

"Good. Change of plans." He guided her toward the front door. "There's a breakfast place down the street I'd like to try."

They walked out the door and headed back onto Massachusetts Avenue toward Dupont Circle.

"There's a patisserie where we can get coffee and pastry, if that's okay."

"Sure." Nancy picked up her pace to keep up with his longer stride. "Is something wrong?"

"Let me kiss you." Sam abruptly stopped, turned to face her, and gave her a hug and a kiss. Out of the corner of his eye, he spotted one of the men from the hotel lobby.

"Shit!" Sam whispered. He grabbed Nancy's hand and kept walking.

"Was it that bad?"

"No. No. Not at all. I needed to look behind us. One of the men from the hotel is trailing us. Another man is diagonally across the street."

"Should I be worried?" Nancy's voice faltered.

"Not yet. I don't think they're going to do anything in such a public place. We'll get our coffee and figure this out."

After they paid for their pastry and coffee, they sat at a sidewalk table in full view of the world. Sam reached into his pocket and pulled out his phone.

"Time to dial a friend."

He dialed a number and waited for his friend to answer. "Trevor. I'm glad I caught you. Are you at home?"

"Sam? What's up? Yeah, I'm home."

"Good. I have a small favor to ask." Sam glanced up and down the street. "I'm about three minutes away. Can you ring me in, then let me out through the garage? I have some unde-sirables following me."

"Sure. Anything for you, buddy."

"Good. Thanks! See you in a few." He hung up and turned to Nancy.

"Let's move. I've got this handled."

When they came to a modern high-rise building with black polished stone, Sam entered a four-digit code into a keypad by the door. A buzzer sounded. Sam pulled on the big glass door and let Nancy enter in front of him. They walked twenty feet into the lobby and stood in front of the concierge's desk where a plump middle-aged woman greeted them. Before she had a chance to finish asking them their names and who they were visiting, the elevator bell rang and the doors opened. Trevor stood in the elevator with a grin on his face and his hand on the door so it wouldn't close. He looked about the same age as Sam, dressed as an athlete turned businessman. His arm muscles bulged beneath his jacket.

"I got it, Marge," he called to the concierge. "They're friends of mine."

"Yes sir, Mr. James."

Trevor waived to Sam and Nancy to join him in the elevator.

"Marge, some men might come to the door with an excuse for you to let them in. They're bad people, and you don't want to open the door for them under any circumstances. Did you get that? Don't open the doors!"

Marge nodded. "Yes sir, Mr. James."

Trevor let go of the doors and pushed the elevator button for the garage.

Sam pointed at Nancy. "Trevor, this is Nancy. Nancy, this is Trevor James, a good friend of mine."

Trevor nodded at Nancy. "Nice to meet you." He turned to Sam. "Where are you guys going? Let me drive you."

"We're going to Georgetown University, but that's probably out of your way if you're going to work."

"Not too much out of the way. I've got time to spare."

The elevator opened to the garage and they walked over to a silver Lexus SUV. Sam and Nancy got into the back seat. As Trevor backed out of his parking space, Nancy spoke up. "Thank you. It's really nice of you to do this for us."

Trevor glanced at her in the rearview mirror and grinned. "This guy saved my ass, and I owe him big time! This is the least I can do."

As they approached the ramp to go out onto the street, Sam put his hand behind Nancy's neck and pulled her head down into his lap. Then he leaned across the seat on top of her. The garage opened out onto a side street, so it was unlikely anyone would see them if they were watching the front door. Also, the rear windows were tinted, but it was best to be overly cautious.

Once they were a couple of blocks away, Trevor said, "I think we're in the clear. You can probably sit up now."

Sam and Nancy raised themselves up and looked around out the windows to reorient themselves.

Trevor glanced in the rearview mirror at Nancy. "What were

you doing down there, young lady? I know he's a handsome devil, but that looked like a compromising position."

Nancy looked back at him through the mirror, seeing the grin on his face. She smiled back at him. "At a time like this, that's all you men can think about?"

"Take it easy on her," said Sam. "I like this one."

Trevor smiled and winked in the mirror at Nancy. "She looks like she can actually keep up with you. There aren't many women who can do that."

"Yeah. She's pretty useful. And I like having her around, so don't ruin my image."

Nancy gently punched Sam in the shoulder.

"I don't have to ruin your image," Trevor retorted. "You can do a good job of that by yourself."

The banter continued as they drove to Georgetown, and Nancy was amused listening to them. But in the back of her mind, she was worried about the meeting with Dr. Higgins.

PART 5

CHANGING THE FUTURE

CHAPTER 22

Trevor dropped them on 37th Street at "The Hilltop" at Georgetown University. It was a short walk from Healy Gates to Healy Hall, distinguished by its tall spire and rough stone façade. They went up the steps, under the triple stone arches, and through the double doors. As instructed, they phoned Dr. Higgins upon their arrival, and their call was answered by his assistant. After a minute's wait, they were met in the front foyer by a young lady with glasses and blonde hair done up in a tight bun. She escorted them through the building, down a back hallway, to a secluded office. She tapped on the door twice, opened it, and as she brought them in, she said with a sweep of her arm, "I would like to introduce you to Dr. Thermopylae Higgins." She departed and closed the door behind her.

A kindly looking, but frumpy man in his late 50s or early 60s stood from behind a large desk scattered with papers. "I'm sorry, she tends to be a bit dramatic. I think she missed her calling in the theater."

Sam stepped forward and held out his hand across the desk. "Doctor Higgins, it's nice to meet you in person. This is my associate, Nancy."

Dr. Higgins reached across and shook Sam's hand. Then he stepped out from behind his desk and turned to Nancy. Instead of extending his hand, he bowed toward her. "It is a pleasure to meet you both. Come. Have a seat." He indicated the sofa in front of a wall-to-wall bookcase.

They both sat, expecting him to pull up a chair, but soon realized he intended to stand in front of them like a teacher talking to students. Other than a neat, military-style haircut, Thermopylae Higgins looked like he had given up caring about appearance. His black trousers were stretched at the knees and the fabric was shiny in places where it rubbed on his desk chair. His shirt was rumpled, as if it he had slept in it. The bulge at his belly led to the quick conclusion that exercise was a foreign concept to him. But he had a pleasant demeanor.

"I've never known anybody named Thermopylae," Sam said.

The doctor let out a sigh. "I'm the victim of overeducated parents with active imaginations. It's a curiosity I have to live with on my driver's license. Nobody actually uses the name."

"Well, I appreciate you taking the time to help us. I hope you can make sense of what we sent you."

Dr. Higgins beamed. "I'm excited about this D2 program. So let's jump right in, shall we?" Dr. Higgins nodded as if everyone was in agreement.

"You're indeed correct this is a program designed to model the future so we can see in advance what is going to happen. It depends on several techniques including complex system theory, behavioral heuristics, and of course, cause and effect modeling."

Dr. Higgins took off his glasses and waved them around in an abstract manner as he continued to talk. "Let me begin with cause and effect since that's so thoroughly ingrained in our western minds.

"We tend to believe that everything happens in reaction to a prior cause. That's not entirely true. There are exceptions. We have to account for mutations and other unexpected outcomes, even when the inputs appear to be the same. Also, you can't have causality with simultaneity. Furthermore, you also can't have causality beyond the event horizon. Thus, we can use cause and effect for prediction as long as we recognize it's not a comprehensive model and won't completely explain or predict the future."

The professor paused for dramatic effect.

"The exceptions to the model of cause and effect are significant and must be considered when foretelling the future. If you believe in cause and effect, as most people do, then you must appreciate the role that time plays in how events unfold. Time is simply the recognition of sequence, one thing happening after another. I use the word 'event' to describe a change in status: a change in location, a change in size, a change in shape, a change in color, etc. An event can only be influenced by something that has preceded it. An input must precede an outcome if the input is to be the cause of the outcome. The definition of simultaneity means if two events happen at the same time, then one event cannot precede the other, and thus cannot influence the other. Even when one event does precede another according to a global clock, there can be no cause and effect if the information from the first event cannot be communicated before the second event takes place. In this way, time is intimately connected to space, because there is a maximum speed at which information can travel across space. Therefore, something happening on the other side of the world cannot influence a decision you're making right now if the information can't reach you fast enough. When considering cause and effect, we must acknowledge there is an event horizon beyond which one event can't influence another within a finite period of time. This limits the amount of real-time data necessary to construct a prediction, which is a good thing, because this is a very, very data-intensive effort.

"The future is an extremely perishable commodity. If you want to influence the future, yours or other people's, you have to act expeditiously. If you need to wait until you obtain more information, or if it takes you a long time to construct a prediction, then you may lose your opportunity to act. It is ironic that prediction is the product of time, but time is the enemy of prediction. Prediction is essential to our lives. There are many things we can and do predict accurately, but the quality of even a good prediction degrades rapidly the farther it projects into the future."

Sam waved his hand to interrupt. "I suppose that's why tomorrow's weather prediction is likely to be accurate, but next week's not so much."

Dr. Higgins nodded. "You're exactly right. Offsetting this notion of limited influence due to time and distance, another concept comes from Complexity Theory that says dynamic complex systems have their own kind of personality. Think of it as system DNA that will produce system characteristics. To the extent that the people on the other side of the world have similar complex system DNA as we do, because we share a similar structure and history, we can make statistical predictions about system events, even though they may be beyond our event horizon. For example, we can predict the way other people will behave when they're terrified. The common characteristics of human behavior mean other people's reactions will be similar to the way we react to the same scary event. 'Fight or flight' is the behavior we associate with a threat. We can also predict how their bodies will react to disease, because we have the same body structures. These are generic system patterns among similar complex systems.

"In summary, if you want to jump forward in time by way of prediction, there is no one perfect way to do it. Most predictions rely too heavily on cause-and-effect modeling. When dealing with inanimate objects, there may be far too many co-dependent variables to construct a meaningful path of cause and effect. You cannot know what every single molecule is doing, but complex system characteristics will follow basic rules. When we bring living organisms into the equation, we need to consider behavioral characteristics. However, it's interesting how often systems involving living agents follow the same system patterns as complex systems that have non-living, or inorganic agents. Here we can talk about such things as self-organized systems, fragile systems, critical nodes, robust systems, and chaotic systems.

"When we want to pinpoint a specific case, rather than a statistical outcome, the preferred tool is massive data collection to build a sequential chain of cause and effect. The trick here is to know how the millions of relevant events are going to intertwine in the sequence of time. That's the brilliance of the algorithms you've given me."

Professor Higgins stopped for a moment as if coming up for air. He looked at Sam and Nancy. "Are you with me so far?"

They both nodded, but they knew Dr. Higgins was saying way more than they understood.

Nancy spoke up. "We understand it's probably impossible to actually travel forward in time, so prediction is the next best thing, or maybe even better. What we don't understand is what this program does that makes it so much better than anything else."

Dr. Higgins paced in front of them. "That's the part I was about to explain. This program combines many different techniques for prediction, but goes a step further. Accurate prediction, when building a chain of events, depends on understanding how everything is going to interweave in the sequence of time.

Inertia is the key to this process. Everything has inertia. Inertia is an omnipresent passive property that resists change. This is what defines time itself. Sequencing in time is determined by the degree of resistance to the forces at play in a system.

"In physics, inertia is an inherent property of mass that opposes any force that attempts to make a change to a body's current state. Inertia is the property that defines the characteristic of momentum in a physical body. The algorithms in the computer program you have given to me have applications well beyond physics, but I'm going to use simple physics as an analogy to explain the broader implications.

"We learned from Newton that a body at rest will stay at rest and a body in motion will stay in motion as long as there is no force applied to it. Imagine there are only two things in the universe: you and a tennis ball floating in front of you. If both you and the tennis ball are frozen in place, and there's just emptiness all around you, then time doesn't exist. Time is a measure of change. If there is no change between you and the tennis ball, then there is no sequence of events, and thus no time.

"Now suppose you and the tennis ball are flying through space at a high rate of speed, but in exactly the same direction and at exactly the same speed. Nothing changes in the relative position between you and the tennis ball. Since there is no background and no way to tell that you're moving relative to anything else, your motion along with the tennis ball is irrelevant. One could argue that you really aren't moving, even if we try to visualize that you are. Motion, or lack of motion, in this circumstance, cannot be measured, and time still doesn't exist.

"When we can measure motion relative to other objects, the simple formula rate x time = degree of change allows us to calculate a future position, or state of change, based on speed and the time during which change occurs. This is called a linear equation, but most of life isn't that simple. Most events in our world aren't linear. The velocity of most things in our world is constantly changing due to changing forces. That means there's a change to the rate of change. The name for a change to the linear rate of change is 'acceleration'.

"Are you with me so far?"

Sam glanced at Nancy, then looked back toward Dr. Higgins. "Anyone who drives a car is familiar with time, distance, and acceleration."

"Quite right. I'm refreshing your understanding. Now, let me give you a simple way to visualize inertia. Let's say you're standing in a train car that's sitting still and you drop a tennis ball. The tennis ball will drop because of the force of gravity acting on it. Gravity is a constant force acting on the tennis ball, so the ball drops at an accelerating rate of speed. The ball will drop straight down, and speed up as it drops. We can calculate the exact time it will hit the floor of the train car if we know the distance and the gravitational rate of acceleration.

"Now, suppose the train is moving down the tracks at a constant speed. To anyone standing in the train car, nothing will appear to be different when the ball is dropped. Since the ball is in motion when it is dropped, its momentum will keep it moving forward at the same rate relative to the train car. It'll land at the same spot on the train car floor and at the same time as when the train was standing still. But to someone standing on the ground outside the train, and thus in a different inertial frame of reference, the tennis ball will appear to travel a greater distance in the same time period due to the horizontal vector from the train's motion. The ball will land in a different place relative to orientation over the ground.

"To further understand inertia, let's assume the train is not moving at a constant speed, but is accelerating as it travels down the tracks. Now, gravity is still acting on the tennis ball, pulling it down, but a new force, from the engine accelerating the train, isn't acting on the ball after it has been released and while it is briefly falling through the air. To someone standing in the train car, the ball doesn't drop straight down. Its trajectory appears to mysteriously bend toward the back of the train, due to the train's acceleration. Likewise, to someone standing on the ground outside, the tennis ball will fall forward from where it started over the ground, but short of where it is expected to hit the floor of the train, because the train has accelerated away from the ball. However, the ball will travel the same distance over the ground as it did before because it started with the same forward momentum, and the force accelerating the train is not acting on the ball. Now we can understand that inertia changes how, where, and when things happen.

"What does this have to do with accurate prediction? If you think of the tennis ball as an event that is liable to influence other events, then the time and distance, and frame of reference from which it is viewed will affect which next events it can and cannot influence. The art of accurate prediction is calculating rates of acceleration to know how different events are going to interweave in time and space. A change in the rate of acceleration is known as the second derivative. I must confess that I don't fully understand the algorithms you have given me, but the good news is it's all coded into the computer program. We can simply run the D2 program. It's just like driving a car, even if the driver doesn't know how an internal combustion engine works. We can try out the program and see where it takes us, even if we don't fully understand it."

"The big question is," Sam said, "do you think this is really going to work and give accurate predictions?"

"I don't know." Dr. Higgins raised both hands with a shrug. "We'll have to run the program and test it. I didn't want to do that without talking to you first. There are certain ethical and security issues we should discuss."

"What are you referring to?"

"I could run this on the computers at Livermore Labs, but that raises the question of under whose authority? And who is going to pay for the computer time? Other people will become involved, and I don't know what your security constraints are.

"As an alternative, you have provided me with codes to the back door of numerous computers around the world. I could use those, but we would essentially be stealing. The good news is that most cybersecurity is designed to protect existing data.

Security is not typically aimed at protecting empty space or unused computing power, because there is no data there to steal. So, we can probably get in and out without leaving a trackable path and without setting off any alarm bells. But we'll be breaking the law."

Sam looked at Nancy, and back at Dr. Higgins. "Well, I think it's time to be upfront about everything here and put all our cards on the table. There are things you ought to know, and once you do, you may want to walk away.

"First of all, we're working in a very gray area. This project is not government or institutionally sponsored. We don't know the rightful owners of this computer program. Ownership seems to be by possession, but that doesn't mean our current ownership is legitimate.

"Second, to the extent that this program may work, it's potentially very valuable. There are people chasing after it, which means they're after us. We believe some people may have been killed in connection with this program. That means your involvement may place your life in danger.

"And then there are the ethical issues of using a program like this, and of course the question of what to do with it. So, if you aren't comfortable with walking on the wild side, now is the time to head for the door."

Dr. Higgins' demeanor changed from a distracted professor to something more focused and serious. "Once I started looking into this, I quickly realized it has immense possibilities and can be of great interest to many people."

Sam leaned into the conversation. "In my experience, governments always manage by crisis. Imagine how amazing it would be if the government could predict what is going to happen and prepare ahead of time. Imagine how our quality of life would improve."

Nancy shifted her position on the sofa. "That's a nice dream, but the Russians are after this technology. Look what Putin did to Ukraine. He doesn't care about the quality of life, except for his own. There's a huge risk if this falls into the wrong hands."

Dr. Higgins nodded. "Like any tool, it can be used for good or evil. The big question is who gets to decide the rules of the game. As you said, possession is nine-tenths. Whoever possesses this will have tremendous power if it works as advertised."

"We've gone way out on a limb to trust you," Sam said. "We hope you're one of the good guys. We're counting on you to help us determine how well it works, and then the next step will be to decide what to do with it. Are you willing to work with us?"

Dr. Higgins smiled. "Of course. I couldn't pass up an opportunity like this. This may be one of the great turning points in the history of mankind."

"Excellent! I guess the next step is to take it for a test drive and see if it works."

Except for her comment about Putin, Nancy had been silent during the whole conversation. Now she spoke up. "You should know this isn't exactly virgin territory. Almost two decades ago, the United States had a program called Total Information Awareness, later renamed Terrorism Information Awareness.

It was a big-data/mass-detection program based on the concept of predictive policing. The program collected detailed
information about people, allegedly to anticipate and prevent
terrorist incidents. The program was theoretically closed down
due to bad publicity over privacy concerns, but like many such
military programs, it never totally died.

"The TIA program morphed into something called Nexus
7 in 2010. Nexus 7 is a data mining program that partly grew
out of work done at the NSA. DARPA took over the program
for wartime employment in Afghanistan. By keeping it secret,
and directing its use toward a war zone, DARPA hoped to avoid
criticism over privacy concerns. The program used data mining
on hundreds of real-time intelligence feeds to make predictions.

"At the same time in Afghanistan, something called the
Synergy Strike Force was using crowdsourcing techniques to
make predictions. So there have been a number of iterations
of artificial intelligence/data-mining programs designed for
predictive use.

"As recently as 2022, the CIA was accused of operating
outside the Foreign Intelligence Surveillance Act, and collected
data on US citizens for two programs operating under Executive
Order 12333. The nature and extent of the data collected were
withheld from the Intelligence Committee and its purpose for
analysis was unknown to Congress."

Sam raised his eyebrows. "Wow. I'm impressed. How do
you happen to know all that?"

"A few years back, I worked with DARPA." Nancy smiled.

"I got to know some of their history."

Sam shook his head. "I had no idea — "

Dr. Higgins cleared his throat. "So, am I to presume you two hacked a military site to get this? If so, why? And what does it mean if there are other copies out there? I guess what I'm asking is, what am I doing here?"

Nancy and Sam chimed in together. "No!"

Nancy took over the conversation. "We didn't hack anything. I obtained this from a British citizen. He had a diplomatic passport, so I believe he worked for the government in some capacity. I considered giving it all back to him and washing my hands of it, but unfortunately, he's dead."

"What?" Sam jolted stiffly erect. "You didn't tell me that!"

"I only recently found out." Nancy looked sheepish. "He was apparently murdered in connection with the break-in at my house. I only found out because the police called me back after you firebombed my car."

Dr. Higgins couldn't keep up with any of this. His expression changed from confusion to worry and fear. "Wait a minute! Wait a minute! You firebombed her car?"

"I'm sorry," Sam said. "It's a long story. We'll fill you in on the background. There are some Russians chasing us and I had to burn her car to throw them off our trail."

"You're getting me kind of worried." Dr. Higgins leaned back and crossed his arms.

Sam took a deep breath, spread out his hands like he was smoothing a blanket, and tried to slow down the pace and the tone of the conversation. "I appreciate your concern, and we're nervous too, but we think we're okay for the moment. Nobody knows you're involved, and we want to keep it that way. We think we're off the grid and not visible, at least for a short period. The pressure is on us to figure this thing out and take the target off our backs. So, do you think you can run a test and see how well D2 works?"

"If you're good with my using the computer resources on the list you gave me, I can get right on it. I expect it'll take hours to scrape the web for data and set up the program, because there's going to be considerable trial and error for me." Dr. Higgins grabbed a pen and pad of paper from his desk. "Are there certain future things you want me to look for?"

As if still in school, Nancy raised her hand. "We want to test things that are easily measurable so we can see if D2 works."

"Good point," Sam said. "How about predicting the stock market? And how about predicting the weather? And how about something more squishy, like predicting tomorrow's top news headline?"

Dr. Higgins rubbed his chin and made a few notes. "The weather is easy because there will be a lot of data points readily available. The only problem is the process might degenerate into crowdsourcing all of the meteorologists out there. That isn't a bad thing for predicting the weather, but it doesn't necessarily tell us D2 is doing anything special. In other words, it may be too easy to get a short-term forecast reasonably correct.

"Rather than trying to predict the whole stock market, I

think we should try to predict a single stock. An index is made up of hundreds or thousands of stocks. There are too many variables that will tend to cancel each other out. What will it mean to us if the program says the S&P index will be up eight points tomorrow and it turns out to be up ten points? We can't tell which of the five-hundred stock price changes the program got right or wrong to arrive at that net result. I think predicting the price of a single stock will tell us more.

"I have kind of the same problem with guessing the top news story. Different publications will pick different headlines. There are only a small number of major stories swirling around, and picking the 'top' story is too subjective. I'd like to suggest something more measurable. What would you think about asking for the number of flights canceled out of Reagan Washington National Airport before noon tomorrow? I have no idea how any computer program could predict cancellations. Flights can be canceled due to weather, mechanical problems, staffing shortages, lack of available aircraft from other destinations, and other reasons. It'll be interesting to see what the program comes up with."

The three looked at each other, then Nancy said, "We won't know what we have here until we try it, and it's unlikely the first try will give us all the answers we want. We probably shouldn't overthink this. I'm fine with using your suggestions and we see what happens."

"Works for me," Sam said.

"Good." Dr. Higgins rubbed his hands together. "I can

spend this afternoon setting things up, and hopefully run the program before the end of the day. Tomorrow we can compare the predictions with the actual results."

"While you're doing that, we're going to have to shop for clothes and find lodging," Sam said.

"Don't you have a place to stay?" Dr. Higgins asked.

"We did." Nancy grimaced. "We were staying at the Washington Plaza — "

Sam gripped her hand. "But some men were following us this morning, so we can't go back there. Don't worry. We lost them — so we're clean now. But our suitcases are still there."

Dr. Higgins cleared his throat. "They set me up in a three-bedroom cottage the university owns. I'm by myself, so it's more space than I need. Frankly, I've been kind of lonely. If you want to stay with me, I have room."

"That would be great!" Sam exclaimed. "Maybe we can meet you there later, after you get started on this project. That'll give us an opportunity to kick around more ideas this evening if we're going to be all together."

Dr. Higgins took a key off a keyring he pulled from his pocket. "Consider it settled then. Here is a key, and I'll write down the address for you. You'll probably get there before me, so make yourselves at home. I expect I'll show up between five and six tonight."

Sam took the key. "Thank you. By the way, I have one favor to ask of you. I sent you access to the program so you could get an advance look, but I want to expunge it from the cloud tonight. I've learned from many years in the financial industry that the longer you're exposed to risk, the greater the opportunity for something bad to happen. I'd like you to download the program to an external, detachable hard drive, or a memory stick that's always kept physically separate from your computer, except when you're using it. I don't want anyone to get access by hacking your computer or by hacking cloud storage. You need to treat this like the most valuable diamond in the world and keep it physically safe."

"That makes sense." Dr. Higgins nodded. "You can trust I'll be extremely cautious."

CHAPTER 23

Sam called the Plaza Hotel and explained they would not be returning. He settled the bill over the phone and asked the hotel to clean out their room. Then he called his friend Trevor.

"I have one more small favor to ask of you," Sam said. "Our suitcases are being held in the lobby of the Washington Plaza under your name. Would you mind picking them up on your way to work tomorrow and storing them at your office? I know you work in a high-security building. I'm suggesting you take them to your office because it's possible there may be eyes following them. I don't want your home life to get mixed up in this. I really appreciate it."

Trevor agreed without any question or comment.

When Dr. Higgins arrived at his bungalow that evening, Sam and Nancy had already settled in.

"We bought some wine." Sam held up a bottle. "Would you like some?"

"Why certainly. Yes. That's very nice of you. I thought it might be easiest if we order dinner in tonight. Does Chinese sound good to you two?"

They both agreed.

"I think I made good progress," Dr. Higgins said. "I ran the program a number of times and gained insight regarding how to use it. As with any computer program, if you ask a question the wrong way, you're going to get a wrong answer or a useless answer. It's important to frame the question correctly."

"Can you give us an example?" Nancy asked.

"Sure I can. First of all, you have to ask about something for which there is data to analyze. I can't ask what color shirt I'll wear tomorrow because my shirt inventory isn't available on the internet. There might be one or two pictures of me wearing shirts on the internet, but that isn't enough to make a prediction. Sufficient valid data is necessary to make a prediction.

"Another example is, I can't ask a completely open-ended question such as 'what will happen tomorrow?' The program wants to have parameters like where, when, and to who or what. I asked specifically for the weather here, at this house, at eight tomorrow morning."

"Did you get an answer?" Sam asked.

"Yes. We will have to see tomorrow if it's right. As I suspected, an answer was produced quite quickly. Most likely, that was because there's a lot of weather data readily available, and the program probably did a lot of crowdsourcing of forecasts."

"For the other questions?" Nancy asked.

Dr. Higgins took a second pour in his wine glass and sat down. "As discussed, I asked for the name of the stock likely to go up the most over the next week out of all the stocks in the Russell 2000 Index. I needed to give it a week to avoid random movement that can occur over a day or two. I picked a discrete set of stocks so we can measure, not only whether the stock goes up, but also does it go up more than the other stocks in the index.

"Finally, as agreed, I did ask for the number of flight cancellations at DCA. The D2 program says there will be twenty-seven cancellations before noon tomorrow. It even provided the names of the airlines and the flight numbers. DCA is a small airport that restricts traffic to flights of less than 1,250 miles. Despite that, there are still hundreds of daily flights spread among a dozen airlines. I will be interested to see how accurate the prediction is. So now we wait."

Nancy pointed out the irony of having to wait. "If we could trust the program, we wouldn't have to wait for the future to happen. That's the whole point of the program. But now we have to wait while we're testing the predictions. That's frustrating. I suggest we don't wait. We should make use of the time talking about more testing we might need to do, so we can get a jump on it. We can also discuss a plan for the disposal of the program. I want my life back, and I would like to know how our task here is going to come to a successful end."

Dr. Higgins nodded. "You make a good point. It's a simple decision tree. If the program doesn't work, then we can give it to whoever thinks they want it, and we're done. If it turns out the program does work, then we can start talking about our next step now."

Sam said. "I'm using the assumption the program does work until proven otherwise. If D2 does work as advertised, it's too important and dangerous to reside in the hands of one person. On the other hand, we can't open source it and make it available to everyone. There'd be total chaos. That leaves us with giving it to an institution or a country."

"Wait a minute," Nancy held up a hand. "The open-source idea may not be unreasonable. If you know anything about complexity theory, complex systems are made up of individual agents operating according to their own individual agendas. Within the system, what one agent does is often canceled out by what another agent does. Internal system forces tend to offset each other, so the system ends up with one net force that trends toward stability. The effectiveness of the computer program's predictions will be largely neutralized if everyone is using it at the same time."

"You may be right," Dr. Higgins said, "but is that the kind of world you want to live in? We would be introducing a new level of internal volatility to the social system that could be extremely disruptive. Keeping with your complexity theory reference, systems with high levels of internal volatility are more apt to have a flatter, wider, normal distribution with fat tails. Let me give you an example. Would you rather ride on a bus where most of the passengers are quietly reading and napping, or on a bus where people are drunk and having political arguments and fistfights? If you think of the bus as the 'system,' ask yourself which bus is more likely to deliver you safely to your destination?"

"You make a good point," Sam said. "But while you mathematicians talk about Gaussian distributions, I can tell you that simple common sense says releasing the program into the wild would be like opening Pandora's box."

Nancy smiled at Sam. "Oh! You know who Gauss was?"

"I might surprise you with what I know." Sam smiled back at her. "You forget that I plot investment risk for a living in my financial business.

"Now that we have all arrived at the conclusion that D2 should probably go to an institution within a country — "

"Hold on," Nancy interrupted. "You jumped to a conclusion. We said it would cause chaos if everyone had the program. We didn't talk about the fact that I'm one person, and I alone had the program until I came to you."

Sam and Dr. Higgins looked at each other. Sam said, "You're right, but you didn't know what to do with the program. And your life is in danger. Any one person who has the program will be under constant threat. History has shown us that power corrupts. Can you think of any one person you would trust to have unrestricted use of this program?"

There was silence in the room. Finally, Sam spoke again

in a flat, calm voice. "I'm not sure the human race is ready for a program like this, but if we're going to place it somewhere, I think it needs to be in a place where it can be defended. I vote the country of choice should be the United States. I'd lean toward presenting this to the intelligence community, but I don't want to see the program weaponized."

"How would you control its future use?" Nancy asked.

"I don't know. I guess it comes down to trusting the party you give it to."

Dr. Higgins shook his head. "You're asking a lot. I have a problem with most of the obvious choices. Personally, I don't trust the organized religions. History shows religion has been the cause of a lot of wars and misery. I certainly don't trust the politicians. I don't trust the military either. I have more faith in the scientific community, but there are a lot of loose wing-nuts there too. I'm short on trust when it comes to something of this magnitude."

Nancy suddenly became more animated. She sat forward on her seat and held out her hands, palms up. "I've got it! Let's use the D2 program to tell us where the D2 program ends up! All we have to do is ask what the status of the program is in one year. If we don't like the answer, then we change the future by changing our decision."

"Now that's an interesting idea." Sam nodded.

"Yes," Dr. Higgins agreed, 'but you can't change the future if you don't know where you started. I think we need to begin by hypothetically picking an organization to place the program with, and then ask what it is being used for one or two years out."

"I'm with you on that," Sam said, "and I'd like to suggest we try the CIA. I have heard good things about Angela Firestone, the director."

"Seriously?" Nancy smirked. "You're worried about it being weaponized and you suggest the CIA?"

Sam leaned back and opened his hands. "Well... I don't want it used for anything short of a dire emergency, but if it needs to be used, I'd want it in the hands of an organization capable of analyzing the big picture and hopefully using it wisely."

Nancy shook her head. "I'm not sure the CIA has a track record that instills confidence."

"Okay, but this is a hypothetical. Let's give it a try to see what the program says." Sam was surprised at the pushback he was receiving from Nancy. He had underestimated her strength of character.

Dr. Higgins stepped in to settle the matter. "It can't hurt to give it a try to ask what happens. Maybe the answer will shed light on how to proceed."

Nancy shrugged and tilted her head in acquiescence. Sam nodded in agreement, being careful not to act as if he'd just scored some kind of a win. This wasn't any sort of a contest, and he certainly did not want to offend Nancy. He was just staying within his comfort zone of organizations he was familiar with.

Dr. Higgins clapped his hands and smiled. "Well, tomorrow should be an interesting day."

During dinner, Dr. Higgins took advantage of a lull in the conversation to gently touch on one of his concerns. "You realize that since the future hasn't happened, there's no way to immediately test a prediction. If we had two programs, we could compare one program's prediction with the other, but we don't. We may come to believe in this program and trust that it works, only to find out sometime in the future that it doesn't. Being wrong could be costly, and I don't know any way of measuring a confidence level ahead of time.

"Furthermore, we're fooling around with time. Time is a complicated thing. There's an old saying that a man with two clocks can't be sure what time it is. This is probably a comment on the quality of clock making more than anything else, but it does raise interesting questions. Which clock is right? Is either clock right? Does it matter?

"In this era of digital streaming, it's often apparent one data feed lags another. You may watch a live broadcast on TV and notice that live streaming of the same broadcast on your tablet is delayed by five seconds. As long as you get the same information in the same sequence, the delay usually doesn't matter. In the case of everybody watching the same feed, the rate of change in the streaming video is constant, and everyone is working in the same time frame. We just have a delay. Suppose the rate of change isn't constant, as in a car race.

"Imagine the Indianapolis 500 race with car 12 and car 16 fighting for the lead. Both drivers see the scenery going past them, but at slightly different rates due to the difference in their speed. The rate of change around them gives the drivers a sense of time, because time is proportional to their distance traveled. But we're used to thinking of time as being constant. What if time is going slower for car 16 and his speed is faster? He's still keeping up with car 12, but car 16 is in a different time frame. Now, the question of who wins the race may be determined by whose time frame is used by the judges. Presumably, the winner is the car that covers the required distance in the least amount of time. You may not observe the winner to be the first car to cross the line if you're in a different time frame. In our everyday life, we don't travel far enough or fast enough, or change our gravitational field sufficiently for relative time frames to matter, but my point is that messing about with time can get complicated."

Sam had listened carefully to follow what the professor was saying. "We know this is complicated. That's why we have you. We hope you're the expert who can guide us through this."

"I'm acquainted with the science, and I can run the program. I'm saying judgement is going to play a role in decision-making. I have no way of knowing in advance if a prediction is good or bad. If you plan to depend on this program, you can build up confidence by testing it, but you can never know with certainty the quality of any given prediction. Your judgement regarding how you use this is going to be most important."

Sam nodded. "I appreciate that, Doctor. You make a good point, and we need to keep that in mind."

As if to lighten the conversation, Nancy put on a big smile

and addressed Dr. Higgins. "Thank you so much for giving us a place to stay. It's very generous of you to take us in."

"My pleasure, my dear. I enjoy having company."

After dinner and small talk, Dr. Higgins excused himself to finish up work before bed. He had a small study tucked in the corner next to the guest bath. His bedroom was on the ground floor next to the kitchen.

Sam and Nancy cleaned up the remnants from their meal and headed upstairs. Two bedrooms were at the top of the stairs, separated by a bathroom. For the sake of appearances, they each took one bedroom. Although the display of decorum was a white lie, it was a show of respect to their host. After lights were out and the house settled down, Nancy left her room and quietly found her way into Sam's bed.

CHAPTER 24

When Sam and Nancy arrived downstairs the next morning, they found a note on the table from Dr. Higgins.

I have gone into my office to get more work done and to run the D2 program again. I'm not swayed by the weather report. It predicted a sunny day with no precipitation and wind 4-7 mph out of the northwest. It appears that is what we have, but any third-rate meteorologist could have probably figured that out. We need to keep testing. This morning, I'll research the number of cancellations at Reagan National Airport to compare with the program's prediction.

Why don't you plan to come to my office after lunch and we can take stock of things?

Have a nice morning.

"Well, I guess we're on our own for a little while," Sam said. Nancy smiled at him. Being with him was like wearing a comfortable sweater. She convinced herself he belonged in her life. "I believe our day should start with breakfast. I'm making eggs. Want some? Coffee will be up in a minute."

"That sounds great." Sam paused with a distant look. "I can't help wondering what the D2 program will say about us turning it over to the CIA. If we decide to follow through with it, I'm not sure exactly how we would get the program into the right hands. We certainly don't want it going through low-level channels. But we can't just walk up to their headquarters, knock on the front door, and say we want to talk to the director."

"Why not? Sometimes the direct approach is the best."

Sam snorted as if he had choked on something. "Are you kidding? First of all, you drive in a long entry road, and most likely you're being surveilled all the way. If they don't know who you are, you're probably not going to be greeted in a friendly manner. Then you'll be stopped at concrete barriers by police carrying automatic weapons. If you can talk your way past the initial inquiry, you'll be directed to a reception center, still separate from the main buildings. There, you'll be vetted and questioned in detail, and you're not going to be able to say you're simply dropping in to see the Director. That would be like dropping in to see the president at the White House. If they don't send you packing immediately, you can be sure you'll have to climb through a long line of subordinates before you're given an audience with the director. How are you going to answer all the questions you're asked? Are you going to say, 'I have something better than a time machine?' How far do you think you can get before being kicked out or arrested?"

"Fine, you have a point. Since going to the CIA was your idea, what do you suggest?"

"That's what I'm puzzling over." Sam ran a hand through his hair. "I don't know anyone to call who can open that door for us."

"I have an idea. What about the cute puppy sale?"

Sam frowned. "What's the cute puppy sale?"

Nancy laughed. "You don't know that one? If you want to sell a puppy, you simply put the puppy in the buyer's arms and let the cute puppy sell itself."

"How does that apply to our situation?

"Simple," replied Nancy. "We tell the director what she's going to do or what's going to happen to her in advance. When our predictions come true, she'll recognize we have something unique and valuable. How can she not want to talk to us?"

Sam nodded. "I'm with you so far, but how are we going to communicate all this advance knowledge if we can't get to her in the first place? As I said, we can't break into the castle."

"You still don't understand the power we have in our hands if this program works. This will be a good test for it. In theory, the D2 program can tell us where she's going to be at any given time in the future. She must have a life outside of the headquarters building. All we have to do is know where she's going to be, and we arrange to show up at the same time. After a little bit of that, she'll realize it isn't just coincidence."

"You're brilliant!" Sam crossed to her and gave her a hug.

"I knew there was a reason I'm keeping you around!"

Nancy laughed and captured his lips, squeezing his ass with one hand. "Let's eat!"

For the rest of the morning, Sam excused himself to check in with his office and make business calls. Nancy took the opportunity to go for a walk around Georgetown and the university campus. She collected Sam at 11:15 and convinced him to take her to lunch at a sandwich shop she had discovered.

They showed up at Healy Hall at 12:30 and were once again escorted to Dr. Higgin's office by the same blonde in a tight skirt and glasses. Her stiletto heels clicked on the floor as she led them down the hall. She knocked twice, opened the door, and with a grand sweep of her arm, bid them to enter the office.

Dr. Higgins rose from his desk. "Perfect timing. I've just finished running the program again." He pointed to the sofa, indicating that they should sit down. "But before we start, let me tell you a story.

"Two men walk into a bar.

"'Welcome gents,' says the bartender. 'Where are you from?'

"The first man says, 'We're time-travelers. We just returned from the future.'

"The bartender is used to strange customers, so he ignores that comment.

"'What can I get you to drink?'

"The first time-traveler says, 'Yesterday, when I was traveling in tomorrow, I ordered the same drink I had the day before. It was quite good! So, I'll have what I had tomorrow.'

"Now the bartender is confused. What is he supposed to do? He says, 'I haven't seen tomorrow, so I don't know what you drink tomorrow.'

"The second time-traveler says, 'Of course you know what he drinks tomorrow. Think about it! Tomorrow he's going to drink exactly the same thing you serve him today.'

"The bartender thinks about it for a moment. As the realization dawns on him, he says, 'So it would seem I can pour any kind of a drink today, and that'll be tomorrow's drink also.'

"The second time-traveler says, 'It would seem so, but be careful what you select. If you change your mind and select something else, you'll be changing his future. And if you change his future, you'll also be changing his future's past, which is where we are today.'"

Dr. Higgins paused. "I tell you this story to emphasize that when you start fooling around with time, it can get complicated. We talked about this last night."

Sam and Nancy looked at each other with confusion in their eyes. Sam said, "When you started off with two men walking into a bar, I thought you were going to tell us a joke, but it's no joke is it?"

"No, it's not." Dr. Higgins polished his glasses on his shirt-tail. "We need to appreciate that the decisions we make going forward will have consequences. This is unfamiliar territory, so we need to think carefully about the possible outcomes."

They were silent while Nancy and Sam considered what he said.

Dr. Higgins continued. "I have both good news, and surprising news, which I guess is bad news. Let me start with the good news.

"I'm getting more confident that the D2 program is legitimate and really works. The weather prediction didn't particularly impress me, but for the second prediction, the program identified Blixen Technology, symbol BLXT, as the top-performing stock. So far this morning, BLXT is up one-half of a percent in a flat market. As I said before, we need to give it more time, but the stock price is going in the right direction.

"As for flight cancellations, it appears the program nailed prediction number three. It came within one count of the total cancellations before noon today. There was a 97.5% accuracy rate on the specific flights canceled, airline by airline. I wasn't able to determine all of the reasons. Weather played a large role in many of the cancellations. I have no idea how the program came up with its prediction of twenty-seven cancellations, but with an actual count of twenty-eight, I'm encouraged to believe it has a method that works."

Dr. Higgins was prone to holding his glasses and waving his hands around when he talked. He now put his glasses back on and started shuffling through papers on his desk. He found what he was looking for, picked up one document, and started reading. "Angela Firestone, director of the Central Intelligence Agency, a statutory position nominated by the president of the

United States and requiring confirmation by the US Senate. She holds a master's degree in International Relations from NYU and went directly to the State Department from school. She was assigned to foreign service with several embassies, and then returned to New York to work as a policy liaison officer with the United Nations. From this position, it appears she had frequent interface with White House policy staffers and came to the attention of the president. Thus, her nomination as director. My sense is that her qualifications are a bit light, but it's a political appointment – so who knows what the president was thinking. Furthermore, to a large extent, the operational side of the agency is run by apolitical professionals, so having a lesser experienced director who is a public face and coordinates with other arms of the government doesn't impair the actual functionality of the agency." Dr. Higgins looked over the top of his glasses at Sam.

Sam felt he needed to say something. "I've heard she's one of the good guys. It's refreshing to have a woman in that position, and perhaps because she is a woman, she has more to prove. She's a straight shooter, not a political animal, and highly competent. At least, that's what I've heard. I've never met her. As for her qualifications, I suspect she might have been working with the CIA when she was on embassy duty. She might have considerably more experience than shows in her official resume."

Dr. Higgins set down the paper and looked them both in the eyes. "There seems to be a problem. I asked the D2 program what would happen if we give the program directly to Angela Firestone. The answer I received is bewildering. The program said it will end up in the hands of the Russians and be used in attempts to influence our political elections, influence our media, support powerful Americans to push doctrines that Russia wants to promote, and to effectively change our culture and social aspirations."

Dead silence filled the room. Sam and Nancy looked at each other, and then both looked at Dr. Higgins.

Mystified, Sam asked, "How does that happen?"

Dr. Higgins shrugged. "I don't get to see the internal workings of the program. I can't tell how it arrives at its predictions. But I've come up with several possibilities. Director Firestone may not be the good person you think she is. If the program is given to her, then presumably it's through her hands that it gets to the Russians. But of course, it's possible someone else at the CIA is a traitor. If someone else at the agency can access the program, then the treachery may have nothing to do with the director. There's a lower probability the program is somehow misused or an accident causes the CIA to lose control of it. We also have to consider the possibility the program is giving us wrong information. Of all the choices, I would place my bet on there being a problem within the agency."

"I guess we aren't giving it to the CIA." Nancy crossed her arms, looking triumphant.

Sam shook his head. "There's more to it than that. If the program is feeding us good information, we can't just ignore it. If there's something seriously wrong at the top levels of the CIA, we should do something about it."

"I'm kind of the outsider here," Dr. Higgins said, "but before you jump to any conclusions, I think you should try to verify the information."

"I agree," Sam said. "It so happens that the director of the CIA reports to the DNI. I have a contact inside the Office of the Director of National Intelligence who might be able to help shed light on Angela Firestone. I'll make a call.

"In the meantime, Dr. Higgins, if you wouldn't mind re-searching Angela's executive assistant and her other top lieuten-ants, maybe you can get the program to uncover some dirt on one of these people. If the program is correct, there must be a bad apple in the group. I know this is kind of an open-ended request, but see what you can do."

Dr. Higgins nodded acceptance. "I don't know what I can find, but I'll give it a try."

"Wow!" Sam rubbed his palms together. "This is certainly not what I expected."

Nancy felt like she was on the edge of the decision-making process, but that was okay with her at the moment. She wanted her life back, and she still believed Sam was the man who could make that happen.

Dr. Higgins said, "Let's regroup tonight at the house and we can compare notes."

"Sounds good." Sam took Nancy's hand in his, stood, and led her to the door. She gave a smile and a small wave of goodbye to Dr. Higgins as they exited.

It was a beautiful day outside, and Nancy would have liked to do some sightseeing and window shopping if their lives weren't in danger. The afternoon was progressing, and she knew Sam had calls to make. They walked hand-in-hand back to the cottage, slowly, to avoid drawing attention. Sam kept muttering about national security being at stake. Nancy didn't have a lot to contribute on the subject, so she kept quiet. When they got to the house, Nancy went to lie down while Sam made his phone calls.

The Office of the Director of National Intelligence was an umbrella organization that extended over the entire intelligence community. The director held a cabinet-level position. Sam previously worked on a Department of Defense project that had overlapped with the ODNI. He didn't have a deep reach into the agency, but he knew a couple of guys who would remember him and might be willing to talk. When he called them, he received nothing but glowing reports about Angela Firestone. The comments were always qualified with "I don't work directly with her," and "This is just second hand from the reports I've heard," etc., etc., but no alarm bells were going off. The only item of concern was a comment that she was struggling. Apparently, a couple of her field operations had failed for unattributable reasons. In spite of her competence and perseverance, she seemed to have had a run of bad luck.

Nobody was holding that against her, but there was a sense something wasn't quite right. Possibly something was wrong with her, or possibly someone was sabotaging her efforts.

That evening, the three of them gathered around the kitchen table and compared notes. Sam reported the background he had gathered on Angela Firestone didn't turn up anything definitively negative. He explained that it didn't absolve her. It just encouraged him to look in another direction to find the problem.

"Well, I have been busy," Dr. Higgins said. "Finding the people that work closely with the director isn't easy. It's not as if there's a company directory to consult. In clandestine service, there are officers at headquarters supporting operatives overseas. There's a lot of additional mission support, with a large group of analysts, and numerous subgroups such as cryptologists, economists, linguists, science and technology, etc. Also, there's the group that prepares the president's daily briefing. There's no way I can be sure who is interfacing with the director. However, I did take a look at a half dozen upper-level people.

"Interestingly, the person who stands out is the most powerful of the group and has the widest range of access. That would be Brandon Kulp, the deputy director. The position is appointed by the president and is not required to be approved by the Senate. The lack of confirmation means his background may not be placed under the microscope like the director. However, one would expect he was thoroughly vetted through the security clearance process.

"This is what I know: Kulp is a first-generation American. He had a French father and a Polish mother who met as a consequence of WWII. Since he already spoke French, which he learned from his father, he elected to study Russian to meet his language requirement in school. He flew helicopters in the Army and then moved into the military intelligence division. When his military service ended, he worked for several policy institutes as a specialist on Russia. He married Karen Whitehall. They have no children. He seems to be a professional politician's friend, but he has never been elected to any office himself. He was appointed to several low-level fact-finding missions to support congressional committees, did some unspecified work for NSA, and then worked for the White House, two administrations ago, on foreign policy. He was a convenient golf buddy for the president. This connection probably influenced his appointment as interim ambassador to Russia when the existing ambassador died unexpectedly from an unknown illness. Kulp was only supposed to be there six months, but his stay stretched out to eighteen months. Upon his return to the states, he found a position with Homeland Security, but that did not seem to be a good fit. From there, he transferred to the CIA as a bureaucrat. This, once again, appears to be due to connections, since he did not come up through the organization and doesn't have the depth of training that one might expect for his position.

"Here's where it gets interesting. The D2 program tells me that Brandon Kulp has a mistress in Russia who gave birth to a son during the period Brandon was there. The program predicts Kulp will have another child with this woman. I'm not finding a separate source to confirm any of this information, but if it's true, it may be the connection we're looking for."

"There you go!" Sam waived expansively. "Either Kulp is choosing his Russian family over his American wife, or the Russians are leveraging his mistress and son to blackmail him into being a traitor."

"You're jumping to a lot of suppositions without proof," said Nancy, "but it sounds like there might be something there. How do we get proof?"

Sam turned to Dr. Higgins. "Earlier, Nancy and I were contemplating how to approach Angela Firestone. We were wondering if the D2 program could foretell where she would be or what she would be doing so we could impress her with our advance knowledge. I wonder if we could do a similar thing with Brandon Kulp? Could the program look into his future and point out any anomalies that might confirm he's conspiring with the Russians?"

"That's an interesting idea," conceded Dr. Higgins. "The problem is how to obtain sufficient data. The internal operation of the CIA is not open source. I don't know how the program could come up with anything meaningful, but maybe it can find data to work with around the edges. It won't hurt to try."

"If you can get me a list of his activities during his off-hours and any predictions about where he'll be, that would be useful. I think I want to try tailing this guy and get a feel for who he is. If you could send me a picture of him, that would be helpful too." Sam pulled out his phone, searching for car rental agencies. "I want to rent a car this afternoon so I'll have the mobility to follow Mr. Kulp."

Nancy stiffened at being sidelined. "If it's alright with you, Sam, I'd like to stay with Dr. Higgins and help him with the D2 program. My strength is data analysis, and it doesn't sound like I'm going to be much help to you. Besides, my face is the one that's going to get recognized, and I don't need to be in harm's way."

Sam looked at Dr. Higgins. "It's alright with me if it's okay with you."

Dr. Higgins smiled. "I'm always happy for the help. Nancy may have a better analytical approach than me on some of these issues."

"Good! It's settled then. I'm off to find transportation and you two geniuses can dig up useful information on what the hell is happening at the CIA." Sam headed for the door.

CHAPTER 25

S am's new rental car was parked in the small driveway next to the cottage, and Sam was on his computer watching the stock of BLXT when his phone rang. Hearing Nancy's voice made him realize how much he missed her in the short time they had been separated. But she was all business.

"I've texted you a photo of Brandon Kulp. We haven't come up with much on his schedule so far. He has clothes at Aster's Laundry on 14th Street ready to pick up, but we don't know when he'll do that. His phone location and credit card history show he's frequently at Off The Record at the Hay-Adams on Wednesday afternoons during the cocktail hour, and he has a dinner reservation tonight at 7 pm at Estelle's across from Franklin Square. Presumably, that's with his wife, but we don't know. I'm calling you now because his phone has just come online. He appears to have left the agency campus heading into the city."

"That's good." Sam glanced at the photo she sent. "I should be able to work with that. Call me if you come up with anything more. Otherwise, I'll see you this evening whenever I get done chasing him around."

She hung up before he could add anything personal. He felt a tiny cut to his self-assurance.

Sam turned off his laptop, grabbed a jacket and a bottle of water, and headed out to the car. Going to Aster's Laundry seemed like a long shot, but it was his best option until later in the evening. Once he arrived, he drove around the block several times until a parking space opened up across the street from the entrance. When he was situated, Sam pulled out his phone and took a longer look at the photo of Brandon Kulp. He might not get much more than a quick look at people coming and going from the laundry, and he didn't want to miss his chance to recognize him.

After half an hour of waiting, Sam called Nancy. "Any chance you're still tracking Kulp's phone and you can tell me where he is?"

Nancy laughed. "Nice to hear from you too! Yes, we're doing fine. Thanks for asking. You have come to the source of all knowledge. We were able to pick up your car rental transaction. From that, we got the LoJack information on your car. It's only supposed to be accessible by law enforcement computers, but we have a workaround for that. I see you're sitting at Aster's Laundry. DC traffic has been its normal state of awful, but Brandon Kulp is heading your way. He should be there in another ten minutes."

"Outstanding! You're a dream come true," Sam gushed. "Remind me to give you an extra big kiss tonight."

"I hope I get more than that." Nancy's tone sent a thrill through him.

"Ahh… yes." Sam grinned. "I'll leave the rest to your imagination. Gotta go!"

Sam hung up and focused his attention on the entrance to the laundry. Sure enough, in less than ten minutes, a black SUV pulled up and double-parked in front of Aster's. It turned its hazard lights on, and Brandon Kulp got out and went in the front door. His dark hair and distinctive goatee made him easily recognizable. Hard to say why, but his body shape reminded Sam of a black wasp. Even the bigwigs had to do menial chores, thought Sam. It reminded him of watching a billionaire money manager walking his dog along the oceanfront in Sea Haven. The dog squatted and pooped. This billionaire, who could have bought the entire town, bent over with a plastic bag and picked up his dog's poop. This was the same man who would have thought it beneath him to pour a cup of coffee for an associate in his office. It was strange how the world worked and where people placed their values.

In a few minutes, Kulp reappeared with an armful of shirts on hangars, which he hung in the back of the SUV. As the black vehicle with its tinted windows pulled away, Sam started the car and fell in line, a few cars behind Kulp. He followed up 14th Street to Massachusetts Avenue NW. At Dupont Circle, the two-car caravan veered off onto Connecticut Ave NW, then Calvert Street to Cleveland Avenue NW.

"Where is he going?" This was taking them away from downtown. His question was answered shortly when they turned left onto Woodley Road and into the Washington National Cathedral. Since it was late in the day, parking was available, but enough cars were still there so another car more or less wasn't going to attract any attention.

Sam pulled into a space far enough away not to be noticed. As he watched, Brandon Kulp got out of his vehicle and walked over to the trees across from the front of the cathedral. A group of three swarthy-looking men stood in the shade, smoking. An animated discussion ensued. Sam studied the men, pretty sure he had seen them before. One of them might have been the guy in the Audi who waved the gun at him. Two of them looked like the men who followed him and Nancy from the Washington Plaza Hotel. "Gotcha!" he said to himself. This was clearly an "off-the-books" meeting, and it could mean that Brandon Kulp was dirty. Whatever was being discussed, Brandon was acting like he was totally disgusted with the men. Clearly, he expected something of them, and he wasn't happy.

Sam watched as Kulp marched back to his car with a frown. Given a choice, Sam decided he should follow the men, not Kulp. They were the new unknowns, and he needed more information about them. Sam lay across the front seat as Kulp made a U-turn and drove past him on the way out. When Sam sat back up, the three men were making their way to a white

Toyota sedan that looked like it had seen better days. The three men should have no reason to think they would be followed, but nevertheless, Sam was cautious when he tailed them out of the parking lot.

Amidst a squeal of brakes and a honking horn, the white Toyota pulled out into traffic. An arm went out the driver's side window with the middle finger raised. As Sam followed, chaos surrounded the Toyota. The driving was erratic and unpredictable. Turns were made at the last minute and from the wrong lane. People were yelling and horns were honking. This was like watching a circus in the middle of Washington traffic. Ultimately, the Toyota ran a yellow light that turned into a red light. The car in front of Sam stopped, and Sam had no choice but to stop and watch his quarry get away. He could only head back to Dr. Higgins' house.

Sam walked in the front door to the satisfying aroma of beef being broiled at a high temperature. Nancy stuck her head around the kitchen door frame and performed an *I Love Lucy* imitation. "Hi honey! How was your day?" This completely disarmed Sam and, with a smile, he let the tension drain out of him.

Sam swept Nancy up in his arms and gave her a big kiss. Nancy pushed back from his chest. "Careful, the kids are watching." She nodded toward the kitchen table.

Dr. Higgins, who was sitting at the table, looked up from

his paper. "Don't mind me, I just live here."

Sam grabbed glasses and a bottle of wine. He sat across from Dr. Higgins and poured two glasses. "Would the cook like some?"

"If it's a party, count me in!"

Sam poured another glass for Nancy, and then raised his glass. "A toast to D2! It seems it's steering us in the right direction."

That got Dr. Higgins' attention. He put down his paper and reached for his glass. "I take it you have news for us?"

Sam nodded with a smile and recounted his adventure following Brandon Kulp. "It seems the guy is in cahoots with the men who've been chasing us. This gives me the confidence to approach the CIA and suggest they need to do a little house-cleaning. Before we even address the future of the D2 program, I think it's incumbent on us to use it to assist with the security of our country."

Nancy stopped what she was doing at the stove and turned toward Sam. "This seems like a big digression from our original objective. Is it really up to us to fix this problem?"

"If not us, then who?" Sam spun his wine glass in his fingers on the table. "This is a matter of national security. If the CIA doesn't even know it has a problem, who's going to fix it?"

Dr. Higgins set down his drink and looked directly at Sam. "What exactly do you have in mind?"

Sam shrugged as if to say that it should be obvious. "To catch a rat, you need to set a trap. I need you two to get me in front of Director Firestone. I need to convince her to set a trap for her deputy director. If Kulp takes the bait, then we've trapped the rat. If he doesn't, either he's very clever, or there's something much more complicated going on."

"I follow your thinking," said Dr. Higgins, "but how are we going to get you in front of Angela Firestone?"

"We go back to plan A," Nancy said. "If we can figure out where Director Firestone is going to be and what she's going to be doing before she even knows, then Sam can impress her with his mystical ability to predict the future. Because it's going to be personal to her, it should get her attention faster and make her more likely to respond to Sam."

Dr. Higgins nodded. "We need to do a complete work-up on Angela Firestone. We need to document her habits, her patterns, her tastes, the touchstones in her life, everything she's connected to. This will certainly be a further test of the capabilities of the D2 program."

"Not a moment to waste," Sam said, "but I think we should start with dinner."

"There you have it!" Nancy waved the spatula toward him. "A man and his stomach!"

After dinner, Nancy and Thermopylae Higgins huddled over his computer and scraped up data on Director Firestone. The more they could find, and the better organized it was, the better the results they could expect from the D2 program. Sam worked on his laptop, catching up with the financial market activity of the day.

Eventually, Sam tired of the real-world news, economics, and business. His mind wandered as he slumped into a more relaxed position. He noticed the corner of a book hidden beneath a blanket on the sofa. He wondered what Nancy had been reading. He looked over at her and Dr. Higgins working on a profile of Angela Firestone. Suddenly, the two events merged in his mind. He was able to see a small corner of a mostly-hidden object and complete the picture of that object in his mind, knowing without question it was a book. He could be certain, based on his experience with the shape of books and the knowledge they are often read while sitting on a sofa. His mind extrapolated a conclusion based on incomplete fragments of data. Nancy was searching for fragments of information on Director Firestone, and from those fragments, she expected to build a picture of the woman – not a picture, a profile. Pictures provided something different than pieces of data. In both cases, the brain was being asked to perform the task of "completion" from fragments of information, through the process of perception. Perception was more than just seeing, hearing, feeling, smelling, or tasting something. Perception involved various cognitive processes required to contextualize and interpret the sensual stimuli into something meaningful.

A visual field was able to provide a great deal more information than could be had from a digitized list of facts or attributes. A visual field had shades of light, a background and foreground, primary objects and secondary objects, things in motion, and things at rest. The brain would be overwhelmed if it reacted equally to all the stimuli coming in through the eyes. The brain adapted to repetitive, static, and unimportant stimuli and treated them as background so it could concentrate on the more important things, first-order objects and events.

A visual field conveyed far more meaningful information than a random list of facts in a database. A visual field had depth, which allows spatial perception. Distance between objects, relative motion between objects, and first, second, and third dimensions helped distinguish relevant and important information. Vision cognition built a hierarchy among the data. The brain used many techniques to extract spatial information. Gradient structure, interposition, aerial perspective, the relative size of identical objects, retinal disparity, and convergence and divergence all sent depth and motion messages to the brain.

From experience, the brain automatically contextualized what it saw. It looked for matches from prior experience. It grouped objects by size, color, and proximity. It assigned importance based on motion or position or relevance. It automatically completed or closed half-hidden objects. The brain could do this much better than a computer, because a computer was only looking for a one-to-one match with the physical appearance of the object. When the brain tried to interpret an object or a partially hidden object, it looked at the full scene as well as the object. It looked at the context, the placement, the degree of cover, and the viewer's experience regarding what might be expected to be found in that environment. This combination of processing capabilities was something still out of reach of computers.

Sam's ability to recognize a mostly-hidden book on the sofa seemed simple compared to what Nancy and Dr. Higgins were trying to do. What if data fragments could be mapped into a three-dimensional picture that helped to define the relative value of each piece of information? What if time could be introduced, and the map could be given motion through time? Was that what the D2 program did when predicting the future? What a marvelous idea.

After several hours of work with Dr. Higgins, Nancy looked over at Sam, sound asleep in his chair. "We've got a man down. I think maybe we should wrap this up and get him to bed."

"We've made a decent start." Dr. Higgins stretched his tired shoulders. "At least the program has identified the director's morning routine for us. That will give Sam a place to begin in the morning."

CHAPTER 26

At 6 am, the alarm on Nancy's phone rang. She turned it off then nudged Sam on the shoulder. "Rise and shine. It's a new day!"

Sam groaned. "What's with the alarm?"

"We've got things to do. Places to go."

Sam rolled over and slid a hand over Nancy's breast. "I know what I'd like to do."

"No, no. We don't have time for that."

Sam took her hand and pulled it down between his legs. "You're going to deprive my friend of care and feeding? He's awake, even if the rest of me isn't."

She squeezed his throbbing member. "Wow. Somebody's up and ready to go."

Sam scooped an arm under Nancy and pulled her on top of him. "You know this is what you want."

"Sam Barron, you're incorrigible! You aren't giving me a

choice, are you?"

"Of course you have a choice. And you're choosing to do exactly what you want — exactly what we both want." He pulled her head down to him and gave her a kiss.

Her hips were already grinding and stroking. Sam matched her rhythm. Yes, this was what she wanted. What better way to start the day? She caught the change in his breathing as she picked up the pace, and she knew she was going to make short work of this. She pressed her hips as far into him as she could, and her insides surged with a tingling rush. Flashing him a big grin, she said, "I've got you now! You aren't going to last. I've got complete control!"

With a hard squeeze, she lifted her hips, then thrust down on him again. She watched as his face flushed red and his body shook with involuntary contractions. She pulled him into her as the tumescence crested in her body with a rush of blood that made her dizzy. She tilted forward in his arms, the two of them panting in silence.

"That was lovely," mumbled Sam. "Now I'm ready to go back to sleep."

"No, no. You can't do that! I told you, you have places to go and things to do."

Sam opened his eyes and looked at her. "What exactly are you talking about?"

"Here's the deal. We discovered last night that Angela Firestone drives her daughter to a private school in the morning. There's a Starbucks Coffee one block down from the school.

After she drops her daughter off, she buys a coffee to get her through the horrendous morning traffic. We know the time and we know the place. It's the perfect intercept for you."

Recollection passed over Sam's face. "Oh, okay. I guess I better get with the program and get my act in gear."

At 7:35, Sam entered Starbucks and dawdled off to the side. He stared at the case of pastries and acted as if he were trying to make up his mind. A few minutes later, his phone rang.

Nancy said, "She just left her car and is walking toward the door. She'll arrive in five seconds."

"Thanks," said Sam as he hung up and pocketed his phone. He stepped up to the counter and ordered a medium Americano.

He heard the entry door open and close, but he resisted looking as he paid for his drink. He could feel the presence of someone walking up behind him. He stood staring straight ahead.

The barista said, "Your drink will be ready in a minute. You can pick it up at the end of the counter." She pointed to her right.

Sam spun 180 degrees to look straight into the face of Angela Firestone. He sized her up quickly. She was about five-ten with a build that was once athletic, but now veering toward pudgy. Her auburn hair was pulled back behind her ears, and her pleasant but ordinary face made her look like any normal career woman and/or mother in her mid-forties. "Good morning, Director! I would have ordered your coffee for you, but you probably wouldn't be comfortable accepting a drink from a stranger." Sam gave her a wide smile. "But I hope we'll be friends soon. Have a nice day!"

A look of confusion crossed Angela's face, then her brow furrowed with concern. But Sam had already turned and moved on. He walked to the end of the counter, picked up his drink, then headed for the door. He thought about turning and waving at her, but changed his mind. He exited without looking back.

Sam hurried down the sidewalk and got into the rental car with Nancy. "I think that went well. We've dropped the first bread crumb. Her curiosity should bring her to us."

Nancy pulled out into traffic and headed back toward Georgetown. "Do you want me to take you to the house? I'm planning to work with Dr. Higgins again."

"Yes, please. I have other work I need to catch up on. I don't suppose there's anything else we can do during the day while she's at the agency."

Nancy shook her head. "We can't get the data we need to make any sense of what she's doing at work. We'll have to stay focused on her personal life. I'll call you as soon as we come up with anything promising."

"Sounds like a plan." Sam sipped his coffee. "Waiting is the hard part."

About 2:30 that afternoon, Sam's phone rang. He was delighted

to hear Nancy's voice. Her tone brought sunshine to him after a tedious day of work and worry. "I have a rendezvous for you this evening," she said.

"She's beautiful, dark-haired, athletic, smart, and her name begins with N," Sam gushed.

She laughed. "Afraid not. Angela Firestone's daughter is going to be performing in a school music recital this evening. This should give you another opportunity to get in front of her."

"Well, that isn't my first choice of how to spend the evening, but I guess it'll help move our project along."

"I'll try to be home by five o'clock so we can eat together before you leave. The recital starts at seven."

"You're doing a great job. I miss you. I hope you and Dr. Higgins continue to make progress."

Nancy sighed. "It's frustrating. Because her daily schedule keeps updating, we keep running the program every hour to see what new data has appeared. We never know when the program is going to come up with something useful. But in the meantime, we're learning a lot more about how the program works. We're getting better at massaging the data set it's instructed to use, so we get more meaningful results. Every once in a while, we hit on something that demonstrates how the potential of this thing can be really scary."

"Yeah, I'm worried about holding on to this program too long. We need to make it someone else's problem. Do be careful. I'll see you soon."

"I miss you too," Nancy said tenderly. "I'll see you soon."

Sam hung up and thought about what he had said. What he wanted to say was, "I love you." He hoped that when she said she missed him, she was really saying, "I love you too." It troubled him he didn't dare say aloud what he felt, but he wasn't sure she was ready to hear that yet.

The balance of the afternoon passed quickly as Sam was diverted by a two percent sell-off in the stock market.

After their quick dinner, Sam asked Nancy if she would be willing to drive him to the recital at the school. "I'm not sure there's parking there, and I don't want the car to be a problem."

Nancy pulled up Google Maps on her phone and went to satellite view. "Much as I'm happy to be your chauffeur, you can see there's plenty of parking alongside the athletic field. You shouldn't have any problem finding a space."

"Well then, I guess I'm off." He looked at Dr. Higgins. "Thanks for your help, Doctor. Keep an eye on her for me. I hope I won't be gone too long."

Sam got in his rental car and headed across town.

It had occurred to Sam he might have a problem with security, but his worries were unfounded. He was able to drive through the school gates, find a parking space, and walk into the auditorium without being challenged by anyone. He took a program at the door and sat in the back of the auditorium. He found the name Firestone listed in the program, so he was confident Angela was there to see her daughter. All he could see was the back of hundreds of heads in front of him, so he wasn't able to find her in the crowd.

As he listened to the children playing various instruments, it reminded him of painful times when he was in school. He was always expected not just to participate, but to excel. So, whether it was an athletic event, a school play, or the debate club, Sam was always nervous when he had to perform. That gut-wrenching feeling came over him now as he empathized with these children. Battling stage fright was an important part of growing up, but necessity didn't make it any less painful. Sam had tried to avoid pressuring his children to perform, but he couldn't avoid having high expectations for them. He wondered if his daughter would still be alive if she hadn't been pushed to excel.

Fortunately for Sam, Joline Firestone performed before the intermission. Sam followed the crowd as everyone streamed out into the lobby. After several minutes of milling about while he searched intently, he spotted Angela Firestone talking to another parent. He approached her from behind and stood near her shoulder. At a lull in the conversation, he stepped around in front of her.

"Good evening Mrs. Firestone. I thought Joline did a fine job. The violin is not an easy instrument. You must have to give her a lot of encouragement."

At the sight of Sam, a slight panic widened Angela's eyes, but she had to maintain something of a poker face because the other woman she had been talking to was still standing there.

She forced an artificial smile. "Thank you. Actually, Joline loves to play, so we don't have to push her to practice."

A man came over and placed a possessive arm around Mrs. Firestone.

Sam stuck out his hand. "Hi. I'm Sam. I was just telling your wife what a nice job your daughter did. You must be very proud!" Sam craned his neck as if to look across the room behind Mr. Firestone. "Excuse me. There's someone I need to catch." Sam stepped around him and dashed into the crowd.

Jacob Firestone tossed a quizzical look at his wife and asked, "Who was that?"

"I don't exactly know, but you can be sure I'm going to find out."

Angela Firestone brightened up her smile, changing the subject. "Let's go back to our seats and enjoy the rest of the performance."

When Sam arrived back at the cottage, he found Nancy reading a book and Dr. Higgins typing on his laptop. A tiny cheer resounded in his mind at the confirmation of the full image of the book he had only partially seen earlier when hidden under the blanket. He didn't recognize the title, though: some old novel.

Nancy looked up from the book. "How did it go?"

Sam shrugged. "As well as can be expected. She's now very aware of me."

Dr. Higgins called over from his computer. "I have fresh output for you. The program tells us there's a 75% chance that

Director Firestone will stop at Harris Teeter's to grocery shop at 5:30 on her way home tomorrow night. Then it goes on to say that around 7:45 there's an 89% chance she'll go for a run along the river. She has a regular route along the Mt. Vernon Trail she likes to jog."

Sam crossed to the dining table and set his briefcase on it. "That's great. I may have two more opportunities to get in front of her. It's time to close on this deal and get an appointment with her."

With his two thumbs, he popped the latches and raised the top of the briefcase. He pulled a fat envelope out and gave it to Dr. Higgins.

"What is this?".

Sam smiled. "That's twenty thousand dollars cash for you. You're spending a lot of time and doing a lot of work for us. I just want to show some appreciation."

The doctor was flustered. "I don't understand. Where did this come from?"

Sam closed the briefcase. "You remember Blixen Technologies? I decided to believe in the program and made an investment. Understand, this is a one-time deal. If I keep doing this, I'll have the Securities and Exchange Commission all over me. Furthermore, it's not part of our mission. One could even say it's morally corrupt. So, thank you for your service. Enjoy it. But that's all there is."

Dr. Higgins looked genuinely embarrassed. "Wow. Thank you. I wasn't expecting this."

"I know you weren't expecting it, but you deserve it. Now I could do with a beer! What say you all? Who wants a drink?"

Later that night, when Nancy tiptoed into Sam's room and crawled into bed next to him, he snuggled up to her and whispered, "I have a surprise for you."

"I like surprises." She slid her hand across his stomach and down toward his groin.

"I hope you really like this one. I opened an investment account at my firm in your name. I put fifty thousand dollars in it for you."

Nancy gasped. "You what?"

"Sshh!" Sam put his hand over her mouth. "Shush. You don't want to wake up the good doctor. I just figured you need a new car, and you have some debts to pay off. I'd like you to be able to start clean when this is all over. I leveraged up my investment in Blixen Technologies with some options. As I told the doctor, it's a one-time deal, but it's almost like free money."

Nancy giggled. "I like this surprise! Sam Barron, you're the best! Now, what can I give you in return?"

"Well, let me see…" Sam acted like he was deep in thought. "I'm sure we can work something out."

The following evening, at 5:25 pm, Sam walked through the entrance to Harris Teeter's grocery store and looked around. He didn't see any sign of Angela Firestone, so he started working on the grocery list Nancy had given him. As he pushed his shopping cart around, he tried not to stray too far from the front door so he could see Angela when she entered. By 5:40, Sam was getting concerned and started thinking about the 25% chance she wouldn't show up. Then a large Dutch apple pie caught his eye and he couldn't resist picking it up and putting it in his cart. It wasn't on the list. If Nancy was anything like his former wife, she would probably give him grief about it, but it looked too good to pass up. As he lifted his gaze up again, Angela was about to disappear down an aisle with her cart. Sam surreptitiously tailed her until she entered the more open produce section. When she was standing in front of bins of tomatoes and cucumbers, Sam approached from the other side of the vegetable stand.

"Good evening, Director!"

"Sam Barron! Are you stalking me? I checked up on you. It wasn't easy to find out at first, but I discovered you've done work for us in the past. If it weren't for that, I'd have you in handcuffs right now and be pressing for a restraining order."

Sam smiled his most innocent smile. "I don't need to stalk you. I know exactly where you're going to be and what you're going to be doing. That's the whole point of this exercise. I can see your future, and it's troubling... very troubling. It's urgent that I talk to you about that, but not here. I'll see you soon. I hope the next time we meet you'll be in a mood to listen to me." Sam turned his shopping cart and headed for the check-out counter.

Angela Firestone stood frozen with a frown on her face.

After Sam left the grocery store, he made a quick stop at a sporting goods store to purchase a sweatsuit. Then he headed for home. When Sam got back to the cottage, the smell of dinner cooking greeted him as he came through the front door. He set the grocery bag down on the kitchen table. "I come bearing gifts."

Nancy looked up from the stove where she was stirring a pot. "Did everything go okay?"

"Yes. I don't know how she identified me. I didn't give her a lot to work with, except my first name and perhaps an opportunity at facial recognition, but she definitely knows who I am. I expect I'll get my audience with her. I hope I can wrap things up tonight."

Dr. Higgins was at his usual position in front of his laptop. "I'd be careful not to give away the store. Remember, we still don't know who can be trusted. Our short-term objective is to lay a trap for Brandon Kulp. We don't want to say too much about the D2 program until we have more confidence about what we're going to do with it."

"I agree," Sam said. "Thanks for reminding me. We're starting to rely on the program like it's second nature, but we do need to maintain secrecy until we get over this first hurdle."

"Dinner is almost ready," Nancy said. "Do you need to clean up?"

"I'm going to change into my new sweatsuit because I need to go for a run after dinner. Whatever you're cooking smells great. I bought some apple pie for dessert."

"Oh, really?" Nancy looked down her nose at Sam. "You certainly will need to go for a run after that load of calories."

Sam exited the room grinning. Who needed a computer program to predict that comment?

A little over an hour later, Sam was sitting on a park bench along the Mt. Vernon Trail, anxiously waiting for Angela Firestone to show up. The darkness made it difficult. He had several false starts when other runners came along. As shapes moved in and out of the shadows between the lights, it was all he could do to try to distinguish male from female body shapes. He was afraid he was going to miss her. But when she did finally come running down the path, there was no mistaking her. Her hair was pulled back into a ponytail, and she had a surprisingly strong gait he hadn't expected from the middle-aged body shape presented by her loose-fitting running clothes. Sam waited until she was past him before he popped up and started a high-speed run at an intercept angle. Immediately, a younger male jogger who had been tagging about twenty-five feet back sped up. When Angela saw Sam, she raised her hand and waved off the eager man sprinting up from behind.

"Brought some protection with you this time." Sam fell into step with the director.

"A woman running alone at night is vulnerable. The government likes to protect its assets. It's good training for the new recruits. It gets them into the spirit of things."

"Well, I mean you no harm," said Sam. "I'm simply here to ask for an appointment. I need to provide you with important information. Do you mind if we slow down and walk?"

Angela eased up on her stride. She put her hands on her hips and settled into a walk while she took a few deep breaths. "What exactly is your agenda, Mr. Barron?"

"As I have been suggesting, you and your agency are in serious jeopardy. I wouldn't be interrupting you like this if I didn't feel it was a matter of national security. I needed to come directly to you, because going through any normal chain of command would risk the information falling into the wrong hands. I only have two requests of you. I'd like an hour of your time in a secure location so I can give you a complete explanation. Second, nobody can know in advance who I am or that you're meeting with me. This needs to be off the books. Don't write anything down. Don't tell your assistant. Don't tell your deputy director. Don't log anything. This is critical. I have access to something people are willing to kill for. If anyone finds out about our meeting, there will undoubtedly be interference. It's not inconceivable that you could be put at risk. I need your help to keep this contained between you and me."

Angela Firestone frowned. "This is irregular. If I didn't have access to your background, I'd blow you off. I don't know whether you're a nut case, or whether I should be terrified. But I'm willing to give you the benefit of the doubt. Let me set something up. How do I get in touch with you?"

"I'm not naïve. I know you have my phone number. You probably have my life history. One thing you may not know is I'm staying with Dr. Thermopylae Higgins at Georgetown University. You should be able to remember his name. The sooner we can do this, the better. I appreciate your trust and your understanding."

"You'll hear from me soon." Angela started back into a jog.

Sam picked up the pace too, and peeled off to the left toward his car.

When Sam got back to the cottage, he was all smiles. He'd barely had time to take a shower, get dressed, and pour himself a drink when his phone rang. He recognized Director Firestone's voice, but there were no introductions, no names.

"A driver named Bob will be out front to pick you up at 8:30 tomorrow morning. Be ready. You know the drill. No weapons. No electronics. Bring a photo ID, preferably a passport." The call disconnected.

Sam spoke out loud to nobody in particular. "Mission accomplished!"

Nancy looked up from the book she was reading. "You got an appointment?"

"Sure did." Sam grinned. "Now we can finally move forward. I think this calls for a toast and then an early bedtime. Tomorrow, the game is afoot!"

CHAPTER 27

The next morning at breakfast, Nancy said she was going to stay at the house. She wanted time to herself, time to relax. What she wasn't saying was she was miffed that she wasn't being included in the meeting with Angela Firestone. She tried to justify to herself all the reasons she was being excluded. Chief among them was the fact she was the recognizable person who had taken the D2 program. If the mole at the CIA recognized her, all of their plans could be destroyed. Nevertheless, it hurt to be kept away from the project she was responsible for from the beginning.

Dr. Higgins said he had work to catch up on. He had set aside other things so he could work on the D2 program. He was still accountable to get his regular work done, and he didn't want to have to make up an explanation for why he wasn't meeting his performance benchmarks.

Sam barely acknowledged their intentions. He was totally

absorbed thinking about his upcoming meeting. At 8:28, Sam pulled back the front window curtains and looked out. A black SUV was parked at the end of the front walk.

"I'm going!" he called out. He straightened his tie, put on his suit jacket, and walked out the door.

As Sam approached his ride, the driver stepped out and walked around to open the rear passenger door for Sam. Nothing was said except for a curt, "Good morning, sir."

Sam got in and sank into the black leather seat. The vehicle had a freshly cleaned smell. Sam waited expectantly for the driver to say something, but nothing was forthcoming. For the next hour, they slugged their way through Washington traffic. It seemed to take forever to get to Route 123.

Even though Sam sat in the back seat between tinted windows, as a matter of protocol, he still put on his sunglasses as they turned off Dolley Madison Boulevard onto the entrance road for the George Bush Center for Intelligence. One never knew who was lurking around, snapping pictures and checking up on visitors to the nation's top intelligence agency. When they came to the first checkpoint, Bob rolled down his window and showed his credentials. The policeman, holding an automatic rifle, exchanged a few words, looked at Sam in the back seat, who had now removed his sunglasses, and then waved them off to the right. They had to pull into a reception area in order for Sam to get his visitor's pass. Inside, at the window, Bob showed his credentials again and explained they had an appointment with the director. He asked Sam for his passport and handed it to the woman. Sam looked around at the few other people sitting on visitor's chairs, waiting. When the woman handed Sam's passport back along with a visitor's pass, it was clear coming through with Bob was a shortcut through the normal vetting process.

They walked out to the car and drove the rest of the way to the headquarters building. The parking lot was huge, and at this time of day, there were no empty spaces. A normal employee would have to park in the back forty and have a long hike to his office. Bob spun the steering wheel and turned into a reserved parking space along the north side of the main headquarters building. The two of them got out and walked around the corner, past the Bubble, to the front entrance. The statue of Nathan Hale was still there to greet Sam with his shiny toe. Sam resisted the urge to reach out and touch the toe.

As they entered the front door, they were greeted by the giant CIA seal embedded in the floor. The room was exactly as he remembered it. The memorial wall was to the right, along with the book of honor. To the left, on the south wall, was the OSS memorial and the statue of Major General William Donovan. Further along, was a security checkpoint that looked like TSA security in an airport. Sam knew he couldn't bring his cell phone, a flash drive, or anything electronic that could carry information in or out. He didn't have anything to put in the tray except his sunglasses and his house key. The guard looked at Sam's passport and compared it to his visitor's pass. Sam pointed to his belt buckle, but the guard shook his head and waved him through the metal detector.

Sam followed Bob up the few stairs in front of them, then down an interior corridor. They walked past a small two-man submersible the CIA commissioned in the 1950s. Sam remembered being surprised at how small and primitive the boat looked when he first saw it years ago. He couldn't help thinking we had come a long way with material science and technology during the intervening decades since it was built. Bob was taking him to the CIA museum, something not open to the public.

"We arrived a few minutes early," said Bob. "I thought we could hang out at the museum while we wait. You might find it interesting."

Most people would consider an opportunity to see the museum a rare treat. The museum was only available to agency employees and the occasional visiting dignitary. Sam and Bob were standing in a wide hallway lined with glass cases full of artifacts, mostly spycraft devices used by CIA officers over past decades. Pictures and posters lined the walls, with written explanations about past agency operations and the history of the various artifacts.

Bob pointed enthusiastically. "Over here is a mock-up of the compound where Osama Bin-Laden was captured. Next to it is his gun. It's a slightly modified Russian AK-47."

Sam had been at CIA headquarters shortly after the gun arrived. Bob didn't seem to know that, and Sam didn't want to rain on his parade. Either Bob hadn't done his homework on Sam, or he was being deliberately kept out of the loop. Sam figured what Bob didn't know, Bob didn't need to know.

A man in dark slacks and a white shirt with a brightly colored lanyard around his neck holding his employee ID came up and whispered in Bob's ear. When the man left, Bob turned to Sam with an apologetic look. "The director is running late. Can I get you anything to eat or drink while we wait?"

"Now that you mention it, I could do with some coffee. It's really hard to find Dunkin' Donuts coffee in Washington, DC. They don't have many in the city."

"You're in luck!" Bob said. "We have a Dunkin' Donuts in the food court. Follow me."

Sam smiled to himself. He was amazed Bob couldn't seem to connect the dots. Sam had mentioned Dunkin' Donuts because he already knew there was one in the food court. But maybe Bob was being intentionally obtuse. Maybe he knew a lot more than he was revealing.

Sam pursued the conversation further. "I know there's a strong connection between Boston and Washington. The capital relies on the academic talent found in the Boston universities. And those Boston folks can't live without their Dunkin' Donuts!"

Bob didn't have anything more to say on the subject. He simply kept walking.

Sam followed Bob down a series of corridors to the food court. Once they were handed their coffees and arrived at the cashier, Sam reached for his wallet.

Bob said, "I've got this. They don't want a credit card. Paying for things here is a little tricky because everybody's identity is protected."

Sam nodded. "Thanks."

Bob pointed to the food court exit. "Unless you want to sit down, we can walk, and I'll show you the CIA art collection."

"Sounds fine to me." Sam followed Bob down more corridors and up a flight of stairs.

Once they entered the lobby gallery, Bob turned Sam loose while he walked over and said a few words to one of the guards. Sam was struck by how eclectic the art collection was. Some items were clearly documenting a historic moment, and happened to be pieces of notable art in their own right. Others were more abstract. Sam wouldn't have known what their intent was if there hadn't been plaques explaining the thought behind their creation. Some pieces were garish and not to Sam's taste at all. Other items, particularly a few of the sculptures, were crafted with a lot of emotion, and had a style and quality that made Sam think he would be happy to have them in his own home to enjoy. Windwalker, a very large sculpture of an eagle in flight, was one such piece that caught his attention.

Bob followed Sam around like a puppy dog. Much like when they were riding in the car, Bob avoided engaging Sam in any meaningful conversation. He didn't ask any questions or solicit any opinions. He would occasionally bring something to Sam's attention, but otherwise remained quiet.

After a while, one of the guards walked over and said something to Bob. Bob turned to Sam and said, "We're all set. It's time to head upstairs."

Once again, Sam followed Bob as they retraced their steps. When they arrived at the elevator bank, Bob held the elevator door for Sam, then entered himself and pushed the button for the seventh floor. Unlike the lower corridors that had people constantly coming and going, when they got off the elevator, the corridor was empty. It was quiet, like a library, and had a 1960s institutional feel. Bob walked a few doors down the hall, then turned and entered a door with a plaque next to it that said "Director." Sam followed and found himself in an antechamber with a female assistant sitting behind a desk. She looked attractive, but an aura about her made him think she was totally unapproachable. She was beyond professional. She seemed scary tough.

Bob addressed the assistant. "Here he is." He looked at Sam. "I'll be available to take you home when you're ready." He turned and went back out into the hall, closing the door behind him.

The assistant nodded at Sam. "You can go on in." She pointed to a door on the opposite side of the room from the hall door.

Sam wasn't sure if he should knock first, but he decided against it. He turned the handle and opened the door.

Light cascaded into the office from a row of picture windows overlooking the top of a forest. Sitting at a large desk in front of the windows was Angela Firestone. When she stood, she commanded the stature of a director. Today, she wore a white blouse, tailored black blazer, and black pencil skirt with accents of gold jewelry. Her face, though pleasant, was intensely serious. Sam quickly confirmed his earlier conclusion this was not a woman to be trifled with.

A smile spread across her face. "So finally, you have your audience." She didn't come around her desk to shake hands. Instead, she indicated the chair opposite the desk. "Sit down Mr. Barron and tell me what this is all about." She sat back down and waited.

Sam had rehearsed his speech a hundred different ways. In the end, he decided to wing it. He sat down and cleared his throat. After a momentary pause, he launched into his presentation.

"Are you sure your office is clean and nobody is listening? No tapes, no transcripts of our conversation, nothing prying eyes or ears can access?"

"You must be kidding!" Angela Firestone chuckled. "I'm not going to detail CIA procedure to you, but rest assured our conversation is confidential."

Sam settled into his chair. "Alright then. Are you aware that several months ago the British lost track of something valuable to them? Perhaps you heard a British citizen named Joseph Campbell was killed on US soil?"

The director nodded. "I'm familiar with the incident. I had a conversation with Sir Reginald at MI6. Of course, he didn't tell me what they were missing or what Joseph Campbell was doing in the United States. Normally we interface issue by issue across lower-level channels, it was a bit irregular to receive an unscheduled direct call."

Sam looked intently at the director. "I would have you think carefully about whether anyone else in your organization had access to that conversation or the information it contained. I have a colleague named Nancy Forrester who is believed to have possession of the information the British lost. Her life is under threat. What the information is and who actually has the information is not open to discussion at this time. What I want to impress upon you is that someone in your agency appears to be behind attempts to obtain the information and pass it on to the Russians. What I'm telling you is you have a turncoat in your midst."

The director leaned back in her chair and brought the fingertips of both hands together. She sat in silence contemplating the ramifications of this news. "May I ask how you know this?"

"How I obtained the information isn't important at the moment. What is most urgent is to verify the information is correct. I don't want to pillory an innocent person. I'm proposing you run a test. If it comes up negative, nobody needs to know we ever had this conversation. No harm, no foul. But if Brandon Kulp is the traitor I think he is, that is something you need to know."

"Brandon Kulp!" The director tilted forward in her chair and both hands slapped flat on her desk. "How could you possibly think I would believe an unfounded claim like that?"

This was where Sam feared he would lose the sale. If he couldn't convince her, they were at a dead end. "I know it's a lot to swallow. If it's true, it upsets the whole balance of your organization. But if it's true and you don't acknowledge it, you're in even worse trouble. That's why I'm proposing a harmless test. You can find out for sure. If I'm wrong, it costs you almost nothing."

A thick veil of silence hung in the room. The director locked eyes with Sam. "You're really stretching here. You have no standing to make these claims. Do you realize it has been almost thirty years since the Aldrich Ames incident and the agency is still recovering from that? In case you don't know, Ames operated from 1985 until his arrest in 1994 and is one of the most notorious traitorous spies in American history. It's a huge black mark for the agency. The FBI now has a Counter Espionage Group at the CIA, and if there's a mole, they should be on top of it. If you have any evidence, we should turn it over to the FBI."

Sam winced at her rebuke. "I'm in a difficult position, because I'm not prepared to give my evidence to you. That's why I'm suggesting a simple test. It shouldn't risk your credibility and it shouldn't risk Mr. Kulp's reputation, as long as he's innocent. The goal is to keep this very quiet."

Director Firestone let out a sigh and shook her head. After a moment's reflection, she said, "I'll give you the benefit of the doubt and listen to what you have to say, but I'm not necessarily going to agree to anything."

"Fair enough. I'm proposing a simple test. Some operatives believe Nancy has information they want. They know her by sight. I suggest that she call in on a CIA public line. You will have told the call center to flag keywords. In this case, it'll be the name, Joseph Campbell. You give instructions that you want information on any call referencing that name routed directly to you. You want to make sure that Brandon Kulp has access to the information, but no direct control over it. He won't be included in any operation concerning the use of that information.

"Nancy will offer to give you a flash drive with information on it. She'll say she doesn't understand what she has, but there's way too much heat on her and she wants protection in exchange for giving you the information.

"You'll put a tail on Brandon Kulp, and you'll arrange a meeting for Nancy to pass off the flash drive to a field officer. This is a low-risk operation. There will be nothing of value on the drive. If somebody wants to steal it, you're happy to let them have it. The objective is simply to see if there is interference with the hand-off, and if Brandon Kulp is involved."

Sam waited nervously for her reaction. The director spun around in her chair and stared out the window. Just then, a Harris hawk flew directly at the window. Sam thought it was going to smash into the glass. At the last minute, the hawk flared its wings and landed on the metal railing that ran across the façade of the building. It sat there staring at the glass, undoubtedly looking at its reflection in the window. But its intent stare made it seem like it was spying on the occupants of the room. Eventually, the director turned back around.

"I don't like the consequences if you're wrong. This has the potential of doing great damage to my relationship with the deputy director. On the other hand, the risk is far too great to ignore if you're right. I feel I'm forced to accept your proposal, even though I find it distasteful. Go ahead and have Nancy Forrester call in with her offer. Any time after nine tomorrow morning should give us sufficient time to get set up."

"Thank you," Sam said. "I trust I'm truly providing a valuable service to you. I'll have Nancy use a burner phone so she can't be traced. She's in real danger. You can always reach me on my phone if you have to. But remember, you can't be sure that you aren't being listened to and watched by a mole in your organization."

"I always worry about that. Thank you for coming to see me." The director stood and nodded toward Sam.

Apparently, she wasn't big on handshakes. "My pleasure." Sam stood as she did, nodded back at her, and made for the door. Just then, the Harris hawk took flight.

Bob was waiting for Sam in the antechamber outside the director's office. He escorted Sam back down on the elevator and they exited out the lobby gallery, with Sam giving his visitor's pass to one of the security guards on the way out. It was an equally long drive back to Georgetown. It made Sam wonder if there was ever a time when traffic wasn't bad in DC.

CHAPTER 28

The following morning after breakfast, Nancy sat at the kitchen table fidgeting. She had a pad of paper in front of her with a script written out for her call to the CIA. Sam had coached her on what to say. Most importantly, he explained she had to include the name, Joseph Campbell. The prior evening, Sam had gone out and purchased a prepaid cell phone — a "burner" phone. He selected a phone without GPS in it. He also purchased another Faraday pouch to keep the phone completely untraceable when not in use.

A little after 9:30 a.m., Sam inserted the battery in the prepaid phone and handed it to Nancy. She dialed the number at the top of her pad. Although she was terribly nervous, her voice was surprisingly smooth. She emphasized quite forcefully that she had important information for the director. The voice at the other end said the director was not available, but somebody would get back to her.

Using her firmest voice, Nancy concluded the call with an ultimatum. "Tell the director that she has two opportunities to call me. She can call between 11 a.m. and 11:05. If she fails to do that, she can call between noon and 12:05. If she doesn't call during those times, she will have missed a very important communication."

After she hung up, Nancy removed the battery from the phone and placed the battery and the phone in the Faraday pouch. She looked at Sam with an expectant face.

"That was perfect," Sam said. "You did a great job. Now we wait. Let's talk about what you're going to say when they call back."

Nancy was relieved the first call was over. She had wanted a more active role, but now that she had one, the tension was gnawing at her. She didn't want to focus on the fact that this was an operation with life and death consequences, but the knowledge of danger lurked in the back of her mind and made her uneasy.

At 10:59, Nancy placed the battery back into her new cell phone. At 11:01, it rang. Even though she was expecting it, the ring startled her. She waited for a second ring, then answered the call. A woman's voice greeted her.

"I understand you have information you're anxious to give me."

"Yes," said Nancy "I — "

"Before we continue, do you have a friend there with you?"

Nancy paused and looked at Sam. "Yes."

"Good. Please pass the phone to him."

Nancy passed the phone to Sam. He looked quizzically at Nancy. "Hello?"

"Hello," said the director. "I wanted to make sure it was you and that we're talking to the right players on the field. You can pass the phone back."

Sam passed the phone back to Nancy. She had the volume turned up and placed the call on speaker.

"Here are your instructions. We've arranged a simple drop for you. I want you to go to Montrose Park tomorrow and take an empty Coke can with you. Tape the flash drive to the bottom of the can with clear packing tape. You can hold your hand over the lower part of the can so nobody will see anything. Across from the armillary sphere is a trash can next to a hedge. At exactly 11:45, I want you to saunter from the armillary sphere to the trash barrel and throw the Coke can into the trash. Don't look at anybody. Don't make any sudden moves. Be as casual as you can and slowly walk back out of the park."

"Excuse me," said Nancy. "What is an armillary sphere?"

"Oh, yes, well, you might know it as a three-dimensional astrolabe. It is a monument with big brass circles that represent planetary orbits. You'll know it when you see it. There is a brick path around the monument, and the trash barrel is immediately next to the path.

"This is a simple, low-risk task. Do exactly what I have told you. Don't do anything to attract attention to yourself, and everything will go fine. Just in case, I'll have A.O. keep an eye on you. If, for any reason, you feel you are in imminent danger, I want you to raise both hands straight up into the air. Got it?"

Nancy was getting nervous. "What's an AO?"

"Oh, sorry, you wouldn't know about Angel Overwatch. A.O. is probably the best sniper in North America. When he was in the military in Afghanistan, he was sent out as an overwatch on high-risk assignments. Often, the soldiers didn't even know he was there. When confronted with deadly situations, there were occasions when enemy combatants simply dropped dead in front of the troops. The soldiers would say, 'I must have an angel watching over me.' Thus, the nickname Angel Overwatch was coined. You will never see him. He'll be up on a rooftop somewhere."

"Okay," said Nancy. "That's all I do. Just throw away the coke can and leave."

"That's it exactly," said the director. "I'm going to hang up now. I expect you at Montrose Park tomorrow. Be punctual. Goodbye." The connection went dead.

Nancy turned to Sam with a pale face. "Seems easy, but I don't know."

Sam smiled and put an arm on her shoulder. "Relax. This'll be a walk in the park!"

"You had to say that didn't you?"

Sam grinned. "I couldn't resist."

When Dr. Higgins arrived back at his house that evening, he found Sam and Nancy working together in the kitchen.

Sam greeted him with a bright smile. "We thought we'd make a celebratory dinner. This project is finally moving forward, and tomorrow promises to be a turning point."

Dr. Higgins set down his briefcase and removed the strap to his laptop case from his shoulder. "I must confess I really enjoy having you two here. I've never eaten so well, and it's nice to have the company."

"It's nice of you to invite us into your home," said Nancy. "Here, try these out." She placed a small plate of crab cakes in front of Dr. Higgins with a dish of tartar sauce. "These are appetizers to get you started. I experimented with Tabasco sauce. Let me know what you think."

Dr. Higgins gingerly tried a few bites. "Excellent!" he exclaimed. "I told you, you're spoiling me!"

As dinner progressed, and more wine was poured, the discussion became more animated and joyful. Everyone was having a good time, and this was clearly the tension release they all needed.

That night in bed, Nancy and Sam's lovemaking was more intense than ever. Whether it was the wine, the celebration, or the tinge of danger and adventure that would accompany tomorrow's events, an effusive amount of athletic sex was followed by a level of tenderness neither of them ever expected to experience after the worn-out relationships and gap of loneliness they had come from. Thoughts about tomorrow disappeared as they lived in the moment and fell asleep in each other's arms.

CHAPTER 29

At 8:30 in the morning, the team leader was in a conference room at CIA headquarters with eight other officers. This was a hastily assembled operation with little explanation regarding the larger issues at play. They had a specific task, and the team leader's job was to make sure everyone was on the same page.

"Leon, you're the pick-up man. Your job is simple: You're to retrieve the package and bring it home. I want everyone to pay attention! The package has no value to us. We don't expect interference, but if there's any attempt by someone to take the package, you're to let it go without resistance or confrontation. Completing the pick-up is not the objective of this exercise.

"Look around the room. Make note of everyone who is here. The objective of this exercise is to identify any player who isn't in this room. Anyone, and I mean anyone, either friend or foe, who is not in this room is a suspect. Your job is to identify and detain anyone who appears to be interested in or engaged in this drop who is not in this room. Do I make myself clear?"

Heads nodded and murmurs passed around the room. The team leader took a moment and stared at his crew intently. He wanted to be sure he had their undivided attention.

"This is tricky. We aren't giving this operation a name. It's unofficial. As you know, we aren't empowered to operate domestically. That's the job of the FBI. Furthermore, we have a civilian making the drop. There can't be any screwups. This needs to go smoothly, low-key, under the radar.

"Spencer, will you raise your hand? Everyone, look at Spencer. He's with the FBI Counter Espionage Group. As you know, the CIA is not allowed to arrest or detain people. If anyone needs to be detained, that's Spencer's job.

"You're now under quarantine. If anyone here has broken the rules and brought a cell phone into this room, you have one minute of amnesty. Bring the phone up and place it on the desk in front of me. There will be no repercussions if you do it now. If you're caught with a phone later, you'll be immediately dismissed and prosecuted to the full extent of the law. In short, your life will be ruined. Any takers? No? Okay then, if you need to go to the bathroom an escort will be provided. You cannot communicate in any way with anyone outside of this room. This quarantine lasts until you're officially released, but the events of today remain classified and are not to be discussed with anyone at any time.

"A.O., who isn't in the room with us, will be out of sight on a rooftop. I don't anticipate he'll have any role to play, but he's our backup. The rest of you know your positions. I want you on site watching the perimeter one-half hour ahead of time, and I want you in position no later than fifteen minutes ahead of time. The drop will be made by a woman about five-eight, slender, athletic, with dark hair. Once she completes the drop, she should be out of harm's way.

"Okay. Let's get this done! Stand by for transportation."

Over breakfast at the cottage in Georgetown, the seriousness of the day spread its tentacles into Sam and Nancy. Dr. Higgins departed for his office, but Sam and Nancy had no particular plans. They struggled to find ways to fill the time until they needed to leave for Montrose Park. They made a feeble attempt at conversation, but quickly drifted off into their own separate little worlds. Sam opened his laptop, but found it hard to focus on anything. Nancy determined housework was the one thing she could handle. She did the dishes, ran a load of laundry, picked up and dusted. The minutes passed by slowly, but eventually, it was time to head for the car.

Montrose Park consisted of a large, open grassy area with mature trees lining its sides. Directly off of R Street NW, a large circle, paved with bricks, enclosed a low garden. In the center of the garden was the monument with the armillary sphere. Behind this bricked area, the grass extended quite far back to a children's park and, off to the right, the Oak Hill Cemetery. Its extensive size, with walking paths throughout, made it a difficult area to police, but this was not expected to be a high-risk exchange. A.O. had an excellent view for hundreds of yards from his rooftop perch across the street. Officers were strategically placed by the public restrooms, on the park bench by the monument, as landscapers out on the grass, and as visitors all the way back to the children's park. It was a beautiful sunny day, but the park was quiet, with nobody in the way of the operation.

Sam parked on R Street, a few yards down from the entrance. At 11:40, Nancy got out of the car and strolled down the sidewalk. She had an empty Coke can in her hand, holding it as if it still had liquid in it. She turned right, off the street toward the restrooms, then turned left down the path that would bring her into the brick circle from the six o'clock position. Once she entered the circle, she ambled along in a self-absorbed manner. She rounded the circle in a counter-clockwise direction, then angled to the right for the trash barrel.

Sam had no role in this operation, but he wasn't going to sit in the car. He got out a few minutes after Nancy and followed her toward the restrooms. Once there, he walked to the right in a direction that kept him under the trees, but within sight of Nancy and the monument. He watched as she feigned taking a final drink from the Coke can, then threw it in the trash. She turned back and continued around the circle toward an exit to the street at the nine o'clock position. Coming directly at her was officer Leon, dressed as a homeless bum in a tattered coat.

He was carrying a clear plastic bag with aluminum cans in it. He passed Nancy and made directly for the trash can where he started digging around. While eyes were on Leon heading for the trash can, a blonde woman with a braided ponytail had also entered the circle from the other direction, pushing a baby carriage. The homeless man pulled the Coke can from the trash and placed it in his plastic bag just as the blonde with the baby carriage approached him. She reached in the carriage, pulled out a Glock 9mm, and aimed it at him. "Give me the bag!"

The man sitting on the park bench spoke into his mic and said, "Gun!"

Just then a voice came over the com system saying, "We've spotted Brandon Kulp near the playground. Detain him!"

The homeless man handed the plastic bag to the woman, and she placed it in the baby carriage. The man on the bench, remembering his priorities, had already started running toward the back of the park. Leon, the homeless man, shed his coat and ran also.

Six officers were closing in on Brandon Kulp from all sides. Suddenly, Kulp's head exploded and he crumpled to the ground, followed by the report of a shot. Immediately, guns were drawn, officers crouched, and eyes were scanning in all directions. A.O. was far enough away that the muzzle flash was within his field of vision. It took him a second to swing his rifle in the direction of the shot. It took him another second to identify the sniper and send a bullet at supersonic speed crashing into his head. There was a loud cracking of branches, followed by a thud, as the body of a Russian sniper fell out of a tree.

Sam watched as the blonde woman pushed her baby carriage around the circle in the direction Nancy had gone. Everyone else was focused toward the back of the park where all the commotion had erupted. On a hunch, Sam followed the woman. He took a direct path toward the entrance and reached the street only about twenty feet behind her. Sixty feet ahead of them, a man lunged out from under the trees and placed a chokehold on Nancy. He dragged her into the street as a white van approached. She was kicking and struggling like crazy, but a sliding door opened on the van, and arms grabbed her feet and pulled her in.

"Nancy!" Sam ran toward her at a full sprint.

The blonde woman stopped the carriage and removed the plastic bag of cans. She stepped between parked cars. As the van approached, she tossed the plastic bag into the open door, ready to leap aboard. Sam launched himself at her, flat out horizontal in a flying superman pose. All he could think was, "This is really going to hurt," but he had no choice. His right shoulder slammed into her upper body, lifting her off the ground. Together, they crashed onto the hood of a parked car. Her head hit the windshield, cracking the glass. The driver of the van was spooked and took off down the street.

Sam grabbed the woman by the shoulders and shook her. "Who are you? Where are they taking Nancy? Who do you work for?"

She was semi-conscious and so groggy she was nonresponsive. Officers ran down the sidewalk and pulled Sam off of her, relieving him of his captive.

Director Firestone was in full panic mode. She had received phone updates from the field and was distressed at the news. Gunshots fired in a public domestic venue! Fortunately, none of her officers were hurt — except for Deputy Director Kulp, who was clearly a bad apple. But to make matters worse, a civilian was kidnapped. What a hell of a mess!

She had her assistant put her through on a secure line to Jean-Jacques Pirou, Chief of Station in London, head of operations for the European theater. "JJ, this is a Code 13. I repeat Code 13. I want you to initiate Operation Reboot. I'm giving you worldwide authority. Things are a mess here at headquarters. The company is under attack and I can't be sure who to trust. You are authorized to send a Flash Worldwide Stations and Bases Cable, eyes only, to all CIA personnel immediately, notifying them the agency has been penetrated at a high level. Give instructions to take the appropriate offensive and defensive measures. I want you to initiate extraction protocols in all sensitive locations, secure all data, lockdown safe houses, and implement full safety surveillance. We have a lot of housecleaning to do. I don't know how far the rot has spread. Put together a team and get this done ASAP! Keep me informed, and be cautious with your communications. Am I clear?"

"*Oui madame*, I am on it."

Next, the director held a conference call with her head of security, information management systems, and the head of the FBI Counter Espionage Group. She requested a lockdown of all sensitive data. Anyone accessing the internal system would need two-step authentication, positive location identification, and a record of their activity. Access to sensitive data would require supervisory oversight. This would place tremendous strain on the system and slow work to a crawl, but it was necessary until they could sort out the extent to which the agency was penetrated.

Finally, she started the build-out of a team to investigate in minute detail everything that Brandon Kulp had been doing over the past months. Travel, contacts, computer use, phone calls, cases he worked on… absolutely everything.

This was a friggin' nightmare, and it was only beginning. Who were these people who kidnapped Nancy? What did they expect to get from her? Who was the woman they detained in the park? At least this woman provided an avenue to pursue the people who were after the information from the Brits. And what was that information? What had Sam Barron gotten himself into? It was time she had another talk with Mr. Barron.

CHAPTER 30

After a checkup by the paramedics and a debrief on-site with the FBI and CIA officers, it was four o'clock by the time Sam got back to the cottage. Mentally, he was in total disarray. How was it possible Nancy had been kidnapped? He had assumed once she made the drop, she would be of no more interest to anyone. What did they plan to do to her? How could he have let this happen?

After sitting in a stupor for an indeterminant period of time, mulling over questions that he didn't have answers to, he finally went upstairs and took a shower. The stillness of the house weighed heavily around him, and his heart was broken that Nancy was gone.

He could only hope she was still alive. If they had wanted her dead, they wouldn't have kidnapped her.

As he was drying himself off after his shower, his cell phone rang. It was Angela Firestone. "I need more information from you, and we need to develop a game plan. I'm disappointed, as I'm sure you are, that this did not work out well. I'm sending Bob over to pick you up at eight tomorrow." With that, the line went dead. It was a command performance.

Dr. Higgins shuffled through the front door at six. He had a smile on his face until he saw Sam. No lights had been turned on. Sam was sitting in the evening gloom with a drink in his hand. Dr. Higgins looked around and asked, "Where's Nancy?" He couldn't have picked a worse opening.

Sam stared straight ahead, and silence hung like an evil spirit in the house. Finally, Sam spoke. "Gone. She was kidnapped."

"What?" Dr. Higgins cast himself left and right and didn't know what to do. Finally, he dropped his briefcase and sat down on the sofa. "What can we do?"

Sam shrugged and sat in silence.

Dr. Higgins looked around and fidgeted. Finally, he asked, "Have you called the police?"

"The police can't do anything, and the CIA has its head up its ass. They didn't have control of the environment. There was poor situational awareness. There was poor deployment of resources. There was no contingency planning. They didn't take the task seriously. They screwed up, and Nancy paid the price.

"At least you'll be happy to know the program appears to have been correct. We caught a rat in the trap, Deputy Director Kulp. He's dead, thanks to the agency's incompetence. Now we can't question him and find out who all the players are. They took Nancy, and I have no idea how to begin to locate her."

Dr. Higgins shook his head. "I miss the girl already. She's something special. You didn't get to see her work with me on the program. She was like a fish in water. She's a natural with computers and data manipulation. She makes it look easy. She was a real asset when she was helping me."

"You don't have to convince me she's something special. I can't believe it was so easy for them to take her."

Dr. Higgins wandered into the kitchen and dug around in the fridge for leftovers. With prodding, he convinced Sam to eat something. A pall of gloom hung over the two of them. There was nothing either wished to contribute in terms of a conversation, so they were left to their own thoughts. Eventually, they found it easy to make their excuses and turn in early for the night.

Sam lay in bed thinking about his new dilemma. The group had not reached a consensus about turning the D2 program over to the CIA. Now, with the agency crippled by a traitor, it seemed like a bad idea. On the other hand, working with Angela Firestone was probably Sam's best chance of getting Nancy back — perhaps his only chance. He needed to solicit her full cooperation and the application of all her resources. But how was he going to do that without explaining what had been obtained from Joe Campbell? Sam wasn't feeling generous about trading Nancy's life for the greater good. He missed her warmth. He missed her mischievous hands tracing the contours of his body. He missed her happy snuggles, and the things she did that made him laugh. He was terrified of where she was and what might be happening to her.

At 7:30 the next morning, Sam's phone rang. It was Director Firestone. "Bob won't be coming for you this morning. Things have changed. I received notice from my Russian counterpart via their Washington embassy. He communicated he was upset about the kidnapping of one of his people. He wants her back. He said he also wants the information she was supposed to have. Apparently, they tested the flash drive she threw into the van. Was it blank?"

"What would be the fun in that?" replied Sam. "The flash drive contained a copy of *Doctor Zhivago*. Perhaps you know it was banned in Russia. You may know, the CIA arranged to have 1,000 copies of the book published and distributed at the Vatican pavilion at the 1958 Brussels World's Fair. I thought receipt of the manuscript might confuse them. They might think it's a cipher."

"Jesus Sam! You don't do anything simple, do you? I asked him where the woman was that they grabbed off the street. He said he didn't know anything about that. I told him Russia cannot abduct a US citizen on domestic soil. That's an act of terrorism. I said he'd better find the woman he says he doesn't know about and return her to me, or I'll go public and create an international sensation so big he'll wish he never took the job he has. And there better not be a hair out of place on our missing citizen or there'll be hell to pay. He said he'd look into it. But then he came back to the missing information and acted like it was something they have a right to and we should provide it. Ultimately, he said maybe there is an opportunity to make a trade."

Sam groaned and rubbed his eyes.

"This was just an opening gambit," she assured him. "The Russians never admit to anything. I think we have enough leverage to get Nancy back, but we need to let the pot simmer for a while. Meantime, I have work to do to get my house back in order."

"I'm pissed about this," Sam said. "This is the biggest Charlie Foxtrot I've seen in all my work with the government! If you want any cooperation from me, you better have an ironclad plan to get Nancy back unharmed."

"I understand. I'll be in touch." She hung up. Sam realized it was characteristic of her to be the first one to terminate every call.

Sam went into the kitchen and found Dr. Higgins, who had not left for his office yet. Sam quickly brought the doctor up to speed on the latest developments.

"I'm wondering if we can use the program to help us get Nancy back," Sam said. "Is it possible for you to run several scenarios to give us a look at what the future holds? We're probably only going to get one run at a rescue, and we want to know we're on solid ground with the probabilities in our favor. I'm not sure how you would set it up, but can you play with variables and see what the future might look like?"

"It's a little tricky without concrete specifics for a starting point, but I can make up details and see how they play out." Dr. Higgins nodded. "Yes. I think what you're asking is possible. Let me work on it."

A little after eleven o'clock, Sam received a phone call from an excited Dr. Higgins. "I've been running scenarios as you suggested. I received a very unexpected result. I've tested it several different ways, and I keep getting the same outcome. Sam, you need to get over here right now! Frankly, I'm terrified."

CHAPTER 31

Sam was sitting across from Dr. Higgins in his office with computer printouts on his lap. Sam looked up from the papers toward Dr. Higgins.

"You're telling me the president of the United States is going to be killed? How confident are you of this information?"

Dr. Higgins pointed to the documents. "It's not me. It's the program. You can see it assigns a 100% probability the United States is going to get hit, and a 73% probability the president will die, based on the fact he's scheduled to be in the White House two nights from now."

Sam shuffled through the papers again. "This is unbelievable. The odds of this have to be a billion to one. How is anyone supposed to believe this? A piece of space junk is actually going to land right on top of the White House?"

"It's just physics and math. If you know when a satellite is going to decompose, you can calculate the orbital decay and identify the targeted impact site. That's all the computer is doing."

"Can we have other scientists confirm this? Why hasn't anyone else raised an alarm?"

Dr. Higgins shrugged. "We could try to get confirmation if we knew how to identify the satellite. With a lot of teasing, I was able to extract the information it is a Soviet craft, but I don't know which one. This program has access to vast amounts of data, but I don't get to see where it's all coming from and how it's being used. All I can tell you is the program has been right so far, so I have no reason to doubt it this time."

"Shit!' Sam shoved the papers aside. "This preempts everything. I need to make a call."

Sam grabbed his phone and swiped through his contacts for the director of the CIA. He turned slightly away from Dr. Higgins and spoke into his phone.

"I need to talk to her. Please, tell her something new has come up. It's extremely urgent and can't wait. I need to talk with her now."

The voice on the other end asked him to hold the line. Generic music blared in his ear.

Sam looked at Dr. Higgins. "Sometimes I wish I had an assistant to screen all my calls."

The music cut out. Director Firestone gave a curt, "Yes?"

He turned his attention back to the phone. "Thank you. I know you're busy, but this takes priority over everything. The first time we talked, I told you it was a matter of national security. Well, this time it's even bigger. I have new information that's time-sensitive and critical. I need to meet with you, and I mean now."

Sam could hear the director sigh on the other end of the phone. "As it happens, I am in a meeting across town. I'll come to you. Meet me at 12:30 across from the South Gatehouse at O Street NW and 37th. I assume you're nearby."

"I am."

"This better be worth it. I really didn't need another distraction. It's been a hell of a day so far."

Sam was about to assure her it would be well worth her time, but the line was dead.

At 12:30, a black SUV came down 37th Street, paused for pedestrians coming out through Healy Gates, and turned onto O Street. Sam was waiting on the corner. The back passenger-side window went down and Angela Firestone said, "Get in."

She leaned forward toward Bob, who was driving. "Go forward a block. Find a parking space, then take a walk."

Sam sat in silence while the car moved forward. He thought about making small talk to fill the void, but this was hardly the time to bring up the weather. When Bob got out of the vehicle and the door closed, the director turned to Sam.

She had a pained expression on her face. "What do you have for me this time?"

Any other time, Sam would have been nervous, but he was

consumed with the urgency and seriousness of the situation. "I didn't plan to share with you the information we obtained from Joseph Campbell, not now while there are other issues to be dealt with. But this is too important. I'm going to gloss over the details, but believe me, there is substance in the background to support what I'm telling you.

"Imagine you're planning an operation and you can know ahead of time how it's going to come out. If you don't like the result, you can change your plans to search for the outcome you desire. We can now do that with a computer model. We should have done that for the drop at Montrose Park. It seemed like such a simple plan. It was arrogant of me to think it would all work out fine. If I had run the program, we might have known we were going to have a problem. What I'm telling you is it's possible to see into the future."

Director Firestone took a deep breath. "I'm skeptical. I'm supposed to take this on faith?"

"For now, yes. How do you think I knew where you were going to be so that I could intercept you? How do you think I knew Brandon Kulp was a mole? I don't have time to demonstrate proof. You need to take what I have to say on faith because it's too important not to."

"Okay. Enough drama. Where are you going with this?"

Sam shook his head, troubled by what he was about to say. "The president is going to be killed. It's up to you to save his life."

She frowned at him sternly. "You're going into serious territory. Threats against the president are not dealt with lightly."

"It's not me — it's the program's prediction. Campbell could have told you the same thing."

She nodded thoughtfully. "Go on."

"You know as well as I do the vice president was selected for political reasons to get votes. Whether you like the president or not, the vice president is not up to the job. Even in the best of circumstances, if the president is killed, it exposes the country to temporary chaos and opens up a weakness. I'm giving you the opportunity to prevent a critical threat to our government."

Disbelief took over the director's face. "And when is this supposed to happen?"

"At 7:45 p.m., the day after tomorrow, a piece of Soviet space junk is going to hit the White House. The president is scheduled to be in residence. You need to change that. You need to get him a safe distance away from the White House. You can't tell him how you know this. There are numerous reasons why, but the most immediate reason is because you'll get laughed out of the room. Just as you're questioning me now, your credibility is going to be severely questioned, and you don't want to give them any ammunition to discredit you. You need to convince the president you have intelligence that his life and his family's lives are in imminent danger. Perhaps you can solicit the cooperation of the Secret Service. The bottom line is, if you're wrong, it's only a slight inconvenience. If you're right, you will save the president's life."

"Why are you the only person who has this information? Where are all the astronomers we have in this country?"

Sam opened his hands in an empty gesture. "I don't know. It won't hurt for you to get **NORAD** involved and **NASA** involved and anyone else you can think of, but if you wait for them to come up with confirmation, it may be too late. You need to get things in motion now. I can offer a plan which you might wish to use.

"As you know, the White House was rebuilt after it burned in 1814. It has had many structural changes and modifications since then, more recently by Franklin Roosevelt and Harry Truman. Given its age and complicated structure, it's not surprising rats have been a constant problem throughout its history. You can use the need to exterminate vermin as an excuse to empty out the White House for a day. After all, it isn't just the president who will be killed when something hits the White House. You want to get everyone out. I propose you bring up this subject at the president's daily briefing tomorrow morning, and then keep constant pressure on to be sure your warning is taken seriously."

The director rocked her head. "If there is truly a threat to the president, they'll just whisk him to the PEOC where he'll be safe. When Roosevelt and Truman remodeled the White House, they built a bunker below the east wing. This is where the President's Emergency Operations Center is located."

Sam nodded. "I know about the PEOC, and I also know about the more modern bunker reputedly built under the north lawn after 9/11, which is deeper and more hardened than the PEOC. But that's not the point. When faced with a threat, you don't take half measures. The safest course of action is to remove the president and get him entirely out of reach from the threat."

"You're not making my life easy, Sam Barron. In fact, it has become a living hell ever since you showed up."

Sam shrugged. "Don't kill the messenger. In the long run, I'm actually doing you a favor."

"And this program you have is what the Russians are after? Is it really that good?"

"It appears to be, which is why we don't want them to get it. In fact, I'm not sure anyone should have it. When you start thinking through the possibilities and the implications, it's downright scary what a tool like this could be used for in the wrong hands. That's why I'm begging you not to reveal to the president, or anyone else, the source of your information. You absolutely need to convince the president to clear the White House, but you cannot tell him why. There's a 73% chance he'll die the day after tomorrow if he doesn't listen to you. You need to be convincing."

"I hear you," said the director. "I guess I have my work cut out for me. When you get out, see if you can flag down Bob and tell him I'm ready to go."

Sam nodded. "Please keep me informed on any new developments regarding Nancy. She's my priority."

As Sam got out of the car, the director assured him she would stay in touch. Bob was lingering across the street. Sam waved to him, then headed back onto the Georgetown campus.

Director Firestone considered requesting an emergency meeting with the president. She could go to the White House with sirens blaring and make a personal presentation to the president. Although rare, it was not unheard of. The drama would certainly emphasize the importance of her message, but it might be too much and turn out to backfire. Also, the president had a public event scheduled, and she wanted to avoid any possibility of the media getting hold of the story. Taking a little extra time to get all her ducks in a row to make a solid presentation was worth the wait.

When the director arrived back at headquarters, she wrote a memo for the team that put together the president's daily briefing. She had thought about the problem on the drive back and decided it was wrong to explain the threat to the president as originating from space. The CIA had no connection to space, other than analyzing data from spy satellites. It would be too easy for her warning to be discredited if she could not provide specific scientific data. Intelligence-gathering was the mandate for the CIA. The keyword to use should be "attack". The president would be advised the White House would come under attack during the following evening. This information was obtained from a credible intelligence source and there was every reason to believe it was true. Unfortunately, the nature of the attack was uncertain. Therefore, it would be difficult to mount a robust defense that had any assurance of success. The path of least resistance was to empty the White House, leaving only essential personnel stationed safely in the bunker. This was a story she could sell, and it would be hard for anyone to push back by asking for specifics.

Item number two on the daily briefing would be intelligence gathered from a Soviet source. A Russian satellite was suffering orbital decay. Rumor had it the debris would be sufficiently dense to reach the earth's surface without burning up in the atmosphere. There was apparently a reasonable probability that the debris would hit the United States. The recommendation to the president was to deploy appropriate resources to verify this information and consider any remedial intervention possible.

The director looked at what she had written and was satisfied that by breaking one event into two events, she had increased the odds of accomplishing her objective. The briefing team would gather at 4 a.m. to put the book together from source information collected all over the world and carefully filtered and vetted. Tomorrow, these two items would be the headlines. Since the Obama administration, the book had been available to the president electronically, but Director Firestone put in a request that this briefing be delivered to the president in person. She didn't go so far as to say "For the president's eyes only," but she did want to emphasize the importance of this briefing. That meant in the early morning hours, a caravan would be assembled outside the headquarters at Langley. There would be a police escort to the White House where the PDB would be delivered by a CIA employee who could provide interpretation and answer questions. Director Firestone could go along and deliver the briefing in person, but that would be irregular and seemed unnecessary. She would rather save her firepower for later on if any resistance arose.

The following morning, Director Firestone sat at her desk with a case of the jitters. How trustworthy was Sam Barron's information? It was her neck on the line. She was placing a lot of faith in something she had no experience with and no reason to trust. She could have simply ignored the information and done nothing. If something bad happened, there was nothing to connect her to it. She could have skated past this and not looked back. But she wasn't built that way. She hadn't obtained her position by playing it safe. She had always done the right thing. She had always followed the moral imperative.

She picked up the phone and called the director of the Secret Service. She put an ingratiating smile on her face as she addressed him, hoping it could be heard through the phone. "Peter, I want to give you a heads up on an important item. To-day, in the daily briefing, the president was advised that there'll be an attack on the White House tomorrow evening. I want to give you a jump on this so you can start planning now. Don't wait until he comes to you, and don't let him brush it off. This is a simple, straightforward decision. If he stays at the White House, there's a high probability he will die. The path of least resistance is to remove him from the area. I'm not telling you where to take him. I'm not telling you how to do your job. I'm just telling you to get him away from the White House."

"Roger. I understand."

"While you remove him and his family, you should remove everyone else. Anybody who stays in that building is standing into danger. I'm advising you of a clear and present threat and giving you the opportunity to save lives. I suggest you increase your perimeter defenses and push your perimeter out as far as you can. I realize the White House is a national treasure and we naturally want to protect it, but I can't tell you how to do that. I can tell you that you'll save lives by emptying it.

"A suggestion for you to consider is to bring in an exterminating company between three and five tomorrow afternoon. Everyone needs to be out due to the potential for harmful vapors. The exterminators need to leave between five and six. The building needs to stay empty until nine o'clock. If you get ahead of the curve with a plan like this, you may be saving a lot of lives, and it won't seem like the president is being scared out of his house. It'll appear to be a coincidence that he doesn't happen to be there."

There was a long pause at the other end of the line. "I'd already heard there was something like this in the daily briefing. I was waiting for more details."

"There probably aren't going to be any more details. If nothing happens, you're probably going to have inconvenienced and pissed-off people, but that's all. If something does happen, you'll be damn glad you cleared the area. There's nothing more I can tell you, except you need to take this seriously."

"Okay, I got the message."

"Thank you, Peter." Angela Firestone sat back in her chair. The psychic energy this was taking was exhausting. Getting through the next thirty-six hours was going to be hard.

Later the same morning, a little past nine, Angela's assistant buzzed her. "The White House Chief of Staff, Geoffrey Hines is on the line for you."

"Thanks, put him through"

"Angela, what is this nonsense about emptying the White House?"

Angela grimaced. "Hello, Geoffrey. Nice to hear from you. Do you like your president? Do you want to keep him alive? Look at the people around you. Now picture them all as dead bodies on the floor. Do you want to repeat your question again?"

"That's a little over the top. You can't just snap your fingers and expect the machinery of government to come to a halt."

"Let me put it this way, Geoffrey. You're being warned of a mortal threat. To ignore it smacks of gross negligence. I might even go so far as to say treasonous. Certainly, White House employees can step away from their desks for a few hours if it means saving lives. We don't pass on warnings for no reason at all. The default position is to save the president's life at all costs. Are you seriously going to try to stand in the way of that?"

"Well, when you put it that way, I guess it doesn't hurt to give everyone a few hours off."

"Thanks for your understanding, Geoffrey. Have a nice day."

Angela Firestone hung up. "What a horse's ass! What did he think that call was going to accomplish? It's hard to fathom how some people rise to amazing levels of incompetence."

Sam went along with Dr. Higgins to his office. The two of them had decided over breakfast to enlist the help of the D2 program to try to sort out the problems they were facing. Although Sam brought his laptop with him, unlike Nancy, he didn't know anything about running the program. He focused on trying to structure the questions to give them meaningful results. Dr. Higgins was in charge of actually running the program.

They tried asking for a look at the future if the president were at a location other than the White House on the following day. The answer was he would remain alive and the world seemed to be largely unchanged. Considering the death of Brandon Kulp, they asked if Angela Firestone would keep her job. The answer was yes, she would. They probed with other questions about the CIA to try to determine the extent of the damage done by Brandon Kulp. The answers were much more ambiguous, because the program was not penetrating the firewalls of the agency. It was hard to determine what was considered normal, but they got a general sense that any damage from Kulp was limited in scope and not degrading the ability of the agency to operate effectively. If anything, the CIA's performance should be improved with him gone.

The most frustrating effort was trying to find out about Nancy. The program had no current information on her location or status. Sam and Dr. Higgins were having trouble coming up with any scenario that could produce a useful outcome from the program. Without knowing the individuals who held her and their ultimate intentions, it was impossible to get anything meaningful from the program. After hours of effort, Sam finally threw in the towel. He told Dr. Higgins he was going to walk back to the house and try to clear his head. Maybe stepping away from things for a while would give him a fresh perspective.

Sam was deep in thought as he walked down the street toward the cottage. He was on the other side of the street as he approached the house, and he looked up for traffic as he crossed in a diagonal toward the front steps. As he looked ahead, he noticed the front door was ajar. A motion caught his eye, like a shadow passing behind the lace curtains on the second floor.

As Sam reached the sidewalk, a man came around from the back of the house, walking down the driveway past Sam's rental car. He appeared to recognize Sam at the same time Sam saw him. The man sprinted full speed toward Sam. Sam had to make a split-second decision. He stood his ground. He put his left foot forward and raised his left arm in a blocking position. His right hand was cocked back to his armpit in a fighter's stance. The man charging at Sam was drawing his right arm back, making it clear he was going to lunge at Sam with a hard right. At the last minute, Sam dropped his left hand, pivoted ninety degrees to the left, and raised his right knee-high to his chest. He thrust out with a side kick that landed squarely in the attacker's solar plexus. The kick gave Sam more than a six-inch advantage to land the first blow. The breath exploded out of the attacker, and he doubled over in pain. His head was down, but tilted to look at Sam. Sam's right fist came down with a hammer blow on the man's neck behind his ear where there's a collection of nerves. The attacker collapsed to the ground.

Sam wasn't going to wait for others to come out the front door. He took off down the street as fast as he could run. As soon as he was out of eyesight from the house, he slowed down to a sustainable jog but kept running.

Sam burst into Healy Hall and ran down the corridor without waiting for an escort. When he came to Dr. Higgins' office, he threw open the door and yelled at the doctor.

"Grab your computer and any papers and flash drives that have to do with the D2 program. They found us! We have to leave."

"What do you mean?"

"There are men in your house. It's only a matter of time before they find your office. Grab your stuff. We have to go."

Dr. Higgins shoved things into his briefcase while Sam snatched up his own computer, and they headed for the door.

"Is there a back exit?" Sam asked.

"Yes. This way. Follow me." Dr. Higgins trotted down the hallway.

After they exited the building, they kept walking past the business school and Regents Hall. They passed up the congested restaurants in Leavey Center and continued until they came to a Starbucks Coffee. They camped in the back of the coffee shop where they had a clear view of anyone coming. Sam pulled out his phone and speed-dialed Director Firestone.

"They found us!" Sam paused to let that sink in. "I encountered men in Dr. Higgins' house, so I grabbed him at his office and we took off. I don't know how they found us. Perhaps they made Nancy talk. There's no way of knowing how much information they have, but clearly, we're compromised. I'm at loose ends now and could use your help."

Her answer was reassuring. "I'm on it. We'll send a team to the house in case they're still there. Are you somewhere safe?"

"I think we're okay for a while. We're at a Starbucks near Shaw Field at Georgetown University."

"Stay there. I'm sending Bob to get you. It might take him as much as forty-five minutes to get there, so sit tight." The call ended.

Sam looked at Dr. Higgins with an apologetic expression. "I'm sorry about all this. We might as well get food while we wait for help."

Wherever Bob was coming from, he managed to get there in less than thirty minutes. When a black Tahoe with government plates paused in front of the Starbucks, Sam motioned to Dr. Higgins and headed for the door. Bob pulled away from the curb as soon as they were in the vehicle, checking his mirrors carefully to be sure they weren't followed. Once they were a few blocks away, he glanced in his rearview mirror at his passengers.

"I've been instructed to take you to a safe house. We have an apartment in Tysons Corner that should suit you. You're essentially going to be in lockdown, so you might need a few things. There's a pad of paper in the side pocket. Write down anything you have an immediate need for and I'll shop for you after I drop you off. Please be sure to give me clothing sizes. Food is being provided. You'll have to cook for yourselves. No ordering out. Stay away from the windows and keep the curtains closed.

"There's an apartment adjacent to the one you'll be in that will have officers rotating through it twenty-four hours a day. Yes, they're babysitting you, but they've been instructed to leave you alone. They're simply there if you need anything.

"Now, we have one quick stop to make. You can let your visitor into the vehicle with you."

Bob pulled off the road and parked in front of a nondescript storefront in a strip mall. Within seconds, a man came out and tapped on the back passenger-side window. Sam opened the car door and the man stepped in. Without introduction, he handed Sam a large phone pouch.

"Turn off all cell phones and place them in here. Don't use your phones. Your life and the lives of the people around you depend on it." He held out a simple phone for Sam to take. "This phone isn't connected to the internet and has no GPS. Even so, save it to use only in emergencies. There's a landline at the apartment that you can use. Obviously, don't say anything that will give away your location. Now, let me see all your other electronic devices."

Sam handed over his laptop and Dr. Higgins did the same. "That's all there is," Sam said. "We left in a hurry."

The man talked while he typed furiously on one of the laptop keyboards. "I'm removing all identifiers from your computers. I'm giving you a new Microsoft account that can't be traced. I'm deactivating all geolocation in your apps and your operating system. I want you to use the ethernet cable at the apartment to connect to the internet. Your IP address will automatically be disguised. Keep a low profile online. Stay off social media. Use your computer for the minimum work you need to do. Got it?"

Sam and Dr. Higgins nodded. "Got it," said Sam.

The man handed all of the equipment back and stepped out of the vehicle. Bob put it in reverse, backed out of the parking space, and got on the road again.

Once Sam and Dr. Higgins arrived at the apartment, they set up housekeeping as best they could. Bob gave the shopping assignment to one of the officers next door. Two hours later, there was a knock on the door and a female officer handed Sam two bags with a change of clothes, toothbrushes, and grooming supplies, along with various other sundries.

Sam smiled politely. She was a young fresh face in her middle twenties. "Just in time for dinner." He looked hopeful. "Do you cook?"

"Sorry. You're on your own with that. If dinner doesn't work out, there's always cheese and crackers to go with the wine." She gave him a big smile and headed back down the hall.

An hour later, the phone hanging on the wall in the kitchen rang. Sam gave a surprised look to Dr. Higgins. "Do we answer it?"

Dr. Higgins shrugged. "Unless it's a junk call, it must be for us."

Sam picked up the phone. "Hello?"

Angela Firestone was on the other end. "I wanted to check in and make sure everything was alright."

"Everything is fine so far."

"Good. Do you still have control of the information we talked about?"

"You mean the program?" Sam pressed his lips together, looking at Dr. Higgins. "Yes. It's with us. I don't think anything at the house would be useful to anyone. We have to assume they checked Dr. Higgins' office also, but he says he didn't leave anything of value."

"I'm worried about Nancy. I'm guessing they forced the information about Dr. Higgins from her. She can play dumb about the program up to a point, but there's a risk that she'll reveal its capabilities."

"I think we can assume they already knew about its capabilities. Why else would they be working so hard to obtain it?" Angela paused. "We haven't made any progress with the woman we detained. We don't even have a definitive ID yet.

She supplied her name, but we can't verify anything. She says she was simply told her job was to obtain the Coke can. She doesn't know anything more." She paused again. "I've been contacted again, and the Russians now admit that they have Nancy. They claim it was a mix-up and she wasn't supposed to be taken, thus the confusion. It was phrased as a happy accident, because now they have something to trade. They're proposing a swap."

"What are we swapping for? I want Nancy back, but we still need to talk about the fate of the program. We can't let the Russians have it."

"I know, but my attention is being diverted with this business about the president. I can't believe the pushback. Something about the way our government works; if you say up, someone is always going to say down — even if it makes no sense. I don't have confirmation yet the president is going to be relocated. I'm trying to stall the Russians until we get past tomorrow. I raised the possibility that they're intentionally throwing their space junk at us. I pointed out this is going to be a public relations fiasco for them. I said we need to address this problem first. Meanwhile, they better be treating Nancy well. I received the typical Russian response. They would neither confirm nor deny."

"Well, I can tell you we ran the D2 program with the premise that the president is absent from the White House. The good news is relocating the president seems to solve the problem. If you can get that accomplished, it appears life will go on without a hiccup."

Angela sounded frustrated. "All I can say is, this program better be right. If something doesn't fall out of the sky tomorrow, I'll have egg on my face, and I'll be tempted to give the program to the Russians with my blessing!"

"Well, we'll know soon enough," Sam mumbled.

"Have a good night, Sam. I need to get back with the director of the Secret Service and make sure he lights a fire under the president's ass. I believe there's precedent for overruling the president when his safety is at stake. One way or another, we're going to pry him out of that house." Once again, she hung up on him, but that was fine. Sam didn't know what else he could say. Tomorrow would determine the fate of the nation.

CHAPTER 32

Sam did not sleep well in an unfamiliar bed. He missed Nancy. He kept thinking about how he was going to get her back, and what was going to happen at the White House. While he was making his morning coffee, he heard a thud at the front door. He looked carefully through the peephole and saw nobody there. Cautiously, he opened the door and stuck his head out. The hallway was empty. When he looked down, he saw a newspaper. Apparently, their temporary incarceration included receiving the daily paper. He brought it inside and closed and locked the door.

When he unfolded the paper, the headline was stark.

KILLER SPACE JUNK TARGETING CAPITAL

Sam stood in the front entry and read the article below the headline.

Scientists at the University of Arizona, working at the Mount Graham International Observatory, have discovered that a satellite, believed to be Soviet, is crashing toward the earth. Density calculations suggest it will penetrate the earth's atmosphere and reach the surface. This observation has since been verified by the astronomers at Caltech's Palomar Observatory and the US Naval Academy Observatory, working with the Department of Defense.

The target zone of impact is the Washington DC metropolitan area, including the federal district and parts of Maryland, Virginia, and West Virginia. Attempts to reconstruct the original orbit and determine the rate of orbital decay are ongoing. Without more accurate data, potentially millions of people are at risk.

An interview with Dr. Alexander Shaw, a highly regarded astrophysicist at the University of Arizona, has produced a dire warning. "When the debris enters the earth's atmosphere and starts to burn up, there will be a brilliant fiery trail through the sky. People are warned not to stay outside and watch. Everybody should be seeking safe shelter. When the debris hits the earth, it may be catastrophic for anyone outdoors. Depending on the angle of impact and what is hit, stone and shrapnel can be blasted for miles around. People should shelter down low behind the most solid structures they can find. Stay away from windows, and stay away from objects that could fall on you." The exact area of impact is not known, and everyone in the Mid-Atlantic area should take precautions.

Sam found Dr. Higgins sitting in front of the TV watching news reports on the impending disaster. Regular programming was preempted by an ongoing series of interviews with "experts" speculating on the expected damage. Roads were clogged with traffic from people evacuating the area. Gas stations were running out of gas. Even grocery stores were being emptied by terrified shoppers who felt the need to hoard. They had a day of chaos ahead of them.

"At least it looks like the D2 program is working correctly. Director Firestone told me last night she was going to be pissed if we were wrong about this."

Dr. Higgins turned to Sam. "Well, that's the good news and the bad news all together. The program may be right, but it's going to be a hell of a mess when this thing hits. Any word on the president? Are they moving him?"

"I don't know for sure. Apparently, they were still arguing over it last night. This should push the issue now that he has a verified reason to get out of the Capital."

The director of the Secret Service went from being busy to having his plate overloaded. He could not delegate fast enough. The potential for a strike by debris from space gave him the perfect cover to prepare for an attack on the White House. He convinced the mayor of Washington, DC to issue a curfew for the city starting at 6 pm. He requested extra resources from the national guard to "protect government assets". He arranged for Pennsylvania Avenue to be closed. A perimeter of marines assigned to the White House would be stationed along 15th St NW and 17th St NW and all the way up to H St to the north.

Reserves would be stationed in Lafayette Square across from the White House. Armored vehicles were being staged in the parking lot behind the Eisenhower Executive Office Building. Additional troops would also be stationed beyond the South Lawn. Increased security was being enforced throughout the day, with everybody coming and going being placed under extra scrutiny. White House tours were canceled for the day. Sources were being queried, but he still had no idea what kind of an attack to expect. All of this preparation was being done based on the warning from the CIA. He hoped they had reliable intel. On the other hand, he would be fine with not having to defend an attack on the White House grounds. Once the shooting started, you could never be sure of the outcome.

The kitchen wall phone rang again in the early afternoon. Sam jumped at the sound of the bell. First of all, he wasn't used to having a landline. Second, it was creepy to be in hiding in a safe house and have the phone ring. Nobody was supposed to know they were there. Of course, when he picked up the phone, it was Director Firestone.

"I'm becoming a believer. We now have confirmation from multiple sources that you're right, Sam. The probable impact zone has been narrowed down to the federal district, but nobody is willing to publicly make that kind of a commitment to accuracy.

"I'm told the president was moved to Camp David at noon.

There was a comment about the irony of moving him to avoid an attack only to have him get hit by falling debris, but Camp David is far enough away from the impact zone to erase any cause for concern. Plus, I'm sure they'll put him in a bunker at Camp David.

"So far, nobody has drawn a connection between the warning of an attack on the White House and the threat of getting hit with space debris. It served my purpose to use the word 'attack' because national defense and the president's security team understand the threat of bombs and bullets, and that is the conclusion they jump to when you use the word attack. The average human brain doesn't know how to calculate abstract risk. I didn't want some expert with a slide rule playing mathematical games with the probability of getting hit by space junk. The president has been moved, and it doesn't matter the reason why. If I get called on it, I'm perfectly comfortable saying a falling Soviet satellite is a form of attack."

"Sounds good to me," Sam said. "I'm eager to move on to our next problem. I'm desperate to rescue Nancy. An exchange might be a viable solution, but we need to discuss the details of how this could work."

"I agree we need to move forward. Let's tentatively plan to meet tomorrow, but I need to see how things go for the rest of the day and get through tonight first. I understand the Russian ambassador has been called in to explain how this space disaster could have happened and why we were not given sufficient prior notice. I really hope they hold his feet to the fire, but I'm not sure that's going to have any effect on our kidnap situation."

Sam spoke up hopefully. "We can threaten them with more bad publicity, but I'm not sure how far that would get us."

"I'm not sure either." Angela sighed. "Think about it overnight and we'll talk tomorrow." Once again, the line went dead abruptly.

Judging from the reports on TV, the frenzy continued to mount all afternoon. Thousands of people in the metropolitan area decided the best option was to get out of Dodge. The freeways which under the best of circumstances operated at a crawl were parking lots. Nobody was going much of anywhere. Other people decided any catastrophe was a good excuse to riot and break into stores. In the less desirable areas of town, looters were rolling shopping carts down the street full of merchandise. The more sensible but least visible people were hunkering down in a safe place hoping they were not in the path of the destruction. The police were overwhelmed. There was a game plan for most disasters, but falling space junk wasn't in the playbook. Instead of being proactive, law enforcement was reduced to being reactive. There was a scattered and disjointed response to 911 calls. In many cases, police forces were held at their stations while their superiors waited to see what the real fallout was going to be and discussed how they should deal with the situation.

At least the White House had a plan, and the director of the Secret Service was working the plan. Employees filed out of the building between two and three o'clock. An exterminating service, which had already been scheduled before knowledge of the falling satellite was public, showed up and actually got to work with liquids and gas designed to get rid of the cockroaches, mice, and rats that frequented the president's house. A few of the White House staff stayed on to supervise the exterminators and make sure none of the furnishings, art, and antiquities were damaged. Everyone was under strict instruction to wrap things up at five o'clock and be out of the building no later than six. By six-fifteen, other than marines and secret service agents on the roof and a skeleton staff in the bunker, the White House was completely empty. A squad of agents performed a final sweep of the building to make sure it was locked down.

Sam and Dr. Higgins could do nothing except wait. The big decision was, did they want to eat dinner before the predicted impact or wait until after? They settled on a compromise of having a beer and a bunch of munchies. Fortunately, their kitchen was stocked with Doritos, pretzels, nuts, Ritz crackers, cheddar cheese, and even Goldfish. For the simple needs of two guys in a bachelor pad, whoever had done the shopping had a discerning taste. The TV was on at a low volume in the background while the two of them talked. They hadn't had the opportunity to truly get to know one another. There had always been pressing business at hand. When Nancy was around, Sam's attention was directed toward her, and Dr. Higgins had been the odd man out. They both missed Nancy terribly, but now a comradery grew between the two of them that hadn't been there before.

They were excited the D2 program was proving its worth by saving the life of the president and, hopefully, many other lives. They speculated how it might be possible to define the conditions under which the program could be used constructively rather than as a weapon. They always ran into the dilemma of how to deal with collateral damage when the future was changed. It was quite possible changing the future for a theoretically good reason might mean someone wasn't born who might otherwise have been a huge benefit to mankind. It was also quite possible an innocent person could be killed because a change caused them to be in the wrong place at the wrong time. Of course, all sorts of lesser events would change also. Who was to say one version of the future was better than another? Sam drew an analogy with permitting a free market to exist unfettered versus empowering a government, a king, or party of elites to control an economy. Could one trust a dynamic complex system to always find an equilibrium? Or could systems become so dislocated, unbalanced, or fragile they need to be coaxed in a direction they might not take on their own? There was something comforting to leaving things alone. Otherwise, one had to answer the question of who was wise enough to know which, among an infinite number of choices, was the best path to take?

At least the two of them could agree that, in this instance, they were both comfortable with saving the president's life. They might be setting in motion unseen forces that could prove disastrous down the road, but based on all the information they had on hand, this seemed like the best decision.

James Patterson, otherwise known as "Jimmy," was a member of the Metropolitan Police Department, the law enforcement agency for the District of Columbia. Jimmy was called in on his day off to help with traffic management. He would have grumbled more, except he was stationed on Pennsylvania Avenue in front of the White House. At least this location was more interesting than the typical inner-city assignment. Jimmy was only twenty-five years old and had been a cop for three years. When he kissed his wife goodbye and headed in for work in the morning, he didn't realize what a strange day it was going to be. Being a lower-level member of the force, he wasn't privileged to see the big picture. He didn't know all the reasons why Pennsylvania Avenue was being shut down, but no question something special was going on. He was aware of the possibility of debris falling from space, but that didn't seem to warrant all the preparations being made around the White House. A half-dozen police from his unit were spaced down the avenue. This seemed redundant, because the street was blocked at each end. In front of him, in Lafayette Square, stood an assembly of national guardsmen fully geared up. He had seen the armored vehicles going past the Eisenhower Building as well as being stationed at key intersections. Something didn't feel right, but his job was to simply follow orders. As the late afternoon dragged into early evening, things grew awfully quiet. He wasn't close enough to anyone to be able to talk, and chitchat on the radio was prohibited. He had spent most of the day on his feet, and by evening, the assignment was getting tedious. His back was sore, and he was hungry. He had to stay until nine, so the evening was going to be a long one. The only consolation was the overtime he was racking up.

At twenty minutes past seven, Dr. Higgins turned to Sam. "Are we really just going to sit here? Do you want to miss out on the biggest event of the decade?"

"What do you have in mind?"

"There's an open-air rooftop lounge. The stairs at the end of the hall will take us there."

Sam rolled his eyes. "Seriously?"

Dr. Higgins shrugged. "Why not? We know the impact is going to be on the White House. We're far enough away it won't be a problem for us. Don't you want to see the light show?"

Sam sighed. "Well, I guess so. It beats sitting around here waiting like two mushrooms in the dark."

Dr. Higgins turned off the TV. Sam grabbed a bag of Doritos, and they headed topside.

Jimmy noticed a murmur among the people around him. Fingers were pointing toward the sky. He turned and looked where they were pointing. A brilliant spec of light twinkled way off in the distance. As he watched, it grew bigger and brighter. He took a quick look up and down the street. All eyes were aimed at the sky. He looked back and was surprised at how much the object had grown. It was obviously moving very fast. Smaller pieces broke away and created little streamers alongside the central fireball. His scalp prickled as he judged it was coming right at him. He unconsciously stepped backward, increasingly nervous. Convinced he was directly in the path, the "Oh, shit!" moment arrived. He turned and ran north as fast as he could.

Sam and Dr. Higgins were scanning the sky from their rooftop position, but they weren't sure exactly where to look. Eventually, Dr. Higgins pointed up at about a seventy-five-degree angle. A bright object stood out clearly against the twilight sky. They watched it get larger and brighter, but it was hard to determine its angle of descent. It was mesmerizing to see it grow. Its brilliance was dazzling, and it left a glowing smokey trail behind. As it got closer, Sam swallowed hard, convinced it was coming right at them. In a peculiar optical effect, his eyes were having trouble interpreting its angle of descent while registering its growing nearness from increasing size and brightness. In a split second, it dropped straight down behind the trees and buildings in front of them.

Dr. Higgins grabbed Sam's arm. "We need to go. Quick!" They ran for the stairwell enclosed in concrete block.

Everything happened so fast. Jimmy barely had time to get to Lafayette Square Park. The remains of the Soviet satellite came down to earth with an incredibly loud shrieking sound. The ground shook with an explosive concussion as the debris wiped out the visitor's entrance at the White House and blew a giant crater into 15th Street. The explosion was followed immediately by a sonic boom. As Jimmy ran, a rush of hot air lifted him up and threw him forward another ten feet. He landed face down on the grass and was immediately showered by a blizzard of twigs and leaves blown out of the trees around him. He screamed, sure he was in the middle of Armageddon.

As Sam and Dr. Higgins ran into the stairwell with the steel door closing behind them, the concussion of a sonic boom echoed in the concrete shaft, the shockwave shaking the building.

"Best we got inside, I think," said Dr. Higgins.

"I believe so." Sam chuckled, shakily. "I would've felt stupid if we got blown off the roof — although, I think that was unlikely."

As they made their way back down the hallway to their apartment, a matronly female officer stood outside their door waiting for them, arms crossed.

"Where have you two characters been?"

Sam looked sheepish. "We figured nobody would be chasing us while the sky was falling. It was quite a sight. Worth seeing."

"I'm sure it was." She pointed to their door. "But you aren't to leave your apartment. You get me in trouble when you do that."

"Sorry," Sam said. "This was a one-off event. Won't happen again."

The two men gingerly walked past her and reentered their apartment. Dr. Higgins flipped on the TV. Like vultures circling a fresh kill, news reporters had already gathered at the scene of destruction next to the White House. The cameramen could not get too close, and news copters were not allowed into the no-fly zone, so the video did not show much, but the verbal description explained the extent of the damage.

The greatest harm to the White House was at the Visitors Foyer in the East Wing. The east side of the wing was torn off and a giant crater was now all that was left of what had been a parking area along E Executive Ave NW. Tons of stone, dirt, and pavement had been blasted from the ground and thrown toward the Treasury building to the east of the White House. The west side of the Treasury building could only be described as a shambles. By comparison, the White House had survived with relatively little structural damage. However, small pieces of high-velocity debris had taken a toll. The White House looked like it had been raked by a 50 caliber machine gun. How far the projectiles had penetrated, and the extent of the damage on the inside was still unknown.

Three marines were missing and presumed dead. Over a dozen marines and law enforcement officers were injured.

Undoubtedly there were civilian casualties, but it was too early to have any numbers. Potentially, the destruction to the east wing meant access to the PEOC was damaged. Anyone in the bunker might be trapped. But that wasn't the kind of news that would be released early on. When viewing the extent of the destruction, it was something of a miracle more people weren't hurt or killed. According to the reporters, it was a fortunate coincidence the White House had been evacuated for a pest control treatment.

The news reporters had already managed to corral key politicians with discussions about making Russia pay reparations for all the damage. At the prompting of the reporters, the conversation was widening into a demand for a proposal to be brought to the United Nations requiring every country to be accountable for the equipment they had in space. Sam could sense the animosity toward Russia for its role in this catastrophe was only in its early stages. The media had hit on a hot topic, and they were going to push it as far as they could.

Sam smiled at Dr. Higgins. "All in all, I'd call our efforts a success. We saved the president, and probably a lot of other lives. I don't think we could have done much better."

"Using this program to change the future makes me nervous, but I have to agree with you." Dr. Higgins nodded in affirmation. "This time I think we did the right thing."

Once again, they both flinched when the phone rang. Thermopylae Higgins looked at Sam. "I'm not going to bother. The call is undoubtedly for you."

Sam walked to the kitchen and answered the phone. He fully expected it to be Director Firestone. He was surprised to hear a different woman's voice.

"Mr. Barron?"

"Yes."

"I'm the assistant to the director. I'm to let you know that Bob will be around to pick you up at eight tomorrow morning. The director sends her apologies to Dr. Higgins. She trusts he can amuse himself for the morning. I remind you to bring your photo ID, and don't bring any electronic devices."

"I understand," replied Sam.

"Thank you. I'll tell the director to expect you. Have a good evening." The line went dead.

Sam turned toward Dr. Higgins who had a questioning expression on his face. "Apparently, you're going to get the morning off tomorrow. I've been summoned, presumably to put a plan together to get Nancy back. Do you have any opinion?"

Dr. Higgins looked off to his left for a moment, then back at Sam. "You tell me the plan, and I'll give you my opinion. Otherwise, no. I don't know where to begin. Rescue plans aren't my area of expertise."

"Very well. We'll have to puzzle over it." Sam moved toward the kitchen. "How about a drink and some dinner while we talk?"

"That sounds like a good plan."

During and after dinner, Sam couldn't help himself from thinking out loud about how to free Nancy. Dr. Higgins was a captive, but a willing listener.

"I'm trying to make lemon meringue pie out of the lemons we've been given." Sam's eyes glazed over as he focused inward on the challenge they faced. "It seems we have a minimum of three or four problems. We wanted to be careful about who ended up with the D2 program, and we wanted to restrict how it was used. Now, unfortunately, the CIA knows not only of its existence, but of its capabilities. Actually, it isn't the CIA. It's just Angela Firestone as far as we know. But the Russians definitely think we have something of value. We need to permanently get them off the scent. Most of all, we need to get Nancy released. Somehow, we need to fit the pieces of this puzzle together to find a master solution that takes care of everything."

"Good luck with that." Dr. Higgins shook his head. He might not have been in complete despair, but he held an air of skepticism. "The Russian problem and getting Nancy back are related. You might find a joint solution there."

Sam looked up at him. "The director was talking about an exchange. But she didn't say what she was thinking about exchanging."

Sam drummed his fingers on the table. "I'm impressed at how well the D2 program works. So impressed, it scares me to lose control of it. However, I don't know how we're going to get Nancy back if we don't do a swap with the Russians. They know they have the leverage. We care more about Nancy than they do about their agent. They're demanding we hand over the program.

"So my question to you is, can we tamper with the program so they think they're getting something of value, but in the end, they're receiving junk?"

"Tentatively yes." Dr. Higgins laced his fingers and leaned back, his speech sliding into professorial mode. "If you want to tamper with the D2 program, you have to first understand what makes this program so special. I'll try to make this as simple as I can. When most people think of predicting the future, they think of a chain of cause and effect. As you know, the typical model for cause and effect is a ball traveling across a pool table and hitting another ball. The collision sets the second ball in motion. This model is only partly correct because it assumes the ball travels in a constant direction and at a constant speed. If you remember, we call this the D2 program because D2 is shorthand for the second derivative. The second derivative is a change to the rate of change.

"Let me give you a real-world example. We teach our children the earth circles the sun, but that isn't entirely accurate. The earth's orbit is not a circle. It's an ellipse. An ellipse is a stretched circle. The sun isn't in the middle of the stretched circle, or in the middle of the earth's orbit. Whereas a circle has one center, called the focal point, an ellipse is constructed with two focal points. Since the sun isn't in the middle, it's closer to one edge of the ellipse than the other. In order for the earth to stay in orbit, the force of gravity pulling the earth toward the sun has to be in perfect opposition to the inertia that wants to make the earth continue to shoot out in a straight line away from the sun. The tug of the sun's gravity is what creates the curve in the earth's orbit. When the earth travels closest to the sun, it is at the perihelion, and the earth changes from going toward the sun to orbiting around and going away from the sun. Most people don't realize the perihelion is reached during winter in the northern hemisphere. At the perihelion, since the earth is closer to the sun, gravity is stronger, so the earth has to move faster along its orbit for forces to stay in balance. This means it travels a greater distance along the line of its orbit in a given amount of time. The earth is farthest away from the sun at the aphelion, where it travels slower to keep the forces in balance. It was a big step forward for mankind when we learned that the heavens are not perfect and the planets do not orbit in circles. My point is the earth is always speeding up and slowing down along its orbit. If you want to calculate the distance the earth is going to travel through space during a given period of time, it's not a linear speed-times-time problem. You must know the earth's position in its orbit relative to the sun. And you must calculate the acceleration or deceleration. Another way to do the same thing is to use geometry with Kepler's laws of planetary motion. This is a simple example that shows our world doesn't operate in a linear fashion."

Sam leaned forward. "I think you're telling me that accurate prediction depends on a complicated calculation for the relative vector and intersection of every event."

"You're right. To expand the discussion of the second derivative, let's talk about Ms. Jones driving down the street on her commute to work. The speed limit is 30 mph, but she won't drive an exact thirty. Her speed will naturally oscillate around thirty. If we want to know what time she will arrive at work, we might think it's a simple time and distance problem using her average speed. We would be wrong. If there are a bunch of stoplights along the way, Ms. Jones will be slowing down to a stop and speeding up again. If there are pedestrians crossing the street, other cars slowing and turning, construction, etc., there'll be more decelerating and accelerating. All of this needs to be taken into account. This is what's special about the D2 program. It doesn't make linear assumptions. Through a myriad of ways, it uses the second derivative to produce a high level of accuracy. But it also builds a matrix that ranges from all green lights to all red lights and every combination in between, calculates time and distance for each event, then assigns a probability to each event. That way, the program can assign a probable time, represented by a Gaussian distribution, to every position Ms. Jones will pass through on her way to work.

"Let's suppose the program calculates exactly the correct time she arrives at work, so it can place her with high probability on a specific elevator to go up to her office. It so happens she meets her future husband on that elevator and they have a son together. Now, to answer your question: What happens if we tamper with the program so a small arbitrary change is introduced? Suppose we make a ten-second change to her timeline by slightly altering the calculations in the program. The program now calculates she will pass through a green light at just the wrong time and be killed by a drunk driver blowing through a red light. This is not an acceptable outcome, so someone running the program will wish to change Ms. Jones' future – I should say her fake future, because of the artificial ten-second change. When a change is made, she won't be killed, but she probably won't meet her husband and won't have his son.

"In this example, creating a false prediction prompts someone to change a perfectly satisfactory real future for Ms. Jones to an alternative in which she will never know what she missed. This may not be what we want to do. Nobody will know the program produced a false prediction due to a tampered ten-second change because the prediction was never tested. Ms. Jones will never know she is going to miss having a son with the love of her life. My point is it matters how we tamper with the program. Depending on the objective, there is a right way and a wrong way to do it. If the program is allowed to predict a true future, and for some reason, that real future is not desired, the program can be run a second time with a deliberate change to the future. If we tamper with the program on the second run and randomly alter its calculations to describe a false alternative future, now there's an observable test. If the false prediction, which was presumably desired, doesn't materialize, it becomes obvious the program is faulty. If little glitches like this create observable failures, it calls into question the credibility of the program."

Sam shook his head. "That was a lot of abstract logic. I'm not sure I completely follow you."

"That was a long but necessary explanation. Let me simplify what I just told you. Suppose the real future is: if A occurs, then B will be the result. B is a desirable result, but we alter the program to tell you instead of B, you're going to get an undesirable X. So, we suggest A- which results in B-. B- is less desirable than B would have been, but you have no way of knowing you could have had B. You believe the comparison is against X, so you don't realize the program is not working correctly.

"To have a measurable result, we tell you A will result in B, but if you accept A+, you will get B+, and B+ is more desirable than B. If the program is altered to produce something other than B+, it'll now be obvious your expectations aren't met. The future is always measured relative to expectations.

"This program uses artificial intelligence. It learns from prior events. If it accepts prior errors as true facts, it may compound its errors over time and eventually become increasingly error-prone and thus useless. So, a small change to the program early on could create a devastating change to outcomes over time."

Sam brightened up. "I can see the beginnings of a plan. Do you know how you could alter the program to make the kind of minute changes you're describing?"

"Well, I would need to think about it and test out ideas. There're a number of ways to cripple the program. But I assume you want it done in a way that's not immediately detectable?"

The conversation continued for many hours into the evening. When Sam went to bed, his mind was spinning with possible ways to get Nancy released. Too much time had passed already, and he was anxious to have her back.

PART 6

FINDING STABILITY

CHAPTER 33

After a short and uneventful drive from Tysons Corner to Langley, Sam found himself once again on the seventh floor in the director's office, sitting across the desk from Angela Firestone. She was effusive with her praise to Sam regarding how her status was elevated in the eyes of the president due to her insistence that he leave the White House. Her standing was also improved with the Secret Service. She didn't expect to receive a thank you from Chief of Staff Geoffrey Hines, but at least he wouldn't be quick to cross swords with her in the future.

The director explained to Sam, "I'm still trying to get back on track after this mess with Brandon Kulp, but it appears the damage is limited. Our confidence level is increasing daily as we're able to identify and contain the fallout from his activities. Now it's time to move forward with neutralizing the Russian attempt to capture the D2 program. We suspect that was a primary reason for Kulp's recruitment as an enemy agent."

Sam shifted awkwardly in his seat. "I've been giving a lot of thought to the problem. The one thing I don't know is how they found out about the existence of the information Joe Campbell brought to America. I assume there must have been a leak in Britain that put everything in motion. But maybe it all started with Brandon Kulp intercepting your conversations with MI6. Either way, we don't know how much the Russians know. They seem to know enough to believe it's important to them to get their hands on the program Nancy took from Joe Campbell. Now that they have Nancy, they've probably learned more about the capabilities of the program."

The director nodded. "We're pretty sure Deputy Director Kulp accessed the information from my conversation with Sir Reginald Huntsman. Kulp tipped off the Russians, so they knew they needed to follow Joseph Campbell when he arrived in the US, and, of course, that led them to Nancy and you. As for what they know, hell, they probably know more than I do. You haven't shared much about this program."

Sam dropped his head apologetically. "I know I haven't explained much. It wasn't necessarily our intention to get involved with the CIA. Nancy and I agreed that what we have is so important, we didn't want to see the program weaponized. We didn't want to turn it over to any government agency without safeguards attached. When we discovered the CIA was compromised by Brandon Kulp, we definitely didn't want to give you any information. Unfortunately, the kidnapping of Nancy and the need to protect the president forced my hand into telling you more than I wanted to."

"That's understandable."

"We call it the D2 program because it employs second derivative calculations to predict the future course of events. You don't need to know exactly how it works. You just need to appreciate its capabilities. Truth be told, I don't really know how it works. I have Dr. Higgins and Nancy for that. But I do know seeing into the future is an incredibly powerful tool that allows one to change the present in order to knowingly manipulate the future. It's a tool so powerful, we definitely don't want our enemies to get ahold of it. Frankly, even among friends, I'm having a hard time coming up with any person or group I'd trust to use this wisely and maintain control of it. The more people who know about it, the more likely we're going to have problems like we're having with Russia."

Director Firestone pulled her mouth to one side and sighed, exasperated. "So how do we get the Russians off our back and get Nancy released? The woman we grabbed hasn't provided us with anything useful. As far as an exchange goes, it seems the Russians don't care as much about their agent as they do about obtaining the program. It doesn't sound like anything is going to make them back off."

"Simple." Sam threw one hand in the air. "The answer is to give them what they want. You're familiar with the term 'buyer's remorse'? We give them what they want and let them figure out that what they thought they wanted is not what they thought it is. They may understand the concept of what the program is supposed to do, but how do they know it really works? If it seems to work when they test it, they're happy and they go away. If, over time, it turns out not to work well, whose fault is that? We can point the finger at Britain."

Director Firestone's eyes grew bigger with realization. "So, you're suggesting we give them a defective program — a program they don't realize is defective. We can do that?"

"Yes indeed!" Sam became more animated. "I've talked at length with Dr. Higgins about it, and he has assured me of several important things with regard to introducing a bug. Time and space are relative concepts that are viewed differently depending on one's frame of reference. For example, special relativity explains why clocks moving at GPS orbital speeds on satellites will tick more slowly than stationary ground clocks. Speed, distance, and gravity play a role in creating time dilation. In order for our Global Positioning System to work correctly, the clocks on satellites have to be adjusted for this time difference. The D2 program has its own internal master clock and then uses calculations like the Lorentz transformation to adjust the timeline in other frames of reference to align with the master timeline. This is how the program determines sequence. Dr. Higgins says he can use a random number generator to make minute changes to event integration with the program's master clock. The changes will be so small, they won't be noticed, but they'll have a cumulative effect over time. Remember, this is an artificial intelligence program. It learns as it goes along."

Angela lifted a finger. "The Russians aren't going to realize what we've done?"

Sam nodded vigorously. "There are millions of lines of code in the D2 program. Dr. Higgins says he can hide a defect in the program so it can't be found.

"Another extremely important consideration is we don't want to give anything to the Russians that can be reverse-engineered. Dr. Higgins assures me he can't sort out the internal workings of the program, and it'll be impossible for the Russians to take it apart. Because the program is always learning as it absorbs new data, it's rewriting its own code. There are changes on top of changes on top of changes. It's impossible to know what the core of the program was versus what's been added over time. If the program has been learning from incorrect data, it'll be impossible to go back and strip out the good from the bad. In other words, the Russians won't realize the program is defective when they receive it. Over time, when they figure out it isn't working properly, it'll be too late for them to do anything about it."

A slight smile worked its way across the director's face. "I'm beginning to like this plan. I assume we keep an unadulterated copy for ourselves. We end up with a program that works, while the Russians have a program that doesn't work, and they think nobody has a good working program."

Sam had now come to the delicate part of his plan. "It's a little more complicated than that. We can bamboozle the Russians and keep a good copy of the program for ourselves, but there remains the question of what happens to the good version that we keep?

"To address that question, if I could beg your indulgence, let me tell you a short story." He looked at the director expectantly.

"I'm listening."

Sam sat back and launched into a tale.

"A long time ago in a land far, far away, there lived a sculptor named Enod. After years of toil, he decided it was time to create his masterpiece. For many years he had been thinking about the perfect woman and how she should appear. The time had come to give life to his vision. He selected a block of the purest white alabaster. For months and months, he feverishly toiled in his workshop, chipping, grinding, and smoothing the physical manifestation of his image of beauty. He created a life-sized forest nymph of perfect proportions. Her naked form revealed gentle curves and delicate features that were pleasing to the eye. The work consumed him, and he poured his soul into his creation.

"When Enod was finished, he moved his statue out into the garden to better appreciate it in the full light of day. Sunlight worked magic on the translucent alabaster and brought life to the stone. The girl's skin was soft and pure. Her face seemed alive with a sultry, flirtatious expression. Her body was sensuous and seductive. Her nubile form was so realistic, it looked like she was about to move. Enod was instantly smitten and sat down on a garden bench to appreciate his work. He sat and stared at the girl, captivated by her life-like presence. Her beauty was overwhelming. When his wife called him for dinner, he ignored her. When she called repeatedly, he did not budge. Only after the sun went down, and his creation disappeared in the black of night, did Enod return to his house and bed.

"The next morning, Enod rose with the sun and took his place in the garden again. Frustrated by his lack of response to her, Enod's wife called his best friend, Tom, to see what he could do. When Tom arrived, he walked into the garden and saw the statue.

"'What a magnificent creature!' he exclaimed, and he took a seat next to Enod. Tom also was transfixed. The two sat there staring.

"Soon, word spread throughout the village. Men and women came to see the amazing statue. All of the men, and many of the women, could not take their eyes off of the beautiful nymph. They simply stood and stared all day long.

"This was a disaster for Enod's wife and for the village. Nobody was getting any work done, and the garden was being trampled. The statue was so incredible, Enod's wife could not imagine destroying it. The destruction of such an amazing work of art would be a true loss to mankind. But for as long as it existed, the village was going to be paralyzed. It was a dilemma without a solution."

Sam paused his story. "What would you do?"

The director looked flustered. "It's your story. How does it end?"

"Enod's wife went out after dark and carefully wrapped the statue in soft padding. Then she tied a tarp over it. She hired a moving company from another village where they knew nothing about the statue. She insisted they show up at first light before the sun rose. Without telling the movers what it was, she had it transported to a storage room where it wouldn't be found.

"When the sun came up and Enod went out to the garden, he was distressed that his statue was gone. As others arrived, everyone asked what had happened. Nobody had an answer. Eventually, life continued in the village as it had been, and the statue became a distant memory.

"It was an imperfect solution, but it met the two objectives. The statue was not destroyed, and the village was no longer paralyzed. It left open the possibility that sometime in the future, a better solution could be found and the statue could be appreciated."

Director Firestone folded her hands and leaned forward on her desk. She pressed her lips together. "So, you're saying the world is not ready for the D2 program. Right now, nobody should have it."

"That's exactly what I'm saying." Sam looked directly into her eyes. This was where he had to close the sale, and her response would mean everything for the future of the world. "Look, you know I have the program and you have the resources to forcefully take it from me anytime you want. I know that. I also appreciate you haven't even asked for it yet. I believe you truly understand how significant the D2 program is, and how dangerous it is. I don't want to keep it. I personally don't want anything more to do with it. But I want it to end up somewhere safe. Since you now know about it, you have become the default choice for its new home. But I mean you, not your organization. The more people who know about the program's existence, the more problems there will be. I'm hoping I can trust you to be the caretaker of this treasure and use your position to place it somewhere safe until it's either desperately needed to save mankind, or until the world is in a better position to use it constructively for good without the possibility of it being misused."

There was a long silence while they stared at each other. Sam's heart was racing. He wanted safeguards. He wanted guarantees, but there was no way to achieve what he wanted. In the end, he had to rely on simple trust. He desperately hoped he could place his faith in Angela Firestone, and that she understood the gravity of the responsibility he was giving her.

The director nodded. "So, when the Russians find they cannot rely on their copy of the program, we admit the same thing. As far as everyone is concerned, it was a nice idea that failed. The world goes on, and this incident is a footnote in history. Meantime, I put the program in a dark hole for an indefinite period. I can live with that. I agree with you, for all concerned, this is something the world doesn't need right now."

"I'm glad to hear you say that." Sam's posture relaxed with relief.

The director lifted a hand with her index finger pointing up before Sam could say anything more. "You do realize we're only postponing the inevitable. Everybody knows we use computer models to predict things like the weather. The models are getting better and better. What's less public is we have sophisticated models to predict the outcomes of different war game scenarios. Gathering data to make predictions is a rapidly growing trend. This D2 program is simply ahead of its time. The science of prediction is coming whether we are ready for it or not. Furthermore, I won't live forever. I'll have to make arrangements to pass this responsibility on to someone else. No guarantee Pandora's box won't be opened somewhere down the road. In fact, you can be sure it will."

Sam nodded. "I trust you'll figure out the best way to make those arrangements. Whether this stays with the CIA or shifts to a better home in the future will ultimately be your decision. I can only have faith you'll make the right decision."

The director remained silent. Sam shifted in his chair and spoke up with a tone that made it clear he was moving on to a new subject. "I'd ask one favor of you. Nancy is basically a good person, but she's been traveling down a bumpy road recently. In view of her sacrifice to this country, I hope you can arrange to have any blemishes removed from her record. She hasn't been at work for several weeks and her employer has probably fired her in absentia. I'm just saying, any help you can provide would be appreciated."

Director Firestone smiled. "Not a problem. Believe me, we looked closely into her background. There's nothing on her record beyond a few vague smudges. She received a notice from the IRS and worked out an arrangement for repayment. Everything is good with that. Nobody has to know or ask what she was doing in the British embassy. She appears to be a very bright, talented young lady. I'm sure she'll bounce back and do just fine. But we need to talk about how exactly we're going to get her back."

"Yes!" Sam bit his lip. "I've been worried that if we do an exchange for the D2 program, the Russians will be suspicious we let it go too easily. I'm not sure they value life the same way we do. If they wouldn't hand over such important information for the life of one person, are they likely to believe we would?

"I came up with a way for you to sell it to them. I meant sell metaphorically, but now that I think of it, maybe you should ask for cash too, or something else you want. Anyway, I think you should tell the Russians the only reason you're agreeing to give them the program is because we have an identical copy. Just as you cannot unsee something you have seen, or unlearn something you have learned, we aren't going to give them the only copy and erase our knowledge of the program. If both countries have the same program, then if the Russians try to change the future, our program will see the change and we can take countermeasures. In other words, each of us can neutralize any advantage the other may think they have. This gets very messy, so the message is they really shouldn't try to use the program. Along the lines of mutually assured destruction policy used with nuclear weapons, this will be a form of mutual deterrence. I think this logic is something the Russians can understand as a reason why we are willing to do an exchange for the program."

The director was scribbling down notes. "So, we give them back their agent and the D2 program. They give us Nancy and some additional 'boot' to even up the deal and make the exchange more believable. I also have to sell them on the concept of mutual deterrence if we each have the same program. Sounds good to me."

Sam leaned forward eagerly. "How soon do you think you can make this happen?"

Director Firestone shrugged. "Time is of the essence. I don't know how quickly they're prepared to move, but if I can get negotiations going this afternoon, maybe an exchange can happen as soon as tomorrow."

"That being the case, how am I going to get the D2 program to you? Bringing digital media storage devices into headquarters is not easy, at least not if you don't want others to know about it."

"You're right." Angela frowned in thought. "I assume everything is on a flash drive? If I go for a run at eight o'clock tonight, can you bring the program to me at the same place we met last time?"

Sam rubbed his chin. "If I can get Dr. Higgins to make the changes we need to corrupt the program this afternoon, then I can meet you tonight. That seems kind of fast, but the sooner we can get Nancy back, the better."

She stood. "Okay. Let's leave it at that. We'll talk more later today."

Sam stood, nodded toward her, and headed for the door. When Sam left the office and entered the antechamber, a young man sat behind the desk instead of the female assistant who had been there before. Sam wondered if this was just a normal rotation, or if Director Firestone was cleaning house after the Kulp fiasco. Sam told the young man he was ready to go, and he was informed Bob was in the hall outside the door.

As Sam left the building and walked past the statue of Nathan Hale, he was reminded that the security of the country and the job of intelligence gathering was serious business. In 1776, at the age of twenty-one, Nathan Hale was captured by the British and executed for espionage. Now, Nancy's life was at risk due to her desire to do the right thing for the protection of her country. Sam was aware of the superstition of placing coins at the base of the statue for good luck when officers of the CIA go off on missions. But Sam was not a member of the CIA, and he felt like he would be an interloper if he participated in any of the rituals reserved for those people who took an oath to protect the United States. He was an Outlier, and was supposed to be working from a distance. He had no business being at headquarters, and he wouldn't be here if the circumstances weren't so extraordinary.

CHAPTER 34

Director Firestone spoke to her assistant and asked to be connected to the Secretary of State. A few minutes later, she was told Secretary Buckley was on the line.

"Harris, how are you? Thank you for taking my call."

"It's good to hear from you, Angela. I understand you're the lady of the moment. We have you to thank for the heads-up regarding the disaster at the White House. Well played! What can I do for you?"

Angela Firestone had started her career at the State Department. She had numerous connections there and was still an insider. Harrison Buckley was a relatively new appointee, but her relations with him had always been friendly since he became Secretary of State.

"Harris, we're in the middle of negotiating a prisoner swap with the Russians, and we thought we might ask them for a little extra to even up the exchange. Do you have any small, non-critical issue hanging out there we could put on the table for you?"

"Well, we have lots of issues with the Russians, but if you're asking for a low-level semi-dormant irritation, that would be the USA-USSR Maritime Boundary Agreement of June 1, 1991. The Soviet Union collapsed before they officially accepted that agreement. We now have a de facto Russia - United States Boundary that our Senate agreed to in 1991, but the Russians never ratified it. This is the agreement that establishes the boundary between Alaska and Russia. It would certainly help to have them step up and sign off on this."

Angela's voice brightened. "That sounds perfect for this situation. We can undoubtedly make it a point of negotiation. We both know they often appear to make a concession, then never carry through, but this may put extra pressure on them for you. Would you like to start the ball rolling by getting in touch with the Russian ambassador? If you wouldn't mind lending me one of your conference rooms, I'd like to meet with the ambassador this afternoon, if you can arrange it. Let him know we're ready to talk about an exchange. If he acts like he doesn't know what you're talking about, remind him we have one of his agents and we'd like to trade her back."

There was a moment's silence while Harrison gathered his thoughts. "We've been busy excoriating them over this falling satellite fiasco. I'm sure the Russian ambassador is not going to be happy to hear from me again, but I expect he'll respond. I'll see what I can do."

"Thank you, Harris. I'll wait to hear from you." Angela

hung up, satisfied that things were in motion.

When Sam returned to the safe house, Dr. Higgins was napping on the couch. He roused himself as Sam came through the door.

"Doctor, I have a project for you. We've agreed to exchange a defective copy of the D2 program. Can you make the changes we discussed last night so the Russians can't tell the program doesn't work perfectly?"

Dr. Higgins, now fully alert, walked toward his computer. "Sure. It's actually easier to break things than it is to create something new. I can slip a random number generator into the program as we talked about. The changes will be so small in the beginning, it won't be obvious that anything is wrong. But as I explained, the cumulative effect over time will cause the complete corruption of the program. It should only take me a couple of hours."

"Excellent!" Sam beamed. "I'd like to be able to do a hand-off tonight. I'll need a clean working copy and a defective copy on two different flash drives."

"I can do that." With a hopeful voice, Dr. Higgins asked, "Does this mean we're going to get Nancy back soon? I miss that young lady."

"Perhaps as early as tomorrow, if all goes well. I'm waiting for Director Firestone to confirm the plans with me."

At 5:30 that evening, the kitchen phone rang at the safe house. Sam got up from the kitchen table and answered it. The familiar voice of Angela Firestone greeted him.

"We're on for eight o'clock tonight. I'll expect to meet you at the same place. I've arranged for one of the officers next door to give you a ride. Be careful. Be situationally aware. I'll have two armed officers tailing me, so don't be surprised. I'll give you the details of tomorrow's plans when we meet."

After dinner, with two flash drives in his pocket, Sam stepped out into the hall and knocked on the adjoining apartment door. A new face answered the door. She introduced herself as Alex. She was attractive, blonde with dark eyebrows and soft doe-brown eyes, about two inches shorter than Nancy, and even slighter of build, if that was possible. Her lean body and youthful appearance made her look like she belonged in high school. She certainly was not what he would expect for an intelligence officer. Sam felt like a strong wind would knock her over, but he was wary about not underestimating her. If provoked, she could probably kick him in the balls, jab him in an eye, and have a chokehold on him before he could blink.

Sam smiled and nodded at her. "I think you're instructed to take me for a ride."

"Quite so. If you're ready, we can leave now." She was all business. She turned around for a moment while she unzipped and removed a loose-fitting fleece. The gun in a shoulder holster was now in plain sight. She reached for a dark blue windbreaker and put it on with the zipper halfway up. Except for her shoes, which looked more like combat boots, she appeared like any other middle-class young lady who might be running an errand after work, but before dressing for the evening.

The drive to the river was conducted in silence. Alex did not seem inclined to talk. If Sam was not so concerned about Nancy and focused on his meeting with Angela, he would have chatted up a pleasant young woman like this. He'd spent so many nights feeling alone and empty, alienated from his ex-wife, that he had programmed himself to reach out to any nice female who presented herself. But ever since Nancy had entered his life, he no longer had a general sense of loneliness. Now, being alone meant specifically missing Nancy. As the prospect of getting her back improved, he became increasingly anxious and impatient.

As they approached the Mt. Vernon Trail, Sam directed Alex to the general area of the park bench where he had previously waited for Director Firestone. When they were within fifty yards, Alex pulled over and parked. Sam got out and headed for the same bench. Alex followed after him, shadowing him by a good seventy-five feet.

Sam sat on the bench, nervously fidgeting with the two flash drives in his pocket until Angela Firestone appeared in her running suit. Sam jumped up and sprinted toward her at an angle of intercept. As he approached, he couldn't think of anything clever to say. "What a coincidence to bump into you," was all he could manage.

"Nice to see you again, Mr. Barron. This actually works pretty well. As long as we keep moving, it isn't easy for anyone to track us with listening devices. I assume your phone is turned off?"

"Better than off. It's in a Faraday bag. No signal in or out. I've seen the demonstration of a cell phone being turned on remotely and the camera activated without the icon showing. Ever since then, I've had a love/hate relationship with cell phones. You're probably aware I went through your agency's surveillance training."

"Yes, but even the best trained do screw up. That's the nature of being human."

Sam turned around and jogged backward. "I appreciate the concept of staying in motion, but do you think we could slow it down a notch. As much as I need the exercise, it's hard to talk when I'm huffing and puffing." After nearly tripping, Sam turned back around.

"You're right. Information takes precedence over exercise." Angela slowed to a brisk walk.

"Are we all set for tomorrow? I brought the flash drives."

Angela looked over her shoulder to check on the two field officers trailing behind them. This time, they weren't new recruits. Alex had fallen in line another fifty feet behind the security detail. Angela returned her attention to Sam. "I spent all afternoon in negotiations. At your suggestion, we're trading for more than just Nancy. The Russians have agreed to revisit a diplomatic issue that has been hanging around for the past few decades.

"I pitched your concept of mutual deterrence, and they

seem to have bought into the idea that what they're getting is an offset to our capabilities. I'm sure they'd like to be the only owners of the program, but that's a nonstarter. Our willingness to make the exchange should now seem credible to them.

"There was a major sticking point. Usually, prisoner exchanges are made across an international border. The Russians claim Nancy is being held outside the United States. I have my doubts, but we have no credible information on her whereabouts. They suggested an exchange at Storskog-Borisoglebsk, Norway, or at sea off of Little Diomede Island in the Bering Strait. Both of those are impractical and would delay things for days. Their concern was that if the exchange takes place in the United States, we could simply round them up after the fact and hold them prisoner while taking back what we give them. It took a lot of assurances to get them to accept a guarantee from us that they'll have a forty-eight-hour free pass for their agents to leave the United States, and they'll have full diplomatic immunity during that time. We stressed that we did not want a repeat of what happened when Kulp was killed."

That statement provided Sam an opening to relate they had run the D2 program again. "Of course, I didn't have the details you're giving me now, but I had to see if an exchange would work out. I felt stupid that we didn't run the program before the meeting at Montrose Park. So, this time we asked for a look at the future based on the exchange we talked about, without specifying a place. We asked specifically if Dr. Higgins, Nancy, and I would survive such an exchange. The answer was clearly in the affirmative. I'm still not comfortable all will be well, because I don't know what data the program used to arrive at that conclusion, but at least we aren't ignoring any warnings."

"That's encouraging," replied the director. "We finally agreed to have the exchange take place locally. The CIA has facilities just off 23rd Street NW by the E Street Expressway. We're moving the Russian agent we're holding to that facility. The exchange will take place nearby in Triangle Park between 20th Street and 21st Street NW. The Russians will enter off 20th Street, and we'll enter off 21st Street. We'll both walk down the paved path that passes behind the General Jose De San Martin Memorial. It's a minor park, and there's no reason to expect people to be on that path. A simple exchange should not attract any attention. It's an open area surrounded by the city. There isn't much opportunity for unseen surprises. There are neighboring rooftops where A.O. can find a perch with good visibility. It's such a small area, we can station men all around the perimeter of the park to be sure we have full control of the situation. Nobody has any incentive to misbehave, so the trade should go smoothly.

"The Russians are insisting on testing the program, or at least looking at it before people are exchanged. They weren't amused by what they found on the last flash drive. They acted as if we had insulted them. I pointed out nobody had represented anything specific was going to be on that disk, and furthermore, it wasn't theirs and they weren't entitled to steal it. So, they have no reason to be insulted. Nevertheless, they're insisting on looking at the flash drive.

"The time for the meet is set for 4:30. That was at the request of the Russians. They said they needed that much time to get Nancy into the city. We should be able to get Nancy back to you about an hour after that. We can do a preliminary debrief at the safe house."

Sam grabbed the Director's arm and stopped walking. "I need to be there. I can't sit at the safe house."

Director Firestone shook off his grip and started walking again. "I know it's hard, but we can't have another civilian getting mixed up in the middle of this operation."

"I'm not just another civilian, and I've been in the middle of this from the start. Furthermore, you need me. I'm the only person Nancy is going to recognize. Who knows what condition she's in and what her mental state is? She's probably terrified. If I can be in her line of sight, she'll know everything is okay and she'll come to me. If I'm not there, she may have no idea what she's getting into. She might just run for her life. I can't predict what her reaction will be. You need to minimize the opportunity for unexpected outcomes."

Director Firestone sighed in resignation. "Alright, you can have Alex bring you tomorrow. But I want it understood you're to hold a position in the background. Nancy will be able to see you, but you must not interfere in any way with the protocol of the exchange. Now, do you want to give me the program?"

Sam reached into his pocket and pulled out the two flash drives. "The red one is the defective version for the Russians.

The blue one is the original working version. That's the one I'm trusting you to put out of sight and out of mind. Obviously, we aren't going to give the Russians access to all the server farms we've been exploiting to run the program, so there's no information about computing resources. They can use their own supercomputers." Sam handed the drives to Angela Firestone.

She took them and zipped them into her jacket pocket.

"I'm going to finish my run. Have a nice evening, Mr. Barron. My team will expect you tomorrow afternoon." With that, she picked up the pace.

Sam curved off to the left and ran a 180-degree arc around the two men who were detailed behind the director. Sam didn't see Alex anywhere and assumed she had gone back to the car. He was startled when she appeared out from behind a tree and ran up next to him.

"You're dressed for a run, but it didn't look like you got much exercise." The tone of her voice and the expression on her face as they passed under a pool of lamplight showed she was teasing him. "You want to race back to the car?"

Sam was surprised by this playfulness. "Seriously?"

Alex picked up the pace, but let Sam catch up to her. When he sped past her, she shifted gears and matched him stride for stride. As Sam continued to increase his speed, she stayed right with him, but her shorter legs were pumping at a faster rhythm. The more he sped up, the more she stuck to him like glue until he was huffing and puffing. The car was in sight about two hundred feet ahead when Alex accelerated away from him and left him in her dust. It was no contest. When Sam reached the car, wheezing and coughing, Alex was nonchalantly standing there as if nothing had happened.

"What was that all about?" sputtered Sam. "Are you trying to make me look bad?"

Alex smiled. "It's called keeping the subject focused on the task. I got you here quickly and safely. If anyone intended to interfere with us, I made it difficult for them. Now hop in the car. It's time to go."

Sam rolled his eyeballs and got in the car. He had suspected he shouldn't underestimate this woman, and this confirmed he was right.

When Sam arrived back at the safe house, he couldn't relax. The thought of Nancy being returned and their problems finally being solved kept him anxious. In his experience, when the finish line was in sight was when things were most apt to go wrong. People let down their guard and failed to focus at the most critical time. He remembered his cross-country training when he was in school. His coach drilled into him not to let up when he got to the top of a hill. *You need to run as hard as you can right over the top of that hill and down the backside. The time you gain there will win the race for you, because everyone else is going to relax when they get to the top. Your job isn't done until you cross the finish line.*

Sam's intensity caused him to draw Dr. Higgins into a conversation about tomorrow. He explained what was supposed to happen and exactly how the exchange for Nancy would take place. "They want to test the flash drive and see what's on it. Is there anything there that will upset them? How will they know it's legitimate?"

Dr. Higgins took off his glasses and rubbed his forehead. "Well, they aren't going to see a Mickey Mouse cartoon. They're going to see minimal instructions and a dot exec file. If they try to run the program without first building a data set and hooking up to a lot of computing power, not much is going to happen. However, I assume they'll have an expert who can actually look at the code in the program. They'll see something they've never seen before. It'll take them a long time to even begin to figure out what the code is doing, but they should realize immediately this is a legitimate program doing something complicated. Most computer programmers won't understand the math, and most mathematicians won't understand how the math is broken apart into code. They're going to have to take a certain amount on faith."

Sam grimaced. "That doesn't sound too reassuring. But in the end, they aren't going to have much choice. We can't stand around for hours while they fool with the program. As long as it has some semblance of being the real thing, I guess they'll just have to accept it."

Dr. Higgins nodded. "I suppose it's just like any commercial contract. Both parties have to believe they're receiving the value they expect. If they don't, there'll be repercussions. We want this deal to be final, so they should be willing to believe they're getting all we said we would deliver."

Sam agreed. "Of course, it isn't our program anyway. It came from Britain. We can always shift the blame to the Brits if we have to."

When Dr. Higgins turned in for bed, Sam stayed up and worried. He realized how much his life had become enriched since Nancy had entered it. He didn't have a clear picture of how things would work out in the long run, but he desperately wanted her to play a central role in his future. He wondered about using the D2 program to look at his own future and plot ways to assure himself of a "happily-ever-after" outcome for his life. Was that something he could feel good about doing? Somehow, it seemed like cheating. At the moment, his primary concern was the next twenty-four hours. He ached to have Nancy safely in his arms again.

CHAPTER 35

When Nancy was hauled into the van, she was immediately thrown face down on the floor and pinned there with one man holding her shoulders down while another knelt on her back. Her arms were pulled behind her, and her wrists were cinched with a plastic tie. A black cloth sack was placed over her head so she couldn't see anything. They lifted her up and sat her on a bench seat with her back against the sidewall of the van. There was a lot of yelling in Russian she didn't understand. The loss of her vision incapacitated her. She couldn't be sure how many people were in the van. It would have been useless to try to kick because she had no target.

Nancy tried counting the seconds between turns and kept track of the number of left and right turns until it became useless. They made too many turns to keep track of, and the starting and stopping in traffic meant her count would be of no value. Twice, the van stopped and the doors opened and closed. People got in and out, but she couldn't tell how many.

Finally, after a long drive, the van stopped, and with one man on each of her arms, she was pulled out of the vehicle and led down a walkway and through a door. She was terrified from the start, but now her anxiety increased. They made several turns, then she was taken down a stairway. Another hall, through a door, and then she was told not to move. The plastic tie on her wrists was cut. She rubbed the sore spots. The bag was removed from her head and she was pushed forward. Before her eyes could adjust to the light, her captors exited the room and closed the door.

When Nancy looked around, she realized she was in a windowless basement. She was surrounded by white-painted cinder block walls and a steel-clad door with a small window to the hallway. A single ceiling light hung in the middle of the room. Along one wall was a steel-framed bed with wire springs and a thin mattress. That was the only furniture. A single sheet had been stretched over the mattress. One blanket and one pillow were provided. That was all. But high up in the corner of the wall near the door was a camera with a blinking red light.

Nancy walked over to the door and pounded on it. After no response, she pounded on it again. Still no response. So she screamed, "Hey! I need to go to the bathroom. What am I supposed to do?" Eventually, she heard the distant sound of a door opening and closing. In a minute, a key was shoved into her door and it swung open. A large, burly, dark-haired man stood in the doorway. He didn't have a mask on, and that worried Nancy. She had seen enough TV shows to know if the kidnappers don't wear masks, that means they don't plan to let the hostage live.

"I need to go to the bathroom," she pleaded.

The man took a step back and blocked the hall to the right. He pointed down the hall to her left and said one word in a heavy Russian accent. "Go."

Nancy went left down the hall, which ended in about twelve feet at a cement wall. To her right was a door to a small bathroom. It had a sink, a toilet, and a small stall shower, about three feet square. There was no window, only a single combination overhead light and exhaust fan. Nancy went in and closed the door. There was no lock on the door, which meant the man could come in any time. She used the toilet quickly and washed her hands and face.

When she opened the bathroom door, the man was standing about six feet down the hall. He walked back to the entrance to her room and waited for her. When she passed in front of him into the room, he immediately closed the door behind her and locked her in. As she listened to his footsteps recede down the hall, she thought what next? She was totally perplexed. They had the flash drive. What did they want with her? She was terrified of the thought she was expendable. If she had no value, they could do anything they wanted to her, including kill her. Her only comfort was that the last thing she saw when she was thrown into the van was Sam running down the sidewalk. Sam would be looking for her. But how was he going to find her?

Nancy sat on the bed and looked around the room. The freshly painted block walls showed no weak spots. She couldn't attack the walls or the cement floor. She couldn't reach the ceiling, and she was being watched by that damn camera. There was nothing she could do.

She thought about what a mess her life had turned into. Ever since she had become involved with Steve, her life had been spiraling downhill. Why didn't she have the self-control to stop stealing? She could have chosen a better way to supplement her income. Was her ego so big she thought she would never be caught?

Getting caught by Sam was incredibly awkward. She was lucky he turned out to be a nice guy. Did that excuse her choice to trade sex for jail? She never should have broken into his house, and she never should have stolen the flash drive from the embassy. The blame was on her for a pattern of bad decisions.

Sam was the best thing that had come out of this whole mess. He was so good to her, and he had no reason to be. Now her life depended on him. She needed him, not just to be rescued, but because she suspected she had fallen in love with him.

Nancy was startled awake when the door opened. She didn't realize she had fallen asleep. How much time had passed? She had no idea. The same burly Russian entered the room and set a tray of food on the floor. He left and locked the door without saying a word. Nancy realized time didn't exist for her. The only way to measure time was with change. She was in a world with no clock and no change except the delivery of food, or her bodily functions. She had no way to tell if it was day or night. They never turned off the overhead light. Presumably, her body would tell her when it was hungry, and she would sleep when she was tired, but that might have no relation to the position of the sun. Perhaps the worst thing was she had nothing to do. She had no present, and she had no sense of what her future might be.

An indeterminate time later, the door opened again. A new tray of food was brought, and the old tray was removed. Along with the food, a pink flannel nightgown was thrown on the floor. The door was closed and locked. Nancy looked at the nightgown. Did that suggest it was now night? If she counted meals from here, maybe she could keep track of the days.

After she ate, Nancy contemplated the nightgown. No way was she going to undress in front of a camera. She could pull the nightgown over her head and undress under the nightgown, but aside from being awkward, even that was out of the question. It was too provocative. She had no desire to give the men behind the camera any reason for their thoughts to stray toward sex. Just the idea of a woman undressing — even if they couldn't see it — started men thinking about the wrong thing.

Nancy had spent far too many years wearing skimpy gymnastic leotards not to notice how men looked at her and the women around her when she worked out. She divided the roving eyes into three categories. The amusing group was the younger boys who were still trying to figure out the female sex. Their faces wore the expression of curiosity and discovery. Gymnastic outfits left little to the imagination. Boys could see curves and bumps in places that were less noticeable in street clothes. Their shy exploration was harmless.

The second group was the connoisseurs. When they scanned her from head to toe, she felt like a work of art. These men looked at her the same way they would look at a fine sculpture. They appreciated the female form. They understood the work and sacrifice it took to hone a body into a tool that had everything that was needed, but nothing extra. They appreciated her skill in a sport that took both strength and precision. These were men who admired her and weren't out to use or abuse her.

The third group was the lewd, lascivious, big swinging dicks who thought all women existed purely for their amusement. They ranged from the lecherous old men to the younger testosterone-loaded sexual bullies. Their eyes would move from her face to her breasts. Even without a tight sports bra, not a lot to see there unless her nipples were showing through. Their eyes would travel down to her legs, rove over her ass if behind her, then back to settle on her crotch. She could read their minds, and it wasn't pretty. As a result, when she wasn't on the gymnasium floor, she learned to dress as defensively as possible. The feminist movement preached women should be able to walk down a public street with impunity, bra-less in a sheer blouse and miniskirt. But that was a fiction. Men are predators. Most have control over their base instincts, but sooner or later you're going to cross paths with the wrong one.

Nancy didn't have any leverage to protect herself from her captors. Simple things like changing clothes or going to the bathroom could trigger a reaction that might end badly for her. The less she interacted with these men, the better. But that damn camera was always watching her. Her best bet was to be as boring as possible. She lay down on the bed fully dressed and pulled the blanket over her.

When Nancy woke up, she needed to go to the bathroom. She pounded on the door. After no response, she pounded again. Then she started talking to the camera. After a few requests, she started yelling. Then the yelling turned to screaming. What was she supposed to do? She couldn't wait forever. She certainly wasn't going to go in her pants. Was she supposed to drop trou and go in a corner? Who was going to clean it up? She was kicking and pounding on the door again, and screaming at the same time.

Finally, she heard a noise. A Russian voice was saying something on the other side of the door. The lock clicked and the door opened. Her captor looked disheveled and unhappy to have been disturbed. Maybe that meant it was still nighttime. Once again, she was walked down to the bathroom and back again without a word. She was put back in the room and the door locked. She sat there in silence for hours.

When the door finally opened again, Nancy was expecting more food, but this time someone different was in the doorway. The man had an aura of command, but he stood there with an orange five-gallon Home Depot bucket in his hand and a roll of toilet paper. "We have business. We cannot always come when you call. If we don't come, you use bucket." He set it on the floor and stepped back into the hall. He returned with a chair. He closed the door, set the chair in front of the door, and sat down looking at her.

Nancy wasn't sure what she was supposed to do. She sat on the bed and waited. He said nothing. She waited. Eventually, she realized this was like the game of stink eye, a staring contest where the first one to blink loses — only this time the first one to speak loses. She wasn't sure what she would lose if she was the first to speak, but she knew she could win this game. She was sitting in this room in silence anyway. It didn't matter if he was there or not.

Finally, the man spoke. "My name is Nikolai. I help you if you help me. There was nothing useful on the flash drive you gave us. I am disappointed."

Nancy waited in silence until it was clear he wasn't going to say anything more until she responded. "I didn't give you anything. If you stole something and did not get what you expected, it's not my fault."

"Clever girl. Okay, let me ask different question. Why you there handing off useless flash drive?"

Nancy thought carefully about how to answer this. She didn't want to give away any information they didn't already have. "I was there to catch Brandon Kulp. That was the only reason."

Andronovich raised his eyebrows. "You work for CIA?"

"No, I don't work for the CIA. They used me to do a job. I simply did what I was told."

"But you took information from the British. Why did you take that information?"

Nancy tried to play as innocent as possible. "I didn't know what I was taking. I needed money. I thought it might be valuable."

"Where is that information now?"

"I don't know."

Andronovich's tone expressed frustration. "How can you not know? Where did it go?"

"I didn't know what to do with it, so I gave it to a friend."

"Where is this friend?'

"I don't know."

"Where are you staying?"

Nancy should have seen this one coming. She didn't have a good answer. "I'm staying at the Plaza Hotel."

"No. You left there several days ago. Where did you go?"

"I went to a friend's house."

"Is this the same friend you gave the information to?"

"No. A different friend. He doesn't know anything about any of this."

"What is the address of your friend?"

Nancy tried not to show the wince she felt. She was trapped. She had to give up the address of Dr. Higgins' house.

Nikolai Andronovich felt like he was getting somewhere now. "Your other friend that has the information. Where does he stay?"

"I told you, I don't know."

"How do you contact him?"

"He comes to see me. I don't know what he is going to do now that I am gone."

"Does your friend work for the CIA?"

Nancy shrugged. "I don't know. I don't think so. He was only trying to help me out."

Andronovich sneered. "So you don't have the information. You don't know what the information is. And you don't know where your friend is. What do you know?"

Nancy's eyes darted like a scared animal. "I don't know. I don't know why you took me. I don't know what you want from me. I'm a nobody. But you can't just snatch someone off the street in Washington DC. There'll be people looking for me."

Andronovich shook his head. "Let's hope there are people who want you. If I can't trade you, you aren't much use to me."

He stood up, picked up the chair, and walked out the door. Nancy was surprised to actually feel relieved when the door lock clicked. She went over in her mind everything she had said.

She hated giving out the address of the house, but otherwise, she thought her performance was pretty good. He seemed to believe she didn't know anything useful.

Hours turned into days as meals came and went. She only saw another human being when she was fed and when she was escorted to the bathroom. She needed to use the bucket only once. When nobody responded to her calls, she placed the bucket in the corner directly below the camera. She hoped that was a blind spot. If nobody was responding to her calls, probably that meant nobody was watching the camera anyway.

After what she estimated was three or four days, she started arguing with herself about taking a shower. She felt grungy and she smelled. She rationalized that if she didn't stay clean, she was likely to get sores and an infection. But that was self-deception, just an excuse to justify breaking her boredom and feeling better about herself. Still, she couldn't get past the fact there was no lock on the bathroom door. Ultimately, she gave in and asked on the next bathroom trip if she could get a towel and take a shower.

She was surprised her request was granted without question. She was given a towel and escorted down the hall. Once in the bathroom, she undressed quickly and turned on the shower. She stood there naked and nervous while ice water came out of the showerhead. It seemed to take forever for the water to heat up. There was only a bar of soap, no shampoo. She rubbed the soap in her hair and sudsed it up as best she could. The shower felt wonderful, and she would have loved to stay and luxuriate in it, but she was terrified the hairy, burly man could come through the door at any moment. She washed and rinsed as quickly as she could. When she was safely back in her room, she felt much better.

The boredom was excruciating and her mind was playing tricks on her. She sometimes couldn't tell the difference between day-dreaming and hallucinations and sleeping. She would believe she was awake and thinking about something, only to wake up and realize she had been dreaming. Time increasingly lost its meaning. When Nikolai Andronovich appeared at her door, she didn't know how long it had been since he was last there. He had a very different demeanor. He came into the room, took her by the arm, and said, "Come. We're going."

CHAPTER 36

The CIA-FBI task force met in a conference room at the CIA facility located off 23rd St NW. It was one hour before the exchange, and they were performing the final review of procedure. The team leader pointed to Bob. "Bob will be escorting the Russian agent and also carrying the package. Alex will be Bob's backup. Alex is not in the room because she's escorting a civilian to the meet. Four of you will be fanned out to the right, and four of you will be fanned out to the left. Our associates from the FBI will be securing the perimeter streets on all four sides of the park. They're working with us as a courtesy because we're operating outside our regulated domain. Since we are not going to detain, arrest, or in any way mix with the public, we aren't in violation of our mandate.

"Let me emphasize this is an exchange. We want the Russians to accept the package and to receive their agent. We don't want anything to interfere with them getting what they want.

In return, we're receiving Nancy Forrester, a civilian who was abducted during a prior operation. There is also a diplomatic agreement as part of this exchange, but that doesn't concern us.

"As usual, A.O. will be on overwatch from a rooftop. This is a carefully choreographed event and there should be no missteps. Everybody knows their job. The Russians have been given diplomatic immunity and free passage. Your objective is to let them come, perform the exchange, and leave without incident. Are there any questions?"

One member of the team halfway back in the room raised his hand. "Sir, why is a civilian being involved in this?"

The team leader looked around the room. "It's been decided at the highest levels, so that's the way it is. But to give you an answer you might like better, I don't know what Nancy Forrester looks like. Do You? We could circulate a picture, but there is nothing better than having someone who knows her on scene. Even more important, Ms. Forrester doesn't know who you are. She will recognize the civilian and go to him. He's the magnet that will attract her.

"Are there any more questions? If not, let's gear up and move to staging."

Alex knocked on Sam's apartment door. Dr. Higgins opened it and pointed to a closed door inside. "He's in the bedroom. He'll be out in a minute." He put his hands in his pockets and rocked on his heels while she stood in the foyer. "I guess this means it'll all finally be over."

"If you say so." Alex glanced around the apartment. "They just tell us what to do. They don't always tell us why."

Dr. Higgins had a low-level security clearance for his work, but he wasn't used to thinking about what he should and shouldn't say. He assumed everyone was on the same page. "We've missed the young woman you're rescuing today. It'll be good to have her back."

The bedroom door opened and Sam appeared. "I guess it's time to head out."

He turned with a bright face toward Dr. Higgins. "You hold down the fort, Doctor. I hope we'll be back shortly with our missing roommate!"

Alex opened the front door and said to Sam, "After you."

Once Sam and Alex departed, Dr. Higgins sat down at his computer. Everyone had expected him to turn over the only good copy of the D2 program. That expectation was exactly why he felt safe by keeping a copy. If nobody believed he still had the program, nobody should be coming after him for it.

Now that he had the details about the exchange, he wanted to run the program again and make sure neither he, nor Sam, nor Nancy were in any danger. After building a new data set and running the program, he did not like what he saw. The program indicated this would be a high-risk operation with a high probability of casualties. He tried to query exactly who would be hurt and how, but he couldn't get specific answers.

He ran the program several times with different questions, which should have pushed the program to scrape for different data, but he couldn't obtain anything more than generic statistics about possible injuries and death. The fact that some of the probabilities exceeded sixty percent, and in one scenario exceeded seventy-seven percent, made him anxious.

The clock on his computer showed 4:28. The exchange was scheduled for 4:30. He wondered what the emergency response time would be after a person in distress called in. He guessed it could easily be anywhere from five to fifteen minutes. If he called 911 now, emergency vehicles might arrive on site just as problems were developing. He moved toward the kitchen phone, but he had a problem. If he used the apartment phone, an address would show up that did not correlate with the place of the exchange. He went into the bedroom, removed his cell phone from the Faraday bag, and turned it on. If nothing happened and it turned out to be a bogus call, they could track him from his cell phone. That wouldn't be good. But he couldn't help believing the program was seeing something legitimate to worry about.

He dialed 911.

"What is the nature of your emergency?"

"I'm at Triangle Park on 21st Street. Someone has been shot. You need to send help now!" He hung up before they could ask him any questions. His hand was shaking as he set the phone down. Now, all he could do was wait.

CHAPTER 37

Alex pulled up and parked on 21st Street NW. Bob, the Russian agent with her blonde hair still in a braided ponytail, and several other team members were staged on the sidewalk. Other officers had fanned out around the park.

"Two minutes until we go," said Bob. He looked sternly at Sam. "Sam, I want you and Alex to stay at least twenty or thirty feet behind me. If you spot anything irregular, you tell Alex, and she'll communicate to me." He then looked at the Russian agent whose arm he was holding. "If you want to stay alive, you'll do exactly as you're told. Okay, let's get moving, slow ahead."

The four of them started walking down the path. Other team members angled twenty-five feet out to the right and left. Once they spotted the Russian group coming toward them from the east, they adjusted their pace to match the Russians so they would meet at the approximate middle of the park. When the two groups were about forty feet apart, they both stopped.

Bob looked back toward Alex and nodded for her to come forward. Alex turned to Sam, and in her most authoritative voice said, "Stay here." She moved up to Bob's position and gripped the Russian agent's arm.

Bob let go of the woman and took a tentative four or five steps forward. He reached into his pocket and held up the red flash drive. Across from him, a geeky-looking thin young man, cradling an open laptop computer, walked slowly toward Bob. Bob continued to walk forward until the two of them met in the middle. Bob handed the man the flash drive, then slowly backed up ten steps. The young man inserted the drive into the laptop and started typing. There was a tense three or four minutes before the Russian looked up and nodded toward Bob. Bob returned to Alex, and the Russian walked back toward his group.

Finally, after a short discussion, the group of Russians parted and Nancy was brought forward. Sam's heart soared. There she was! He couldn't believe how excited he was. It took all his control not to run forward.

Bob took the Russian woman by the arm again and pointed down the path. "You can walk slowly to your people." He let go of her arm and moved to stand behind her.

As the woman moved away, Bob said to Alex, "You can return to Sam. I'll wait here."

Officer James Patterson of the Metropolitan Police Department still couldn't believe how lucky he was. How many people could say they barely escaped being hit by a falling satellite? He was banged up from being thrown during the impact, but he had miraculously survived! The department had given him a couple of days off, and now he was returning to work for an evening shift. He was wearing chino pants and a windbreaker. His service revolver was hidden under his jacket. As he cut across Triangle Park on his way to the stationhouse, he looked like any ordinary tourist.

Jimmy entered off Virginia Ave and walked past the San Martin memorial statue. He cut through the trees behind the statue and came out onto a grassy area in the middle of the park. The grass was bisected by a path where he saw two women walking toward each other. One had bleach blonde hair and was built like a Swede or Norwegian. The other was tall and slender with beautiful black hair. He was thinking what a contrast they made as they passed each other about eight feet in front of him. As he walked between and behind each of them, something struck him as odd. They seemed tense, or nervous, and their stride was kind of wooden.

Nikolai Andronovich had released Nancy and told her to walk forward. He was watching their agent coming toward him when he spotted a man coming out of the trees to the left. The man was walking straight toward both women. Nikolai was immediately nervous about having an unexpected player on the field and instinctively reached for his gun. He held it by his side as the two women passed each other and the man went in between them.

Jimmy's training kicked in. He knew when people got nervous or scared and focused on a problem, tunnel vision sets in. It was a natural human instinct, but not what he wanted when needing situational awareness. He would have to force himself to expand his field of vision and even swivel his head.

Jimmy looked to his left and saw a man standing in the path staring at the dark-haired woman coming toward him. Strangely, he wasn't moving or speaking. Other people were farther back, also standing and staring.

Jimmy looked to his right and saw a cluster of men staring at the blonde coming toward them. One of them had a gun in his hand, hanging by his side. It took a moment to register. A gun! Jimmy reached for his service revolver, pivoted one hundred degrees on his right foot, stepped forward with his left foot, and gripped his gun with both hands as he aimed it at the man. He yelled, "Police! Drop your weapon!"

When a policeman contemplates shooting his gun, he has to take numerous things into consideration. Are there civilians in the line of fire? Is there a justifiable cause? Is his life or the life of a civilian in imminent danger? Are there likely to be racial overtones or political ramifications? Is he going to be pilloried on social media?

Nikolai Andronovich had no such concerns. In one swift move, he raised his gun and shot officer James Patterson in the forehead. As soon as Bob saw Andronovich's gun go up, he reached for his own gun. Andronovich saw the motion out of the corner of his eye and swung his arm to the left. He had Bob in his sights and squeezed the trigger.

A.O. was watching the whole scene through his scope from a rooftop. As soon as Andronovich shot Jimmy, A.O. fired a shot straight into Nikolai's left chest. His heart was shredded, but not before Nikolai squeezed off his second shot. The impact of the bullet that hit Nikolai caused him to twist to the left. The bullet meant for Bob shifted three feet to the left and slammed into Nancy's back. As she slumped forward, Bob caught her. He slowly lowered her to the ground.

Eyes that had been full of sparkle at the sight of Sam a moment ago went dead. Bob placed his hand on her neck searching for a pulse. Sam screamed and bolted forward, brushing Alex aside as she returned toward him. He ran up to Bob and shouldered him away from Nancy. He took her face in two hands and called to her as his eyes welled up in tears.

Bullets were now flying everywhere. It wasn't clear who was shooting at who, but shots were ringing out and bullets were ricocheting off the pavement and thudding into trees. Bob shouted, "We've got to go! She's dead, Sam!" He grabbed Sam by the collar. He yanked Sam to his feet and hustled him back toward Alex. Sam was screaming and resisting. Alex grabbed an arm and helped haul Sam back to the street. The two officers shoved Sam into the back seat of the car, and Bob said to Alex, "Take him home." As they left, ambulances and police cars were racing down the street with sirens blaring

CHAPTER 38

By the time Alex returned Sam to the safehouse, he had the demeanor of a zombie. His face had no expression and his eyes were blank. He got out of the car and walked toward the building like a sleepwalker. When he entered the front door of the apartment, he walked straight past Dr. Higgins, into his bedroom, without saying a word. The expression on Dr. Higgins' face turned from expectation to confusion.

Alex briefly explained to Dr. Higgins what had happened. She concluded by backing toward the door. "I am so, so sorry." The door closed and there was silence. Dr. Higgins was dumbfounded.

Several hours later, well into the evening, the kitchen phone rang. Dr. Higgins answered. Director Firestone asked to speak with Sam.

"I don't think Sam is in any condition to come to the phone right now," replied Dr. Higgins.

He heard the Director sigh. "I understand. I'm sorry about the way this turned out. I don't know how we could have foreseen the peculiar set of circumstances that led to this outcome. It's tragic to lose Nancy. Please let Sam know we'll take care of all the final arrangements for her. I'll call back tomorrow to give him the details. Thank you for your help on this project, Dr. Higgins. I assume you too got to know Nancy. Let me offer my condolences to you."

"Thank you," said Dr. Higgins, and the call was concluded.

Before going to bed, Dr. Higgins knocked on Sam's door and asked if there was anything he could get him. There was no reply.

It was almost ten in the morning before Sam came out of his room. He was greeted by a suitcase sitting by the front door. Dr. Higgins was in the kitchen putting dishes away.

"What's this? Are you leaving?" Sam asked.

"Yes. I'm glad I got to see you before my flight. I'm going back to California. I don't want to go back to the house in Georgetown, and all this business with you and Nancy has knocked me completely off my stride in terms of completing any more work here. They need me back at Lawrence Livermore, and that's where I'll be most comfortable."

Sam felt even more dejected than he already was. "I'm

sorry to see you go, but I guess I can't blame you. I appreciate the help you gave us. It meant a lot to have someone we could work with and someone we could trust."

Dr. Higgins shook his head. "It's a damn shame to have a fine young woman like Nancy killed for no good reason. I don't understand why it had to happen. I don't understand why the program said all three of us were going to come through this okay. I'm beginning to think the D2 program, good as it is, can't be relied on as perfect. I guess random volatility can always creep in when you least expect it. It's just a damn shame, in this case, that it had to mean the loss of a life such as hers."

"I know." Sam hung his head. "This is something I'm never going to get over."

After Dr. Higgins departed, Sam sat in the empty apartment by himself. He had nothing to do except contemplate the rest of his life. He was on the edge of an abyss. He had taken two steps forward and three steps back. After dwelling in a wasteland after the death of his daughter, Nancy came along and filled a giant hole in his life. He had felt so good when he was with her. Now he was left lonely, empty, and forlorn. He felt cheated by life.

He wondered if he had somehow brought this on himself. *Pride goeth before destruction, and an haughty spirit before a fall.* Had he been too confident? Had he overplayed his hand? *Better it is to be of an humble spirit with the lowly, than to divide the spoil with the proud.* He did not believe the meek would inherit the earth. He always believed that he needed to fight for what he wanted.

Perhaps he had been wrong. Was this his comeuppance?

The kitchen phone rang and startled him out of his reverie. When he answered it, he expected the now familiar voice of Angela Firestone. "Sam, I'm so sorry about Nancy. From what I know, she was a lovely young woman. We're indebted to her for her service to this country."

Sam had nothing to say and held the phone in silence.

"The agency is taking care of all the final arrangements. We plan to have a service in three days. We haven't been able to locate any family members. We do have a list of her phone contacts. Aside from her roommate, it mostly seems to be associates she worked with. We'll make sure they all receive a notice." Again, a long silence.

Finally, Sam spoke up. "I don't plan to stay around. It's time to go home. I've never been one to participate in goodbyes. I'd rather just remember the time we had together."

"I see. I'd like to ask a favor of you. Before you leave, I'd like to go over some details with you. Call it a debrief. Bob is pretty upset about the way things turned out. I've given him a couple of days off. I'll have the officer next door drive you to my office tomorrow morning, if that's okay. If you want to schedule an eleven o'clock flight or later, she can then take you directly to the airport."

Sam gave out a lackluster sigh. "I guess that'll work."

"Good! I'll see you tomorrow." The phone went dead.

Sam stood there and stared at the phone on the wall. None of this had much meaning anymore. He wasn't sure what the point was of rehashing what had happened, but it probably wasn't going to be easy to book a flight before tomorrow anyway.

CHAPTER 39

The next morning, when there was a knock on the apartment door, Sam opened it expecting to see Alex. She would have been a bright spot in his day, but it wasn't her. It was the middle-aged female officer who had scolded Sam and Dr. Higgins when they had come off the roof from watching the satellite crash. She wore a serious face, but was polite and pleasant enough.

Sam was once again driven to CIA headquarters. The check-in process was now a familiar routine. He was escorted without delay to the director's office. There, he found Director Firestone sitting behind her desk, backlighted by a bright sunny day pouring through the picture windows.

"Have a seat, Sam."

Sam picked one of the chairs opposite the desk and sat down. He was no longer nervous about being in the office of the director of the CIA. Anger and bitterness had subsided and given way to a numbing brain fog. He hadn't arrived at acceptance yet. He was still overcome with loss. Emptiness was the predominant feeling. He felt hollowed out.

The director continued. "This isn't the triumphant celebration I had envisioned. I'm devastated about the loss of Nancy, and we have a lot of explaining to do with regard to how a policeman was shot and why his killer will never be apprehended. What were the odds things could go so wrong?"

Sam spoke in a voice barely above a whisper. "I remember a saying about the best laid plans of mice and men. Deep down, I think we all know there's no such thing as absolute certainty. No matter how sure we are of something, there's no guarantee. There are too many variables…"

She waited in silence, as if expecting him to say more. Eventually, she raised her eyes to look directly at Sam. "We did accomplish the objective of giving a faulty version of the program to the Russians. With all that happened, I don't expect them to question our intentions. As long as the program appears to work for a while, I doubt they'll come back at us. I hope this whole episode is now behind us."

Sam finally looked up and met her gaze. "This has been a fiasco from the start. I had a gut feeling the whole premise of the program was flawed. I knew it had the potential to be very dangerous. How can it be good to tamper with the future? Everything has a cost. There's always going to be collateral damage. I had some long discussions with Nancy about complex systems. She was pretty keen on the subject. She told me all complex systems trend toward increasing levels of stability. But underneath that trend, there's always some random volatility. You can count on the larger trend toward stability to prevail over time unless a new exogenous force interrupts the system trend. The D2 program has the potential to be the kind of exogenous force that can throw our civilization into chaos. I hope you appreciate how important it is that you don't succumb to the temptation to use it."

Angela Firestone nodded and clasped her hands. "I do believe I understand what you're saying. I hope I will be a good custodian for the responsibility you've given me.

"In that respect, I do have a question for you. It concerns Dr. Higgins. I understand he was the person who primarily operated the program. Are you aware of him using the program for anything personal?"

Sam was surprised. "No. He seemed to be a dedicated scientist. It didn't occur to me he would do anything nefarious, if that's what you're implying."

Angela shrugged. "I don't know that I'm implying anything. We deconstructed the events of two days ago to try to understand how we could have done things better. In the process, we learned that the 911 call for the ambulance was made by Dr. Higgins. The strange thing is he wasn't there, so how did he know anybody was shot? Even stranger, he made the call well before any guns were fired. Why would he do that?"

"That is odd." Sam tapped his fingers with his thumb, thinking. "Especially because we ran the program together to test the outcome of our planned exchange. The program said Nancy and I and Dr. Higgins would all survive the exchange. We had no concern about any problems. Obviously, the program was wrong, but I don't know how he could have known that."

"Well, it gets more curious. As you perhaps know, Dr. Higgins flew back to California yesterday. His ticket was processed and he was checked off on the passenger manifest. We even have video of him getting on the plane. However, he never arrived in California. We have a video stream of everyone getting off of that plane, and he's not in it. He hasn't checked in for work and can't be found anywhere."

Sam frowned. "That makes no sense to me. I don't know how that can happen."

"I've been thinking about it." Angela leaned back in her chair. "Is it possible he changed his future? I assume when you do something to change your future, you're changing everyone else's future at the same time. We all go along for the same ride. But what if when you change your future, the old future keeps going on without you? Is it possible Dr. Higgins jumped to a new future and we are still traveling along in his old future?"

"That's crazy!" Sam scoffed. "I don't see how that's possible. Are you suggesting there are an infinite number of futures all spread out in front of us?"

Director Firestone frowned as she studied Sam. "I don't know. I'm asking you. There's a mystery here we can't explain. Maybe we'll never know the answer. But Dr. Higgins is missing."

Sam shook his head. "I have no idea. I don't think that's the way things work, but I really don't know. Maybe he discovered something he never told the rest of us about."

The director threw open her hands. "I don't know how much we should worry about it. Maybe we'll find the answer in time. Perhaps he'll show up."

She stood and walked around her desk. For the first time, she held out her hand to Sam. "Thank you for your service, Sam Barron. You've helped me and you've helped your country. I hope you can find some peace. The world will never know what an important role you played, but don't think it isn't appreciated. We can all sleep better because of people like you."

Sam shook her hand and said, "I'm grateful to have had the opportunity to work with you. Thank you for trusting in me."

Angela smiled. "Perhaps there'll be a time in the future for us to work together again. Now get out of here. Your file says you're an Outlier. You should never have been here in the first place. Have a nice trip home."

As the black SUV made its way back out the access road, Sam put his sunglasses on and reached for the Boston Red Sox cap he had left on the seat. *You never know who is watching.* He was being driven directly to Reagan National Airport. As the vehicle turned into the traffic on Dolley Madison Blvd, he sank into the leather cushion of the back seat and pondered his situation. Now he was going back into the ordinary, everyday world that had no idea what he had just been through. A strange and tangled chain of events had involved him with Nancy and the Russians and the CIA. "I wonder if the D2 program could've predicted all of that," he thought to himself. Then he had a disturbing idea. "I wonder if I should have used the program to look at my long-term future? What would I have seen? — It's probably best not to know, considering how things have gone so far." A rush of sadness overtook him. He had gained so much, then lost everything. How do you come back from that?

Loneliness seemed to be his lot in life. After all, he was an Outlier. He was the lone wolf who worked on the outside. He would never enjoy the fellowship of belonging that came from being in the inner circle. Anonymity was his weapon, but it was a heavy weapon to bear.

The reality of the moment was the hum of tires on the road and the monotony of traffic all around him. The sun penetrating the dark privacy glass of the vehicle felt warm on his face. Tension drained out of his body as the weight of recent responsibility poured off of him, but it was replaced by a black hole of emptiness. He thought to himself, "My future will come soon enough. Right now, I'm consigned to a bleak present. There isn't anything in my life to get excited about. The world at large is in its own dark place with nasty politicians, class warfare, contentious ideological struggles, racial and religious strife… It makes me want to crawl under a rock, but that's not my nature. Somehow, I need to pick myself up and continue to fight the good fight. I suppose I should see what's been going on during my absence from the office."

Sam dug his cell phone out of the Faraday sleeve in the side pocket of his luggage, which he had left in the car while visiting Director Firestone. As his cell phone powered up, he saw he had a pile of email messages. The first one was from his son in England. It said, *"Rachael is pregnant. You're going to be a grandfather!"*

Maybe there was something to look forward to after all.

EPILOGUE

The bullet hit Nancy like a sledgehammer. While her brain was trying to process what happened, her muscles let go and her body crumpled. The pain was enormous, and she struggled to breathe. She had been staring at Sam's face, but it was replaced by a blur of blue sky spinning above as she twisted and fell. She was vaguely aware of arms grabbing her before everything faded to black.

When Nancy opened her eyes, she couldn't make sense of where she was or what had happened. Lying flat on her back, all she could see was the white framework of metal straps holding squares of institutional soundproof ceiling tiles filled with little pinholes. Her brain couldn't come up with an explanation for what had gone before. She took a breath and realized it hurt. She became aware of whirring noises and beeping noises behind her. A hand gripped her arm and she turned her head in the direction of the touch.

A nurse in a pale blue uniform looked down on Nancy. "I'm glad to see you're awake. You've had a rough go of it. You've been out for a couple of days. I don't know how much you remember, but you're safe in the hospital now."

Nancy tried to talk, but only a scratchy breath came out as her dry throat froze up and she ended up coughing.

The nurse held out a cup with a straw. "Here, have a sip of water."

Nancy struggled to raise her head enough to drink. "What hospital is this? Where's Sam? What time is it?"

The nurse looked very sympathetic. "I'm sorry, but we're under strict orders not to talk to you except to give you medical instructions. I don't know anything about you. I don't even know your name. You're under full quarantine. Now that you're awake, someone will be here in a while to talk to you. In the meantime, the best thing you can do is rest."

The nurse turned and walked away, leaving Nancy to her thoughts. Looking around the room, it looked like an ordinary hospital room. Hers was the only bed, and she could hear equipment operating behind her that she couldn't see. A white curtain on a ceiling track was pulled partially around her bed. The curtain blocked her view out the window, but daylight passed through the fabric. She felt incredibly heavy and lethargic. A steady background of pain held her prisoner.

She tried to make sense of how she got here, but her head was filled with a jumble of images. As she tried to sort through them, she drifted back off to sleep.

+≥====≤+

Several hours later, well into the afternoon, Angela Firestone entered Nancy's hospital room with her coat draped over her arm. Nancy was dozing and didn't see her come in. "Hello, Nancy! I'm glad to see you pulled through. We were pretty worried about you."

Nancy opened her eyes and tried to make sense of who this woman was. Angela could see the confusion on her face. "I'm Angela Firestone, director of the CIA. We were never formally introduced, so there's no reason you would recognize me. However, I've come to know a great deal about you. I've come to understand what Sam Barron sees in you."

"Sam," murmured Nancy. "How is Sam?"

Angela smiled. "Sam is fine. He's back in Massachusetts."

"Can I talk to him?"

Angela shook her head. "Well, here's the thing. Sam thinks you're dead. We all thought you were dead. It was thanks to Dr. Higgins arranging to have ambulances on-site that you had any chance at all. The doctors worked long and hard to save you. We all assumed you were gone. When I was notified you were hanging on to life, I had you classified as a 'Jane Doe' and placed in quarantine. What you may not realize is that this whole affair is far from over. At some point, the Russians may well become dissatisfied and come looking for you. Unfortunately, you still have the shadow of danger hanging over you." She paused to let that sink in.

Nancy had a tremor in her voice when she spoke. "So,

everyone thinks I'm dead? Sam thinks I'm dead?"

"That's the way things stand at the moment, and I think it's in your best interest to keep it that way. I can arrange for you to start over with a clean slate. As I said, I've gotten to know you, and I think you could be an excellent resource for my agency. We can give you a new name, a new life, train you, and give you a new job that I suspect you'll be very good at. You'll be in a very unique position of having no prior history. You'll be a ghost. You can be anyone you want to be and move in any crowd you choose to associate with. If you accept my offer to work for me, you'll occupy a very special position."

Nancy was struggling with a rollercoaster of emotions. Her life may not have been that great, but she had never contemplated giving it all up. "What about Sam? Can I ever see him again?"

Once again, Angela shook her head sympathetically. "I don't envision that being part of the program. It opens the door to too many risks, and I don't see an upside for you. Our character sheet says he's not a people person. His contract profile says he operates best when he's alone."

Nancy looked deflated.

"You don't have to make a decision right now." Angela put her coat back on. "We'll talk again tomorrow. Get some rest." With that, she turned and left.

Ten months later, Nancy had an assignment that took her

up to the Canadian border. It was mid-afternoon as she was driving through Massachusetts. It had been a long haul from DC headquarters and she was ready for a break. She couldn't resist checking into a motel for the night in Sea Haven. There was still plenty of light left in the day, and she decided to poke around before getting dinner. She drove down to the docks and parked far enough away from Bartlett's Landing not to be noticed. It had been a sunny day inland, but the coast was shrouded in fog. It was thick, but not so thick that she couldn't see the length of the docks. She casually walked past the marina and looked for Sam's sailboat. Her heart sank when she saw it wasn't in its slip. Had he sold his boat? Had he left town? She could find out if she really wanted to, but she wasn't sure she wanted to torture herself.

She continued walking along the waterfront. The fog became increasingly dense as she approached the harbor entrance. She passed the last of the tourist boutiques and ice cream shops, and headed out onto the path along the top of the breakwater. After walking hundreds of feet to the end of the breakwater, the fog closed in behind her so she couldn't see the land she just left. She stood there in the cool moist air, staring into nothingness, contemplating how much had changed over the past year. So much had happened, yet here she was, standing in the same town, alone in the fog. The loneliness was the hard part. She really missed Sam. As she stood there, a sound drifted across the water, through the fog. It was the haunting wail of a bagpipe playing a bittersweet dirge. Her heart beat faster and she smiled to herself. But her chest ached with emptiness. "Would she ever see Sam again? Could she ever recapture the special time they had together? Sometimes it was better not to know. Sometimes it was better to live with hope."

THE END

Thank you for reading this book!

ABOUT THE AUTHOR

Penny Lane is a fictitious person who lives in Maine. She enjoyed writing this book but doesn't want her mother to know that she's the author. She likes puppies and pine forests. She likes the ocean and warm sunny days. She doesn't like dealing with people and their problems on Monday mornings when she's trying to start the week with a fresh attitude. In fact, she doesn't like Mondays, and she doesn't particularly like problems on any given day. She doesn't like most people very much either. That's why she lives alone in a cottage in the woods. That's also why there is no email for her provided here, and no Facebook or Twitter account for her. She prefers to be a ghost.

If you like this book, please tell your friends and write a good honest review online. Perhaps that will encourage her to write another one.

www.OutlierTheBook.com